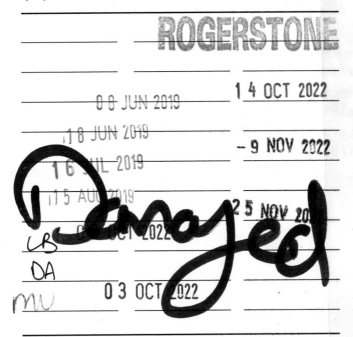

Mark Griffin began his writing career with three successive years of gold medal awards in the Hampshire Writing Festival. In 1996 he moved to Los Angeles, where he turned his attention to acting, script writing and development.

After returning to England, Mark continued in this profession, and in April 2012 was shortlisted in the top five out of 3500 entrants in a national crime thriller writing competition sponsored by Random House Publishing and the Daily Mail for his debut, *When Darkness Calls*. This is the first book in a series starring criminal psychologist Holly Wakefield and DI Bishop of the Met Police.

When
Darkness Calls

Mark Griffin

piatkus

PIATKUS

First published in Great Britain in 2018 by Piatkus
This paperback edition published in 2019 by Piatkus

1 3 5 7 9 10 8 6 4 2

A CIP catalogue record for this book
is available from the British Library.

ISBN 978-0-349-42073-8

Typeset in New Baskerville by M Rules
Printed and bound in Great Britain by
Clays Ltd, Elcograf S.p.A.

Papers used by Piatkus are from well-managed forests
and other responsible sources.

Piatkus
An imprint of
Little, Brown Book Group
Carmelite House
50 Victoria Embankment
London EC4Y 0DZ

An Hachette UK Company
www.hachette.co.uk

www.littlebrown.co.uk

Dad – thanks for those bedtime readings of *The Travels* by Marco Polo and *The Voyages and Adventures of Vasco da Gama*. Mum – thanks for always insisting I carry a book when I travel and for introducing me to the Moomins, the Hardy Boys and *Sparkling Cyanide*.
Love always.

One

Ten Years Ago

The blade made a staccato hammering on the chopping board.

Chicken, carrots, potatoes, a sprinkling of salt, and the baking tray was pushed into the oven and the door closed in one fluid motion. Natasha Sickert checked her watch. Four thirty in the afternoon. No rest for the wicked. She took a packet of ready-made pastry from the fridge and started to roll it out on the counter. Her husband preferred home-made but she just hadn't had time today. She wiped the perspiration from her brow before lining the tray, and smudged some flour on her forehead. She had wiry arms – thin but strong – and she wasn't afraid of hard work. She was thirty-seven, with hollow cheeks and watery blue eyes, as if she was about to cry. But Natasha didn't cry any more. She had stopped crying a long time ago. From another room the phone began to ring. After three rings she turned towards the corridor that joined the kitchen.

'Richard? Are you going to get that?'

No answer.

1

She closed her eyes and allowed herself a moment, then wiped her hands on her apron and was about to leave the kitchen and answer it herself when she heard him pick up. Her husband had a deep, stuttering voice and she could hear him talking, but it was muffled, only reaching her after travelling through two walls. She hoped it was someone trying to sell him something. The conversation stopped within a minute and she caught sight of his shadow as he made his way up the stairs. He was a big man, over six feet tall, but he always managed to move quietly when he wanted to.

She filled the pastry with a tin of peaches and sprinkled brown sugar over the top. There was a clunk from upstairs, the familiar sound of the immersion heater turning itself on. Richard was running a bath. She checked her watch again and shook her head. She didn't think she'd ever understand her husband.

Two hours later Richard left the house, leaving the front door open. His eyes were normally round and dark, like doll's eyes, but tonight they looked washed out in the street lights. He crossed the front lawn and stood in the middle of the road, content to stand and stare at the neighbours' houses, seemingly unaffected by the cold despite being completely naked. Then he dropped to his knees as a car approached from around the bend. There was a squeal of brakes as it swerved to avoid him, and in the beam of its headlights the driver saw that Richard's body was splattered in red. The driver put his hand on the horn. Richard watched the car disappear and his thin lips formed the beginnings of a smile.

Within minutes, neighbours gathered curiously at their front doors as a blue police light strobed across the street. Sergeant Echeos and DI Combs were first on the scene, the call from

Richard's neighbour, seventy-two-year-old William Gardener, having been logged at the station by the duty officer at 18:58. Despite being exhausted from double shifts DI Combs was suddenly very much awake when he saw the state of the man in front of him. Richard was shivering uncontrollably, and Combs placed a blanket over his shoulders.

'I'm s-so sorry to have caused such a nuisance, Officer.'

'That's all right, sir.' Combs hunkered down next to him. He smiled gently. 'The neighbours said there was an incident with a car?'

'Oh no, Officer,' Richard replied. 'The incident is in the bath.'

Two

Holly Wakefield stood behind the desk in her classroom at King's College on the Strand. She was wearing black trousers, a white shirt and a black tailored jacket. Her brown hair was pulled into a ponytail that normally had a life of its own, but at that moment she was motionless, deep in thought, oblivious to the thirty-two students who were sitting in front of her, waiting.

'Okay, here's one.' She looked up. 'Psychopaths don't seek therapy willingly.'

The gauntlet had been thrown down. The students stared back at her, mental cogs kicking up dust.

'Who said it? Come on.'

A girl with blonde hair raised a hand.

'Seto?'

'Well done, Abigail. Yes, Michael Seto. Quote: "Rather, they're pushed into it by a desperate relative or by a court order. To a psychopath, a therapist is just one more person who must be conned, and the psychopath plays the part right until the therapist is convinced of his or her rehabilitation." End quote.' She took a second, then:

'Get this next one and I'll buy you coffee. "He has acquired

4

a psychiatric hunting licence to kill." A hunting licence to kill. Love that.' A sea of blank faces. 'Do you want a clue?' She didn't even wait for them to answer. 'A sign for Cain.' Started to pace from side to side behind her desk, her ponytail swaying gently. 'I've gone all biblical on you . . .'

A male voice from the back of the class. 'Luis Hutchins?'

'No, Ben. Come on. *An Exploration of Human Violence.*' Another hand went up.

'Patrick?'

'Fredric Wertham?'

'Thank you, Patrick! Yes. Coffee for you.'

'White, two sugars, miss.'

'Thought you might be. Someone find me the quote.' Pages turned until Sarah took the lead.

'"A defendant may be declared insane, spend some time in an institution, and then be completely free without any parole or other supervision. If he ever commits another murder, his lawyers can point to his insanity record – and every prosecutor knows that de facto he cannot be convicted of first-degree murder. He has acquired a psychiatric hunting licence to kill."'

'Thank you, Sarah. There's a scary thought for a Monday morning. Here's another one. Peter Sutcliffe, aka the Yorkshire Ripper, is serving twenty concurrent life sentences for murdering thirteen women and attempting to kill seven more during the '80s in Yorkshire and the Greater Manchester area. In 2011 he was denied parole after thirty years behind bars, but in October 2015 he was out in public, without handcuffs, being escorted to an NHS eye clinic for a cataract operation. Let loose among us. How does that happen? His psychiatrist and the former clinical director of Broadmoor, Doctor Kevin Murray, stated he posed a "low" risk of reoffending. A low risk.

I wouldn't trust him with a gummy bear. Have any of you read Murray's psychological analysis of the Ripper?'

There was a universal shaking of heads.

'Read it by candlelight and you will shit yourselves.' She glanced at one of the many transcripts on her desk. It was one she knew by heart anyway. 'Let's move on to Sutcliffe's modus operandi. How did he express himself? The marks and wounds he left on the victim's bodies are like a written signature. Now, the signature of the killer is unique and is carried out purely for emotional satisfaction. It does not necessarily contribute to the death of the victim. Give me an example of a premeditated signature.'

'Rearranging the victim after they've been killed?'

'You're on fire today, Ben. It's called posing the victims. Turning them face down or face up, propping them up as if still alive; it can also be interpreted as a ritualistic trait. Now, this is the important bit: as they adapt to their crimes and environments, and as they become more efficient, a serial killer may change their MO but very rarely will their signature change. Give me one of Sutcliffe's signatures.'

'Didn't he use a screwdriver?'

'Yes he did, and the more women he killed the more frenzied he became. This can be evidenced by what we term overkill. For example, one woman, Emily Jackson, was stabbed fifty-two times.'

The bell rang, signalling the end of class.

'Okay – homework. The Yorkshire Ripper's signature was a deep wound to the stomach of his victims inflicted after hitting them on the head with a hammer. As part of his defence, his three psychiatrists, Doctors Milne, McCulloch and Kay, each diagnosed encapsulated paranoid schizophrenia – he was instructed to kill prostitutes on God's behalf, ridding the world of such undesirables. His hatred of women, however, especially prostitutes, and the sexual excitement derived from inflicting these types of wounds were more likely the true driving forces. Where did his fetish for deep wounds in the abdomen originate? Give me two thousand words on this.'

She started to put her notes away as chairs scuffed on the floor and the students stood up. 'I'll give you a clue,' she said. 'According to some, it involved a very creepy Victorian waxwork exhibit in Morecambe. I will see you next Monday. That's it – get out of here, you schizoids.'

Three

The grey clouds that had blocked the sun all morning were still there. A procession of heavy showers that chased across the city like thick smoke.

The roads through London were always busy at this time. Holly drove along the curve of Embankment and tapped a tune on the steering wheel as rain drummed on the car roof and spattered off her windscreen. She loved her MG. Bright red, 1982 – she liked to think of it as a classic. She opened her window slightly so she could benefit from the air and smell the rain. London rain. Slightly salty from the Thames. Sometimes the great river would be hidden from view by the traffic but then she would come to a gap and see the lights and masts of the boats at her side. November had broken, and in another month the traffic would be bumper to bumper as Christmas revellers and shoppers saturated the city, lured by the promise of bargains.

She checked her watch. Nearly three o'clock so she cut through Westminster, past Belgrave Square Garden and soon found herself on Cromwell Road, all the stores waving the sale flags ubiquitous at Christmas. Within five minutes she was in a quiet residential street with Georgian houses either side, and pulled into the driveway of the Wetherington Hospital. It had a grandeur about it, with fluted columns at the entrance and a façade of white stone, converted in the 1980s when gentrification had been all the rage. Holly navigated the speed bumps and parked in an NHS Staff Only space which had her own name. The footpath was bordered with azaleas and ended in the hospital's solid metal door. Above it a security light nestled next to a wide-angle camera that captured everything that came along the path and entered the car park.

She swiped her pass card in the door scanner and was rewarded by a heavy thunk as the magnetic connection was broken and the door opened to her touch. Inside it was warm and bright from the overhead fluorescents. She made her way to the security check where she walked through the metal detector and Edyta, the guard, signed her in and rummaged efficiently through her handbag.

'Afternoon, Holly.'

'Hi, Edyta. I still can't work out where the weekend went. How's Mike's leg?'

'The plaster comes off next Saturday. He's been at it with the knitting needle again. I wouldn't mind but he unravels my jumper every time.' She handed back Holly's bag. 'Have a good one.'

She passed through to the locker room where she donned her white doctor's coat and picked up her clipboard. Walked the long corridor, exchanging greetings with other doctors and nurses, on her way to the treatment rooms which were housed in a separate building. Beside the circular reception desk there was one door that led further inside. The ward sister was putting files into little stacks when Holly approached.

'Hi, Jackie, busy day?'

'You could say that. There was no hot water in the men's showers, for starters.'

'Cold showers in an asylum? What is this, 1869?' She picked up her checklist and her brow creased. 'How's Lee today?'

'I'm so sorry, sweetie, but Lee had a bit of a turn this morning.'

'Oh, no. He was doing so much better on the risperidone.'

'It was pretty bad. He's been segregated.'

'Is Max in his office?'

Jackie nodded. 'He's expecting you.'

Max Carrington, the hospital administrator, said nothing as Holly walked around in a little circle in front of his desk. Her hands were clasped in front of her so tightly that the knuckles were white.

'You should have called me, Max. I know him better than anyone.'

'I'm not disputing that, but—'

'So what happened?'

Max took off his glasses and squeezed the bridge of his nose as if he had a headache coming on. 'He had a strong delusional episode. He began to self-harm. The alarm was raised and when the orderly opened the cell door Lee attacked him.' He was squinting at her so he put his glasses back on. They had thick lenses that made it difficult to read his eyes.

'Is the orderly okay?'

'It was Alan, one of the new ones. He was a little shaken, that's all. I've spoken to him and he isn't going to lodge an official complaint.'

'Good. Thank you, Max. Okay – so I'm here now. Get Lee out and let me talk to him.'

'You know I can't do that.' The glasses came off again. The thumb and forefinger went back to the bridge of his nose. 'We cannot show preferential treatment. The board would go ballistic.'

'Max—'

'No, Holly. Listen, please. Lee is ... he's one of our difficult ones. Three years in Parkhurst now ten years here. He's segregated until tomorrow. It's not going to happen.'

'Don't take him out then, but how about you let me in?'

'Jesus Christ, Holly. He's a killer. You know how dangerous he is.'

'He listens to me, Max, you know he does.' She dropped her voice. 'I will take full responsibility for any outcome. Please.'

Lee Miller was playing solitaire when Holly entered the cell. There were hard lines on his face and it was grey, as if the blood just didn't want to go there. He had no eyebrows left and only a whisper of ginger hair. He sat behind a trestle table, keeping his eyes down, hidden, turning the cards, seemingly oblivious to her presence, but she knew he was watching her. The silence, apart from the gentle flipping of the cards, was absolute. Then he lifted his head slightly and that small movement seemed to bring the rest of his body to life.

'Hello, Holly.'

It was an invitation.

'Hello, Lee.' She took off her jacket and lowered it on to the back of the chair opposite. Stood for a moment watching him, then eased the chair out and sat down as quietly as she could. 'How are you today?'

'Better for seeing you. How were your Monday-morning students?'

'Good. Some promising ones. They're starting to quote Seto.'

'He's overrated. Newman and Lykken always have me on the edge of my seat. But now class is out and you're back here for the rest of the week, among the evil.'

'Evil dwells "not in the spaces we know, but between them".'

'Lovecraft.'

'Well done.'

He still wouldn't make eye contact. Kept his head down, eyes on the game.

'What happened, Lee?'

She reached across the table with her hand and let it rest within his reach, well aware of the cameras watching. At that moment he looked up. His glassy eyes were bright blue and cracked with little red veins. Amid the bruises on his face she could see that he had been crying. He laid his own hand on the table, close to Holly's but not touching.

'It doesn't matter. You look tired. Late night?'

'You could say that.'

'New boyfriend?'

'No.'

'What then?'

'Work.'

His eyes narrowed a fraction. 'I can still tell when you're lying.'

'I'm not lying. What happened, Lee?'

'Ah, we're back to me again, are we?'

'Yes.'

'My favourite subject.' A pause. 'Apart from you.'

12

'Come on, let's talk.'

'Do we have to?'

There were a few seconds of stalemate but then he dipped his eyes and she took that as a signal to press on.

'How bad were the images, Lee? What did you see?'

He pulled his hand away and looked suddenly vulnerable.

'What I always see. The monster.'

She waited.

'Not in the empirical sense of the word. But the monster nonetheless. I thought it was going to find me this time. I had to stop it. The only way I could stop it was to give it my blood. So I started to cut.'

'What with?'

He held up his hands and splayed his fingers. 'They didn't clip me very well last time. Naughty.' He lowered his hands and sighed. 'How's the orderly? I hadn't seen him before. It was a shock to see an unfamiliar face coming through my door. Does he have a grey beard?'

'No.'

'Hmm. Someone does. Someone with a grey beard I saw.'

'What made you stop?'

'I thought I was going to kill him. I mustn't be doing that now, must I?'

'No.'

'He kept saying my name. "Lee, it's okay, Lee. It's okay, Lee. I'm here. I'm here." I was going to ask him if he really was here in a literal, quantum physics sense, but at that point I felt sorry for him. Anyway, what's done is done. I'm sure he'll be fine.'

'He is.'

'Requested a transfer?'

'No.'

'He's a keeper then.' He smiled but not with his eyes. 'I shall look forward to getting to know him.'

'I don't want you hurting any more people, Lee.'

'That's not up to me. That's up to the person who whispers inside.'

'Tell me about the monster again.' A pause. 'Where did you see it?'

'Home.'

'Home?'

'Yes.' Barely audible. 'A grey beard ... I don't ...' He paused. Concentrated. 'I could see him through the gap in the cupboard doors. Flashes of him. Moving so fast. Silver and red. And the doors I was hiding behind. They wouldn't shut properly. I was desperately holding the edges with the tips of my fingers. Kept thinking they would slowly open and he would find me ...' He faltered and seemed to retreat. 'No, I don't want to. I don't want to remember. Not now. I just want to play the cards.'

'We can play together?'

'Not today.'

'I don't want you to shut down, Lee. You're doing so well.'

'Am I?'

'Yes. You're sleeping better. Your moods have improved, you've got your appetite back.'

'Appetite for destruction. I'm lonelier than ever.'

'I'm here, Lee.'

'But you're not, are you? You're not here. You're outside looking in.'

He was starting to get upset.

'No, I'm inside, Lee. I always will be.'

He stared at her for the longest time and when he eventually

14

tore his eyes away he screwed them up as if in pain. She leaned in closer. 'Am I lying now?'

'No.' Barely a whisper.

The seconds dragged into minutes of tense silence until there was knock at the door. It opened and an orderly stepped inside.

Holly turned. 'Already?'

The man nodded.

She stood up and put her jacket on. Lee picked up the cards and began to turn them over again as if their conversation had never taken place.

'Is it cold outside?'

'Yes.'

'Stay warm then, Holly.'

'I'll try.'

She left the cell. A knot was already forming in her stomach when she heard the heavy echo of the metal door clanking shut behind her.

Holly was exhausted when she finally got home.

It took her nearly twenty minutes to get off the Cromwell Road and another twenty to clear Hammersmith. By the time she reached her own street in Balham, south-west London, all the spaces had been taken and she had to circle back on herself half a dozen times before she finally got lucky and managed to park.

The street was crammed with people; teenagers laughing and smoking and glaze-eyed men and women desperate to get home after a day at the office. The Christmas decorations were already up outside the Bedford pub, a local venue for live music and comedy, and she glanced through the windows as she passed. It was already filled with people, but the lighting was so bad they looked like smudges in the background, shadows against the bar.

She stopped at her local mini-market and grabbed milk and a container of luxury hot chocolate.

'Pulling an all-nighter?' Jatinda Gill asked as he packed her items away.

'It gives me super powers, J.T.'

'You said that last week,' he smiled. She paid for everything, picked up her bags and walked back out into the busy street.

A turn on to Northwest Lane and a hundred metres on the left was her block. Flat 17, on the fifth floor. She had saved and saved and bought the flat six years ago and it had turned into a renovation job that had taken three years to complete. She had learned to plaster, plumb and paint and when she had finally finished she couldn't have been happier. There was nothing she liked more than coming home.

She took the lift up and stood for a few minutes in her doorway, content to stay in the darkness. She moved towards the bay window in the living room and stared down at the traffic five storeys below. The red and white car lights sparkled like blurry gems as the drizzle slanted first one way and then the other. She let herself become mesmerised until a sudden gust of wind rocked the window and she pulled the blue curtains closed.

She was too tired to eat so she poured herself a glass of red wine then lay back on the sofa. Checked her watch. It was almost midnight. Raw-eyed and sleepy, she picked up the post and went through the motions. Free pizza – bin it. Fifty per cent garden centre discount, credit card offers – bin. Bank statement – put to one side. And then an envelope, handwritten, and she recognised the writing immediately. She opened it and pulled out a reunion invitation from her old school. Blessed Home, a school that she had been sent to when she was ten. She flicked through the pages and was soon lost in memories, smiling when she saw an old black-and-white photo of herself among the other children. So young then, so naïve. She flicked the television on, watched for a minute then closed her eyes. She wasn't interested in the channels, just a companion while she tried to sleep.

Four

Holly was asleep on the sofa when her mobile rang. She was so groggy she kept her eyes shut as she fumbled it to her ear and cleared her throat.

'Hello?'

'Holly Wakefield, please.'

She didn't recognise the voice. 'This is Holly.'

'This is Detective Inspector Bishop from the Met.'

'I'm sorry, who?'

'DI Bishop. I'm phoning from the Metropolitan Police.'

She sat up, opened her eyes. 'Is everything okay?'

'You're on our call-out list, Miss Wakefield. I'm sorry about the time but this is important.'

'Sorry, your what?'

'Our crime scene call-out list. You teach forensic psychology at King's College one day a week and are employed by the NHS as a criminal behavioural analyst. You wrote your doctorate on "The Parody of Parole in Modern Society". We've used it as a reference before. You offered your services if we ever needed—'

'Oh, God, sorry. Yes, now I remember. I volunteered over five years ago.'

'You did, Miss Wakefield. And tonight's the night.'

An hour later Holly had showered, dressed and found herself driving through a small village in Surrey. The road was narrow with no street lights but the stars were bright, the moon a blue disc. Gravel crunched under her tyres as she approached a rambling two-storey mansion in the shadow of massive trees. There were no flashing lights or sirens, just an ambulance and half a dozen police cars that sat like sleeping lions in the driveway. She slowed and parked, staring at the pair of floodlights that had been erected at the top of a set of wide stone steps by a heavy oak door where two police officers stood guard. It was all so sudden and surreal, she felt as if she was watching a scene from a movie, but then one of the officers saw her and the spell was broken. He approached and raised a hand in caution as she got out of her car.

'Can I help you?'

'My name's Holly Wakefield. DI Bishop asked me to come over.'

'I'll need to see some ID, please?'

She reached back into the car, pulled out her handbag and handed over her NHS medical staff pass. He gave it a cursory glance.

'Hold on.' He turned away and pressed a button on his shoulder radio. He spoke so softly she couldn't hear what he said but within a few seconds he turned and motioned her to follow him. He didn't say another word as they walked to the house.

At the top of the steps he said, 'Would you mind waiting here one moment?' Then he whispered something to the other constable on guard, opened the big wooden door and disappeared inside. Holly got a glimpse past him. Below a carved oak staircase were more spotlights, forensic kits and rolls of police tape. Cameras flashed as police officers and plain-clothes detectives moved among the shadows with silent purpose. She stood aside as a SOCO team exited, smudges of red on their white scrubs. Their faces were strained. Something had rattled them.

'Miss Wakefield?'

The voice belonged to a man who made his way over from within the circle of light. He was smiling genially although it had obviously been a rough day. Six foot tall with dark brown hair; she guessed he was in his early forties. His face was a little rough, weathered but not beaten, and he had a slight limp. She moved forward when he offered his hand. 'I'm DI Bishop, senior investigating officer – we spoke on the phone. Apologies again for calling you at this ungodly hour, and thank you for coming over.' His voice was gravelly and she wondered if he smoked.

'Anything I can do to help.'

He nodded and passed her a pair of booties and latex gloves. She realised her hands were shaking. Whether he noticed or not was hard to tell.

'Sam Gordon, our normal profiler, is away, and our back-up, Natalie Wilson, is on maternity leave, not that these names will mean anything to you, but I need someone's eyes on the scene tonight.' He paused for a second. 'I know this is your first call-out so let me tell you what I need. Any ideas, thoughts, first impressions, no matter how crazy they may seem. And it goes without saying, this is strictly confidential. Not a word of what you see gets out.'

'Of course.'

'Good.' He swallowed hard. 'It's a bit of a messy one.'

Bishop led her across the hall and through a dining room that was set for dinner. White plates, silver cutlery, white napkins and decanted red wine played host to the nineteenth-century landscapes hanging on the walls. They passed through another door, along a wood-panelled corridor, the only sound their footsteps on the tiled floor and the click and whir of cameras behind them.

Bishop stopped beside a door that stood slightly ajar and turned to her.

'We've got five minutes before pathology takes over.'

He stepped inside. She followed. The room was rectangular and very large. Hundreds of books lined two of the walls and opposite were massive bay windows covered by green velvet curtains. An anatomical skeleton hung on its stand in one corner by a mahogany desk and there were coloured prints from *Grey's Anatomy* on the walls. Centre stage, draped across a chair like a ghastly exhibit, was the body of a man. A tan belt had been tightened around his neck and he had been eviscerated – cut down the middle from chest to navel.

'His name is Doctor Jonathan Wright. The other victim, his wife, is on the sofa by the bookshelves.'

Holly said nothing. She clasped her hands together and her fingers began to flutter like tiny birds. A nervous habit she had picked up when she was, what, ten years old? When she knew she should be doing something with her hands but didn't know what it was. When she wanted to help but didn't know how.

'You okay?'

She nodded. She remembered the only other murder scene she had ever walked into and it all mashed together in an

21

incoherent vision of red. Her chest was tight, and she could feel her heart smacking against her ribs with every beat. She wanted to turn around and walk away, to get out of there as fast as she could, but her legs wouldn't respond. Then somehow, inexorably, they started to move until she found herself next to the doctor's body. The smell immediately caught in her throat and she wanted to gag. The acrid taint of death, sweat and excrement.

His twisted face was white. His mouth sagged to one side and his blue eyes were open, but they were glassy and bloodshot, like a dead fish's eyes. His trousers were pulled down to his ankles and his hands were tied behind his back. The cut in his abdomen was perhaps ten inches long, the exposed internal organs grey, and the dried blood looked cherry red in the light from the chandelier above.

'Who found them?'

'Their niece. Alexandra. They were supposed to be having a dinner party at nine. She came over at seven thirty to help and found them like this.'

Holly walked slowly over to the sofa and knelt beside the woman. She looked like a discarded mannequin. Her face was pushed into the blood-soaked cream sofa and a cushion had been placed on the back of her head. Whoever had tied her hands behind her back had dislocated one elbow with the force and it jutted awkwardly towards the ceiling. Around her neck was a belt, this one thin and black, and underneath it the skin was red raw. Her purple blouse was ripped from top to bottom and she was wearing a black skirt that had been cut or torn down the middle and spread open like a bat's wings.

'What was her name?' Holly asked.

'Evelyn.'

'Evelyn.' She hesitated and then said softly, 'Was she raped?'

'It would appear so.'

'Evelyn.' Holly nodded, frustrated now at her own quiet. She wondered if Bishop was waiting for her to say something. Something meaningful. Anything. She took a deep breath, closed her eyes and tried to empty her mind and focus on the present. The bodies . . . Start with the bodies. Get a feel for the place, she told herself. Come on, you can do this, you can. You must. What about the bodies, Holly? What's so special about them?

'Evelyn is face down. Jonathan is face up. Exposed. Open. The killer. He's . . . '

'He?'

'Without question. He's not scared of making a mess either. It's so excessive. Almost too much. Not the anger, that's real. But the bodies – they've been intentionally left like this. Not concealed or hidden away, but placed where they would be easily discovered. So they would shock whoever found them. The doctor on his back, his wife on her front, degraded. It shows us his mastery over them. He got pleasure from demonstrating their vulnerability. The murder was simple, but what he's done to the bodies afterwards, that's him.' She took a moment. 'Can I smell smoke?'

'There were papers of some kind smouldering in the fireplace when we got here. Our lab boys have already taken them away.'

She nodded and stared at the marble fireplace. Above the mantel was a smashed mirror, on the floor below, a jigsaw of glass reflections.

She headed over to the anatomical skeleton. Empty eye sockets. Stupid grin. On the desk by its side there was an appointment book, some post, magazines, a quill pen, a white glazed phrenology head and a small brass bell. She picked up the bell. It rang, tinny, and quite loud. She was careful to put it back exactly where it had been.

'Doctor Wright retired five years ago. According to his niece, he still saw some of his old patients for check-ups every now and then. We're going to be talking to them tomorrow. Apparently they were both well liked and active in the local community.'

'What sort of doctor had he been?'

'He used to specialise in reconstructive plastic surgery, skin grafts for burns victims. We're going to look into his past cases, see if there's a disgruntled ex-patient, but it looks highly unlikely. We're also going to be looking into his accounts to see if he owed any significant amounts of money to anyone. Some sort of motive.'

'I don't think this was about money.'

'No.' Bishop turned to the door as the coroner, Angela Swan, entered. In her fifties, she was wearing scrubs which covered her from head to toe.

'Hello, DI Bishop.'

'Morning, Angela.'

'And you must be our temporary call-out?'

Holly was still staring at the desk. Something was bothering her but she couldn't tell what. She was quiet for too long and Bishop said, 'Holly?'

'Sorry, yes.' She looked up and gave Angela a wan smile.

'Get her a coffee, Bishop, she looks ill.'

Holly waited outside the front door by the stone steps, staring into space, drained. It had grown colder and the rain flashed

24

like silver needles as it blew past the halogen floodlights. She looked up as Bishop appeared and offered her a cup of coffee in a polystyrene cup.

'You probably won't sleep much. If you're going to be awake, might as well be wide awake, right?'

'Thanks.'

She smiled, touched, and took a sip. It was exactly what she needed. She wanted to get rid of the taste in her mouth. In fact she wanted to get rid of the taste in her body, under her skin, the images she saw whenever she closed her eyes.

Bishop sat down next to her with a coffee of his own. He seemed content to sit in silence and Holly was glad for the quiet. She thought she had hardened herself over the years with the thousands of case photos she had seen, but witnessing violence first hand was a very different animal.

'It never gets easier,' he said, as if reading her thoughts. 'I was working robbery when I got my first murder. A fifty-two-year-old female taxi driver had her skull bashed in with a ball-peen hammer. She was slumped over the steering wheel. When I opened the car door it looked like she was asleep. You know – nodded off after a long shift. Then I saw the hole in her temple, the pool of blood in her lap and on the rubber floor mat. The whole car smelled of vanilla. One of those air fresheners hanging from the rear-view. I can't stand vanilla now. Maureen Thyme her name was. Robert Stokes was the man who killed her.'

'You got him then?'

'Oh yeah. Fingerprints, blood. He even had the receipt for the hammer in his wallet when we arrested him. He was sentenced to twenty-seven years in prison, got out after twelve. Was back in prison six months later for GBH and assault. Now

25

he's serving time for rape. This time he probably won't get out.' He took a sip of coffee. 'It's ironic, isn't it? I finished my shift at seven but ended up chatting to the duty officer because Sergeant Ambrose was going to be late. His wife's expecting their first. The call came in at seven thirty-five. If I had left the station when my shift finished I'd have been off the rota, would have got home and watched an hour of mindless television, had a drink. Still been asleep now.'

'Bad timing.'

'For the bastard who did this, yes, because now I really want to catch him.' He tilted his head and narrowed his eyes. 'Tell me what you think.'

She hesitated, hoping her voice was as calm as she was pretending to be. 'I don't think this was a spontaneous killing. I think it's more likely to have been premeditated, and whoever is responsible didn't attempt to make it look like anything else. Didn't even try to throw you guys off the scent.'

'Why?'

'I don't know yet. After his fifth victim, Earle Nelson, aka the Gorilla Killer, believed he was uncatchable, that a divine right had been bestowed upon him to kill.'

'After his fifth victim? Did they catch this Nelson guy?'

'Yes. But not until he'd killed another fifteen people.'

Bishop huddled in his jacket and stared at his own breath as it formed a circle of mist in front of him. 'First impressions. What do we look for?'

'Our killer's got a record. A bad one. He's done this before, that much is obvious.' She turned to him and felt a tingle of anticipation in her spine despite the chill. 'We've just got to find out where and why.'

26

Five

When Holly woke she was stiff and had a gnawing headache.

She got up, pulled back the curtains and saw the faint glow of the winter sun reflecting off the windows of the flats opposite. She took a long hot shower, dressed, and went into the living room. There were fresh bluebells in a vase on the coffee table, a Harland Miller Penguin Plays original oil above the fireplace 'Death – What's In It For Me?' and the rest of the room was filled with bookcases – volumes on criminology and psychology, with a shelf for case files. She stared at the folder that Bishop had given her, and caught herself wringing her hands on her lap. She opened the file, on which someone had written simply 'The Wrights', and the date. Photos showing the bodies from every angle, with abbreviated notes scribbled in the margins that she didn't understand.

She stopped on a photo of Evelyn. The coroner had turned her on to her back, and her head had tilted naturally down and to the right. She had beautiful blue eyes. Holly passed a finger over the photo as delicately as if she were reading Braille.

The phone rang. It startled her. She didn't recognise the number but picked it up.

'It's Bishop.'

'Morning,' she said.

'How you feeling?'

'Drained. As if I'm hung over.'

'Yep. It can do that to you.' A pause and she could hear papers rustling in the background. 'Reason I'm calling: I have the debrief at eleven but thought you might want to come to the autopsy first. Sometimes it's better to see things rather than read about them.'

She checked her watch. It was 9 a.m. She had thought about breakfast but decided against it. 'Shall I meet you there?'

'Sure, it's the Wessex county coroner's office near East Street.'

Holly parked in the underground car park and took the lift up to reception. Bishop was waiting for her in one of the chairs, thumbing through a magazine. He smiled when he saw her, although he looked tired and she wondered if he had had any sleep at all. He led her back into the lift and pressed a button. The door closed and they started to ascend.

'When was your last autopsy?' he asked.

'Seven years ago. A horse, actually. Friend of mine had recently qualified as a vet and asked if I wanted to watch. I think I must have had an empty calendar that week.'

'Obviously.'

The lift opened on to a bright white corridor and the clinical smell wafted over her. She had been expecting it but it came as a surprise. Bishop led her to the first door on the left and reached for the handle. 'After you.'

Harsh neon strips lit the white-tiled floor, which sloped slightly from two walls down to a narrow gutter in the centre. The bodies lay on separate stainless steel autopsy tables, each covered with a white sheet.

Angela Swan was already there, standing between the tables, and she didn't look over when they entered. 'I've made a preliminary examination, but for your benefit I'll start with the good doctor, if you don't mind.'

She walked over to the white sheet on the left. Without her SOCO suit, Holly could see she was in her mid-fifties, with a fine-featured face and white and grey streaked hair. Above her hung a microphone into which she talked as she worked. 'The time is 9.45 a.m. on Tuesday 7 of November 2017. Angela Swan, DO, performing the autopsy on Doctor Jonathan Wright. The body was presented secured in a green body bag and wrapped within a white sheet.' She pulled back the sheet, revealing the head and upper torso. The doctor's face was pallid, almost pale blue, and his arms looked rubbery and hairless. 'The victim is naked. The body is cold and non-embalmed. Lividity is fixed in the distal portions of the limbs. A brown leather belt was removed earlier, labelled Exhibit 203A. Said belt had been tightened around the upper neck with a buckle. An extra hole had been cut into the leather to keep the belt tight – possibly a means of strangulation. See Appendix Two of my notes.'

Holly was standing to one side next to Bishop. It was chilly and she wished she'd worn a heavier jacket.

'The body is that of a normally developed white male. Measuring seventy-one inches and weighing two hundred and six pounds, generally consistent with the stated age of sixty-two. The eyes are open. The irises are brown and corneas are cloudy. Petechial haemorrhaging is present in the conjunctival surfaces of the eyes.'

29

Swan stood back and seemed to notice Holly for the first time. 'How are you enjoying the case?'

'Every time we meet there's a dead body in the room.'

'Nature of the beast,' said Swan. 'My kids aren't exactly lining up for work experience day. Bishop, I presume you're interested in the belts?'

'Please.'

'The one used around the doctor's neck was indeed his own and appeared to have been pulled from his trousers. The extra hole is more like a slit and would have been cut with a knife, possibly the same one that was used for the evisceration. Identical findings with the wife's belt. Probably hers, and the extra notch had been added in the same way.'

'Was she wearing the belt with the skirt?' Holly asked.

'No. No loops.'

'So the killer could have got it from her wardrobe?'

'Possibly. Yes. Removal of the belt around the doctor's neck revealed a ligature mark which will be in the report as "Ligature A" – immediately above the laryngeal prominence. It's approximately one inch wide and encircled the anterior of the neck.' She lifted the head gently. 'Much less prominent on the posterior of the neck, suggesting a gap between the ligature and the skin and consistent with hanging or violent strangulation. However, the skin shows no petechial haemorrhaging, which would indicate the belt was applied post-mortem.' She frowned, examined the neck again and then brought a large magnifier down from a pulley above the table and stared through it. 'You're not squeamish, Holly?'

'No.'

'Come closer then. I think you might find this interesting.'

Holly hesitated, then stepped quietly up to the table. She didn't feel the chill any more.

'There.' Swan pointed a finger. 'Underneath the red. See the slightly darker shade? A thinner strip encircling the neck.'

'Another ligature?'

'Correct.' She moved the magnifier away. 'We'll call this Ligature B.' She spoke into the microphone. 'This second horizontal mark observed on the victim's neck is dark red and encircles the neck one inch below the laryngeal prominence. In contrast, this mark does show petechial haemorrhaging and is consistent with a soft material, such as a length of fabric. Maybe a tie or curtain cord. Any trace evidence recovered from the scene that might assist in its identification, Bishop?'

'Nope.'

'He's very tidy, this killer of yours.' She placed a hand gently on the doctor's neck by the Adam's apple. 'Autopsy will undoubtedly show a broken hyoid bone.' She turned to Holly. 'I think you'd better step back for this, squeamish or not.'

Holly retreated to Bishop's side.

'Bishop?' Swan asked.

'Go ahead.'

Swan pulled the sheet down to the thighs.

'The body has been eviscerated from the sternum to the navel by a single cut in a diagonally downwards direction from left to right across the abdomen at approximately thirty degrees to the horizontal. The cut is consistent with the blade of a very sharp knife, at least six inches long, which would explain the damage to the internal organs. There is significant ante-mortem haemorrhaging, left upper chest. The evisceration would have been performed post-mortem.'

'Any hesitation marks?' Bishop asked.

The magnifier came down again and Swan took her time examining the skin around the cut. 'Nothing on the epidermis. One mark on an adjacent rib, anterior left side, that mirrors the cut almost exactly, which I conclude would have occurred as a result of the evisceration. No, this guy didn't have any second thoughts.'

'What time was he killed?' Bishop asked.

'I can be more accurate after I've opened him up and examined the stomach contents, but going by body temperature and rigor mortis, I'd estimate time of death at between five and seven p.m. last night.'

'Immediate cause of death?'

'Asphyxia due to ligature strangulation.'

She walked over to a bench where she had a cup of coffee sitting. 'What time's your debrief?'

'Twenty minutes.'

She took a quick sip then put the cup down. 'I'll get a move on then. Give you a quick synopsis now and you can read the full report later.' She changed gloves and moved over to the other white sheet. Holly found herself edging forward.

'The time is 9.58 a.m. on Tuesday 7 November 2017. Angela Swan, DO, performing the autopsy on Evelyn Wright.' She pulled down the white sheet and exposed Evelyn's naked body, gleaming china-white in the lights.

'The body is that of a normally developed, well-nourished Caucasian female measuring sixty-three inches in length and weighing one hundred and forty-four pounds; appearance generally consistent with the stated age of fifty-seven years. The body is cold and non-embalmed with declining rigor. Unblanching lividity is present on the anterior of the body in the regions of the feet ... the calves ... the abdomen, particularly on the left side ... the left arm, and the neck.' She brought the magnifier down. 'A one-inch-wide black belt was closed around the upper neck using the buckle. This belt, Exhibit 203B, was removed earlier by me. The opposite end of the belt was tied in an overhand knot.'

'No prints?'

'That would have been nice, wouldn't it? The eyes are open, the irises blue and corneas cloudy. The skull is symmetrical and there is evidence of extensive trauma in the infraorbital foramen and the squamous section of the frontal bone. A blunt-force injury with multiple cranial fractures resulting in a craniocerebral injury. The first wound measures approximately three inches in diameter; the frontal wound is larger at approximately five inches in diameter with a multitude of bone fragments from both fractures penetrating the underlying fascia and brain tissue. Depth of penetration of the first blow is approximately two inches, the second, approximately four inches.'

'Weapon?'

'Probably a flat-head hammer. The second blow was the one that killed her. Both blows would have been delivered in a single downward arc to the anterior of the head, at between an eighty and a one-hundred-and-ten-degree angle.' A moment. 'He's tall.' She moved her hands slowly along the china-white arms. 'The hands and nails are clean and have no evidence of injury. No defence wounds of any kind on either of the victims, which suggests there was no struggle.'

'He attacked very fast then.'

'*Blitzkrieg.*'

'Who do you think he attacked first?' Holly asked.

'Interesting question.' She thought for a few seconds then

turned to her. 'Almost impossible to tell until I've looked at the stomach contents.' Swan moved lower down the body. 'She wasn't raped as we first suspected. However, she was penetrated with a straight-edged blade which caused multiple lacerations and perforations. There is also evidence of soot deposition and searing to the skin. He burned her. Not with a cigarette though, something equally small but very regular and smooth. There are eleven marks in all. I'll number all of them for reference but my system may not correspond to the order in which they were received. All the injuries will be post-mortem, unless otherwise specified.'

'Cause of death?'

'Blunt-force cranial trauma.'

Bishop nodded slowly. Holly thought he sounded almost reluctant when he asked his next question.

'What do you think, Angela?'

'I wondered when you would ask. If it was just the doctor's body I'd say only a slim possibility. The ligature strangulation is similar. The evisceration is at odds but the injuries to the wife's genitalia and the burn marks are almost identical.'

She took off her gloves, pulled down her face mask and sighed.

'It's exactly like the other one.'

Six

'Which other one?'

They were driving through Hammersmith towards Fulham police station in Bishop's car. The mid-morning traffic lined up in front of them in a never-ending parade of headlights and tail lights. It was raining and the sky was like slate.

'Her name was Rebecca Bradshaw,' Bishop said. Holly sensed he wanted to say more but was keeping quiet. They stopped at a red light. He took a cigarette from his pocket and lit up. 'Sorry. I'm down to one a day.'

'That's okay. I don't mind.'

He cracked the window a little and the smoke drifted lazily outside. 'I should have told you, but I didn't know for sure they were connected until now. You say the words "serial killer" and it's like shouting "shark" on a busy beach.' He took a moment. 'Should I be shouting "shark"?'

In at the deep end. Her voice faltered slightly. 'Possibly. Tell me more about her.'

'She was a flight attendant for British Airways. Her body was found in her flat in St John's Wood on 18 October. She'd had her wrists slashed, been strangled post-mortem and had been burned and penetrated with a knife. A constable named Siskins found her. He'd only been with the force for four months. A web designer bored with his everyday life who wanted a career change and a bit of excitement. Shook him up pretty badly. He handed in his notice a week later. I presume he's designing web pages again.' For what seemed like a long time, neither of them spoke. Then Holly said:

'Were there any other similarities?'

'The mirror in her hallway had been smashed.' A beat. 'What's that about?'

'Doesn't like reflections? Doesn't like seeing himself? Don't know.'

He gave a brief shake of his head and his face looked almost ghostly in the dim light.

'Do you like any of them?' he asked.

'Who?'

'Your patients. The killers you look after.'

'I won't lie. They're hard work. They're demanding, sometimes violent, but at the same time it can be incredibly rewarding when one of them makes a breakthrough.'

'Do they get cured? I mean, can they go on to lead productive lives?'

'Some of them. Most of them can't or won't be helped. But they are better off in hospital than prison. And the public are better off too.'

'Why?'

'Prisons don't know how to deal with them. Serial killers are a different breed. They're not drug dealers, gang members, one-off murderers. They have a whole variety of problems that most people can't even pretend to comprehend.'

'And you can?'

'Sometimes. A lot of the time I can't. I don't think anybody can ever really understand someone else. You put a socio-path in a prison and they'll flourish because it creates a false reality for them. Model citizens when they live in a cell for twenty-three hours a day, and when they talk to their friendly in-house doctor they can make it appear as if they are learning to cope with their tendencies. But when that killer or rapist is released early on a doctor's recommendation, within a month they have raped or killed again – happens all the time. The doctors are dumbfounded. "They were doing so well, we don't understand ..." The reality is, you give a killer sudden free-dom with virtually no restrictions and they will reoffend. It's in their blood.'

He didn't say anything, merely nodded.

She carried on: 'Like the scorpion and the frog.'

'The what?'

'One of the first things we were taught at college when I was studying criminology was the story of the scorpion and the frog. There are different versions but this is the one that stuck with me. A scorpion walks down to the edge of the river, spots a frog and asks it to carry him across to the other side because it can't swim. The frog says, "No way. You'll sting me." The scorpion is horrified and promises he won't; he says he will owe the frog a huge favour. The frog, being a trusting old thing, finally agrees and the scorpion jumps on to his back and the frog hops all the way across to the other side of the river. As the scorpion slides off the frog's back, it stings him. The frog looks at him, incredulous, and with his dying breath asks, "Why did you sting me, knowing I would die? I don't understand." The scorpion just smiles and says, "Sorry, it's in my nature."'

Bishop gave a thin smile. 'Poor Mr Frog.'

'Never trust a scorpion.' She paused, a little reluctant to continue. 'There's one patient that I am close to.'

'A killer?'

'Yes. He's also charming, smart and funny. And he's really trying. He knows that things aren't working properly in his head and he wants to fix them. He wants to be normal.'

'I lost track of normal twenty years ago.' Bishop took another quick drag and threw the cigarette into the street as if he had a grudge against it. A spray of orange sparks that ended in a hiss. 'I got a phone call from our profiler, Sam Gordon, earlier this morning. There was an incident with his wife and she's taken a turn for the worse, looks like he won't be coming back for a while. I need to know if you can stay on.'

She didn't hesitate. She would have to rearrange her college rota, her visits to Wetherington, but it was doable. 'I'll need to see the case file for Rebecca Bradshaw as soon as possible.'

'I'll have a copy of everything ready for you at the station.' She thought he looked suddenly relieved. 'What do you think, Holly? Going to pull a rabbit out of the hat for me on this one?'

'I can try.'

'Good.' He rolled up the window. 'You need to meet the team.'

Seven

At the task force briefing, wall boards were covered with glossy photos of the victims and the interior and exterior of the crime scene and surrounding area. Holly hung to one side as a dozen or so police and special officers arrived, and found herself moving further away from Bishop until she was resting against the photocopier by the back wall. There were ten officers in all, five male, five female. Bishop was talking to a young sergeant by one of the desks. He was shorter than Bishop with light brown hair and eyes that matched the sky. He nodded and left the room carrying a file folder. Bishop waited until everybody had settled and the chatter had died.

'Let's get straight on.' He turned to the incident board. 'The two victims are husband and wife. Doctor Jonathan and Mrs Evelyn Wright, sixty-two and fifty-seven respectively. Both were brutally murdered, one by asphyxia with a fabric that we have not traced, the other by a blunt instrument trauma to the head. No sign of the weapon. Evelyn was assaulted and Jonathan eviscerated. We have not located the knife either. They both lived in a very desirable village called Abinger Hammer in Surrey. Nearest major town, Guildford. Theirs was a large Georgian house, with a two-hundred-yard gravel drive from a B-road that runs east to west through the village. The nearest neighbours are about fifty metres away. The couple were respected and well liked and the proud parents of two children, Connie and Stephen, who are both in their mid-twenties and living away from home. The daughter is a financial adviser at City Tech in Woking, the son a mechanical engineer with his own company who has settled in Brighton. Both have been informed and are awaiting formal interviews with us today. Bethany, you'll be liaising with them I believe?'

'Yes, sir.' Bethany, petite, fair-skinned and intense. 'They're both going to be here in about an hour I think, so I'll have my first chat with them then.'

'Are you going to their offices?'

'Later today.'

'Take a couple of PCs with you, check out their neighbourhoods while you're there.'

'Are we looking into them? The brother and sister?'

Bishop hesitated. 'Yes, but I'm pretty sure only to eliminate them from our enquiries. Run the usual checks into the family's finances anyway.' He pointed to another section of the board where a photo of a young woman with long dark hair was pinned.

'This is Alexandra, their niece. She was the one who discovered the bodies. She's nineteen, both her parents are deceased and she appears to have been very close to both Jonathan and Evelyn. This was backed up by a conversation with the two siblings. She's already spoken to the CSM and given a report ... Do we have that yet?'

A uniformed officer raised a hand. He held enough manila folders for everyone. 'Shall I distribute these now?'

'No, wait till we're done. Bethany, no one has been assigned to Alexandra as yet, but if you could come up with a time frame for counselling. Understandably, she's pretty shaken up.'

'Who were the other guests?'

'The next-door neighbours. Bill and Janice Anglesey from one side, Mr and Mrs Fenbourne from the other. They all turned up at eight fifteen, saw the police lights and were obviously horrified. We're getting detailed statements from them now. Checking the house phone records, mobiles and computers as well, to see who the doctor and his wife have been talking to these past few months.'

A phone rang on one of the desks, loud and shrill.

'Can we have the switchboard take all calls until we're done please, somebody? PC Prior.' The constable with the folders picked up the phone and whispered into it. Bishop carried on. 'We're still waiting for the final autopsy results but first impressions suggest both the doctor and his wife were killed in the living room which used to be the doctor's consultation room, between five and seven p.m. Let's talk about access.' He moved over to an aerial view of the property. 'Like I said, this place is fairly remote. There's a river at the end of the back garden. They don't have a boat and the mooring looks unused but we need that checked. Access by land: there is only one main road, the A25, that goes all the way through the village. There are smaller subsidiary roads on both sides: White Down Lane and Raikes Lane to the east where the A25 leads towards Dorking and the A24. And to the west, Hackhurst Lane, Beggars Lane and Wonham Way through the adjacent village of Gomshall and eventually Guildford. There are no speed cameras on the A24 and the closest CCTV is at a Shell garage on the A246 approximately nine miles away. The number 9 bus uses the

A24 through the village and the number 13 bus comes in from the opposite end originating in Guildford. Get the shifts of all the bus drivers and interview the ones who were working from midday to eleven p.m. on the day in question. Assuming the bus company has regular customers, try to get statements from them, especially the ones who prefer sitting on the upper decks – they may have seen something. Sergeant Ambrose, could you check on that?'

'Yes, sir.' It was the officer with the fair hair and blue eyes who had been talking to Bishop earlier. Holly hadn't noticed him come back in.

'I need someone to head up house-to-house in the local villages. Knocking on doors. Mosely, are you up for that?'

Mosely grimaced. He was a big man in plain clothes and looked like a rhino in a suit. 'I'm still working the Gordon case, sir, unless you want me to switch?'

'No, stay with that.' Bishop took a second. 'Erm ... while we're on the subject, I'm sure most of you know that Sam Gordon is away on compassionate leave, so for those of you who missed my morning briefing yesterday, this is Holly Wakefield, our behavioural analyst on the case.' He looked around. 'Where are you, Holly?'

'Over here.' She raised a hand in greeting and everyone turned to look at her. She licked her lips and managed a tentative 'Hi'. Bishop took back the reins. 'Holly came to view the crime scene last night and will be drawing up some kind of profile in the next twenty-four hours. Who wants house-to-house?'

'I'll do it.'

'Thank you, Sergeant Crane.' He was young, early twenties, with a determined smile. 'There are only twenty-odd premises in the village so it shouldn't take too long. Also, check to see if there are any dog walkers; if there are, get a statement and find out their routes. They'll know the area better than us. Maybe they saw something.'

He moved across to the photos of the crime scene.

'Forensics are still working the rooms and I don't expect them to be done anytime soon. So far nothing on the bodies but every contact leaves a trace. There will be silent witnesses somewhere – and hopefully they'll be speaking to us soon. As for motive, we have none as yet. There appeared to be nothing stolen, and I think Constable Jacobs is running an inventory check against their latest home insurance policy which, lucky for us, was renegotiated only nine months ago.'

'I'll have it on file by this afternoon,' said Jacobs.

'Not exactly much to go on at the moment, so we apply the old maxim: "Find out how a person lived and you will find out how they died." What habits, hobbies, leisure routine did the victims have? Where did they frequent? Check out the local pubs, churches, betting shops. They're both retired but they will have had friends and old work colleagues. Someone, some-where will have seen something or know someone. Sergeant Williams, take a three-man team with you.'

'Yes, sir.'

'What are we doing with the media?' Another woman in the squad. She was hidden among the masses but Holly made her out. Tall and slim, holding a pen and notebook in her hand.

'Nothing yet, Kathy, although I'll need you to draft a press release by tomorrow. They know it's something bad but at the moment not a word, please.'

An older man had appeared at the back of the office, decked out in a starched uniform with the shoulder insignia of a chief constable. He was tall and grey-haired, with an authority that didn't need to flaunt itself. He nodded once at Bishop then turned on his heel and disappeared.

'One more thing,' said Bishop. He paused until he was sure he had their attention. 'Angela Swan is in the middle of the autopsy but it appears she will conclude that this is the same killer as the Rebecca Bradshaw case.'

Holly looked at the sea of faces watching Bishop. Everyone listened with rapt attention, some wrote notes; a few stared into space, deep in thought. He carried on: 'I'm hesitant to use the phrase "serial killer"; you all know the connotations that come with that, so I won't for now. But we have to be aware that it is a possibility. Rebecca's murder was three weeks ago now so we need to reread every statement, every assessment, every witness report and compare it to what we're going to find with this one. Something connects the victims – we need to find out what. Mosely, make copies of everything available. We'll have another briefing at six o'clock tonight. Preliminary findings. You know your roles. Briefing material along with the policy file from Constable Prior – I know most of you are up to date but please reread. Ambrose, you're going to be taking deputy SIO on this.'

'Thank you, sir.'

People started to move around and talk, phones were picked up, numbers dialled and Holly found herself lost in the maelstrom of bodies.

'Kathy Pembroke.' The press officer introduced herself. They shook hands.

'Holly. Hi.'

'We'll have a chat at some point. Legal aspects, if that's okay?'

'I'll make sure I'm available.'

Kathy nodded and left, and Holly saw Bishop had turned back to the crime scene photos. She made her way over to him.

'It's going to be hectic. Sorry,' he said.

'I'm up for it.'

He nodded, and Holly thought he looked pleased. 'Tomorrow afternoon then. Some sort of profile, yes?'

'Yes.'

'Good.' He turned and gave her a fleeting smile as Ambrose approached. 'Sir?'

'Sergeant Ambrose, this is Holly.'

They shook hands. He was younger than she'd first thought.

'Nice to meet you,' she said.

'Likewise.' He smiled and handed her a file. 'Rebecca Bradshaw.' He immediately turned back to Bishop: 'Sam Gordon's come in. He's in your office.'

Bishop winced. 'He's not supposed to be here.' He looked to Holly, 'Look, I've got to deal with this so . . .'

Bishop walked away. Ambrose hovered, awkward.

'Welcome to the squad, Holly. How many cases have you worked?'

'This is the first. It's not something I . . . Sam's your regular profiler, right?'

'Yes. His wife was attacked last week. Acid thrown in her face. Quite bad. Hence the compassionate leave. He's part-time, semi-retired anyway, but it's not pleasant. We're trying to work out if it's retribution for an investigation he's been involved with.'

'Has he worked a lot of cases?'

'A couple of dozen over the past five years or so. His wife used to come in sometimes. Bring us cupcakes. She's nice. Janine.'

Holly thought he looked desperate to get on so she decided

45

to make a move herself. 'I'll leave you to it, Sergeant. See you tomorrow.' He waved absently, already starting to skim through a thick file he had picked up from a desk.

Holly followed the corridor, trying to remember the way she had come in. She passed numerous officers and plain-clothes detectives and then she saw Bishop at the end of the building talking animatedly on the phone. He hung up and Holly watched him as he entered an office and greeted a man who was sitting in a chair, head buried in his hands.

Eight

Rebecca Bradshaw had been killed on 18 October 2015 between 4.30 and 6.30 p.m.

She was thirty-nine years old, five feet five inches tall and weighed one hundred and twenty-four pounds. There was no evidence of rape, but there were multiple cuts and stab wounds to the vaginal area with a sharp-bladed implement as well as a series of curve-edged burns along her inner thighs. She was identified by her mother on the day of the autopsy.

She had suffered frenzied cuts to the radial arteries on both wrists which had caused rapid exsanguination resulting in severe hypovolemia and death. Initially, the first officer on the scene, PC Siskins, suspected a suicide but when the coroner discovered she had received a blow to the back of her head and the ligature mark around her neck was deemed to have been applied post-mortem, it was concluded that suicide was highly improbable. The Met Serious Crimes Squad was notified of this finding immediately.

Holly put the autopsy report down, went to the kitchen and made a new pot of coffee, her mind working overtime. She had already rifled through her shelves, and over every available surface were dozens of old case files. They contained notes, some handwritten, on various killers. Grainy enlargements of murder weapons and crime scenes. Pages of descriptions, lab reports, testimonies, and graphic photos, with headings such as 'Autopsy', 'Witness statements', 'Psychological assessment', 'Sociopathic tendencies', all lined up and placed in order. She took a deep breath, picked up the phone and dialled. It was answered within two rings.

'Wetherington Treatment Centre.'

'Hi, Jackie, it's Holly. How's the madhouse?'

'Smells like wet clothes and floor polish, how's you?'

'Surrounded by paperwork and lots of questions. I'm afraid I'm going to have to reschedule my rota, I'm consulting with the Met on a case.'

'No problem, I'll let Central know.'

'Thanks, Jackie.' She poured herself a coffee with her free hand and grabbed a long-forgotten biscuit from a tin on the counter. 'I'm also going to need the names of all the NHS watch-list transfers in the last five years.'

'All of them?'

'No – only the ones predisposed to strangulation and or sexual humiliation.' She felt suddenly drawn and tired. 'How's Lee?'

'He's doing well. He came out of solitary three hours ago. Ate his favourite dinner. Roast beef and veg.'

'Good. Tell him . . . tell him I'll be in as soon as I can.'

'I will do, Holly. Bye.'

'Bye.'

She hung up and checked her watch. It was eight thirty p.m. She hadn't eaten properly for over twenty-four hours. She took one bite of the biscuit and threw it in the bin, went back into the living room and stared at the daunting amount of material in front of her. She had a sudden thought, remembering a quote from one of her books. FBI profiler John Douglas had always said, 'If you want to understand the artist, you have to look at the painting.'

She took down her Harland Miller painting above the mantel. The wall stared back at her. A blank canvas but she had to start somewhere. She grabbed the photos of Rebecca, Jonathan and Evelyn and stuck them up in a line. Then she joined them together with a black felt pen and wrote their names and the dates of their murders underneath. She added a crime scene photo under each one and put a detailed map of London and its surrounding counties to their right. She circled the murder sites and measured the distance between them. Approximately thirty-five to forty miles. That was quite a distance.

She rummaged through the files and picked up the police report and subsequent investigation on Rebecca Bradshaw. No witnesses. All of her friends had been interviewed, statements taken, and every one of them had an alibi. There was no CCTV on her street, no unusual cars or people were seen hanging around in the weeks before or after. She turned to the statement by PC Sean Siskins and read it again.

I approached the residence, Flat 3, Acacia Place St John's Wood, accompanied by a friend of Rebecca's, Marissa Stokes, a purser with British Airways who lived within the area. She and Rebecca had known each other for three years and she described her friend as 'an easy-going spirit, kind-hearted' but there was also a 'tough edge' to her and she wasn't a pushover. Marissa had first alerted the police when Rebecca hadn't turned up for their post-work drink at the Judge & Quill on Rothery Road at 6 p.m. on Tuesday 18 October.

They had both flown in from Chicago that morning and were looking forward to three days' leave. She was concerned because Rebecca was never late and they had talked earlier in the afternoon, confirming their meeting. It was 9.07 p.m. when I arrived at the residence and knocked on the front door. There was no answer. I shouted, 'Rebecca, this is the police!' three times and then twice through the letter box. Still nothing. I told Marissa I was going to open the door and asked her to stay outside and wait for me. She said she would. I used the key given to me by Mr Eric Khan (real name Mohammed Khan), the landlord, who said he could not assist because he had to take his mother out for her birthday dinner at a local Thai restaurant (the booking was confirmed by me later that evening and Mr Khan and his mother were there for four hours). Regarding Rebecca, Mr Khan said she always paid her rent on time and was very pleasant but he didn't see her much because of her flying schedule.

I turned the key in the lock and opened the front door. It was a typical 1960s council flat. I switched the hall light on. It didn't work and on inspection I discovered the bulb had been removed. I got out my torch but left the front door open as well so I could see properly. The hallway was dingy but had bright orange carpet. I then noticed the hall mirror had been smashed although it was still hanging on the wall. The hall had one door to the right that opened on to the living room and carpeted steps leading upstairs to the left. Ahead was the kitchen, the door was open. I called out 'Rebecca' several times and identified myself but again there was no reply. I quickly checked the living room and kitchen and as I turned to head up the stairs I noticed that Marissa had entered the flat. I instructed her to stay where she was and asked her not to touch anything. She nodded and put her hands in her jacket pockets. I continued my search by ascending the stairs. At the top of the landing there were three doors. Marissa shouted up that Rebecca's bedroom was at the far end so I headed in that direction.

The bedroom door was closed. I pushed into it and I thought it was stuck against the carpet because it stopped moving after about twelve inches. The lights were off so I reached my hand through, flicked on the switch but again, it didn't work. I shone my torch inside the room. From where I was I could see a shelf and part of the far wall. It looked as though she was in the middle of redecorating. I pushed a little harder and despite some resistance the door opened another twelve inches, enough room for me to put my head around the side and have a look.

The body was facing me, leaning up against the foot of the bed. I realised then that it was one of her legs that had been resting against the door that had created the resistance. I deduced from the description Marissa had given that it was very likely Rebecca Bradshaw sitting in front of me. She was dressed in a short black skirt with a white blouse and no shoes. Her head was bowed down, resting against her chest. I couldn't see her face or if her eyes were open or closed and it appeared as if she had a thin plastic yellow belt fixed around her neck. Her arms were placed either side of her body, facing upwards. Each of her wrists had been slashed quite violently. There was an enormous amount of blood on the pale carpet, by the wrists and hands and also along the outside of the thighs and calves down to the feet where it had pooled. I thought about entering the room to check to see if she was alive, but I knew she probably wasn't because the blood looked as if it had already congealed. So I stayed exactly where I was as I didn't want to contaminate the scene. I immediately called for the paramedics, told the station of my situation and then radioed my sergeant to get here as soon as possible and seal off the flat. I then put a call in to the coroner's office. The woman would have to be officially pronounced dead before we could begin our investigation.

Holly put the report down. Thoughts hesitant. How did he do it? How did he get into Rebecca's house? Did she let him in? No. Why would she? Only if she had known him, but this guy can't form friendships with women. Deep down, he's terrified of them. Especially someone like Rebecca. Smart. Resourceful. Outgoing. She'd eat him up and spit him out.

A stranger then? Smarmy. Talking his way inside like a cheap weekend salesman. Wouldn't work. She worked with 'smarmy' every flight. No. Rebecca was a smart cookie. She'd know better than to let a stranger in the house. And even if he had forced his way inside, there was no blood spatter on the walls or ceiling when the hammer had come down on her head. There's a point, Holly. Think. She was attacked from behind. So she hadn't turned around. She hadn't seen him. It was a total surprise. No defence wounds on her hands or body, just like Evelyn. A surprise in her own home – which meant what? What did it mean, Holly? How would someone surprise me here?

She looked around her flat and got up. Started to pace. The only way you could surprise me was if I didn't see you. Hidden somewhere? Behind the doors? Possibly. Wait for me to come close to you and then ... No. That wouldn't work. Too many things could go wrong. I might see you. Sense you. The lights hadn't been working though, had they?

Holly turned off all the lights in her flat. Everything looked familiar but it was somehow foreign now. She opened the front door, stepped outside and came back in, closing it behind her. Eyes still adjusting to the darkness.

Rebecca comes home. Feels her way past the open front door. Closes it behind her. Even darker now. Lock it like you always do. Now you're trapped but you don't know it yet. Everything's okay. Turn on the hall light. The dull flick-flack. The bulb has gone. Happens all the time. Walk forward to the living room, try the light in there. Same thing. All of them have gone? That's weird. No it's not, Rebecca. A fuse then. Hate that. Where's the fuse box? In the bedroom. Maybe use the torch on your phone now to go upstairs? Maybe not. Could be in your jacket or purse. Hard to get to and it's not like you don't know your way around your own home, is it? Up the stairs we go then. Dragging your flight bag in the darkness. Bump. Bump. Bump on the steps. Hope you don't annoy the neighbours. Take the left. Open your bedroom door. The soft scuff on the carpet. That familiar sound. Heightened by the darkness but everything's still okay. Flick the switch. This light in here has gone too. Definitely the fuse. Curtains are drawn as well. That's odd. I don't remember doing that before I left. Maybe I did? No ... why would I draw the curtains? Let go of the suitcase. Staring at the curtains. Walking over now. I don't remember ...

THWACK!

The hammer comes down.

Holly winced. She could almost feel the blow. The immediate ache of pain. The inevitable deafness in her ears and then the carpet rushing up to meet her. And it's all over. So sudden. A life wiped out. Only one conclusion.

He was already inside.

Like a spider in the lair. Except it was her lair, you bastard.

It was her place of safety but he had made it his. His domain now. Waiting for her to come home from Chicago. Handing out her final packets of peanuts and smiling goodbye. Catching the crew bus to Hatton Cross. Driving back. And he's waiting with the lights off. Rebecca couldn't see a bloody thing.

This guy's a planner, Holly thought. A meticulous planner. How long did you watch her for? Weeks? Months? She replaced the file and picked up the investigation report. She flicked through it, picking up relevant information as she went.

The day's flight manifesto had been obtained and all the passengers on BA 1543 from Chicago had been contacted as it was first suspected a traveller might have been the culprit, but even after cross-referencing the passenger list with Interpol and the Home Office no names were flagged. At the time of the report, seventy-eight passengers had responded and been cleared. All of the BA flight crew were interviewed and asked specific questions about Rebecca, her passenger relationships on this flight and any others that stood out. Leads were followed up but after three weeks all alibis had been verified. Attention turned back to Marissa for information as she seemed to be Rebecca's closest friend; she gave an honest account of the flight attendant's life. Rebecca was a *'lovely person who would do anything for anyone. Everybody liked her and she didn't have any enemies'.* Her ex-boyfriend, Martin Cornwall, with whom she'd split up in June, was devastated by the news and had an airtight alibi. He worked in the City as a trader for JP Morgan and had last seen Rebecca three months previously. Her mobile was discovered in a handbag in her bedroom and all her calls were analysed. There were no strange or withheld numbers, simply a catalogue of regular communication to close friends and work. She had no siblings and both her parents were deceased.

Holly stopped reading, took a red felt pen and drew a circle with a question mark above all three victims. *Why these three? What did you see in them? Were they weak, were they vulnerable? What is it about them that we don't know yet?* Holly needed to step into his shoes. However unpleasant it was, she knew she had to think like the killer. She wrote down Domination, Manipulation, Control next to the question mark, then Bed-wetting, Setting fires, Cruelty to animals. It was known as the triad of homicidal symptoms. Three events that were early signals of sociopathic behaviour.

'What did you fantasise about when you were young?' she said aloud, and then to herself: *Are you refining this fantasy with each kill? What was the difference between Rebecca and Evelyn? And was Jonathan just in the way – an afterthought because he happened to be there, maybe not part of the original plan? But you had to make it look good, didn't you? You had to push the boundaries, try something different, try to make us believe that you didn't mind him being there. The overkill. The evisceration. Or maybe not. Maybe it was a refinement of the fantasy. Maybe the doctor was the intended victim—*

The phone rang. She jumped before snapping it up.

'Hello?'

'It's Angela Swan from the coroner's office. I have an answer to your question.'

'What question?'

'Who was killed first. It was Evelyn, by about five minutes. Which makes me think she was alone downstairs when she was attacked. Her husband would have been getting ready in the bedroom, then he came down, discovered her and met his fate.'

'Thank you, Angela.'

'You'll have the full report by tomorrow afternoon.'

The line went dead.

Holly hung up and looked back at Evelyn's photo. It wasn't much but it was a start. She immediately dismissed the thought of Jonathan being the main target. It wasn't about him. He was stronger than his wife, more of a direct threat, and yet the killer had gone straight to her, killed her first because that's where most of his anger lay. Towards the woman. She wrote, '*Sexually immature, incompetent*'. No rape but a manipulation of the bodies, masturbation probably, although he would have been careful, but definitely no intercourse.

So what was it about Rebecca and Evelyn? What connected them together and, more importantly, what connected them to this killer? They were both well liked, apparently; Evelyn was happily married with two doting children, active in the local church and community and the chairperson of local charities. Rebecca had a lot of friends, loved her job and had that sunny disposition that all flight attendants seem to be born with.

She reread part of Marissa's statement where she had described her best friend: *A lovely person who would do anything for anyone. Everybody liked her and she didn't have any enemies.*

'No enemies.' Holly raised her head and gazed at the bloody crime scene photos of Rebecca Bradshaw. 'Sorry, Rebecca, but that can't be right,' she whispered. 'Somebody really hated you.'

Nine

Holly got the call from Wetherington Hospital at 7.20 in the morning.

Jackie informed her that Max Carrington and Judy Olsen had scheduled an emergency meeting with her before her rounds.

'What's it about?'

'I don't know,' replied Jackie. 'They're keeping quiet.'

When she arrived at the clinic, she was ushered straight into Carrington's office. He was sitting behind his desk and the moment she entered, he pinched the bridge of his nose and started shaking his head feebly. Judy Olsen was one of the more senior directors of the facility. She was in her sixties with terminally short hair. Holly hadn't seen her for months and the sexagenarian smiled and stood up when Holly entered and they shook hands.

'Lovely to see you again, Holly. Sorry to have to bring you in like this. But we've had a request' – she passed over a thin folder – 'from the judiciary review board regarding Lee Miller's case. It's been thirteen years since Lee was found guilty of murdering Ryan Abbotswood. Lee's lead therapist, Mary Sharpe, has made wonderful progress but she's not been as effective as we had hoped. He's not opening up to her. Ryan's family want closure and there are still a few blanks in his report that need filling in.'

'Such as?'

'The review board are curious about the room where the body was found.'

'The room.'

'Yes. His room. He had a special name for it. I don't ...'

'He called it the Red Room,' Holly said.

'Yes. That's right. The Red Room. Why red?'

'Red. Often signals danger. Stop signs are red. A red alert? It's the highest level of threat, isn't it. Which means people have to ... What actual colour was it? I've never seen the photos. I mean, it wasn't painted red, was it?'

'No, it was magnolia or something,' Judy said. 'Or grey. Maybe it was grey.' Judy sat on the edge of the desk. 'This proposition is unorthodox, as you know, but we're hoping you can break through to Lee. If he is forthcoming, it may help his parole.'

'Parole? He's never getting out. We both know that.' She felt herself faltering. 'Is there anyone else? I mean, there are fifty-three therapists here. Perhaps—'

'We've been rotating therapists for over a year now. You should have been informed.' Olson shot a look at Carrington. Carrington glanced away, reddening slightly. 'The judiciary have been very patient but are coming to the end of their review, Holly. They need an answer within two weeks'

'Two weeks? Jesus, that's not enough time to—'

'It's a tall order, I know,' Judy said.

'It's ridiculous. How can I get that sort of information out of him in two weeks?'

'It may be Lee's only chance.'

Holly put her shoulders back. 'All right. Fine, I'll do it.' She walked over to the door but lingered, not quite wanting to leave yet. 'When do I start?'

'As soon as possible.' This from Carrington, who had somehow managed to find his balls again.

Olsen shot him a look and he withered. Her tone softened.

'Thank you, Holly. I really mean that.'

A soft electronic click and the door opened.

Lee was sitting on the floor, the epitome of defeat; leaning back against the wall, his head resting on his chest, both arms wilted across his lap. Holly watched him for a while, entered and sat down cross-legged in front of him. She took a deep breath. Composed herself.

'Do you remember this?' she said. 'In the field, at the beach, wherever you are, you're always in reach. Come on. Do it with me. Lee?'

He looked up at her slowly, eyes intolerably sad.

'I know why you're here, Holly. This won't work.'

'It could.' She took her time. Then delicately. 'There's talk of a possible parole.'

'There's talk of another Brexit vote but I'm not holding my breath.'

'Lee . . .'

'Don't. You could have at least smiled when you said it, Holly. Those words mean nothing. It's what's behind them that matters. What's in your eyes.'

'This goes all the way up to Judy Olsen. I want to help so much but . . . I feel if I don't at least try then I have failed you.'

'Nobody has failed me. It's just the way things have turned out. Telling you things about that night . . . Do you really want to know what happened?'

'If it will help you.'

'I don't know if it will.'

'You and Ryan were close.'

'Don't start.'

'I've already read the file, Lee.'

'Don't fucking start!' He took a moment. Took a breath. Teeth gritted. 'I don't want to tell you things.'

'Why not?'

'I . . . I don't want you to think I'm a monster.'

'I don't think you're a monster, Lee. That has never been an issue at all.' She took a moment. His eyes were flitting from side to side. She needed him to come back to her.

'Have you eaten?'

'What?' He turned. Faced her. 'I'm not on a hunger strike. I like the food here, as it happens. Although I was horribly perturbed to have been told that in the outside world they have changed the name of my favourite dessert from Spotted Dick to Spotted Richard. In case some poor soul is offended by the vague physical attribution to a lump of cock.'

She couldn't help smiling. 'That's ridiculous. Where did you hear that?'

'Mrs Beeton would turn in her grave. It's lovely to see you smile.'

She nodded. Then – 'I had no idea they had been pushing this on you for nearly a year.'

'Trying to fit a square peg into a round hole. Some of the therapists I found amusing at times. They have nothing but water between their ears.'

'What about Mary Sharpe?

'As blunt as a spoon.'

'I hope—'

'"Hope is the thing with feathers, that perches in the soul. And sings the tune without the words and never stops at all."'

'That's beautiful.'

'Emily Dickinson.'

She shook her head. 'I can't ...' the thought trailed off into nothing and they sat in silence for a while. 'What do you want, Lee?'

'I want to be free of me. Inside. I want to be free.'

'Then I think this could really help. The room where Ryan was killed. Why did you call it the Red Room? That's all they want to know.' She stared at him but now she hoped he would look away. He didn't.

'Your face looks strange today,' he said.

'What do you mean?'

'I don't know. The thoughts come into my head and I say them. Today is the last day I'll see you like this.'

'Don't talk like that, Lee.'

'Like what? A manic-depressive sociopath with suicidal tendencies? Me, me, me.'

'Maybe they need to adjust your medication.'

'My medication? Put the pill in front of me. This will help. Let my eyes grow heavy. Nothing can hurt me any more?' He suddenly stood up and started pacing, his head tilted at an awkward angle looking back at her. 'I'm sick of the magical words, the whispers that mean absolutely nothing. Put a sign around my neck. Do not fucking disturb! Oh, the bountiful land of milk and honey. It is a figment of everyone else's imagination, including yours, but not mine, because I know better. I don't think you realise how fast I'm sinking.' He paused and his eyes were like lasers. 'Do you?'

She found herself shaking her head.

'Don't shake your head at me! You don't know. The next time I'm never coming back, am I?'

'Lee, don't talk like that! They want me to help you. Talk to me, for God's sake! Tell me about what happened in that room.'

'I've already gone to the other side. They show me things when I'm asleep. They don't think I see, but I see everything!' He stopped pacing and stared at her, his shoulders hunched, his hands like twisted claws. 'I see everything. Sentenced to keep drifting further and further away from reality. I'm sick of wearing this mask. I should just let it slip once and for all and embrace who I really am.'

'I know who you really are, Lee. I've seen you. You're not—'

'Yes,' he whispered, but it had the beginnings of a snarl. 'And I've seen you . . . remember?'

Holly walked briskly away from the interview room and headed towards the exit. She clutched the case notes to her chest, her emotions so pulverised she couldn't even speak. Jackie said something to her as she passed, but it was distorted, some other language, and Holly couldn't face her so she carried on past the security checks, pressed the buzzer and exited the building.

It was raining hard as she walked to her car, but she found it cathartic, washing away her sins and letting them swirl in the mud along the pavement until they disappeared down the drain. Once inside she straightened herself up and took a deep breath. Then she caught sight of her reflection in the rear-view mirror and started to cry. Great sobs that heaved through her body. A slough of despair that seemed to have a life of its own and never wanted to end. But it did end. And when it did, Holly found the strength from somewhere, wiped away the tears and started the car.

Ten

Holly entered the incident room and smiled an apology for being late. The smile was false and all too brief but she hoped Bishop was too busy to notice. He stopped whatever he was saying as she pushed her way through the assembled task force and sat on one of the empty desks. Bishop was standing in front of them all and he waited for her to settle before he began again.

'Sergeant Williams has put together a profile of the victims and in summary we've got our work cut out for us. Mr and Mrs Wright were the quintessential older couple living in an English village: well liked, regular churchgoers, charitable, no financial problems, paid their taxes on time in the years they worked, had decent pensions and a sizeable amount in stocks and shares. Nothing that was hidden and everything divided three ways in their wills. Their routine as such was simply that. Very routine. Driving to Waitrose twice a week, Tuesdays and Fridays, for grocery shopping and a coffee. No long journeys except for the occasional visits maybe twice a year to Brighton or Woking to see their children. They were both keen gardeners, entertained once every few months with the local villagers and would either watch television or read books from their extensive library in the evenings. His old clinic partner, Doctor Hatcher, had nothing but praise for him and his wife and there were never any lawsuits or complaints made against him or his practice.

'There you have it. If we were hoping for hidden bank accounts and illegal offshore trading deals that had gone horribly wrong to provide some sort of motive, we're sadly disappointed. Jacobs, enlighten us on the inventory.'

'Disappointing again. The only thing missing of any note seems to have been a bit of cash that was hidden in a biscuit tin in the kitchen.'

'How much?'

'The niece thinks about fifty pounds. I mean, they have some nice paintings, really nice, worth thousands, and some silver as well, but none of that was touched. Everything of any value seems to have been left in place. Whoever did it, didn't seem to want to take anything.'

'Unless they were disturbed and didn't have the time.'

'Right. I'll bring you a full copy of the report after this. And the paper that had been burned in the fireplace – it was an old National Trust membership renewal form for Mrs Wright. So . . .'

Bishop nodded. 'Kathy?'

'We've got the press release going out today. The tabloids are already frothing at the mouth to get into this, for obvious reasons. It's been cleared by legal and we're keeping a few things out; firstly, that it appears to be the same killer as Rebecca Bradshaw, and secondly the smashed mirror at both crime scenes. Now, if some of the press do cotton on to the fact that it is the same killer, I will deal with it. If any one of you gets asked probing questions, on no account try to answer them because they can cut and paste whatever you say. All enquiries of that nature get channelled through me, please.'

'Thank you, Kathy,' Bishop sighed, staring at his hands, before he looked up at the group. 'This is the second murder that we know about. Three victims so far. I'm hoping there aren't more that we haven't linked to this guy yet but I have a feeling I may be wrong. Therefore I want an inventory of unsolved cases to be made a priority. Let's go back through the last ten years. Um . . . ' – he looked around the room – 'Sergeant Karanack, you're taking point on that, please. Take two researchers and start digging.' Karanack, Asian, slight of build, raised a hand to acknowledge. Bishop paused. 'I'm now going to pass you over to Holly, who's had a look at all the evidence and may have some insight as to what we're dealing with here.'

All eyes turned to her. She could have heard a pin drop. The crowd gathered in front of her weren't young adults, fresh out of college, desperate to learn, they were police men and women and violent crime specialists, highly experienced agents who had seen more death than she cared to imagine. She tried to conjure the friendly and jovial faces of one of her classes at King's College, but there was hardness in these eyes, chips of flint and steel that had seen too many unforgettable things. Some were no doubt jaded, too many shifts, too many marriages, but each one of them had a certain confidence about them, an astuteness you could only earn out in the field. It was intimidating. She took a breath.

'Good morning, everybody,' she began. 'I agree with DI Bishop: I don't believe this is the beginning for him. These were not his first kills.' She turned and glanced back at the board, took her time. Shot a look at the sergeant. 'Karanack, right?'

'Yes.'

'Look for similarities in the old case files. Not just the victims and their ages, but the method. Focus more on female victims but don't entirely discount men. Priors will definitely include attempted rapes and possibly murders. Check the database of all known sex offenders. The double strangulation, the sado-masochistic aspect and the slashing of the wrists are key here.' She wrote on the board: *Domination . . . Manipulation . . . Control.*

'Domination, manipulation and control.' She turned back to face everyone. 'These are the three most common motives of a serial killer. With each of his victims so far he has exercised all three. This killer likes his drama as well: the placing of the bodies, the dramatic theme, the fact that in both murder rooms the victims had been left in the dark. Constable Siskins found Rebecca at night in her bedroom. Both the hall and bedroom light bulbs had been removed, and according to Alexandra the lights in the main rooms were off when she arrived at the Wrights' house. Her uncle and aunt didn't answer when she called out their names, which already had her slightly worried, but then when she went into the living room and turned on the lights . . . well, there is perhaps nothing more terrifying than someone entering a room and suddenly coming face to face with that nightmare scenario. He wanted to create as much shock as he possibly could in whoever discovered the bodies. That is him. His behaviour. And his behaviour will reflect his personality.'

She pointed back to the crime scene photos. 'This is some sort of fantasy for him. Fantasies that would have developed when he was very young. Note the almost identical injuries to

Rebecca and Evelyn. The relationship between sex and death. It's very specific. Which brings me to another indicating factor, which is that he killed Evelyn first.'

'That doesn't make sense.' It was Ambrose. 'Her husband would have been more of a threat.'

'Correct. But what this shows us is that his anger was primarily aimed at her. He hated her. The two blows to her head obliterated her face and the cuts on her wrists were frenzied, to say the least. And then, after the kill, both victims were strangled post-mortem. That's another signature. Again, the sado-masochism. But the killer isn't directing his anger at what was the initial cause.' She took a second to collect herself, hoping she wasn't going too fast or leaving anything out.

'What was?'

'I'm sorry?' The question disorientated her.

'What was the cause then?' It was Bethany asking the question.

'Oh. Erm . . . there will have been a whole collection of factors but he will probably have been abused as a child. It could have been his mother. It would have been a dominating figure, most probably female, but she won't be around any more. She'll be dead, I think, whether by his hand or not it's impossible to tell right now. That's what . . . that's part of his history.'

There were no more questions so she moved on.

'On the face of it, these killing appear to be random. The victims are very different from each other. A different geographical area, a different economic and socioeconomic bracket, but I think that's misleading. I don't think he knew them as such. They were strangers but I don't think they were haphazard. Something binds them together. If we can look at the geographics for a second.' She went over to the map on the incident board and circled the two murder sites.

'Wherever he lives, I don't think this killer would want to kill on his own doorstep even though the travelling is minimal. It's too dangerous. There would be too many opportunities for someone to recognise him. It's approximately thirty-five to forty miles between the two murder sites. That's a big distance to cover, which again makes me believe that these aren't random attacks. Rebecca and Evelyn weren't people he saw on the same street while he was going about his daily life and noticed them as potential targets. Which draws me to conclude that he probably doesn't live in or near Abinger Hammer or St John's Wood. Plus, the immediate areas around the kill sites are what we call the buffer zones. He won't live there – much too dangerous for him. So we should discount these two areas. Our killer is therefore a commuter, a traveller who either searches for a suitable victim away from his home, or finds potential victims by some other means and then chooses which one to kill depending upon their location. Ideally' – she drew a circle between the two murder sites – 'the killer should be based somewhere between the two areas.' She took a breath. 'But that would be too easy, wouldn't it?'

It was rhetorical but she heard a few of the squad say, 'Yes.'

'So, if they're not simply vulnerable victims, which I don't believe they are, then our killer has chosen them for a specific reason. Which means he has a mission.'

'What sort of mission?' Kathy asked.

'I don't know yet.' Holly's gaze wandered back to the crime scene photos. 'Some kill for lust, some for the thrill of it, some for profit. Whatever it is in this case, it would have evolved from a fantasy created in childhood. Sutcliffe's mission was to get rid of prostitutes. He saw what they did as wrong and unclean. He actually thought he was doing them a favour and redeeming them, purging them of their wrongdoings. He was surprised they weren't grateful as he was killing them. This killer's mission or his motivation is going to be complex and will make his kill choices confusing and practically impossible to predict. Let's look at him for a while.' She went over the board and attached an 8 x 10 sheet of white paper. She lifted her pen as if about to write in the middle, but after hesitating for a moment she put it down and turned back to the room.

'This is him,' she said flatly. 'This is our killer. We can't see him yet, can't see anything at the moment, but he is here in this room, judging us, watching us, waiting for us, knowing that we are looking at the photos of *his* victims on *this* board in *this* police station. He is out there somewhere, preparing for the next one – because he will continue to kill. He has to; he is addicted to the feelings he gets when he does. What he is doing is completely rational to him so there is no reason for him to stop. Will he suffer from a conscience, guilt, compassion? None of the above. Think of a shark in a cage full of bleeding fish. He sees himself as the master of his domain. He can pick and choose. I don't think you need to get bogged down in this, but we should explore what made him like this and in order to do that we need to go back further.'

She wrote the pertinent headlines by the side of the paper as she spoke:

'As I touched on earlier, he would have had an emotionally harrowing childhood contaminated with abuse from a relative. It might be an idea, when we look at sex offenders' records, to cross-reference them with old juvenile records and check for any homicidal traits at an early age. You may find notes from previous psychological profiles or hospital records. Were they bed-wetters? Had they tortured or killed animals? Were they arsonists? If they were predisposed to all three of these tendencies, put them at the top of the list—'

'Sorry, Miss Wakefield . . .'

She looked over at the man who had a hand raised. He had short cropped hair and spoke with a strong eastern European accent.

'What is this guy? A sociopath? What?'

'That's a good question,' she answered and shrugged wearily. 'Clinically speaking, I don't know what he is. After he is caught, we might begin to understand but even then I wouldn't be too sure. It's not as simple as putting these types of people into little boxes. He could be a paranoid schizophrenic. He could be psychotic. He undoubtedly has sociopathic tendencies. I would say he's quite smart, above average IQ, possibly college-educated; he will probably be single, live on his own or with a relative. More likely a relative, as I think he would find it hard to cope by himself.'

She found herself standing up and pacing as if she were back at King's College. 'I put him in his late thirties or forties – this is too sophisticated for anyone much younger. A white male. He'll be dishevelled-looking, scruffy hair, probably dirty clothes. Unshaven. Height, minimum five feet ten inches tall, according to the blood spatter at the Wrights' residence. Workwise, it will be blue collar. Something that doesn't pay too much. He's not rich. So, cars maybe, or a production line. Possibly engineering. We should cross-reference the employees at their son's engineering company. Check for criminal records or maybe a fired employee—'

'Someone with a grudge against the son?' Crane offered.

'Good idea, yes.' She took a second. 'It may also be worth checking into the day-release programmes that some psychiatric units and prisons offer. The majority of patients and inmates are escorted, but some are allowed out on their own recognisance. So a heads-up on that as well. One thing that's interesting here is that, although he is asocial, he seems to be well organised. It appears he took the knife with him on each occasion. In other words, it was premeditated to the nth degree. He knew exactly what his victims were doing, and his timing was impeccable. He will be interested in how the police are progressing, will probably follow the press closely on these cases and may even call up to offer help or ask if he can be a volunteer. He may even turn up at the scene of the crime.'

'You're joking?'

'No. He'll be fascinated by what you're doing and ask all sorts of questions. 'What's going on? I was passing and I saw the flashing lights. I read about this in the papers, how's the investigation going?' Record everything, if you can, because if you do hear or see him you can't make the normal common-sense judgements with this guy. His body language, his gestures, things he says – they're all there to deceive. If someone is really calm or really helpful, be suspicious. Take nothing at face value because the normal rules won't apply with him. I know this isn't an exact science and I know . . . ' She was going to say that she wasn't Sam Gordon but she thought it would be tactless so refrained. 'I'm just trying to offer as much scope as possible.' She paused. 'One other thing: I'm thinking he may have been waiting inside Rebecca's flat when she came home. That's how he managed to surprise her in the bedroom. How he got in, I have no idea. A skeleton key? Do they still work? I don't know. But something to think about.' She exhaled and shot a look at Bishop. 'I've written up a summary. Could someone maybe photocopy it and distribute?'

'You got this guy's address as well?' Bishop smiled.

Someone in the room laughed.

Holly smiled. Soon, hopefully. But she kept that thought to herself.

'Ambrose, get some copies made, please.' Bishop turned to Holly. 'Thank you. Now, let's crack on, people. Briefing at two p.m. tomorrow for updates. Let's see where we are by then.'

'Sorry, guv.' Kathy stood up. 'The family are holding a press conference tomorrow evening at seven thirty at the local village hall where Evelyn volunteered. The vicar has organised it. Stephen, Connie and the niece, Alexandra, will be there. It's an appeal for witnesses to come forward, and also for the locals to become involved. We're going to ask them to help with a search of the local area.'

'Yes, thanks, Kathy. I'll be there, as will a few local PCs. I imagine the whole village will turn out.'

'Can you film it?' Holly asked.

'The press will do that for us,' Kathy said.

'No, I mean, can you film it facing the other way? Put a camera on the audience. He might show up, you never know. It depends how bold he is.'

'Okay,' said Bishop. 'We'll get on to that. Anything else, anyone?'

'Oh ... one more thing, actually.' Holly chose her words carefully. 'I don't know any of you yet. Not really. But I do know killers.' She swallowed hard. 'This is the most important thing in his life so he will be thinking about it every minute of every day. From now on we have to do the same.'

Eleven

'I wasn't being entirely facetious when I asked whether you'd come up with his address as well. That was a pretty thorough profile.'

Bishop was sitting behind his desk, in the same office where Holly had seen him meeting Sam Gordon yesterday. It was smaller than she had expected, with one window that looked out on the red brick wall of the building opposite. There were filing cabinets to his right, a bookshelf on the far wall with more files, and his desk was in the middle of the room, with two comfortable chairs opposite. The only splash of colour was a bright pink orchid that sat to one side of the desk. She wondered whether Bishop had bought it himself.

'Thank you.' She was seated in one of the chairs and unconsciously played with a loose thread on the arm as she talked. 'I don't want to play it down but the majority of profiling isn't rocket science, it's merely a process of elimination. If you take twenty random serial killers throughout time, ninety per cent of them would have been blue collar workers, college educated, single, had trouble forming relationships with women, lived with a relative and were physically and or mentally abused when they were children.'

'What about the other ten per cent?'

'They'll have the same abusive background but they'll be harder to catch. They'll be smarter, more devious, very aware of police procedure. They'll be charming, persuasive, but it will all be an act, a façade. Deep down, they still won't be able to get along with people. Did you ever read about Ted Bundy?'

'A little.'

'He was the epitome of handsome and charismatic. Killed at least thirty women. Ironically, he was arrested for a broken rear light on his car. The police found a crowbar, handcuffs, ski mask and an ice pick in the boot, thought he was a burglar.' As an afterthought: 'He used to impersonate a policeman sometimes when he was looking for a victim.'

'You're joking?'

'Officer Roseland was the name he gave himself. It's how he gained their trust. A lot of sociopaths crave authority. I wonder if our killer does that?'

'Dresses up as a policeman?'

'It's a possibility. John Christie was a policeman. Well, he joined the Police Reserves during the Second World War. That's when he started killing.'

'You're like Wikipedia for the damned, aren't you?'

'I'll take that as a compliment, DI Bishop.' She smiled. 'Our killer may have tried to join the police at some point. His whole youth he would have been branded a loser, someone inadequate, someone with no authority. It makes sense that his fantasy would be to become someone of power and respect. Look at me now? I'm the cop, the one who decides whether you go to prison or not. Or in his case: I'm the killer, the one who decides whether you live or die. He wants what he never had. He thinks he's getting it, as well.'

There was a knock at the door.

'Come in.'

It was Jacobs. 'Inventory list on the Wrights'.' He handed it over and left. Bishop started to flick through it, then placed it on his desk.

'May I?' Holly asked.

'Sure.' He passed the folder over. 'You think we missed something?'

'I don't know. Part of me thinks he took a trophy of some sort, a memento. Not something obvious. It will be something personal, something small.'

'How personal? Like a lock of hair?'

'Anything that he can look at, touch or smell, to relive the excitement of the kill. Reassure himself that he is the dominant one, the one in control.'

'Swan went over all three bodies. None of the victims' nails had been clipped, there was no pubic shaving, no hair cuttings. I mean it could be as simple as a photo or a pair of earrings, right?'

'Yes.'

'Then that's going to be like a needle in a haystack. Or maybe this killer didn't take anything.'

'I think he needs to, Bishop. Like I need my coffee in the mornings, he'll want something to wake him up when he's feeling low, give him a boost when he feels resentful or the anger builds. It's not a choice. It's a compulsion.'

'So what do we do? Go through everything at the property, start downstairs and work our way up?'

Holly shook her head, deep in thought. 'There's the

possibility he went upstairs to get the belt that he used on Evelyn, so we should start in their bedroom. Where the victims slept.'

Bishop leaned back in his chair and sighed. Holly thought there was a greyness under his eyes that hadn't been there before.

'What did you make of Rebecca's case file?' he asked.

'Too early to say. I think the rage is growing, but it seems so controlled at the same time. I don't suppose I could see her flat?'

'Landlord's already cleaned it out, repainted and re-rented.'

'That was quick.'

'Life goes on. As for skeleton keys, you don't really need them these days. It's relatively easy to pick someone's front door lock. The only thing locks do is give an illusion of security. The reality is far from that.' He took a packet of cigarettes from his desk drawer and pulled one out. He stared at it for a while then shifted his attention to Holly. 'Everything else okay?'

The question caught her off guard, but she didn't want to lie to him. 'No. One of my patients is . . . I've been asked to elicit answers from him. It's . . . hard to deal with sometimes.'

'The guy you're fond of?'

'Yes. He'll be fine. He just needs . . . '

'You?'

'Clinically, probably not.'

Bishop nodded. 'Hmm.' Holly was about to ask him what he was thinking when he suddenly stood up, stretched and yawned loudly. 'I spend half my life sitting down. I need some fresh air. Clear my head.'

'You want company?'

He stared at her and put his cigarettes away.

'Sure. Okay.'

They left the office together but when they opened the station door their reactions couldn't have been more opposite. Bishop winced and Holly smiled like a little kid.

'It's snowing,' she said. 'I love the snow.'

'You do?'

They watched the flakes falling and swirling as if conducted by an unseen maestro.

'Plays havoc with my joints.' He groaned and put his hands into his jacket pockets.

'Grumpy Detective Inspector Bishop. We're alive, aren't we?'

'I guess,' he managed.

She glanced at him and he looked like a child who had just been chastised. She could see from his frown that there were deep thoughts whirring in his head, but she had no idea what they were. It irritated her but it also stirred feelings in her that she thought had long since disappeared.

'I'd better go home,' she said finally.

'Eight o'clock tomorrow morning. I'll come pick you up?'

'Okay. Thanks.'

She turned away and walked towards her car, all the while thinking, Do not slip in front of him, you idiot. Do not slip. She didn't, but when she opened the car door and turned back to say something else, Bishop had already gone back inside.

Twelve

Parking her car, she walked as fast as she could, turned a corner and headed towards her flat. The snow had finally eased, but the air was still damp and every now and then the wind would blow wisps of white from the leaves of the trees. A taxi shot past her, showering the pavement, its yellow light glaring as it disappeared down a side street.

'The more featureless and commonplace a crime is, the more difficult it is to solve,' she recited under her breath. 'But these crimes are anything but featureless, Holly. There is so much going on here and I think this is the tip of the iceberg.' She opened the front door of the apartment block and waited for the lift, her mind spinning. 'He covered Evelyn's face with a pillow and pushed her head into the sofa. Because she knew him?'

The lift door opened. She stepped inside and pressed the fifth floor.

'I don't think so. My guess is he did it to degrade her. He wouldn't even look at her when he assaulted her. Evelyn's body position was very different from Rebecca's, so he's altered his MO slightly, he seems to be have become more refined with this kill.' The door opened at the third floor and a man got in.

He didn't press a button and Holly barely noticed him. She continued in a half-whisper. 'And this will continue to evolve. It will become more masterful, more creative perhaps.'

'Are you a writer?'

'I'm sorry?' She looked up at him. Clear dark eyes, attractive, a nice suit. She couldn't remember seeing him before.

'You were talking aloud.' He smiled. 'I couldn't *not* hear you.'

'Oh. Sorry. No, I'm not, um . . . a writer.'

'Okay.' He smiled again. 'Peter, by the way. I moved into number seven.'

'Holly.' She offered her hand. He shook it. His hands were warm and smooth. 'I'm at number three.'

'I know,' he said. 'I saw you go in the other day.'

The lift stopped and the doors opened. He let her go first and the two walked together in silence along the corridor until Holly stopped at her front door.

'Bye, then,' he said over his shoulder as he carried on walking.

She nodded, gave him a vague wave and disappeared into her flat.

She made herself a hot chocolate and settled down in the living room, lay back on the sofa and stared at the ceiling. She did nothing for a few minutes, her mind flickering from one mental image to another, from one scenario to the next. Then her eyes fell on the reunion invitation from her old school so she picked up her phone and dialled.

'Hello. Blessed Home.' A woman's voice, soft and lilting.

'Maureen.'

'Yes.'

'It's Holly. Holly Wakefield.'

'Holly?' The woman faltered but Holly knew she would be smiling. 'How are you, my child?'

'I'm very well thank you. How about yourself?'

'Not getting any younger, but not feeling any older.'

'That's a good sign.'

'I think so too.' A pause. 'Will we be seeing you at the reunion? Zoe and Joanne are coming, along with Selina and Rhonda. Do you remember Michelle?'

'Yes. How is she?'

'Very well. Looking forward to seeing everyone. It's going to be quite busy. We have one of the girls flying over from France.'

'Really?'

'Valerie. She's married now with two children. Two girls.'

'That's lovely.' Holly was finding it hard to speak and at first she couldn't work out why. But then she realised it was the case. It was affecting her more than she thought it would.

'Holly?'

'Yes, sorry.'

'Will we be seeing you?'

She bit her lip. 'I'm not sure. I'm helping the police with an investigation and my hours are crazy. I don't know if I'm going to be free.'

'That's okay.' The reply was immediate, non-judgemental. Holly felt even worse. 'More importantly, are you taking time for yourself?'

'Trying to.'

'Well, look, if you can make it, wonderful. If not, I will say hello to the girls on your behalf. Do you talk to any of them?'

'No, not really. They leave messages. It's silly, I have their numbers, but I—'

'You know you should. They see you as a sister. Part of the sisterhood. Always remember that.'

'I know.' She could feel the first sting of the tears and she closed her eyes, wanting to move on. 'I had better go. I'm sorry, I um ...'

'You never need to apologise, Holly.'

'I know. Thank you.' She hung up and took a deep breath. She was angry at herself, which was a good reaction. She should have been. She had a habit of doing this. Of pulling back inside herself, retreating to the safety of her flat and destroying any possibility of a relationship. She had been like that ever since she was a child, and despite years of therapy and counselling she still favoured the call of isolation over the pull of friends and companionship.

'"I think you would rather be alone than with anybody,"' was what her first boyfriend had told her shortly before they broke up. They were both eighteen and his name was Ralph. 'Wreck-it-Ralph', she had called him afterwards but she knew that deep down he was right. She glossed over intimacy, skating across the surface of anything meaningful that could be developed. It was so much safer that way. The fear of being abandoned loomed ever large in her imagination, the fear of losing everything she cherished.

She let her eyes wander over to her incident board and spent the next ten minutes adding more photos of the victims and their homes and then she highlighted key phrases from the police reports and stuck them on the far left. She took her marker and linked everything with black lines, but when she finally stepped back she saw the empty space where the killer should be, circled with a question mark by its side. She stared at what she'd done with a ferocious determination, as if by staring at it the answer would magically reveal itself.

She had a sudden thought, grabbed the phone and dialled. When he answered, she thought he might have been asleep.

'This is Bishop.'

'It's Holly.'

'Hey.'

'I'd like to talk to Alexandra tomorrow. The niece who found the bodies. Would that be possible?'

'Sure. I'll sort it out with Bethany. She's the liaison officer, she'll be present at all times.'

'Were you sleeping?'

'Trying to, yeah.'

'Sorry if I woke you.'

'It's okay. Let's push the house search then. Say eleven?'

'Perfect.'

A pause.

'Is it still snowing?' he asked.

She went over to the windows and pulled back the heavy curtains. 'No. It's stopped.'

'Good.' He coughed once and sighed. 'Night, Holly.'

The line went dead. She turned back to the status board again, brain whirring. Serial killers. They didn't appear very often but when they did they got everybody's attention. *Okay – so now you've got our attention, what do you want?*

She stepped back and uncapped her pen with a sharp click. *What do you really want to say?*

Thirteen

Alexandra Lymington was on the sofa in her flat. She sat very upright, face impassive, her eyes red-lidded and watery. It was a one-bed flat with an en-suite and a kitchen and dining room running into one long strip. The place was sparse, almost clinical, and there were surfaces that Holly suspected would normally have propped up framed photos of her uncle and aunt. She could understand why Alexandra had put them away. Out of sight, out of mind. Bethany entered with three cups of coffee on a tray, handed them out and took a seat next to Alexandra on the sofa. Holly was opposite in a rattan armchair, the sort that sometimes creaked when you moved, but this one was silent and the arms well worn. There had been a coffee table between them but she had asked Alexandra if she could move it to one side. She didn't want to break the space.

'I'm thinking of getting my hair cut,' was the first thing Alexandra said, and she looked suddenly broken. Her eyes roved from Holly to Bethany like a wounded animal. 'I don't know why. I've always liked my long hair but maybe now I should change it.'

'I can understand that,' Holly said. 'You feel as though you need to change something. As though that will make things better. Start afresh.'

'I think so.'

Alexandra dabbed her eyes with a tissue. She seemed so young and bright. She was handling herself incredibly well and Holly admired her. She knew the girl was coming apart, but on the surface she was still desperately trying to look composed and strong.

'Thanks for agreeing to talk to me, Alexandra,' Holly said.

'Alex please. Nobody calls me Alexandra. Too much of a mouthful.'

'Alex then. Thank you.'

'That's okay. Bethany said you're a profiler or something?'

'In a way, yes. I try to look at various clues and help the police. Point them in a certain direction.'

'Do you understand the sort of person who does this type of thing?'

'No.' She thought a moment. 'Yes. I can understand why they do it. But as a person I don't understand them. Does that make sense?'

'I think so.' Alex's eyes were becoming watery again. Holly tried to distract her.

'Nice coffee by the way.'

Alex suddenly laughed.

'Yes. I'm very particular about my brands.'

'So am I.'

There was a silence. Holly smiled and waited. She knew Alex wanted to talk but it was a question of letting her do it in her own time.

'I want to know how I can get rid of the images in my

head,' she began. 'I'll never forget it, will I? I'll never be able to erase them.'

'No, you won't.'

Bethany gave Holly a harsh look as if she had overstepped an invisible line. Holly didn't care.

'You can deal with them, though. You can make them become more ... acceptable. But it takes time. It takes a lot of time. A lot of hard work. A lot of understanding. Not about what went on, what happened with your uncle and aunt, but about you. About how *you* see things. Don't look for answers from the person who did it, or the whys, because you won't find them. You need to try to look at things differently.'

'But my life will never be the same again.'

'No, it won't, but you don't need it to be like this. It's more—'

'I keep thinking if only I'd got there ten minutes earlier ...'

'Then you probably would have been dead too and we wouldn't be having this conversation.'

'Maybe I could have saved them.'

'No. The person who did this ... the man who did this, is incredibly strong. He wouldn't have looked at you with pity or remorse, or thought, "Oh, she's so young, I shouldn't kill her." He would have come at you just as fast, just as viciously and I'd be talking to someone else – your cousins, probably – and Bethany wouldn't be here and you wouldn't be drinking that coffee. So be grateful that you arrived at the house when you did. But what I want to ask you now, Alex, is what do you remember?'

'I ... well, I've said everything to the police. I've already given statements.'

'No, no. I know that. I've read them. You were coming over to help with the dinner party. You'd got dressed, and decided to drive over an hour early.'

'That's right. Partly to help, but mostly because I liked being with them. Spending time with them.'

'Okay. So, you entered the house . . . '

'I rang the doorbell first but there was no answer. I rang it again. There was still no answer.'

'Was that strange?'

'No. It's a big house. My uncle is quite deaf and has arthritis in his legs so can't move very fast and I knew my aunt would be preparing everything. She was always busy. I had a key so I let myself in.' She paused and Holly thought she seemed to sink into a moment of personal reflection. 'As I stepped inside, I shouted, "Hi! I'm here!"'

'No reply?'

'No. Someone will normally shout something, but I thought they might not have heard, so I went into the kitchen – I'd bought them flowers, tulips. I put them in a vase, went into the dining room and left them on the table. Then I walked through to the living room.' Alex hesitated. Her face became locked in an expression of dread. 'The um . . . the um . . . the lights were off.'

'Yes.'

'So I turned them on. Turned them on and . . . walked inside.'

'What did it feel like, Alex?'

'Feel like?'

'Yes.'

'I don't understand.'

'The room itself. How did it feel when you walked inside?'

'It was too bright. I had to squint. All the lights had come on together. The chandelier, the sidelights. There are spots on the walls for the paintings and they were all on as well. And it felt . . . '

'Go on.'

'There was, um . . . It felt sticky.'

'Sticky.'

'I think that's the best word to describe it when I walked inside. It felt hot and sticky in there, like when you get off a plane on some tropical island and it hits you hard in the face. And then when I saw . . . the first thing I saw was my uncle.' She took a breath. 'I thought it was clothes to start off with. Clothes that maybe my aunt had pulled out of the washing machine and thrown over the chair. But they were glistening red. There was something almost alive about them, as if they were still moving somehow, but they weren't. I don't know. I took another step inside the room and then I realised what they were. And then I saw my aunt on the sofa. I called out her name but she didn't respond. I knew she was dead but I couldn't quite believe it. Part of me wanted her to answer, to move, to do anything other than lie there looking at me but . . .'

Her head fell into her hands.

Bethany moved to her side and put an arm around her. 'Well done, love, well done, Alex. I know this is so hard, but you've done so well.' She glanced at Holly and mouthed, 'That's enough.'

Holly didn't move. She sat and stared at Alex, willing her to look up. 'Alex?'

'I think Alex has had enough for today, okay?' Bethany said.

Holly nodded and got up. She picked up her handbag and moved towards the door. Alex looked up at her, her tired eyes like slits, her nose snotty and wet. Holly stayed where she was. She didn't speak for a while. Was very quiet and very still. Then she said, 'Do you think he was there?'

'Holly, please—'

'What?' asked Alex, and her mouth twisted as if she was sucking a sour sweet.

'Did you think he was still in the room?'

Alex looked away, and then when she turned back her voice was husky, as if she had scarred vocal cords.

'Yes.'

'Tell me.'

'After the initial shock of finding them I thought, Oh my God . . . seeing them, my aunt on the sofa, my uncle . . . I mean, Jesus . . . what sort of an animal does that?'

Holly shifted position and crouched down on one knee, leaning forward slightly, never breaking eye contact.

'What did you feel, though, Alex? Apart from the disgust, the repulsion. What were your senses telling you? Was he still there?'

Alex closed her eyes, squeezed them tight. 'Yes, I think so.'

'Watching you?'

'He could have been anywhere.' She was getting stronger now, more in control of her emotions. 'He could have been standing by the curtains, he could have been by the desk, he could have been by the bookshelf. It's almost as if . . . if he'd stayed perfectly still, I wouldn't have noticed him. If he'd kept absolutely quiet, I wouldn't have heard him. All I was doing was looking at my aunt and uncle. I couldn't . . . I couldn't focus on anything else.' A breath. 'Although I could smell something.'

'What?'

'Burning from the fireplace.'

'Paper.'

'Yes. Somebody had burned some paper and I could smell it in the fire. It reminded me of Christmas . . .'

Holly took Alex's hand and squeezed it tight.

'Thank you, Alex. Thank you very much.'

Fourteen

'It looks empty already, doesn't it?' Bishop said.

He had parked his car and now he and Holly stood on the gravel driveway staring at the Wrights' residence. She nodded, amazed at how much smaller the house looked in daylight. A PC stood by the front door. He was brushing his trousers off as they approached and Holly wondered if he had been sitting down until they showed up. She wouldn't have blamed him.

They pushed under the incident tape.

'Where are the SOCOs?' Bishop asked the PC.

'Three round the back and two in the kitchen, I think, sir.'

'No one in the bedrooms?'

'They were cleared yesterday, sir.'

Bishop turned to Holly. 'Upstairs?'

'Upstairs.'

They went through the hallway, past the living room and dining room and started up the wood-panelled staircase. Elaborately framed canvas portraits hung every few metres, the men and women all looking arrogant and haughty – the children looking lost. Holly stopped at one: a young girl holding a posy of flowers, a somewhat tired expression on her face.

A relative of the Wrights? She doubted it. She was about to move off when she realised Bishop was still a few steps behind.

'You don't have to wait for me.' He was putting on a brave face but Holly could tell he was having trouble with his leg.

'How did you do that?'

'My gimpy thigh?'

'Yes.'

'Got hit by a car. I was out of uniform as well, which made it even more annoying. Don't mind someone trying to run me down when I've got my badge on but when you're in your civvies on a day off it makes you feel ...'

'Anonymous.'

'Right. Come on, let's keep going.' They continued up the stairs. 'Hit and run. Never caught the bastard either. Spun around like a wooden top, hit the pavement hard and blacked out. Lucky really. Cracked my patella, busted my femur, managed to flatten my toes as well somehow. I guess he drove over them. Seven years this month. Spring and summer are fine but it's the chill coming into winter that gets to it.' They were at the top of the stairs now. 'Used to be as fit as a fiddle but I don't think I'll be signing up for the London marathons any more.'

'You've done them?'

'Three. Everyone should do a marathon.'

He led her to the master bedroom. It was as grand as the rest of the house. A large mahogany sleigh bed with matching furniture, a bookcase with bestsellers and antiques magazines, heavy, pale lemon wallpaper with tiny black flowers, a deep cream carpet and a walk-in wardrobe.

'Drawers or wardrobe?' Bishop asked.

'Wardrobe.' They both put on latex gloves and went through

to the walk-in. It was large, with dozens of hangers, his clothes to the right, hers to the left.

'Start on the outside and we'll meet in the middle?'

Holly began fanning through Evelyn's clothes, feeling along the linings of the dresses, counting the buttons of the blouses.

'How about you?'

She was glad he was talking to her. It was taking her mind off the task. She felt like an intruder. Gawping at a dead woman's clothes, groping into her personality.

'What?'

'Do you run, yoga, weights? What's your thing?'

'Nothing really. I walk when I can, try not to eat too many microwave meals.'

'You a vegetarian?'

'God no. I can cook though. Well, it's not exactly *Masterchef*. Do you cook or . . .'

Bishop didn't answer for a while and Holly wasn't sure if he had heard or not. 'Bishop?'

'Yeah, sorry. Try to. Hard to have regular meals because of the shifts. You know? Wasted food ending up in the dog.'

'You have a dog?'

'No. Figure of speech. Do you?'

'No.'

A silence as they carried on searching, getting closer to each other. Gloved hands whispering across silks and cotton. They finished somewhat disappointed.

'Nothing,' she said.

They exited the walk-in and continued the same systematic search with the chest of drawers. 'Ed Gein took his victim's bones and used them to make things – cereal bowl, corset, masks from human faces. Dahmer kept their heads and genitals in a freezer. Ed Kemper, well, he turned his mother's head into a dartboard.'

'One hundred and eighty,' Bishop whispered.

'Exactly. But Swan said there was no evidence of nail clipping, pubic hair cutting . . .'

'Blood?'

'It's a possibility. Take a small vial, stick it in a box. But blood dries over time, changes colour, so when he looks at it again it won't be the same as it was on the kill. Bright red and full of oxygen. It will be dull. Black. It won't give him the same thrill. No, I don't think he took blood. There was nothing taken from Rebecca Bradshaw's body either, so if there was anything, it has to be something else close to the victims.'

Having thoroughly searched the drawers, Holly sat on the bed, unconsciously running her gloved hands over the surface of the quilt to feel the fabric. Then she got up and wandered over to the window, stared down at the gardens below. Evergreen bushes backed on to the river and the lawn was close-cropped and neat and surrounded by mature trees whose branches were leafless and looked dead. She spotted the three SOCOs in their white boiler suits, moving around the bushes like stealthy snowmen.

'Did they search the river?'

'Divers were there all morning. Found the usual trash, but no knife. Which either means it's still out there somewhere or he took it with him.'

'Maybe it's his lucky knife.'

'Like I have my lucky socks?'

'Could be part of his MO. Using the same weapon,' she sighed.

'What's wrong?'

'I don't know. He will take a trophy of some sort . . . '

'Do you want to check the other bedrooms? There are three more.' Bishop had joined her at the window.

'No. If he went anywhere, he would have come in here.'

She turned back to the bed, had one last look around the room, then headed to the door. Behind her she heard Bishop following but the footsteps stopped and there was a light thumping sound. She turned. 'What was that?'

'The bed had been moved. Probably by SOCO. I shifted it back.'

'How could you tell?'

'The indentations in the carpet. They were slightly off.'

'Show me.'

Bishop went to the left corner of the bed and shifted it slightly to the right. 'There.' The round indentation of the ball foot was slightly out of sync. She crouched down and shone the light from her phone underneath, panning slowly from left to right. She felt Bishop next to her.

'I don't see anything.'

'Neither do I.'

She stood back up and grabbed the same edge of the bed and started to heave it. It was surprisingly light and skidded across the carpet with ease. They both stared at the carpet, as if answers would suddenly appear.

'It was probably SOCO who moved it.'

'I can find out,' said Bishop, already getting ready to move it back. Holly stopped him and pointed to the wall that had been revealed behind the headboard. A small section of the wallpaper had been cut out, maybe four or five inches square.

'Maybe they were thinking about redecorating?'

'Maybe,' said Holly. She was stuck in a thought, frozen in

the moment. 'Redecorating,' she whispered. 'Who else was redecorating?'

'What?'

'I don't know. Something.' A beat as she racked her brain. 'Rebecca Bradshaw. I think PC Siskins said something in his report about how he thought she'd been redecorating.'

'I don't know. I don't remember.'

'Why did he think she'd been redecorating? Where are the extra crime scene photos?'

'They'll be on file at the station. You want me to have them pulled up?'

'Please.'

'You think this guy took a piece of wallpaper?' he asked.

'It's strange if he did – it's not very personal to the victims, but maybe it means everything to him. Again it goes back to the "why?". What made him kill? What's the link? Perhaps I've been looking at this from the wrong angle.'

'What do you mean?'

'His motivation. Perhaps whatever is making him do this . . . ' she trailed off and felt suddenly very tired.

'Holly?'

She was glad Bishop didn't push her for more. 'Or maybe you're right. Maybe the Wrights were simply thinking of redecorating.'

They went downstairs and Holly stopped in the hallway. Motioned to the living room.

'Is it clear for us to go in?'

'Sure.'

She led the way, Bishop playing shadow behind her until they were standing in the centre of the room. She felt a lot more comfortable here than she had the first time she'd seen it, when she'd stumbled over her words, desperate to say something vaguely meaningful. Now it felt as if she had started to belong here. In this room. The killing room. It looked empty now that the bodies had been removed, but the bloodstains were still rich and the smell ever present.

'The killer may have been here when Alex found them.'

'What? Are you serious?'

'Watching her.' Holly's eyes took in the room and rested on the curtains. 'Maybe behind there. Maybe crouched behind the desk. Maybe behind the sofa where Evelyn was.'

'How do you know?'

'I don't for sure, but Alex thought he may have been. She said she sensed him.'

'Jesus Christ.'

'The ultimate thrill. Witnessing the first sharp intake of breath, the terror in her eyes.'

'It would turn him on?'

'Undoubtedly. Alex said the room felt sticky. Hot. When she flicked the switch all the lights came on: the chandelier, the spotlights, the side lamps, everything. Highlighting his work. Roll up, roll up, the circus is in town and have I got a show for you ...'

'But you don't think it was about the doctor, do you?'

'No. I'm even more convinced he was a distraction. Smoke and mirrors. Trying to send us off in the wrong direction. Evelyn was the target, the one that he wanted to kill. I think he knew about the dinner party, though. I think he knew guests were coming. Hence the elaborate set-up. What a surprise that would have been for them all, but instead Alex turned up early, by herself.'

'So he was interrupted?'

'I'm beginning to think so. I think the murders had been done, the stage had been set, but he hadn't made his escape yet. Alex surprised him, but he didn't panic, did he? Just stood there. Daring to breathe as he watched her walk in here and see the horror. In Rebecca's murder there were no witnesses; the kill was quite mundane compared to this. Private even, in her own bedroom. No witnesses with Rebecca, so this is an escalation, a slight adaptation. He might look for the same thrill in his next victim.'

'Someone watching?'

'Possibly.' She shivered involuntarily and turned back to Bishop. 'Jesus Christ, this guy is ...' hard to find the right words ' ... darkness itself.'

Bishop walked over to the remains of the mirror. The scattered fragments on the ground. When he turned round he was frowning, trying to work something out.

'Say he was here,' he said. 'Would that make our timeline different?'

'When did she phone the police?'

'The call was logged at 7.35 p.m. The local guys got here within fifteen minutes. Closed off roads, set up a cordon, took care of Alex. They didn't even come in here. I gave them specific instructions – stay the hell away until I arrive on scene. I made it here at 8.12 p.m. They'd done a good job. Sealed off and untouched. How it should be.'

'Where did Alex make her call from?'

'The kitchen.'

'He could have slipped out while she was distracted.'

'Yes,' he conceded, 'or maybe he left before she got here. Maybe she was imagining things. I mean, I wouldn't blame her. When we were in there with the bodies I had a feeling someone was watching me too.'

'You did?'

He shrugged. 'Call it paranoia. I don't know . . . It wasn't a pleasant room to be in, was it?'

'No.'

They got outside, dejected, having learned nothing really. Big black birds called out from the tops of the dead trees as they walked to the car. Holly turned at the noise, as if seeing a glimpse of something in her own future. She heard Bishop turn the ignition and took one last look at the house. Condensation covered the lower windows and the midday light rippled and bounced off the frost. A small bird appeared, flickering from one perch to another. A robin, she thought, or a linnet. Then its wings rose to the light, flapping once more before it seemed to evaporate in the sun.

They pulled out of the driveway back on to the road and the trees swept by in a blur of dark branches. Bishop clocked Holly in thought, and as if the silence bothered him:

'What are you thinking?'

'I honestly don't know.'

But as they passed the village hall she wondered if the killer really would turn up tonight.

Fifteen

He arrived at the village hall at six forty-five.

He was impressed at how calm he felt, but it may have helped that he had kept his promise – he wasn't high and hadn't had a drink all day. The car park was full and the narrow country lane had vehicles parked for fifty yards in both directions. He had spotted several vans with catchy logos and satellites on their roofs and suspected they must be the news crews that were inevitably attending. This was important, after all. He watched a few more people arrive in the darkness on foot, talking quietly amongst themselves before disappearing inside the hall. He made sure no one was behind him, and entered the little wooden building himself. It smelled damp and earthy like his old school sports hall, and after moving slowly through the murmuring crowd he managed to find a seat near the back, by the toilets. The heating was making him yawn and he wondered if he might nod off at some point, but after a few minutes he realised this might be more fun than he had thought. Nobody knew why he was there.

There must have been forty or fifty people in all, most of them local, he supposed. The majority were older than him and wore serious expressions on their faces. There were a few younger ones, teenagers, but he presumed they were only there because their parents had dragged them along to show support. The reality was they would probably rather be at home watching YouTube or posting on Facebook. A camera flashed and he noticed an area at the front and to his right where the journalists, photographers and film crews had set up. He could see the expectation on their faces. Voice recorders primed, notebooks turned to clean pages – hounds sniffing for blood.

They were all watching a gathering of rather self-important looking people at the front of the room. There were five policemen – he had expected more – who were all standing with their hands by their sides, not sure where to look. There were several people dressed in suits who looked as if they wanted to say something, and a clergyman who looked a hundred years old with wispy grey hair and massive blue parka. The vicar took the big parka off, shuffled to the front of the group and waited calmly for quiet. Speaking softly, with a grimace as if he had constipation, he thanked everybody who had come tonight to offer their support to the grieving family. He talked about the horrible deed that had been done within their little village and how the perpetrator would be answerable to God – who worked, apparently, in mysterious ways. There was a smattering of applause and then he introduced the children of the dearly departed to the gathering.

The eldest turned out to be their son, Stephen, and the man disliked him immediately. He looked snobbish and was wearing a posh suit and had a smarmy side parting. The two women standing on either side of Stephen he found more palatable. The sister was called Connie and she was wearing a dark blue dress. She had long blonde hair which she stroked back behind her ears, and had a habit of playing with the fringe at the front like a cat does with a ball of string. The other woman was quite a bit younger and shorter with curly dark hair. Alexandra was her name and the man thought she really was quite pretty. He felt the beginnings of an erection when she started to talk. She wore jeans and a black jumper, nothing pretentious about her, and he even felt a pang of pity when she waxed on about her dead uncle and aunt, especially so when one of the women in the crowd next to him whispered that 'it was her that found the bodies'.

The three talked for about ten minutes about their dead relatives, blah blah blah, and how much they would miss them, and they each thanked everybody for their continued support in their time of need. When they had finally stopped waffling the man heard a few sniffles from members of the audience and someone to his right blew their nose quite loudly. Next up in the parade was a surly-looking detective. He introduced himself as Detective Inspector Bishop and thanked the family for their bravery in coming forward, and everybody else who had gathered there to offer their help and condolences.

He talked about the crime itself but didn't reveal anything that hadn't been mentioned in the press. Spoilsport! The man wondered if the detective was married and, if he was, what his wife looked like. Probably ugly. Bishop was past his prime physically but there was something about his eyes that frightened the man. They were very intense. As if he could look right at you and know when you were lying, as if he could see through to your core and wheedle out the truth that was hidden deep down. At one point he thought the detective was staring at him. He felt decidedly uncomfortable and asked himself, not for the first time, if he had made a mistake in coming here. To be on the safe side, he turned away from the detective and focused on the woman next to him. He pulled a remorseful face and asked if she needed a hug. She said no, a bit rudely he thought, and by the time he turned back the detective was looking away and he felt safe again. The detective was going to be a bit of a challenge, especially during the next part of the plan. He would really have to prepare himself for that. After all, he was going to be having a one-to-one with Detective Inspector Bishop very soon.

As the night wore on and the tears continued to fall from the dreary relatives and friends, he started to get a bit antsy. He felt suddenly exposed, though he couldn't work out why. It came as a relief when the speeches finally stopped and everybody got up and started chatting. An old woman with a bent back pushed a trolley out from some hidden room, with mugs of steaming drinks, biscuits and slices of lemon drizzle cake. He took a thick slice of the cake and washed it down with a mug of sweet tea. He made sure he wiped the mug clean before he handed it back, then went to find the toilet.

When he returned, he noticed the police constables had split everybody into groups of about ten. He wandered over to the closest gathering and started to listen.

'Each group will have an officer assigned and each officer will be given a certain section of the local area to search. It will all be within a two- to three-mile radius. We'll go through the fields in a grid system, and we'll concentrate on the sides of the roads, footpaths etc. We're looking for footprints, cigarette butts, anything that could have been left by the perpetrator. Obviously, if we find a cigarette butt, that doesn't mean that the killer smoked it or was even there, but we will bag it all the same and take it back to the station as possible evidence for the future. These are arable fields and I'm told they should be empty this time of year, so look for anything that doesn't belong there.'

'Like what?' someone asked.

'An article of clothing perhaps, a large stick. Discarded food packaging. Anything that stands out. Now you're all local so you know the land better than we do – in that sense your eyes will be sharper than ours.'

'Jonathan and Evelyn had a big garden, didn't they? Do we search there as well?' an old woman asked.

Ooh. Good question.

'No,' the police officer said. 'That's off limits to the public, I'm afraid.'

Killjoy.

An elderly gentleman cleared his throat and said, 'The Tillingbourne runs through the village. Our house backs on to it. We could all meet there. Use it as a base.'

The man felt compelled to add to the scenario. He couldn't believe what he was about to do but he felt a shiver of excitement when he opened his mouth.

'Good idea,' he said. 'What time shall we meet?'

'Say nine o'clock?'

Nine o'clock tomorrow was agreed by everyone including the constable and by then the man knew he had well and truly infiltrated. He gave a fake name and address as planned and as it was getting late he thought he should probably leave. He didn't want to press his luck any more, that wasn't part of the master plan. Also, secretly, he really didn't think he was ready to accidentally bump into Detective Inspector Bishop quite yet. Thankfully the man and his intense eyes were nowhere to be seen, but he did spot the niece, Alexandra, and emboldened by his success so far he wandered over to her. She turned at his approach but somehow she didn't look pretty any more, just sad.

'I'm so sorry for your loss,' he said softly.

'Thank you.' She tried to smile but he thought she looked uncomfortable. He squinted awkwardly, briefly wondered what it would be like to kiss her and then headed to the door. He scored another slice of lemon cake from a tray on the way out – something to look forward to on the long bus journey home – and shook hands with the vicar, who was waiting at the entrance like a gracious host.

'Same time next week?' he wanted to say as he walked past, fighting the urge to laugh. He gave one last look over his shoulder, waved to Alexandra and then stepped out into the starry night.

He had no idea a camera had been filming him all evening.

His name was David Eagen.

Sixteen

Holly woke before dawn to the smell of early-morning coffee spilling through her flat.

She had set the percolator for 5.35 a.m. and by 5.50 she was stretched out on the sofa with her first cup. Bishop had sent the extra crime scene photos from the Rebecca Bradshaw murder but they lay untouched on the coffee table. She allowed her eyes to close. The past week had been intense, to say the least; her Monday-morning students, Lee at Wetherington and then a call from Bishop at an ungodly hour that ended with her walking into a scene reminiscent of one of Blake's illuminated manuscripts. She hadn't slept properly since the case had begun, she'd barely eaten and now she needed to decompress, to turn off from the murder and mayhem. She put on Radio Two and settled against the cushions. Huey Morgan was raiding his personal record collection and between tracks there was some easy banter. A late eighties throwback made her smile. The Stone Roses and 'Fools Gold', Ian Brown whispering the lyrics.

She stayed like that for the next few hours, half-listening to the words of the songs as they floated over her. Memories flitting in and out of her mind – childhood and early teens at Blessed Home, hitting her twenties with Oasis and 'Wonderwall', Blur and 'Parklife' and ending with Chris Isaak's 'Wicked Game'.

But underneath the calm exterior and the gentle tapping of her fingers on the arm of the sofa, her subconscious was working overtime.

'You think too much,' Nathan Sylvester, head lecturer on criminology, had always told her. 'Stop thinking, Holly.'

'And how do I do that?'

'If you can work that out you'll make a fortune,' he had laughed. It was fair to say he was her first real crush. She was never one to mix with boys her own age. What was it, maturity? Humour? Or absent-father syndrome? Nothing had ever happened between them – he was married with a child – but she had enjoyed spending time with him, enjoyed picking his brain and soaking up his knowledge and mentorship. He still cared deeply for her; they spoke at least once a month on the phone, and because he considered himself old school he insisted on writing letters to her several times a year.

'Sit down and try to work out the answer to something and you probably never will, but give yourself a distraction and suddenly the words will come to you, the feelings. Always trust your feelings, your instincts. That's what saved you from the sabre-tooth tiger, the famine and the drought all those thousands of years ago.'

She was getting hungry now so she made herself a ham-and-cheese sandwich and switched to Earl Grey tea. She kept the music playing – Depeche Mode and 'Personal Jesus' – but turned her attention to the crime scene photos.

It didn't take her long to find the photo she wanted. It was labelled Exhibit 79C and had been taken from the foot of the bed and showed Rebecca's headboard and bedside cabinets. A neat square had been cut from the wallpaper on the right-hand side. Wallpaper that was pink with fluffy clouds. She called up the station and asked for Bishop. He was in a meeting so she left a message with Sergeant Karanack to call her back.

She got up and wrote the word 'Wallpaper' on the incident wall beside the main suspect. So this was his souvenir? His keepsake. He wasn't taking anything personal from the victims. He was taking something from the crime scene itself. Something that was personal to him. *What is it about the wallpaper that means so much to you?* She didn't have wallpaper in her flat, it was painted, so she tried to remember what wallpaper she'd had as a child in her room at Blessed Home. What was it? Bluebells. Tiny blue flowers scattered on white paper. How could she ever forget? She had stared at them through tears when she had first arrived and then as the nights had passed she had grown to love that wallpaper. She used to pretend it was a blanket of beautiful flowers that her parents had laid down for her. Holding her at night. Keeping her warm. Keeping her safe. She stayed mesmerised until the phone rang. It was Bishop and she told him what she had found.

'You ever seen anything like this before?' he asked.

'No. It may be a coincidence but—'

'I don't believe in coincidences. We find one more and it's definite. Two's a coincidence, three's a crime.'

'I've never heard that, but yes.'

'Look, late notice I know, but are you free?'

'Yes.' She instantly regretted saying it so fast. She had a life outside of this, didn't she? Outside the criminology at King's College, the patients of violent crime at the hospital. Outside her flat. She didn't, though, and deep down she knew it. 'What's up?'

'Afternoon briefing. Make your way down if you've got nothing else to do.'

'I'll be there as soon as I can.'

She decided she'd better jump in the shower first and cranked up one final tune whilst she got ready. 'Songbird' by Charlotte Campbell.

'They said it would rain today, but the sun shone. You said that you'd stay today, but you're long gone . . .'

Seventeen

'You're desperate for a smoke, aren't you?'

'Yep.'

'Don't mind me.'

'Not in front of the orchid. Bad for its circulation, apparently.'

How ironic, Holly thought. Bishop was willing to quit for the sake of the plant on his desk, but not for his own health.

'I know you're analysing me now, so what does that say about me?'

She laughed. 'You don't want to know.'

They were sitting in his office. She had given him the brief on the wallpaper find again, and shown him the photos.

'We've got to make sure the press don't get hold of this,' he had said. 'It's way too speculative anyway. God knows what they'd make of it. Let's keep it between us at the moment, okay?' A pause. 'After the story broke a couple of journalists asked if we'd brought in a profiler.'

'What did you tell them?'

'That we're consulting with numerous individuals within and without the police force to assist in our enquiries. Kept it as neutral as we could. We didn't mention your name.' He sat back and started playing with his pen. 'Karanack went through the cold case files going back ten years. A few had some interesting similarities, mainly the handiwork with the hammer and the knife, but no penetration and none with the round burn marks that we found on both Rebecca and Evelyn. What do you think they are? Some sort of branding?'

'It's possible. Were the numbers similar?'

'Evelyn was burned eleven times, Rebecca seven.'

'Let's hope they're not incremental then, otherwise there'll be four bodies in between that we haven't found yet.'

'And six before Rebecca,' he added. 'We ended up with half the squad going through the entire list of known sex offenders, rapists, anyone with a record predisposed to sexual humiliation, and exhausted every one of them. We're still waiting for the NHS roster of inmates and psych patients to come through, including the day releases and any on parole for good behaviour. I don't know how many there will be but the options are narrowing. How much leeway have we got with regard to this guy's MO?'

'Not much. These kills are too specific. Too unique. It's possible there are bodies out there that we will never find and therefore never be able to connect to him. What about John and Jane Does?'

Bishop almost laughed. 'Where do you want me to start? At least a hundred and fifty to two hundred bodies turn up every year. That's minimum. Most are found by dog walkers, joggers, mushroom foragers. Usually in the winter months when the shrubs and bushes have died back. Too mutilated or decomposed to ever identify.'

'I didn't realise it was that many.'

'I think between the Met, Kent, Essex and Sussex forces

we've got about four or five hundred on file that we can't identify – and they're the ones we know about. God knows what the true number is.'

Holly thought he seemed nervous today, or perhaps the case was getting to him, as it was to her. He picked up a photo of Evelyn from his desk, stared at it for a while, his face inscrutable, and then gently put it down.

'Need to bring something up,' he said.

'Go on.'

He was stalling and looked down at the photo again.

'The interview with Alex. Bethany was concerned you pushed her too hard. Some of the things you said to her, Bethany thought were inappropriate.'

Holly felt her cheeks flush. 'I'm sorry. I don't think I did, but—'

'You don't need to apologise. It was brought to my attention and I had to mention it now you're part of the team. That's all. Bethany's a great liaison officer, has been for the last eight years and she's worked with more victims than I've had hot dinners. There are some things that the professionals help with and other things that we do, okay? You help profile the killers, we catch them, and the counsellors are the ones who take care of the victims. Feathers are always ruffled when someone comes in from the outside, sometimes the nest gets disturbed as well, but you know now so . . . onwards and upwards.'

Holly knew Bishop would make a mental note and file it away. It was a mark against her even though he was trying to be casual about it. Eventually she spoke: 'All I wanted to do was find out how she felt. Not what she saw or what she thought happened, but how she felt. It works well with my patients and I thought it might be useful with Alex.'

'And I think it worked this time. Don't take it personally.'

'I won't,' she said. But she knew she would.

There was a knock at the door. Ambrose entered, followed by Crane and then Bethany. They tried to make themselves comfortable in the cramped space but it wasn't going to happen.

'Jesus, I need a bigger office,' Bishop said. 'Sit down – I don't care where, even on my desk if you have to. I hate people standing up in front of me.'

Bethany took the chair next to Holly but effectively ignored her, Crane perched himself on the windowsill and Ambrose sat on a box of files.

'All right,' Bishop continued. 'First things first. Let's have an update, please, in the order of occurrence. Ambrose?'

'Search of the interior of the Wrights' house yielded nothing in terms of a weapon of any kind, either a knife, hammer or a material that could have been used for strangulation. All the kitchen utensils that could have fitted the wounds were collected, tested. No blood, no latent fingerprints, no foreign DNA. The immediate exterior, the front and back gardens, the bushes, were all searched by three squads, and we brought in a couple of K9 units but nothing so far. There is a river at the bottom of the garden' – he checked his notes – 'the River Tillingbourne. We thought the killer could possibly have used the river as his method of transport, but there's a lock system on either side of the mooring jetty that was closed for three days due to dredging further upstream, so there's no way he could have utilised it. We wanted to get some divers further up the river, half a mile either side of the property, but we're still waiting on Thames Valley to give us permission, likewise for a warrant.'

'Which judge did you go to?'

'Judge Harvard.'

'Okay. He's generally pretty good about things like this. Follow up this afternoon.'

'Yes, sir.'

'Bethany, how were the family?'

'Absolutely devastated. The brother and sister first. They both earn good money, have no financial worries as such. Good credit, no debts apart from the normal mortgage and a few credit cards each, but they both live well within their spending capacity. Stephen is twenty-seven, the older of the two siblings – he's an engineer in Brighton. His company is successful, he's well liked by staff and clients alike. No family grudges there. He usually comes up once a fortnight to see his mum and dad, would have been there next Saturday.'

'What about the sister?'

'Connie. Twenty-five, a financial wizard in Woking. Like her brother, doesn't overspend, doesn't drink, doesn't smoke, very clean-cut and healthy-looking considering the long hours she works and the stress she faces at her office.'

'How much money does she deal with?'

'Approximately sixty-five million pounds' worth of funds. She's never been investigated by the Financial Conduct Authority for impropriety and her accounts are transparent. She was very open with me about all her dealings – says she has to be, due to the latest regulatory regime and new financial tort laws.'

'The niece who found the bodies? Alexandra?'

'Nineteen, sweet kid, seemed to be in a bit of a daze. She kept crying. I don't blame her though.' Bethany shot a not too subtle look at Holly, which didn't go unnoticed by anyone in the room. Holly bit her lip and said nothing. Bethany skimmed her notes. 'She really did look upon Jonathan and Evelyn as her parents – she lost her mum and dad when she was fifteen. Car accident with a drunk driver on the M3 towards Basingstoke.'

'Did they raise her?'

'Pretty much. She stayed with them through school until she moved out of their house when she was seventeen; they bought her the little flat in Albury which they helped her to decorate.'

Holly looked up at that. 'Who did the decorating?'

'I'm sorry?'

'The decorating? Was it her or did they hire someone?'

'I have no idea. I didn't ask.'

Holly looked at Bishop and he backed her up. 'Could you find out, please, Bethany?'

'Yes, sir.' Slightly ruffled, but she immediately returned to her notes. 'She still stayed with the Wrights quite a bit though, would have stayed that night too, since she was going to the dinner. She works at an animal shelter in Albury and is training to become a vet.'

'Could she cover her mortgage with that?'

'No mortgage. The Wrights paid cash for the flat in 2013. She's got clean credit and no debts. She's enrolled in the Victim Support Programme and starts with counselling next Tuesday. I'm helping her with that. I'm going to go with her to the first one, if that's all right, and then she'll be assigned a full-time liaison officer.'

'Good call. Any run-ins, any of them?'

'Connie has had three parking tickets over seven years, traffic school in 2013 for speeding on the motorway. I mean, they're all really clean, sir.'

'Then thank them and remove them from the enquiry.' He moved on. 'Crane, what about the neighbours?'

'Immediately to the east there's Mr and Mrs Fenbourne. Seventy and sixty-nine years old. They've known the Wrights for the past thirty years, both used to be patients of his. They were having a new burglar alarm put in when I went to see them. Suitably shocked and upset. They were two of the guests that were coming to dinner that evening so it really affected them. They had nothing unusual to report from the previous two weeks; no strange cars or vehicles, no taxis, didn't see strangers in the neighbourhood who didn't belong, no unusual phone calls or hang-ups.'

'What about to the west?'

'The Angleseys. They only moved there three months ago from Holland Park in London. They're younger, both in their fifties, he's retired, used to be a professional golfer. His wife works from home running her own interior design company. They have no children. Again, nothing to report on unusual activity, although because they haven't been living there that long they would be the first to admit that they really don't know everybody in the neighbourhood. But again, no nuisance phone calls recently, no unusual vehicles spotted and nothing else to report. They're thinking of moving again now.' He skipped back a page. 'Sorry, the Angleseys would also have been guests at the Wrights' that night. So, along with the niece, that completes the seven table settings.'

'What do they drive, out of curiosity?'

'She's got a Range Rover, a new one. He's got a Mercedes.'

'Right.' Bishop mulled something over in his mind then patted his jacket, took out his cigarettes and put them on the desk.

'Buses, Ambrose?'

'Two routes towards the village converge on to the A25.'

Ambrose checked his notes. 'The A24 and B2126 from the east and the A248, that's the Chilworth road, from the west. Five different bus services, but only two go past the house. The number 22, which heads east to Dorking, and the 38, westerly to Guildford, which stops about eight hundred yards from the house by the public footpath. They run a regular service, twice every hour from eight a.m. to seven p.m., then once an hour between seven and eleven p.m. We managed to get interviews with both bus drivers from that evening. Their routes have regular passengers and neither reported seeing anybody they didn't recognise.'

'Did the Wrights ever take the bus?'

'Not very often. The driver of the 38 remembered the wife from a couple of occasions but that would have been over a year ago and he doesn't think he ever saw the doctor on his route.'

'Passengers?'

'Interviewed a couple but they're proving harder to track down. We've circulated flyers at the bus stations within a five-mile radius asking for help, anybody who was travelling on the bus that evening, etcetera, and I think we've got a helpline set up through HQ – right, Crane?'

Crane nodded. 'Yes. We've established an 0800 number with a dedicated response team. It patches straight through to anyone on the task force that's available.'

'Okay, good,' said Bishop. 'I don't want any witnesses having to leave messages.' He gestured for Ambrose to carry on.

'Three train stations in the vicinity, the closest being Gomshall, about a fifteen-minute walk from Abinger Hammer. The other two are further west, Chilworth and Shalford – that's definitely a car or bus journey. No CCTV. We interviewed staff at all three ticket offices and nobody reported anything suspicious, just the usual slew of late-night commuters and a few people coming back from the pub. We put up police incident posters asking for witnesses who travelled at the times we specified, and so far, we've had about twenty calls but nothing of any substance.'

'Dog walkers, birdwatchers – what did we find?' Bishop was playing with his pen.

Crane said: 'The nearest animal shelter is the one that Alexandra works at. Doubles up as a vet's surgery and they have three dog walkers on their books. All are women and none of them were walking the route either that day or the day before. They tend to avoid the road immediately opposite the Wrights' property, the A25, because it's too narrow to walk dogs safely. That's it so far.'

'House-to-house?'

'Twenty-three houses in the village, nearly all on that one strip of road spread over approximately one and three-quarter miles. Most of the residents have lived there for at least twenty years and all knew the Wrights quite well. One house is empty and is up for sale' – a quick check of the notes – 'the owners, a Mr and Mrs Pettiman, having moved back to Scotland. Six couples were away that evening at various functions. We're checking alibis, but they're all being very cooperative for obvious reasons. The remaining households were all at home at the time of the incident, eating dinner or watching TV. None of them saw or heard anything out of the ordinary, with the exception of one couple, Margo and Geoff Giles.'

'What about those two then?'

'The husband, Geoff. As he was pulling the curtains in the living room he said he thought he saw someone walking past his drive and along the road.'

'What time?'

'About five fifteen he thinks.'

'Any description?'

'No. There are no street lights. It's pitch-black out there after five this time of year.'

'If it was pitch-black, how could he have seen someone?'

'Because they were carrying a torch. He thought it might have been a dog walker.'

Bishop took a second. 'Was this dog walker going to or from the doctor's house?'

'To the house, sir. From the west.'

'The walker was coming from the west ...' Bishop unfolded a map on his desk and studied it. 'Mr Giles didn't hear a car?'

'No, and they haven't got a telly so he said they would have heard it.'

Bishop traced a finger along the route. 'There's no access to this road other than through everyone's gardens on the north side or over the river on the south side. So, if they were walking from the west they must have come from the direction of ... Gomshall. Where's that empty house you mentioned?'

'It's right there, sir, at the end of the village.'

'How long has it been empty?'

'Two months.'

'Get in contact with the owners—'

'The Pettimans.'

'Right, and ask them if we could look inside as soon as possible. Don't freak them out, tell them it's routine. And find out who the estate agent is. They must have left keys with someone.' He took a breath and stood up. 'Okay, I think we're done.'

'Thank you, sir.' Ambrose got up and stretched his legs, dislodging a file as he did so. 'Sorry.'

'It's fine, leave it. I'll get it.' Bishop collected up the file and restacked it. A second as he looked them all in the eye. 'Go on, get out of here. Have a great weekend.'

Bethany and Crane left but Bishop put a hand on Ambrose's shoulder.

'You look knackered. You didn't have to come in, you know that, right?'

'Yes, sir.'

'How's Claire?'

'Not sleeping much.'

'And you?'

'I'm coping.'

'Your wife is due any day now. Don't miss what I know will be one of the most beautiful experiences you will ever have. Not for this. We're dealing with death every day here and you guys are about to be dealing with a new life, so . . . that's your priority from now on and that's an order.'

'I don't want to—'

'You won't lose SIO on this, okay? It's yours. Always has been.'

'Yes, sir. Thank you.'

'Go home, Sergeant. Be with your wife.'

Ambrose looked relieved. He gave Holly a little smile, then said to Bishop, 'What are you going to do, sir?'

'Don't know. Stay here for a bit with Holly. Try to look important.'

Ambrose nodded and left, closing the door behind him. Bishop sat down again and picked up his cigarettes. He fidgeted with the packet, shaking his head slowly.

'I can't stand it,' said Holly. 'Go and have your smoke.'

'Maybe I should.' He got up and made for the door. 'Fancy a coffee afterwards? We can go somewhere. Get out of here.'

'That sounds good.'

He left and she stayed where she was, staring at the pink orchid on his desk. And for the second time she wondered who had bought it for him.

Eighteen

They went to a small Italian restaurant, about a hundred yards from Fulham Broadway tube station. A bustling high street of independent shops, bars and restaurants. Christmas shoppers passed them by, coats flapping in the wind, scarves and winter hats bobbing with brilliant colour.

The place was crowded, but Bishop knew the manager and he had organised a table for them at the rear so they wouldn't be disturbed. For the past forty minutes they had been going over the finer points of the case.

'About sixty volunteers turned up to help with the searches around the village this morning. Some came in from as far as central London. That's one of the things I like about police work,' Bishop said.

'What?'

'Human beings coming together in times of crisis. Working with each other, with people they don't even know, wanting to help make it right again. Take away some of the pain.'

'And will they?'

'You know they won't, but sometimes it's nice to have others around you.' He paused. 'A few items turned up. Some clothing. Bottles, usual crap. The lab boys are sifting through it but I'm not holding my breath. We're going to ask Alex to come in and watch the video from the village hall, see if she remembers anything or anybody that stood out. You never know, we might get lucky.'

'How often do you say that?'

'Every day.' A beat. 'Are you back at Wetherington soon?'

Holly gave a ghost of a nod, upended her coffee cup and drained it.

'How's your man?'

'He's not my man,' she scolded playfully.

'The one you like then.'

'The judicial review board are talking possible parole. I don't know if it's even feasible yet. We'll have to see if he wants to play ball. But Lee is—'

'Lee – that's his name?'

'Yep. He's definitely one of a kind. I've also had a new patient assigned to me. Very exciting. A certain Roland Cinzano.'

'You know the party's over when there's nothing left except the Cinzano.'

Holly smiled. 'Not his name, but he likes to think it is.'

'What's his story then?'

She was about to launch into it but realised her coffee cup was empty. She checked her watch. 'It's after six. If we're going to talk about Mr Cinzano, I need something sweet.'

'Like what?'

'Hot chocolate.'

'Really?'

'After six my sweet tooth kicks in. I'm hungry as well now. Do you want to grab something to eat?' A few people had entered and were starting to sit at the round wooden tables. 'Or do you have to get back?'

'No, I'm good for a while.' He checked his watch. 'I don't know. They do a good steak here and I'm pretty picky about my steaks. I like them rare.'

'Loser.' She smiled. 'I like mine raw.'

There was an open bottle of red wine and a wooden bowl of fresh salad. Bishop and Holly both had chargrilled steaks that sweated blood when they cut into them.

'Roland Cinzano has been a patient at Wetherington for over ten years now. He ran a very successful dry-cleaning company. Killed his business partner in August 2006. Strangled him with his own belt then tried to dispose of the body by cutting it up and putting the bits out with the rubbish. Unfortunately for Roland, rubbish collection was only once a fortnight and the remains started to smell. Staff also thought it strange that his business partner had apparently left on holiday without mentioning it to anyone, so they called the police.'

'He claimed insanity?'

'Diminished responsibility.'

'Right, like the famous Twinkie defence in the States.'

'Not as spectacular, but a worthy comparison. Although Roland, give him his due, is unlike any sociopath I have ever come across.'

'How so?'

'A sociopath is generally devoid of emotion, will kill without knowing why it's wrong and won't care, but with Roland ... Roland shows empathy towards people.'

'It's not a trick?'

'No, he really does feel remorse.' A moment. 'Not like our guy.'

'Our guy ...' Bishop nodded and re-filled their wine. 'Okay, Sociopathy 101. Let me give you a recap on the textbook version you schooled us in the other day.' He gave a thin smile. 'We're looking for a white male. Probably in his thirties, maybe older. He's physically big and strong. Has incredible self-control and won't be prone to panic. Was abused. Maybe started some fires and killed a few pets as a kid. Can't foster relationships. Might be on meds but is smart enough and familiar enough with police procedure to not leave clues, apart from the ones he wants us to find. Like the smashed mirror. He also takes his own knife and possibly his own belt with him.'

'Exactly.'

'How's the steak?'

'Perfect. Thank you.' She took a sip of wine. 'Do you know who Thomas Bond was?'

'No.'

'He was the Whitechapel pathologist during the Jack the Ripper murders. After he performed the autopsy on Mary Kelly in 1888 he told the police that the killer would be physically strong, quiet and harmless in appearance, possibly middle-aged, and neatly attired, probably wearing a cloak to hide the bloody effects of his attacks.'

'So in essence Thomas Bond was the first profiler?'

'I think he probably was. But you see, that's the advantage that most serial killers have. They can hide in plain sight because they look just like everyone else; they have jobs and nice homes, some have families and some go to church.' She glanced around the restaurant at the intimate tables, the hum of conversation, the smiling faces. 'There could be a serial killer in here now. Ordering food, holding hands with the person opposite, smiling at the other people in the restaurant, being charming to the waiters, and yet underneath they could have the darkest of secrets, the blackest of hearts.'

Two tables away was a man in his forties with a thick mop of black hair and wire-framed glasses. He had on a duck-egg blue shirt and as he ordered a glass of wine Holly thought she could detect a slight Scottish drawl. She dipped her head in his direction.

'Him.'

Bishop turned around. 'Seems like a nice chap. What's he got, pasta? Yeah, the pasta here is good. His partner ... what, maybe his brother, a friend or—'

'Lover,' said Holly. 'Could be another Dennis Nilsen. He killed fifteen men between 1978 and 1983, practically under the noses of his neighbours. He hid bodies in the garden and under the floorboards and nobody knew. He would dismember them and hide them in the wardrobes until the smell got too much, then he would chop them up and either burn them on a bonfire or flush them down the toilet.'

'What made him do it?'

'He couldn't relate to the living. A living, breathing person meant nothing to him. He was obsessed with his grandfather, was convinced that this relative was the only person he could love and would therefore love him in return. The trouble was, his grandfather was dead. So, he had to have dead people in order to express those feelings. It was the only way he could truly *feel*. He regarded it quite scientifically after he had been arrested; he felt he suffered from a "pseudo-sexual, infantile love which had not yet developed and matured". Apparently, the sight of his victims was bittersweet in the end – after all, it only offered a temporary relief.'

'Nilsen,' Bishop said. 'He's the one who got caught when he blocked up the drains with the remains of the bodies, right? Neighbours complained. Dyno-Rod sent someone and when they opened the drain cover they discovered it was packed with flesh and bones.'

'That's the one.'

'Classy kind of guy.'

Holly nodded to the man sitting in the alcove behind them. Bishop had to turn to get a look and saw a bald man in his fifties, again with glasses, a nice suit, tie, shiny shoes.

'John Christie.'

'Are you serious? Does he even look like him?'

'What does a serial killer look like, Bishop? You, me? The guy in the alcove? The chef who cooked our food? Christie murdered at least eight women, including his wife, by strangling them at his flat in Notting Hill. When he moved out of his house, three of his victims were discovered hidden in a cupboard in the kitchen. His wife's body was found beneath the floorboards of the front room.' She motioned to the front of the restaurant. 'And then there is the ultimate . . .'

A large group of people were entering and taking seats by the window. A mixture of lookers and suits, beautiful women on either side of men from the city, dripping with jewellery and watches, perfume and attitude. One man stood out from the rest, and Holly had recognised him. Handsome and charming, with dark hair and a movie star smile. He opened a bottle of champagne and filled everyone's glasses. He had an air of charm and self-assurance about him. When the bubbles settled, he saw Holly and Bishop staring at him and raised a glass to them both. Holly smiled back and raised her glass in return.

'Do you know him?' Bishop asked.

'Met him the other day, as a matter of fact. He lives in the same block as me. On the same floor.'

'Oh,' said Bishop.

'Anyway, for purposes of our little game, he's the classic Ted Bundy. He killed at least thirty women, some say sixty. Battered and strangled them all, then buried them in fields. He decapitated some of them and kept their heads at his home, partially hidden on his shelves like trophies. Death right in front of your eyes. His dirty little secret.'

In a daze, Bishop slowly turned away from the crowd and focused on Holly again. His blue eyes were shadowed by the candlelight and for the first time she found him hard to read.

'Sorry,' she said. 'Am I—'

'I don't know, Holly. The word "obsessed" comes to mind.'

'I'm probably not the best company. I just want to catch him.'

'So do I.'

'And I don't think he's going to stop. Not until he is caught or killed.'

Bishop finished his wine and stared at the glass as if it were a crystal ball. 'But we don't even have a name. Let alone a face.'

'But he does have a name,' Holly insisted. 'And he does have a face.'

She thought he was about to say something when a shadow crossed over his body.

'Everything all right, Mr Bishop?'

The waitress had arrived to take their plates.

'Fantastic, Simona, thank you very much.' He leaned back and cleared his throat. 'Oh, and a hot chocolate to go.' She nodded and left them alone again.

'What were you going to say?' Holly asked.

'Doesn't matter,' he said. 'I could do with another smoke.'

They were walking in the small park off Musgrave Crescent. People were wrapped up like mummies in coloured scarves against the cold and dead twigs snapped like bones under their feet.

'What made you want to become a policeman?'

'Hmm?'

'What made you join the police?'

He took a final hit on his cigarette and ground the remains under his foot.

'I was army before this. AAC for six years. That's Army Air Corps. An engineer on the Chinooks. They're the big troop carriers. Double blades. Like flying an HGV.'

'Were you in Afghanistan?'

'Started off in Kenya, then did my three tours of Afghanistan. Came away without a scratch. Well, a few paper cuts, but they don't count.'

'Why did you leave?'

'Same reason most end up leaving: medical discharge. Saw too many IEDs. Friends. You know. Thought I'd give this a go. I knew I had some skills. Realised I should try to apply them. And I still wanted to piss off my father.'

'Really?'

'To a degree. We didn't exactly get on, plus I couldn't stand the thought of a nine-to-five office job after I was demobbed. And, believe it or not, I wanted to make a difference.'

'And did you?'

'What, make a difference?'

'No. Piss off your father.'

'Yep.' He smiled wryly. 'To start off with, anyway. And then somehow he became proud of me. Fucker. That wasn't part of my master plan.' A pause. 'How about you, Holly? What made you want to look inside people's heads?'

She gazed up at the darkening sky and tucked herself deeper into her jacket. 'I didn't do it to piss anyone off. Or maybe I did. I needed to understand things. I liked the idea that if you could understand what motivated people to do bad things, you could stop them. You could talk to them or persuade them not to do it again.'

'And can you?'

'No.' She didn't sound bitter or angry, just matter-of-fact. 'Maybe it's like all jobs though. You go into it thinking you're going to change the world but, in reality, all you end up changing is yourself.'

The wind had picked up and they headed along a gravel path towards a lake. Couples were walking hand in hand. There was an echo of light laughter.

'Are you married?' she suddenly asked.

'No.' A pause. 'Engaged once, but it didn't work out. How about you?'

'No. Never been engaged either. Married to my work. Sad but true.'

'Nothing sad about that. I'm sure Wetherington takes up a lot of your time anyway. Makes it hard, right?'

'It does, but the hospital's been good to me. I take things too personally, that's all.'

'I know you do,' he said. 'The doctor and his wife? You always call them by their first names, Jonathan and Evelyn, because it makes it more personal, right? Makes it seem like you know them. You know them, you have one hell of a motivation to find their killer.'

'You're wasted as a detective inspector.'

'Yeah, tell that to my boss.' He stopped walking for a second, rubbed his right knee.

'Cold getting to it?'

He nodded, but wanted to carry on moving. 'I don't know. It's all a compromise, isn't it? Life. Marriage. Everything in this world seems so fucking twisted sometimes.'

She wanted to disagree but knew he was right.

'What about your family, Holly? Sisters, brothers? Mum and dad, what are they up to?'

'One brother.'

'Older or younger?'

'Older.'

'Was he spoiled more than you?'

She laughed. 'Maybe. No, my parents both passed away when we were young. A sailing accident.'

She saw him falter for a second out of the corner of her eye, and shake his head. 'I had no idea. That's—'

'Do you remember your parents when you were ten years old?'

'No,' he admitted.

'I do. It's like they're frozen in time. A snapshot. I hold them there at that age. I still think about them the way they were. They never grew old to me. Never will.'

'What happened?'

'We used to go down to Falmouth beach once a year, worship the sun, find crabs among the rocks. Then one year my father announced he was going to buy a boat. I'd never seen him smile so much. He really was like a little kid at Christmas. My mum hated the idea at first but then the day we went out on our first sailing trip she began to love it. In fact, I think she loved it more because my father loved it so much and she'd never seen him so happy. It was like being free, he used to tell me. Out on the waves, going wherever the wind took you. We were going to have amazing adventures together, he told me. It was small, only one sail and enough room for four people, but it felt like the best sailing ship in the world. We went all around the harbour on that first day and I pretended I was Vasco da Gama, off on a voyage of discovery, finding new lands, discovering treasures never before seen.'

They had stopped walking and now and the two of them stood facing the small lake. She felt her eyes shining with the memory.

'And then it ended three months after our first trip. We had gone down to the beach on the last week of the summer holidays. My brother and I were dreading going back to school so we set sail one more time and spent hours fishing next to a buoy. Didn't catch a thing, but it never mattered, it was the thrill of watching the float, seeing it bob in the waves and suddenly dip and dive when something took a bite. My mum made me a pirate's hat from a newspaper and I thought I was Blackbeard, holding on to the tiller and eating crab-paste sandwiches for lunch. In the afternoon, we came back to the beach but my dad wanted to take my mum out again on their own. Take her for a spin, he said, and they'd laughed. He asked me and my brother to hold the fort for them while they were gone, so we stayed on the beach guarding the towels and sunscreen, with knickerbocker glories and plastic spades . . . ' She stopped talking and looked at Bishop. He was staring at her. Very quiet and very still.

'You don't have to . . . '

'I never talk about it, but sometimes I need to.'

She turned her attention back to the lake as if her memories were replaying on the glassy surface. 'There isn't really much left to the story anyway. They simply never came back. They drifted further than they should have, the wind picked up, the currents took them out and they capsized. My father was knocked unconscious and my mother drowned. They found her body three days later in a rock pool further up the coast. My father was in hospital for a week, but never regained consciousness.'

'Jesus. I'm so sorry, Holly.'

She took a moment then said: 'Thank you.' He looked apologetic, and totally helpless. 'I used to say, "Oh that's okay, shit happens" when people told me how sorry they were. But now I don't, now I've learned to say thank you.'

'What happened afterwards? I mean, where did you . . . who looked after you both?'

'We had no relatives and unfortunately we were separated when we were placed in foster care. It wasn't much fun. I loved my brother. Missed him so much. We never really got to see each other although we did write.' She paused. 'I got lucky. I was moved into a place called Blessed Home with other children like me who had either lost their parents or been abandoned, or worse. I was under the care of the most amazing woman. Her name was Maureen and she became my guardian, my surrogate mother. I stayed there until I was seventeen and then I made my own way.'

She felt Bishop's hand on her shoulder and it made her shiver. He withdrew it immediately.

'Oh, I'm sorry,' he said.

'No, it's fine. I'm . . .'

She shook her head, annoyed with herself for going so far.

She liked Bishop, trusted him too, but now that she had told him she could never un-tell him. She didn't know where to look so she looked to the sky, where the clouds had turned black and were scudding sombrely across the heavens. The first spray of rain stung her face and she pulled up her hood to bury her face.

'We should get back,' she said.

They started to walk to the car. A heron flapped lazily in front of them and landed with a gentle splash in the lake. A quick preen and then it stood stock still amongst the reeds, barely visible.

'In plain sight,' Holly said.

'Hmm?'

'Nothing. Just being obsessive,' she whispered.

They sat side by side in his car but didn't say anything until he had pulled over and parked at the kerb outside her flat.

'Monday morning – the empty house in Abinger Hammer, if you want to tag along? Got the lockbox combination.' Bishop sounded hopeful.

'Sounds good to me.'

Water pattered on the leaves of the trees and drummed on the car roof.

'You going to make a run for it then?' he said.

'I can try.' She managed a smile but it was weak. 'Night, Bishop. Thanks for the steak.' They looked at each other and she could feel a rising warmth inside her. She imagined his hands touching her. The pressure of his fingers on her naked back.

'Night, Holly.'

She ran to her front door, thinking of his lips, and all the while wondering what it would be like to kiss them.

Nineteen

The weekend had gone faster than she had hoped.

Holly had spent most of Saturday on the sofa in her pyja-
mas catching up on paperwork and had ended up watching a
movie in the evening. Sunday she spent nearly all day in bed.
Snatches of sleep, punctuated by bowls of chicken broth soup.
Then back to sleep and sporadic dreams of sharp knives and
dark places. So when Bishop picked her up at eight on the
Monday morning, and they drove through south London,
she felt as though she hadn't really had a day off. Hooking
up with the A3 after Battersea, they made good time towards
Guildford, the commuters all heading the other way. Bishop
took a left on to Merrow Lane by the River Wey and then the
A25 carried them to the pretty little village. They were both
quiet on the drive but Holly didn't mind quiet. Quiet was good
sometimes. Quiet meant not having to try.

When they pulled into the driveway of the empty house
there was a squad car already waiting for them and Bishop
gave Holly a half-smile and said, 'Let's see what they've
learned so far.'

He had requested two PCs to be present while they

conducted the search – Lipski and Harrowman, both women, both young and both eager to prove themselves. Harrowman was painfully thin, almost malnourished, Lipski pear-shaped and pale, and Holly wondered which one would last. Which one would fight the good fight, be as incorruptible as possible, learn something every day and grow hardened to the awful reality of police work. She followed Bishop as he approached them and watched him casually lean against the bonnet of their car as he introduced her. She knew what he was doing. He turned to her and gave her a wink. The PCs had been there for at least thirty minutes, maybe more.

The four of them completed a circuit of the periphery and concluded the house was very similar to all of the other houses in the village; large, detached, with a curving gravel driveway and massive back garden full of mature trees, thick bushes and well-maintained flower beds. It also backed on to the river, which drifted sluggishly to the east.

As promised by the estate agent, Mickey Munroe from WW Estate Agents, the key was in a lockbox by a flower pot. Holly noted that it hadn't been disturbed or forced in any way and when Bishop punched in the code, the key dropped into his palm.

He opened the front door and the smell wafted over them immediately. Fresh paint. A stark contrast to the Wrights' residence. How had Alex described it? Sticky. Yes, that made sense. Sticky and red and claustrophobic. The owners of this place had obviously slapped on a fresh coat of emulsion to try and encourage viewings, and it was a good sign. No smell of decomposing bodies lurking in the cellar or underneath the floorboards or spreadeagled on the couch in the living room. The search was systematic, from room to room, wall to wall, looking for anything out of the ordinary – an ornament on the floor, a drawer left open, a light left on.

Holly checked every window herself, but found each one secure, with no sign of tampering. Upstairs it was the same story. Four bedrooms and two bathrooms; nothing disturbed, no drawers open, no curtains hanging loose, no windows slightly ajar, no cracked panes. She was staring out of the master bedroom at the view when Bishop entered the room and joined her.

'Beautiful place, isn't it.' He rested one hand on the window frame as they watched a pair of swans glide effortlessly across the river below, orange beaks dipping into the frosty surface. It seemed so idyllic, so peaceful, Holly felt as though she could have stayed there forever. Then her eyes lifted from the river and her expression changed.

'I hadn't realised the river curved quite so much,' she said. 'You can see the rear of the Wrights' property from here. Even into the bedrooms.'

They both stared, a heavy silence between them. Bishop said it first.

'You think he could have watched them from here?'

'An empty house. Perfect location. Great vantage point. We're east-facing, so the sun would set behind us, making it almost impossible for the Wrights to see whoever's here. Observing their house, waiting for Jonathan and Evelyn to get ready for dinner, counting the seconds until the sun went down so he could exit here and walk along the path in complete darkness.'

'Past the Giles' house,' said Bishop, 'a single torch lighting his way.'

'Jonathan had arthritis and he was deaf. He wouldn't have

heard anything that was going on in the living room. What our killer did to Evelyn would have taken three, four, five minutes perhaps. He had all the time in the world. He knew Jonathan was going to come down eventually, but he didn't know when. Maybe he even timed him coming down the stairs when he was watching him from here.'

'No signs of a break-in anywhere downstairs though. No footprints in the flower beds. No forced entry.'

'Which means he used the key.'

'So he either made a copy or knew the lockbox combination.' Bishop pulled out his mobile and dialled. 'Mr Munroe please ... Yeah, I'll hold. Tell him it's Detective Inspector Bishop. We're at the Pettimans' house in Abinger Hammer.' A pause. 'Mr Munroe, yes ... Hold on, I'm going to put you on speaker ... We need a list of all the people who came to view the property. Their addresses, telephone numbers and what times their appointments were.'

'Why is that?'

The voice was very clear and clipped and Holly had a sudden image of Mr Munroe on a galloping horse, sipping brandy from a silver stirrup cup while the hounds bayed behind him.

'To help with our enquiries, sir.'

There was a horribly long moment before Munroe asked, 'You didn't find anything bad there, did you?'

'No, it's fine,' Bishop assured him.

'Thank God for that. I've had a few sleepless nights, what with the old ... you know ...'

'Yes, sir. I do. Thank you for your time, Mr Munroe.' Bishop hung up, pocketed his phone as Lipski and Harrowman appeared at the door.

'Can't get into the garage, sir. No batteries in the remote.'

He looked almost apologetic when he stared at them and issued his challenge.

'All right, which one of you wants to go get some double A's?'

The two rookies left together. While they were gone, Bishop and Holly skirted the premises once more. When they were done, Bishop slumped on to the porch steps and treated himself to a cigarette.

'You sleep over the weekend?' he asked.

'A little. You?'

'Same.'

She watched him sucking the cigarette as if it contained all the answers, and then he glanced up, looking at her but not seeing her. She sat next to him and they shared a moment of personal silence, mentally cataloguing everything they knew, and she found herself clasping and unclasping her hands.

'If he watched them from the bedroom,' she said, 'he may have been planning this for a long time.'

'Is that normal?'

'Most serial killers are opportunists. They happen to find the right person at the right time. Sutcliffe, Ridgway, Fred West ...' A pause. 'John Wayne Gacy was a planner. He killed teenage boys. The press nicknamed him the "Killer Clown". He devised a character for himself and used to dress up as "Pogo the Clown" and do fundraisers for charities and children's parties.' She frowned slightly. 'That's the thing – and I can't stress this enough: he will be someone people know. The next-door neighbour, the charity worker, the man who helps old ladies across the road, the policeman, the fireman, the paramedic. Hidden right out in the open. His beautiful little secret.'

'His beautiful little secret,' Bishop repeated. There was a lull and then he stood up. Lipski and Harrowman had returned with the batteries and a cardboard tray of takeout coffees.

Bishop clapped when the garage door groaned and swivelled upwards, revealing a sparse and clinically clean interior. Workbench on the left with neat boxes of nails and screws, discarded paintbrushes and a few tins of the new white emulsion; a row of tools hanging from brackets on the right-hand wall – a collection of hammers, saws, a spirit level and a drill. At the back, a large white freezer, humming quietly to itself.

The first thing Holly thought was, wouldn't it be interesting if there was a body in the freezer, curled up and stiff with a sugar coating of ice. She knew there wouldn't be, though – it wouldn't fit the MO. This killer liked people to see exactly what he was capable of doing, he craved an audience, and when Bishop lifted the lid, she was suitably relieved. No body, just a single rather sad-looking box of vanilla choc ices crumpled against one of the wire racks.

'Search this place,' Bishop said. 'Everywhere.'

Holly and Bishop looked on as Lipski and Harrowman moved the freezer away from the wall, checked underneath and behind the workbench and opened tins of paint. After five minutes, however, they came to the rather stilted conclusion that there was nothing of any interest.

They were getting ready to leave when Bishop suddenly turned on his heel and walked back to the freezer, opening the lid. He pulled out the box of choc ices and Holly thought he was about to help himself to one, but then the bottom flipped open and a hammer, smeared in black, fell out and clunked on to the concrete floor.

Twenty

'Jeff Larson, thirty-nine, one murder, two attempted. Used a hammer on his girlfriend, strangled her post-mortem.'

'What does the asterisk by his name mean?'

'That means it was my investigation. I got the collar.'

'Nice.'

'Thank you. I'm here all week. Try the veal. Actually, no,' Bishop added. 'Strike him out. He's in Broadmoor, eligible for parole in 2019.'

It was late afternoon now and they had been stuck in Bishop's office ever since they had returned from Abinger Hammer. He was behind his desk, Holly at his shoulder, scrolling through a list of possible suspects with similar MOs on his computer.

Holly went and sat on the office sofa, where she had left a mound of watch-list predator case files and read out the next one from her pile. 'Noah Gross. Convicted of rape.' She scanned the page, didn't try to hide the sarcasm in her voice. 'Oh, that's a shame, he had a heart attack in 2016. Died of complications in January this year. Why was he even sent over as a suspect if he's dead?'

'Welcome to my world. Put him in my out-tray. Permanently.'

Bishop moved on to the next one. 'Raymond Theroux. Forty-two, three rapes, one attempted, cleared of manslaughter through lack of evidence. Nicknamed himself the New Forest Strangler.'

'Original. Still inside?'

'Recently transferred to Rakemoor. Should be out in eight months in time for Valentine's.'

'Nick Whitticker,' said Holly. 'Two rapes, one pending, pleaded diminished responsibility ...'

Bishop brought him up on his screen. 'Went on parole three weeks ago and ... nope, no good. He was inside when Rebecca was murdered. Got arrested for a DUI.' He carried on reading. 'Jesus ...'

'What?'

'It's gross.'

'You started this.'

'Gareth Craven. Likes to do things with dogs.'

'A zoophiliac.'

'They've got a name for it?'

'Everything's got a name. Necrophilia.'

'Dead people.'

'Autoplushophilia.'

'Auto-what?'

'Arousal from cartoon-like stuffed animals.'

'You're making this shit up.'

'I'm serious. You never fancied Mickey Mouse?'

'Minnie Mouse, yeah, obviously, I'm only human, but—'

'Don't even get me started on lithophilia.'

'Go on.'

'Finding gravel and stone a turn-on.'

'You're joking?'

Holly found herself laughing at the expression on his face. 'That's why they call it crazy paving,' she said.

'All right, I'm crossing Gareth Craven off the list. He's gone.'

There was a knock and Karanack stuck his head around the door. 'Sir, we've had a call. A bloke says he killed the doctor and his wife.'

'Did he give a name?'

'Actually, he did, sir. Says his name is David Eagen.'

'Eagen? Is he on our list?' He turned to Holly.

'Not mine.'

Bishop looked him up and a mugshot of David Eagen appeared on his screen. 'David Eagen. Thirty-three years old. Spent five years in Belmarsh for raping a sixteen-year-old girl named Juliette Billington back in 2009. Released May 2014. Threatened a prostitute last month with a knife then stole her car.'

'Did he cut her?'

'No. The woman refused to press charges and prosecutors had to abandon the case. On the lesser charge of vehicle theft, he was cleared as it could not be proved he stole the car intending to "permanently deprive" the victim.'

'He got off on a technicality?'

'Yep. The judge sent him to spend a week in a mental institution for assessment under the Mental Health Act, but he was then released as it was the equivalent of serving time. What do you think?'

'Not our guy,' she yawned.

'Shame.' A pause. 'Go on. Go home. Get some rest. Come back tomorrow.'

'No way. You said you'd include me as much as you can.'

'You're a real glutton for punishment, aren't you, missy?' He smiled at her and then hung his head in exhaustion. 'Does he want to make a statement, want us to pick him up?' he asked Karanack. 'What's the deal?'

'Said he's more than happy to come in and have a chat.'

'Have a chat? Great.' He rolled his eyes. 'What have we got free?'

'Number four.'

'Go get him. No lights, no commotion. Let me know when he's here.' To Holly: 'You can watch through the one-way.'

Bishop led Holly downstairs and showed her into the observation room. It was narrow and small, with four chairs and a shelf that ran the length of the one-way mirror. The interview room beyond was bare save for a table with two chairs either side. It was being readied for Eagen by an officer she didn't recognise who was setting up the voice recorder and making sure everything was working as it should. He placed pens and fresh pads of paper where Bishop and Karanack would sit. Holly felt as if she was at the theatre and waiting for a show to begin.

'I'll be wearing an earpiece so you can talk to me if you want.' Bishop was putting it on as he explained. 'The microphone is there on the shelf, so talk normally.' He opened the door and called to someone: 'Could you take him in, please?'

They watched through the one-way as Eagen was shown in by Sergeant Crane. After Crane exited, Eagen murmured quietly to himself for a while, and then stared up at the left-hand corner of the room where the camera was positioned.

'There he is in all his glory,' Bishop said. 'What do you think?'

Holly scrutinised him as if he was in a petri dish. Eagen was fair-haired and so pale and skinny he looked like a grey ghost.

His eyes were like saucers and he was wearing filthy jeans and a T-shirt. As he splayed his fingers on the desk she noticed his nails were red raw and split.

'He's on something,' she said.

'Meth. Maybe heroin.'

'At some point, he's going to come down without a parachute.' She felt Bishop shift next to her and smiled. 'Maybe you can give him a hug.'

Some of the other squad members entered the room, curious as to what was about to happen. Jacobs was there, along with Lipski and Kathy, the press liaison officer. Then Chief Constable Franks entered and Lipski had to leave to give them more room.

Bishop did the introductions. 'Sir, this is Holly Wakefield, she's been standing in for Sam Gordon.' Franks leaned towards Holly and offered his hand. 'Chief Constable Franks, thank you for your help.'

'My pleasure, sir.'

Franks turned to Eagen, watched him for several seconds then nodded to Bishop. 'Are we ready for this?'

'Yes, sir.'

Bishop left and a minute later he and Karanack entered interview room number four.

They took a seat opposite Eagen, and Bishop placed the case file on the table between them. He turned the voice recorder on.

'Today is Monday 13 November 2017. I am Detective Inspector Bishop from the Serious Crimes Division of the Metropolitan Police. I will be conducting the interview. Present with me is . . .'

'Sergeant Karanack.'

'And the time is 4.27 p.m. We are interviewing David

Eagen, who has come to the station voluntarily regarding the double murder of Jonathan Wright and his wife Evelyn at their house in the village of Abinger Hammer in the county of Surrey last Monday evening. Could you state your name and address, please?'

Eagen swallowed hard, then puffed himself up like a peacock.

'David Eagen. No fixed abode.'

'David Eagen, you are hereby cautioned, although you are not under arrest and you are free to leave. You have the right to seek legal advice as there is no solicitor present at this interview. Do you understand?' Eagen said nothing. 'Mr Eagen?'

'Yep.'

'You have something to tell us?'

Eagen shook his head, then nodded. 'He was a doctor, right?'

'Yes.'

'Okay. I went there to get a nose job for my girlfriend. But he fucked her up. Made her look like a pig. So I killed him.'

'Are you serious?'

'Yeah, she's really fucking ugly.'

Eagen smiled but there was no warmth in his eyes.

'I meant are you serious about your confession or are you just here to waste our time?'

'Where's your shrink?'

'What drugs are you on, Eagen?'

'The blue ones. I wanna see the shrink.'

'Why?'

'What's his name, the chap with the bald head? I've seen him before. Gordon, right?'

'Sam Gordon, that's right.'

'Where is he?'

'He's not here.'

144

'What do you mean he's not here?'

'He's not working this murder investigation.'

'No?'

'No.'

'Why?'

'I don't think that concerns you, Mr Eagen.'

'Maybe it does.'

'Where's he going with this?' Franks said in the observation room. Nobody had an answer.

Eagen shifted in his seat. 'Who's working the case then? I know you guys will bring in a profiler for a serial killer. It's protocol. You didn't mention them in the papers.'

Holly leaned in to the microphone. 'How does he know it's a serial killer? He can't know about the link with Rebecca.'

'What are you talking about, a serial killer?' Bishop asked. 'Are you saying you've killed other people, David?'

'What?'

'Are you saying you've killed other people as well?'

'Maybe. Maybe I have, yeah. But you won't ever find them because they're buried.'

'Buried?'

'Yeah. You'll never find them.'

They held each other's gaze, like two fighters circling each other in the first round. Eagen looked away first.

'All right,' he said, 'let's say I didn't kill anyone else, but I still want to know who the shrink is.'

'Why, David?'

'Why not? Aren't I entitled? They're gonna assess me, aren't they?'

Bishop leaned forward over the desk, claiming the space. 'I don't get it, David. Why are you so interested in our psychologist? You had an evaluation last month after you assaulted a woman with a knife. You want another one? How about I give you one? Time-waster. What do you need? A soft bed and a warm meal? That why you're here?'

'Give me the fucking shrink's name! The one who's working this murder!' He banged his fist on the table. It made everyone jump, even in the observation room.

There was a taut silence that stretched until Bishop said, 'Calm down please, Mr Eagen.'

Eagen took a deep breath but Holly could see he was screaming inside. There was an aggressiveness that hadn't been there before and she watched him with fresh eyes.

'I want to know their name,' repeated Eagen, quieter now, although his face was still stained red.

'That doesn't concern you.' Bishop sat back again and started to play with his pen.

Holly felt herself edging forward. She wanted to be in the room with Eagen, wanted to be able to see into his eyes, close-up. Why was this so important to him? Why was he so interested in which psychologist was working the case? She turned to Kathy.

'What was the name of the other psychologist who works with you? The one on maternity leave?'

'Natalie Wilson.'

'Has she ever come into contact with Eagen?'

'I doubt it. She's only ever worked two cases. Not killers or rapists either. She focuses more on the legal aspects.'

'Then what about Sam Gordon? Has Eagen ever been involved with him in any way?'

'Sam has always worked murder with the serious crime squad. Never sexual crimes.'

'What about his wife? Janine. What does she do?'

'She's an accountant, volunteers at a homeless shelter once a week.'

'Which shelter?'

'I don't know. Sergeant Mosely is working the assault case, he'll have all the details.'

Holly remembered Mosely, the officer who looked like a rhino in a suit. She made a mental note to talk to him, to clarify this line of enquiry. She glanced into the interview room, where it appeared Bishop was content to let Eagen stew in the silence, and checked through his arrest sheet again. Born into poverty, his story mirrored that of thousands of other young offenders. Small crimes at first, judicial slaps on the wrists alternating with visits to HM Prison Feltham for juvenile offenders, and then his first charge of domestic abuse when he was twenty-three. He had been sentenced to seven months in Pentonville, a closed prison, Category B, and apart from a few drugs charges and one for intimidation, he appeared to have stayed out of trouble until the rape of Juliette Billington eight years ago. After release he had spent the next two years on an Offender Behaviour Programme, but again seemed to have slipped, given the recent incident with the prostitute. Holly put the file to one side and stared at Eagen. She came to a decision and spoke quietly into the microphone.

'Tell him my name.'

There was silence. Bishop was pretending to write something down. He looked up at Eagen but still said nothing.

'It's okay, Bishop. Tell him.'

His nod was barely perceptible. He put down his pen and leaned across the table, his face a picture of concern.

147

'David. I need you to answer me honestly, okay?' A resigned sigh. 'I know you've been been trying to go straight. Keep out of trouble. But what you're telling me today is worrying. You understand that, right? So if you think that our psychologist can help you in some way, help you to stay out of trouble, then I'd be happy to fill in the gaps for you. Would it help you to know their name, David? Would that make it easier for you to talk about this?'

'Nicely done,' Holly whispered.

Eagen hesitated. For a second he looked panicked but then nodded slyly.

'Yeah. That's why I want to know who it is. I wanna connect with them, you know? Make me better.'

Bishop nodded and smiled.

'Her name is Holly, David.'

'Holly?'

'Yes.'

'Like in mistletoe?'

'I guess so. Yes, like a sprig of mistletoe.'

'Like a sprig of fucking mistletoe. It's Christmas all round then, isn't it?' Eagen smiled, satisfied. He stayed staring at Bishop for some time but then his eyes faltered and the surface of the table became his new best friend. 'Have you done your Christmas shopping yet, DI Bishop?'

'No, I haven't. Have you?'

'Yeah.'

'What have you got your girlfriend?'

'What girlfriend?'

'The one who you want to have a nose job.'

'Oh, nothing yet. Maybe get her some condoms.' Eagen swallowed hard, his eyes wandering around in their sockets.

'Holly,' he said again. He scratched his nose, cleared his throat and shot a look at Karanack.

'Oi, choirboy. Is my lawyer here yet?'

Karanack kept quiet. Bishop answered for him.

'You declined a lawyer, remember?'

'Changed my mind.'

'You want a lawyer now?'

'Why not? I know my rights.'

Bishop's shoulders sagged. He reached across to the voice recorder. 'This is DI Bishop. The time is 5.54 p.m. I am now terminating the interview because Mr Eagen, who originally volunteered to help us with our enquiries, has now decided he wants a lawyer.' He clicked it off, got up and headed to the door.

'Wait. Ask him how tall he is,' Holly said.

Bishop rolled his eyes and turned back to Eagen.

'One last question, David. How tall are you?'

'What? Five nine, five ten.'

'That's what I thought he'd say,' Holly continued. 'According to his arrest record, he's five foot five. His height is inconsistent with the blood spatter on the ceiling. Unless he committed the murders standing on a chair, which I very much doubt, he's not our man. Show him the photos.'

Bishop stood still for a few seconds and Holly knew he was weighing up the odds, deciding whether or not to play her hunch. Then he opened the case file and slammed several of the crime scene photos on the desk. A look of horror flashed across Eagen's face.

'Jesus Christ . . . What is that?'

'That's the body of the doctor you murdered, David.'

In the next moment, Eagen was sick by the side of the table.

149

'For fuck's sake,' he protested. 'I didn't do that. Jesus, get that shit away from me!'

'It's not him,' Holly said.

Bishop moved to the corner of the room, half-turned away from Eagen. He lowered his voice: 'You knew that, right?'

In the observation room, everyone looked at Holly.

'Suspected. He wants the glory without the crime. Did you know that sixty people confessed to murdering the Black Dahlia?'

'What are the odds we can beat that?' Eagen was wiping his mouth with a tissue when Bishop turned back to him. He glanced at Karanack.

'Get the little prick out of here.'

'What do you think?'

The question came from the Chief Constable, who was lingering in the doorway of Bishop's office. Bishop was behind his desk and Holly was standing by one of the filing cabinets.

Bishop shook his head. 'We've got to let him go. The CPA will laugh at us, we've got absolutely nothing on him. He's already retracted his original statement. He said he'll admit to wasting police time, but apart from that ...'

'Bottom line: do you think he murdered them?'

'No, I don't, sir. No.'

'Miss Wakefield?'

'He didn't do it. There's something going on with him but I don't know what it is.'

'Fine,' said the chief. 'We can't charge him so we've only one option. Let him walk.'

Twenty-one

Sergeant Mosely was just as Holly remembered him. A large man, over six feet tall, with fists that seemed to be bunched and angry, as if underneath the uniform there was something simmering. But his eyes grew soft when he smiled.

'Sergeant Mosely,' he said. 'Nice to meet you, Holly.'

'Likewise,' she said, and she decided there and then that if she was ever in a cage fight she'd want this guy next to her.

'So you think there might be a connection between David Eagen, Sam Gordon and Janine?' he said.

'Eagen was really pushy about Sam Gordon working the case, but when he found out Sam wasn't involved, he withdrew his statement and wanted out. Can we find out if Eagen ever had contact with either of the Gordons?'

'I've already put in a call to Sam. He said he doesn't remember the name, but he's re-checking his files.' He led her over to a computer terminal and tapped a few keys.

'What do you want to look at?'

'I know it's a long shot but I want to see if Eagen was involved in the attack on Janine. Is this it? Is this the CCTV?'

'Yes. I'm bringing it up for you now. We already had a clip

post-offence, the attacker fleeing the scene. But now we've got the attacker arriving at the scene.' He pointed to a map on the wall. 'Here's all the CCTV. Green ones are council cameras, blue ones are private. The first images were captured by private cameras at 9.44 p.m. Here comes the assailant. Good shots of him and his clothing here. It's all dark, jeans, jacket and he has his hood up, maybe even a scarf across the bottom of his face. He's wearing gloves on both hands. Hands in pockets to start with, then he has a cigarette here ... '

'Where is this?'

'Off Loughborough Road, Lambeth. It's 9.47 now. Janine finishes her shift at ten so he's basically waiting. See? Walking up here, past Crowhurst Court. Fast-forward and he comes back again. Repeats that route until 9.57.'

'Killing time.'

'Waiting for her to come out. The shelter's around the corner on Overton Road. So he'd obviously scoped it out and knew her route and timeline.'

'Have we got any previous footage so we can verify that?'

'No, all the private CCTV was wiped after a week and the council cameras are wiped after two.' He waited. 'This is approximately three minutes before she was attacked. So, we switch locations now, this is a council camera outside the shelter, and there's Janine leaving the building with two other volunteers. She's the one on the left, wearing the light coat. They chat for a while, then her two friends head off to the left, wave goodnight to Janine, and she starts to walk up Overton Road towards the Loughborough intersection.'

'What did her two friends say?'

'They didn't see anything. They both live a few streets away in the opposite direction to the route Janine takes.

She always parks her car up there because it's the only way she can join the main road without getting caught up in the one-way system. He's at the corner watching her now but she obviously can't see him, or if she does see him she doesn't view him as a threat.'

'How many other staff at the shelter?'

'Varies week to week. That night there were nine active volunteers with forty-three homeless. We talked to all of them and no one saw the attack or mentioned anybody new in the area. They're pretty tight with each other, so they would have noticed an outsider.'

'It might be worth going back there, showing them Eagen's photo, see if it rings any bells?'

Mosely pointed to the screen.

'Here it comes now. He's walking out from behind the wall. Janine is still a good fifty metres away. Watch . . . there.'

'What did he do? Rewind and freeze-frame it.'

'Okay. Here we go. He's right under the street lamp. See how the light is reflecting off his face?'

'That's weird. What is that? Flare-up?'

'That's what I thought at first, but look at the next few frames. See how when he turns the street light picks up his eyes. But there's nothing there.'

Holly squinted at the image and gave a strained smile. 'He's wearing a mask.'

'Yeah. Plain white, plastic probably. A Phantom of the Opera kind of thing.'

'He obviously knows there's CCTV around here. Or maybe he knows her? Maybe that's what it is. Can you print me off a copy of that?'

'Sure.' He pressed Play again. 'Okay, frame by frame, here

we go. He's got both his hands in his jacket. Holding the container in the right-hand pocket – you can see the bulge.'

'What was the container?'

'Looks like a water bottle, but it won't be, it will be aluminium with a screw top. He takes the top off there – look – as if he's about to have a drink, approaches her – BAM – throws it straight in her face. She reacts, doesn't know what's going on yet and then the pain hits her and she screams, falls to the ground. He looks left and right, checking to see if anyone has seen him, puts the cap on the bottle, fumbles it, drops it, picks it back up and walks away. Doesn't start running until the next street. Didn't want to attract attention to himself. CCTV follows him there, brings up—'

'Can we get any close-ups, or is this it?'

'This is it, I'm afraid. Okay . . . CCTV follows him when he takes a left on Robsart Street. Another camera picks him up on Stockwell Park Road about sixty seconds later. And then we lose him after that.'

'So what's around that area?'

'Loads of abandoned places. Offices, old shops that are closed and boarded up, empty warehouses. Any CCTVs have been vandalised and not repaired. So we lost him.'

'Hostels, doss houses?'

'Not officially. A lot of people living rough, though. We canvassed the whole set-up, but nobody's saying anything. We think if whoever did this lives in the vicinity, then he might be one of their own so they're circling the wagons.'

'I'd be surprised if he did stay in the area,' Holly said.

'Why?'

'If you're going to attack someone, especially with acid, you're not going to do it on your own doorstep. You want to be able to get away and stay away.' Holly leaned against the desk. 'Do we have any idea where Eagen lives?'

'He's one of the ones that stay under the radar. I made a few phone calls before you came over and according to a PAYE from Jobseekers he's on the payroll at a garage in Shoreditch. The manager, Jamie Nettles, confirmed he works there as a mechanic on and off, but he hasn't seen him in months. He admits paying him cash in hand when he does turn up. No real problems with the other employees. When he's there, he works hard. He does like his beer and drugs though. Couple of times Nettles has had to have words with him.'

'What about?'

'Turning up late. High on the job. Usual stuff.'

'Have you got any other leads?'

'Janine can't remember anything. A vague recollection of a figure in front of her and then everything changed to a blur. She had her eyes squeezed shut after that.'

The video was still rolling and Holly saw more figures appear next to Janine. 'Who are they?'

'They're residents from the opposite side of the street. Heard her screaming. When they found out what had happened they rushed back to their house, turned on the garden hose and reeled it out to her. Lucky they had one.'

'And they didn't see anything?'

'Curtains drawn, watching TV.'

'Can we work out how tall . . . ' She trailed off, started again. 'How tall is Janine?'

'She's five foot seven. Why, what are you thinking?'

'I'm not sure. I mean . . . Christ, it could be Eagen. The body type, the height. He's only five foot five.'

'It's a possibility.'

'Could you make copies of some more stills of him from this footage, different angles, front and back? I want to compare this guy's walk, his stance, to the CCTV we would have got of Eagen walking into the station this evening.'

'Sure.'

Holly stared at the screen, unwilling to take her eyes off the freeze-frame of the man in the mask. *Is that you, David Eagen? You took a hell of a risk coming here today. Why would you put yourself in the firing line?*

'Doesn't make sense, right?'

She snapped out of it; didn't realise she'd been talking aloud. 'He was high. Maybe a spur-of-the-moment thing, but he definitely didn't come here to talk about the murder of Evelyn and Jonathan. The moment he realised Sam wasn't working the case, he hightailed it out of there. But why give a false confession just to talk to Sam?'

'There's been no press about it. He wanted to see what damage he'd done? To gloat?'

'So Eagen throws acid on Janine for ... whatever reason. For revenge, for something. She has to be the link, but what has she done?'

'She's done nothing.'

Holly spun her head around at the unknown voice. She recognised the man immediately. The man who'd had his head in his hands in Bishop's office last week. He looked in his sixties but perhaps he was younger. He seemed tired – beyond tired, as if in the grip of a profound fatigue.

'Holly, this is Sam. Sam Gordon.'

They shook hands.

'I'm so sorry,' she said.

156

'Thank you,' he replied rather curtly. 'DI Bishop has been telling me you might have a theory?'

'I don't know.' She recoiled at being put on the spot. 'It's a bit of a stretch, but . . . we've interviewed this man, David Eagen. Do you recognise him?'

Mosely handed over a mugshot and Gordon took out his reading glasses and balanced them on his nose.

'No, never seen him. What is he?'

'A rapist.'

'Well then.' He looked disappointed. 'I wouldn't have dealt with him. I mean, it's a possibility he was on the periphery of a case, but highly unlikely.'

'He seemed very interested in you.'

'In me?'

'He came in earlier this evening for questioning about the murder of the doctor and his wife. I don't know if you've been following the case—'

'A little.'

'He wanted to know if you were working on it, wanted to know if you were here, at the station.'

'I'm sure I haven't seen him before. I've been through all my old files going back to my college days, trying to find out who the hell did this, and he's definitely not one of mine.' He handed back the mugshot and leaned against a desk.

'He's a loner, a bit of a vagrant,' Holly continued. 'It's possible he's been to the shelter that your wife worked at. They may have met, talked. Perhaps she told him about you.'

'Janine would never do that.' It came out fast and furious. He stood up quickly. Turned away and turned back. 'She knows not to talk about work outside of the home. But you think there's a possibility that he's the one who attacked her?'

157

'Physically, he appears to be the right shape and size, but it's flimsy.'

'Can we bring him in again? Maybe bring him in and ask him directly about Janine. That might rattle him, make him talk about it, maybe even confess.'

'It's a possibility,' said Mosely, but he didn't look enthusiastic.

Gordon folded his glasses and put them neatly away. 'And he confessed to the murders of the doctor and his wife?'

'Initially, yes. Called up and said he wanted to talk about it.'

'But you didn't believe him, Holly.'

'No. He withdrew his confession immediately after the session in the interview room. It would never stand up in court now and, more importantly, he doesn't fit the profile. He's a convicted rapist, yes. But he's not a killer and there was no rape with either Evelyn or Rebecca.'

'Was there penetration in these attacks?'

'Yes.'

'I haven't seen the photos. Would it be possible to?'

'I can't make that call. It has to come from Bishop or the SIO,' Mosely said.

'Who's SIO?'

'Ambrose. He's taking leave at the moment, though.'

'SIO on leave during a triple murder? What's that about?'

Neither of them answered.

'Right, I'll talk to Bishop then.'

He was about to leave when Holly said, 'How is she?'

'Not good. Coping. They're being very good at the hospital. She's having a second skin graft at the end of the week. We're hoping it's going to take – the first one didn't do well.

It's time. Time, healing. No, she's lost the sight in her left eye. Permanently. This isn't . . .'

He left the room without finishing the sentence.

Holly was in Bishop's office, watching him water his orchid with some bottled water. At first she had thought he was smiling, but now she could tell he had a scowl on his face. He threw the empty bottle in the bin and sat behind his desk. Arms up, above his head.

'The blood on the hammer found in the Pettimans' freezer. It's not a match for either Jonathan or Evelyn.'

'You're joking.'

'Wish I was.'

Holly couldn't have been more surprised. 'Have they tested it against Rebecca's DNA?'

'Not a match for her either. The report came through from the forensic team about twenty minutes ago. Doesn't match anybody in the database, cold case or otherwise. There were traces of blood, skin cells and minute fragments of bone.'

'No hair?'

'No. No other fibres. Some dust, but nothing out of the ordinary.'

She sighed, starting to lose faith. 'Do they have any idea how long the hammer was in the freezer?'

'The house has been empty for two months, so we've got up to eight weeks to play with. I did ask them that and they said' – he glanced down at the report – '"Blood crystallises under zero-degree temperatures. Therefore, the hammer and materials investigated could have been there for five days or five months."' He let the report drop on his desk. 'There's going to be another body out there somewhere,' he said. 'How long before we find it?'

'But it proves he was there. I don't believe he chose that house at random to hide the hammer. He would have watched them.' She tried to think it through, work it out, her hands drawing diagrams in the air.

'He gains entry, searches the property, goes upstairs and finds that vantage point. Sees the Wrights' residence. Perfect location. He's found his hide. He watches them in front of the television, making a drink, getting ready for bed. Biding his time. He's not going to kill them that night, but he knows now he can watch them at his convenience. And after he put the hammer in the freezer he also removed the batteries from the garage remote so the estate agent couldn't get inside. Have we got the list of viewers from the estate agent yet?'

'Still waiting. I'll put in another call.'

There was a knock at the door and Crane appeared.

'Sir, the niece, Alexandra, is here.'

They followed him into the incident room.

Alexandra was with Bethany, Jacobs and Kathy. They were watching the video from the village hall. The camera positioned at the left of the stage had captured nearly all of the participants. The villagers were assembling after the initial talks, grouping themselves around their allocated police officer.

Jacobs pointed to one of the men, who seemed to be constantly looking at the camera. 'Who's that?'

'His name is Geoffrey Harris. He's a tennis coach at the local school,' said Alex.

'What about him?'

'No. I think he's married to someone in the village. Wait a minute.' She had seen something. 'Go back.'

The video rewound and played again.

'Him,' Alex said.

'Jesus,' said Bishop under his breath. 'It's Eagen.'

Alex turned, suddenly aware of the newcomers. She smiled at Holly then spoke to Bishop:

'He came up to me at the end.'

'Pause it,' Bishop ordered. The screen was stopped and showed David Eagen crossing the frame. 'What did he say?'

She looked back at the image for a few seconds, her brow furrowed. 'Sorry for your loss or something. It felt weird.'

'Why?'

'I don't know. He's not a local. I didn't recognise him.'

Bishop was pacing in his office.

'He was there, right in front of me! What the hell is he playing at?' His face was impassive but his eyes were cold. 'Send some PCs out to the village immediately. Get statements from everyone who was there at the meeting. Knock on all their doors. Talk to anyone who spoke to him and try to find out how the hell he got there. Where did you drop him off?'

'Address in Waterloo, sir.'

'All right. Go around there now. Send two cars. Find the bastard. In fact, I'll come with you.'

'Yes, sir.' Crane left and closed the door.

Holly kept her voice as calm as she could as Bishop stood up, put his jacket on and walked towards the door.

'It's not him. Physically and mentally, he doesn't fit the profile. He didn't kill Jonathan and Evelyn and he didn't kill Rebecca.'

'You said the killer might show up at the village hall. Eagen did. You said he might be blue collar. Eagen's a mechanic. You know I don't like coincidences. We've got to bring him in.' He reached for the door handle, but stopped when she said:

161

'What did you think of him, though? You were sitting in the room, right opposite him – what did you think?'

'Apart from being a – what do they call it? An oxygen thief . . . ?'

'But do you honestly think he did it?'

'No. No, I don't. But he's hiding something. He knows something.'

'You're right, he does. On the surface, Janine's attack and the double murder don't seem connected. But underneath there's something going on here. Something that . . .' She took a second. 'Maybe he attacked Janine. Maybe he . . .' Another breath, another thought. Then she shook her head. 'When you pick him up, will you let me talk to him? I want to find out why he was so interested in Sam.'

'Sure. Um, I've had a thought . . .'

There was an uncertainty in his voice that Holly hadn't heard before. 'I've been thinking about his whole interest in the psychologist from a different angle.'

'What do you mean?'

'He may not have come here to find out about Sam. You're the shrink. You're the one working the case. Maybe he came here to find out about you.'

Holly had added the CCTV photo of the 'man in the mask' to her incident wall. Underneath was the mugshot of David Eagen, with a question mark and the words, *Not the killer but involved?* Alongside that was a map of south London which she had decorated with coloured pins that detailed the addresses of the homeless shelters. He was there somewhere, but trying to track him down had proved useless. The Waterloo address he had given the police earlier that evening was a fake and Bishop had phoned her an hour ago to say that Eagen was nowhere to be found. But was he on the run or merely hiding?

Let's have a real good look at Mr Eagen. A convicted rapist. His first victim that we know of was Juliette Billington. Sixteen years old, a pupil at Selsdon High School in Croydon. She was attacked in a park, dragged into some bushes while she was walking back from a night out with the girls in Southwark. South London again. Eagen seems to stay in that one area, then. No reports of him ever doing anything north of the river. The prostitute he attacked last month was in Kingston. He's got a pattern. Likes to stay close to home, but not too close obviously. However, it makes it easier for him to disappear afterwards. Familiar territory.

And today? Why come in to confess to a murder he didn't do? Did he do it? No. Physically he's too short, mentally he doesn't have the cold detachment to cut someone open from chest to navel, and why wouldn't he have raped Evelyn or Rebecca? He had the time, the opportunity. No. Not him. So why phone the police with a false confession? What does that say about his personality?

Perhaps Bishop was right and he just wanted attention. A hot meal and a warm bed for the night. But if he had wanted that, he would have stuck to his confession until we had found zero evidence against him after twenty-four hours, and then had to release him. If that isn't his motivation, what is? To find out about the psychologist? About Sam Gordon? But why? Sam Gordon has no record of him and nor has his wife Janine. Perhaps Eagen visited the shelter a few times but, if so, they'd never spoken. The other volunteers said they had never noticed him. If he had ever caused problems there, they would have made a record of it.

Eagen is sporadic. He's not a man who is organised. He seems to move from place to place quite freely with no real attachments. Not like our killer. Our killer is methodical. Our killer knows exactly what he's doing. He has a plan. I don't think David Eagen has a plan. I think he's too impulsive and he loses his temper too fast. You saw him in the interview room, Holly, when he suddenly shouted and banged the table when he wanted to know the name of the psychologist. There was rage there. His hands were shaking. Same as they were when he tried to put the lid back on the bottle of acid. He dropped the lid. Had to fumble and pick it up. Our killer's not like that. Our killer can murder with the cold detachment of an embalmer. He can slash someone's wrists while reciting a Shakespeare sonnet.

She felt as though they were being distracted. Being moved away from the murders of Evelyn, Jonathan and Rebecca because they were concentrating on David Eagen and the acid attack – and even that link was an assumption. It always came back to the why. The motivation. He was a rapist. Why would he suddenly turn into an acid-thrower? There were too many unanswered questions, too many loose ends. She felt surrounded by dark alleyways and dead ends. The answers were there, she knew that. The answers were always there. Sometimes you had to change the angle you looked at things.

Stop thinking, Holly. Stop thinking.

She took a step back, pulled her focus away from the wall and leaned back on the sofa. She grabbed a blanket and wrapped it around her shoulders. It was warm in her flat but she felt a sudden chill. Maybe Bishop was right. Maybe Eagen had come in today to find out about *her*. Did that worry her? Frighten her? No, it didn't. She'd faced rapists and killers before. She'd seen them up close and personal.

She forced herself to stare back at her incident wall. The empty sheet of white paper with the question mark by its side called out to her. 'Who am I, Holly? Who am I?' She narrowed her eyes and glared.

I'm getting closer to you.

I can feel it.

But this guy was different. She thought of Rebecca, a woman whom she had never met and only knew through autopsy photos; she thought of Evelyn and Jonathan, a loving couple brutally murdered in their own home; and then she thought of Alex, the young woman who had seen the horror within.

Her hands started to shake with anger and she gripped the arms of the sofa till her fingers hurt.

'I will find you,' she whispered. 'I will fucking find you.'

Twenty-two

'What is this?'

She was reading from a sheet of paper that Bishop had just handed her. It was Tuesday midday. She had already been to Wetherington that morning and given her initial assessment on Roland Cinzano and now she was back at the station. Walking the corridors to his office, and despite his bad leg she was having trouble keeping up.

'We've expanded the criteria to include suspects in non-homicides. Anybody with a record who—'

'Bishop, please,' Holly said. 'This guy has killed before. I know it.' She carried on reading. 'And you've included men who target men?'

'Yes.'

'That's wrong. This guy, whoever he is, hates women. Not men. Not boys or girls, but women.'

'Why can't he hate men as well? Why can't he just hate everything living? I'm sure there are people like that.'

'I'm sure there are, but not serial killers. They have a very specific reason for choosing their victims; there's almost no crossover, race to race, men to women, and very little women to children. They generally stick to one type of target because that's their psychosis.'

They turned a corner. Holly pressed on.

'Daniel Camago killed women and girls only, over three hundred, he claimed. Fritz Haarmann, The Vampire of Hanover – twenty-seven boys and young men. No women, not interested. Ahmed Suradji – he killed eighty-plus women and girls, used to think killing them would give him magical powers, but again, no crossover. No men or boys. Dean Coril, the Houston—'

'Christ, Holly! Enough with the Sickopedia. I don't need your almanac of cannibals or twisted fucks, okay? That doesn't help me today!'

They entered his office and he slumped behind his desk.

There was silence between them but it was simmering, as if either of them could explode at any second. Bishop eventually sighed, broke the ice.

'I'm sorry. I'm tired today. I'm not sleeping well and this case is starting to bug the shit out of me. I know you know killers. You see them every day, deal with them every day and most of my time is spent doing paperwork, making sure the squad is happy, the team is gelling. Taking care of the most mundane things in the world sometimes, but—'

'I'm sorry too. But Evelyn was the target. I'd bet my life on it. The coroner concluded the previous victim was murdered by the same killer. Why would he suddenly target a man?'

'I don't know.' Bishop looked as if he was about to get up but then sank down again. 'I feel like we're taking one step forward, two steps back at the moment.'

There was a knock at the door and Crane entered.

'Any news on Eagen?' Bishop barked.

'We've got cars patrolling and local informants are working

the streets but nothing so far. The narcs are getting involved as well, they know Eagen of old, but again, he's staying out of the light.'

'What about the NHS list of day releases?'

'Full Sutton, Rampton and Bayview Psychiatric Hospital are coming in now.'

'How far back have you cross-referenced?' Holly asked.

'Ten years.'

'Make it fifteen,' she said.

Bishop turned on her. 'You're looking at tens of thousands of criminals! Some of the cases aren't even computerised going that far back. You'd have to go over to the National Archives in Kew Gardens.'

'Maybe there was a ten-year gap because he was in prison? Maybe this guy killed. Got put away and is now out and killing again?'

'And maybe Jonathan could have been the target?'

Stalemate.

Bishop shrugged. He automatically reached for his cigarettes but then tossed them on to the desk and closed his eyes. 'I need to go for a walk.' He got up without saying another word and left his office. Holly stared after him until he disappeared from sight. She got up and paced. Anxious. Why was he so stubborn? Why wouldn't he listen to her? Reaching out she touched the soil on Bishop's orchid. Dry. She filled up a Styrofoam cup and proceeded to empty it out. Crane came in. Saw what she was doing. Looked alarmed.

'You shouldn't um . . .'

'What?'

'No, don't do that. That's Bishop's thing. It's his . . .'

'It needed some water.'

'No. It's ... it's for his other half.'

'Other half?'

'Her favourite flower. He buys them for her.'

'I didn't know he was married.'

'He's not. His fiancé ...' He looked out of the office window, squirming uncomfortably. 'I thought he'd have told you by now.'

'Told me what?'

When Bishop returned to his office Holly stood up. She felt awkward and embarrassed. He saw her and smiled. Tried to put her at ease.

'Sorry if I was ...'

'No ... No.'

'Feel better now. Got some fresh air.' A pause. 'What's wrong?'

'I tried to water the orchid and then Sergeant Crane came in. And ...'

'Crane?'

'He told me what happened. To your fiancé.'

'Oh Jesus.'

'He told me.'

'Christ, he shouldn't have said anything ... it's ah, Jesus ...'

'If you want to talk about it ...'

'No! I don't want a fucking therapy session!'

'Okay.'

'I've been through that. I've done it.'

'I wasn't talking therapy. Just me. If you want me to listen.'

'What did he tell you?'

'Told me you'd lost your fiancé and a baby when you were both in the army.'

He stared at the floor for a while before looking up at her.

'Yeah, that's about it. That about sums it up.' He shook his head. His eyes wandered around the room and eventually came back to her. 'What? Do you feel as though I need to tell you about it? I mean, you told me your secret tragedy so—'

'No, you don't have to.'

'Don't look at me like that. I feel as though I'm back on the fucking couch.'

'I'm sorry.' She looked away.

'Four years,' he said. 'Therapy. I quit after that. I didn't want to do it any more. I didn't see the point. Didn't solve anything. It made me deal with anger. Yeah, I dealt with the anger. But I couldn't get over the guilt. Still can't.' He sat on the desk. 'We'd seen each other the month before. A bit of R&R. Talked about marriage. Family. Kids. You know.'

'Was it hard? I mean, both being in the army. Not seeing each other every day.'

'No. Something you sign up for. You get used to it. It's easier in a way because it's part of the problem. You know? If they're not there then you have nothing to worry about but when they're next to you, especially in a war zone, all you do is worry about them. She was stationed in Charikar. I was in Kabul, an hour away. Nothing but shitstorms and uncertainty in between. We had made a pact before we were stationed. On no account do we go see each other, no matter how much we want to. No matter what. I told her: never. I would have hated that. Worrying about your partner as they put their lives at risk to catch a glimpse of you for a few seconds. Some of the troops did it. Little excursions across the no man's land to meet up with their lovers. Something idiotically romantic about it. But she wanted to. Didn't tell me she was coming that night. Wanted to wish me happy birthday. Tell me about the baby

170

as well. Tell me she'd found out she was pregnant. She'd made it to within half a mile of the camp when she stepped on the IED. We all heard the explosion. Sirens went off. Everyone fell out of bed. It was 3.02 in the morning. Word came back about twenty minutes later of a casualty. We all thought it would be a local. Some sheep farmer or insurgent. But no: a white woman, dressed in civvies. She would have been killed immediately. They found her dog tags a hundred yards away. Brought them back to me the next day. That was it.' He was looking back at her now, his face resigned with the gentlest of frowns but she noticed his knuckles were white where he was gripping the desk.

'I'm sorry, Bishop.'

'I don't celebrate my birthday, by the way. Just so you know.'

'I'll remember that.'

'Let's call it a night, shall we?' he said.

'Yes. Let's.'

Bishop went to the door. Shouted:

'Crane!'

'Don't be mad at him. He's not . . . '

Crane arrived a few seconds later holding up a massive file, his wrist straining under the weight. 'Got the transfer list, sir. You want me to start going through it?'

'I'll take it,' said Holly. She walked over, grabbed the file with both hands and before Bishop could say anything she was already heading out the door.

Twenty-three

She had taken the file home and the rogues' gallery lay like bloody confetti at her feet.

It was a systematic search, checking their MOs, seeing if there were any similarities and then finding out if they were still behind bars. So far nothing. Full Sutton and Rampton had been pored over, slowly, meticulously and twenty minutes had stretched to an hour. Then another hour. She only had Bayview to do, and as she flipped open the front cover and started to search through the contents, she ran her finger down the page over the list of names.

Colin Ireland, fifty-two. Strangled five gay men he picked up in pubs. Convicted 1993. 'No,' Holly whispered. 'No evidence of homophobia with our victims.' Rahan Arshad, thirty-eight, murdered his wife Uzma and three children. Convicted 2007. Nope, family connection not relevant. David Tiley, forty-nine, murdered his fiancée and raped a carer. Convicted 2007. Too feeble. Glyn Dix, fifty-four, stabbed and chopped up his wife, Hazel. Convicted in 2005. Interesting. Holly went to the section on Dix.

'Glynn Dix was found guilty of murdering his wife, Hazel,

at his house in Redditch, Worcestershire, on 19 June 2004. Dix and Hazel made love before rowing over what TV channel to watch. Dix stabbed her three times. He used a knife, hacksaw and scissors to cut Hazel's body into sixteen pieces at their home ... she suffered multiple stab wounds ... life imprisonment ... previous conviction for murdering his first wife, Pia Overbury, in the 1970s.

'No, not you ... this killer doesn't prey on family members.'

She went back to the contents page. Trevor Hardy, sixty-one, 'the Beast in the Night', killed three teenage girls. Convicted 1977. *Teenagers? No, that's not your style.* Anthony Arkwright, forty, hacked three people to death. Convicted 1989.

'Arkwright; a petty criminal ... youth custody sentences for burglary and disorder, a six-month jail term. Boasted to friends that one day he would be as famous as Jack the Ripper ...' Holly stopped reading and looked at his photo. A mouthy kid with spiked blond hair.

'After getting the sack from his job in a scrapyard he went crazy and started a fifty-six-hour killing spree. Killed his grandfather first, stabbed him in the neck, then finished him off with an axe and a hammer. Next victim was his neighbour ... whom he disembowelled with a surgical precision that criminologists later said was remarkably similar to the technique used by Jack the Ripper ... draped his entrails around the room ... internal organs scattered across the corridor and hallway.'

Could be you, Arkwright. Where are you now? She flicked a couple of pages – Broadmoor. She made a note in the margin and circled the telephone number.

Next up, Anthony Entwistle, fifty-seven. A double rapist, killed a girl, sixteen. Convicted 1988. *Possibly* ... She turned to his case notes. *No, not you, you're too short.* Michael Smith, fifty-six, convicted in 2007 of killing with a bottle while on parole. *No.* Mark Martin, twenty-eight, wanted to be a serial killer. Killed three women. Convicted 2006. *No ... you like homeless women, you're a spree killer.* Viktors Dembovskis, forty-five, killed Jeshma Raithatha, seventeen years old. Convicted 2006. *No.* Stephen Ayre, forty-six, raped a boy while on parole for murder. Convicted 2006. *No.* Peter Moore, sixty-eight, mutilated and killed four men 'for fun'. Jailed in 1996. *Homophobic again – you're not our killer.* Richard Sickert, thirty-nine, killed three women, the last of whom was his wife, slashed their wrists, no rape but penetration ... convicted in 2007. Holly stopped on the entry. She found herself unconsciously imagining the crime scene. *No rape but penetration.* She'd heard of him and would have read about the crime ten years ago but she couldn't recollect the details. She pulled out a separate manila folder which had the name Richard Sickert stamped across it. Richard had been tried and convicted for killing three people: Kate Wendell, Rudy Esters and his wife Natasha.

Sickert's first victim was a prostitute named Kate Wendell (Police Report 37809B). Her body was found in the water between two boats in Canary Wharf on 7 May 2006. She had been strangled and her neck had been broken. There was no evidence of any sexual interference. She was twenty-two with blonde hair and green eyes and had been working the city streets, notably in the East End, for three years. Her friends had described her as 'the girl-next-door type': sweet, a little lost, but with a good heart. She had no tattoos or any other distinguishing physical features.

Sickert's second victim was Rudyan Esters, Rudy to her friends (Police Report 26557D). She was forty-five years old and was killed on the morning of 3 July of the same year. Rudy was of Indian origin, born and raised in Streatham, South London. She moved to Farnborough with her family and in 2004 set up a tattoo parlour in Aldershot on 7 Upper Union Street, with her husband Aaron Esters. Her body was found in their parlour by Aaron, horribly mutilated. She had been strangled twice, penetrated with a straight-bladed knife and had a series of circular burn marks along her inner thighs . . .

Jesus Christ . . . Holly picked up the Wrights' autopsy report and studied the photos of Evelyn's body. There on the thighs, the series of eleven circular burns. This is it, Holly thought, this could be him . . . How many burns on Rudy?

There were sixteen burns across Rudy's inner thighs, eight on each leg.

Even in the old photos, the marks were almost identical. Whatever was used, it was the same implement. She carried on reading. No knife was ever recovered and the burns remained a mystery. Rudy's husband was immediately eliminated from the police enquiries as he had an airtight alibi and according to all witness accounts was devoted to his wife. They were both looking forward to starting a family.

Richard's third known victim was his wife, Natasha Sickert (née Atkinson). She was strangled and mutilated in the family bathtub on 8 October 2007. Her wrists were brutally slashed and she too suffered similar burn marks on her inner thighs.

That was two out of three with the same burns. She flicked some pages and came to the trial transcript. According to his testimony, Richard killed her because 'She kept talking loudly and wouldn't get out of my head' (page 139). He went on to say (page 140) that after he'd killed her, he 'went downstairs, ate some of the lovely peach cobbler she had made and watched *I'm a Celebrity ... Get Me Out of Here'*.

The coroner's report stated that Mrs Sickert was actually killed between 4 p.m. and 6 p.m. on the day in question. The prosecution had tried to discover Richard's movements between 2.30 p.m. and 4 p.m., but apart from a trip into town no other sightings or evidence was ever forthcoming.

Richard Sickert had been arrested when he walked naked out of his house into the street and sat down in the middle of the road. A car nearly ran him over, but the motorist managed to avoid him and a neighbour called the police. When the police arrived at 7.12 p.m. he was still sitting in the road and the two officers at the scene saw immediately that he was covered in blood. They called an ambulance, thinking Sickert had been hit by the car, but soon realised it was someone else's blood. An immediate search of the house followed, and his wife was found in the upstairs bathroom. He was arrested at 8.18 p.m. that evening and officially charged at 3.24 a.m. the following morning by Detective Inspector Simon Combs. The charge was murder.

Holly's memories were being jogged now. The case was coming back to her. Something else as well. Something that was said at the trial. She carried on reading, her coffee forgotten and cold.

Natasha met and married Richard Sickert in 2003. Theirs was described by her family as a whirlwind romance. They had only been seeing each other for three weeks when he proposed to her. She said yes, though her family were reluctant to give their blessing. According to testimony at the trial, Mary and Peter Atkinson, Natasha's parents, had their doubts about Richard's mental state when they first met him.

Trial transcript (page 224), Peter Atkinson on the stand:

'He was paranoid. Kept thinking we had something against him, or knew something about him. I never trusted him.'

Trial transcript (page 312), Mary Atkinson on the stand:

'After they were married, we saw very little of our daughter. She was meek and bullied by him. I wish we would have stopped it. But we couldn't see. Nobody could see what a monster he was.'

The prosecution wanted the maximum penalty after Sickert admitted to the killings of Kate and Rudyan as well as his wife. However, the defence presented a clear case of insanity, and with the evidence provided by the defence psychologist, Doctor Seymour Andell, Sickert was classed as insane and sentenced to thirty years in a psychiatric hospital rather than a maximum security prison. The Honourable Mr Justice Hogarth was dispirited by jury's verdict but had to concede the defence had put forward an airtight case. On sentencing (Trial transcript, page 1045) he said:

'It is a shame that I cannot send you to a secure facility where other murderers are confined, but there is no doubt in the jury's and in my own mind that you are indeed insane. As for rehabilitation, I believe there will be none. You are so depraved, and have gone so far into the dark realms of the human mind that I fear you will never see the light again.' Then he added, *'If you never walk free, Mr Sickert, I will not lose any sleep.'*

The trial at the Old Bailey ended on 13 February 2008 and Richard was transported to Bayview Psychiatric Hospital in Hastings where he began his sentence.

Holly turned to DI Combs's testimony. Trial transcript, page 207:

Q: How long have you been a detective inspector?

A: Eleven years.

Q: Have you worked on many murders?

A: As DI, I've worked on fifty-seven, but this was only the second where I was first on the scene.

Q: Run us through the events on the evening of 8 October 2007, if you would.

A: I was on standby at the station, nearing the end of my shift, when the front desk received the 999 call from Mr Gardener, at 6.42 p.m.

Q: Did you take the call?

A: The call was taken by PC Rachel Strettons.

Q: Your Honour, we have her testimony, but thought it unnecessary to bring her in.

JUDGE: Thank you.

Q: We also have a recording of the conversation, if it pleases the court.

JUDGE: Maybe later, if we have to, but I think it unnecessary at present.

Q: Carry on, please, Detective Inspector.

A: Constable Strettons informed us immediately of the situation. I told her to call an ambulance and have it sent to the address, and then Sergeant Echose and I drove over ourselves.

Q: What information were you given about the situation?

A: We were told a man was sitting naked in the road, covered in blood and apparently injured.

Q: What were your first thoughts?

A: That the man had been hit by a car.

Q: How long did it take you to get to Mabley Street?

A: Approximately ten minutes.

Q: Tell us what you saw when you got there.

A: We saw the accused sitting off to the left of the road, on the kerb. He was naked and covered in a red liquid which I believed to be his blood.

Q: How did he appear mentally?

DEFENCE: Objection. Speculation. DI Combs is not a psychiatrist and cannot therefore comment on my client's state of mental health.

JUDGE: Sustained.

Q: Did Mr Sickert appear normal to you?

DEFENCE: Objection.

JUDGE: Sustained.

Q: Did Mr Sickert say anything?

A: Nothing. He just sat and stared straight ahead.

Q: What did you do next?

A: I approached him from the side, slowly, and called out his name.

Q: Did he respond in any way?

A: No. I thought he'd been badly injured, because of all the blood, so I thought he was in shock. He looked pale and I thought he may have been rocking.

Q: Rocking?

A: Yes, you know, backwards and forwards a little.

Q: What was the light like?

A: There was a streetlight nearly directly above him, so I could see him pretty well.

Q: What next?

A: I approached after putting my gloves on and very cautiously started to examine him. I wanted to see where he had been hit and what injuries he had sustained.

Q: And what were the results of your examination?

A: It was cursory but I could find no evidence of any trauma whatsoever. Which worried me considerably.

Q: Why?

A: Because if it wasn't his blood, whose was it?

Q: What was Sergeant Echose doing at this point?

A: He was talking to the witness, Mr Gardener, and taking his statement.

Q: Exhibits 7 to 12, Your Honour. Witness is still on hand for recall.

JUDGE: Noted.

DEFENCE: No objections.

JUDGE: Continue, please.

Q: Could you tell us what happened next?

A: I put a blanket over Mr Sickert's shoulders, as it was starting to get chilly, and then Mr Sickert said, 'I'm so sorry to have caused such a nuisance, Officer.' He had a bit of a stutter. I replied, 'That's all right, sir. Um . . . the neighbours said there was an incident with a car?' And then the accused said, 'Oh no, Officer. The incident is in the bath.'

Q: In the bath?

A: That's correct. In the bath.

Q: What did you do then?

A: I called over to Sergeant Echose and asked him to take care of Mr Sickert as I thought it very necessary to check out the house.

Q: You didn't ask the sergeant go with you?

A: No. The ambulance still hadn't arrived, so he remained with Mr Sickert.

Q: Carry on.

A: The front door was open, so I entered and proceeded into the hall.

Q: Your Honour, I submit the floor plan of the Sickert residence.

JUDGE: A copy, please. Thank you.

Q: In fact, Inspector, in your official statement, Record 278A, you described the house as 'morbid', did you not?

A: I did.

Q: Explain.

A: When I first entered I felt claustrophobic and I couldn't explain it. It just ... the whole house felt morbid.

DEFENCE: Objection, Your Honour. Prosecution should be presenting facts, not feelings.

JUDGE: Overruled. I want to hear this. Go on.

A: I've seen many crime scenes but have never felt like I did in that house. There was a horrible loneliness about it, as if it were soulless.

DEFENCE: Objection, Your Honour, are we going to have a séance next?

JUDGE: In light of the charges, it might not be a bad idea – then we could all go home very quickly, Counsel.

DEFENCE: Apologies, Your Honour.

JUDGE: Carry on.

Q: Describe the home for me, Inspector.

A: It was a typical 1970s ex-council house. A bit messy, damp. I looked off the hallway into the living room first.

Q: Was everything as it should have been?

DEFENCE: Leading.

Q: Rephrase. Was the house tidy?

DEFENCE: Asked and answered. Witness has stated it was messy.

Q: The living room. Was everything in place?

DEFENCE: Your Honour ...

JUDGE: I'll allow it. Answer the question.

A: Yes, it was. Apart from the coffee table. It had been turned over and smashed.

Q: Describe it, please.

A: It was 1970s, wooden but with a strip of ceramic tiles

along its centre. They were brown and orange with flowers, the tiles.

Q: Exhibits 13 to 23, Your Honour. Photographs of the coffee table and accompanying tiles. And you say it was smashed?

A: Yes, it had been turned over and smashed. A lot of the tiles were on the carpet. There were shards and broken tiles everywhere.

Q: Exhibit 26 – shard of one of said tiles, recovered from the bathtub. Were there any other signs of violence in that room? Any signs of a struggle?

A: No. Everything else was quite normal. I concluded at the time that, for whatever reason, someone had decided to break the coffee table.

Q: Did you notice anything else in the room that might be relevant?

A: A single glass of whisky on the mantelpiece. Initially, I thought it belonged to the accused, but when I examined the glass I saw that it had traces of lipstick on it.

Q: What did you do next?

A: I went out of the living room, through the dining room and into the kitchen.

Q: And what did you see in the kitchen?

A: There were two dresser drawers open. There was a cooked roast dinner on the countertop and a dessert.

Q: Was the table set for one or two people?

A: One.

Q: Had any of the dinner been eaten?

A: No. But it looked as though someone had eaten some of the dessert. Peach cobbler, I think.

Q: Only the one bowl?

A: Plate, actually, but yes. One plate and one spoon.

Q: Any signs of a struggle in the kitchen?

A: No.

Q: Where did you go next?

A: Upstairs. As I passed the front door to get to the stairs I saw that the ambulance had arrived and so I knew Mr Sickert was being examined. I went upstairs and stopped on the landing.

Q: Why?

A: I was deciding which way to go first. I nearly always go left first at a crime scene, it's a habit I've developed, but I could see the bathroom to the right so I decided to check there first, based on what the suspect had said.

Q: So you went straight to the upstairs bathroom. Describe what you saw.

A: The light was off . . .

Theatrics again. This had to be their man.

A: . . . So I pulled the cord and it came on and . . . well, it was a mess. There was blood everywhere. The floor, the shower curtain, the walls – they were all covered. Not spots but smears, as if someone had wiped their hands across the walls. The whole room was covered. Even some of the ceiling was red.

Q: Tell us what was in the bath.

A: I pulled the shower curtain back. It was damp and heavy. The victim was lying in the bath. There was a man's belt around her neck. It was very tight.

Q: Exhibit 53, Your Honour. Carry on.

A: Her eyes were open and her skin was a very pale, almost white. There was some residual water at the bottom of the bath but it was pinkish and darker red, as if some blood had settled.

Q: Did you try to resuscitate her?

A: No. I knew she was dead and I didn't want to disturb the evidence.

Q: Next?

A: I immediately called for additional paramedics, told the station of the situation and then radioed my sergeant at 8.10 p.m. to detain Mr Sickert for further questioning. At 8.18 I made the formal arrest myself.

Holly remembered reading this years ago but she had forgotten so many details. She flicked forward a few pages. The coroner's report.

Q: We all have a copy of the report, Your Honour. The jury have been instructed.

JUDGE: I will reiterate. Members of the jury, you are about to see photographs and hear testimony from the coroner's office. This is never a pleasant experience. If any of you need time or would like a break during the proceedings, please let me know. Thank you, Mr Weeks. I think we're ready.

Q: For the record please, Mr Anderson.

A: My name is Ronald Anderson. I am fifty-three years old and have been the chief Middlesex Coroner for the past twelve years.

Q: How many autopsies have you performed?

A: Over thirteen hundred.

DEFENCE: No need for credentials here.

JUDGE: Carry on.

Q: In the early hours of 8 October 2007 you were called to 83 Mabley Street to examine the body of a woman found in a bathtub.

A: That is correct.

Holly went back to the beginning of the file. Randomly opening pages and reading excerpts. She stopped suddenly.

There was a glimmer of a memory. Something had caught her eye. She had glossed over it before, but whatever it was, it was lingering in the back of her mind and becoming more insistent by the minute. She had seen something that all her instincts told her was important. She was tempted to put the transcripts down and take another break but felt herself opening the pages again, flicking through the notes. Where was it? Who was on the stand? One of the neighbours? No. It had to be the policeman, Combs. The arresting officer. The first on the scene.

A: No. Everything else was quite normal. I concluded at the time that, for whatever reason, someone had decided to break the coffee table.

Q: Did you notice anything else in the living room that might be relevant?

A: A single glass of whisky on the mantelpiece. Initially, I thought it belonged to the accused, but when I examined the glass I saw that it had traces of lipstick on it.

That wasn't it. Not the lipstick.

A: I nearly always go left first at a crime scene, it's a habit I've developed, but I could see the bathroom to the right so I decided to check there first, based on what the suspect had said.

Natasha's body in the bath. No, what Holly was remembering was oblique to the original statement. It was as if it was an afterthought in his testimony. She had read his original statement and whatever it was that she was remembering, she knew it wasn't in there. It was something he had forgotten about and, if he ever remembered, deemed it irrelevant, but then he had brought it up in cross-examination later. She flicked forward.

Q: And what did you do then?

A: I went downstairs. Oh – I kicked something that had been

on one of the steps. Heard it roll down the carpet and hit the floor. It made a ringing noise.

This was it . . .

Q: Like a phone?

A: No. When I got to the bottom of the stairs it was lying on its side. I hadn't noticed it on the way up because it was dark. It was a small brass bell.

Holly straightened, riveted, and then started ransacking the files. Everything was a mess, she should have organised . . . There it was, Jonathan and Evelyn Wright. She pulled the file to her and searched through the photos. There was one in particular she wanted to find, and the more she looked for it, the more frustrated she became. Until finally, she found it and pulled it out. A photo of the Wrights' living room, taken from the left-hand side as you entered. In the background the curtains, in the foreground the hanging skeleton and the desk, and on that desk, the diary, the phrenology head and . . . a bell. The one she had picked up and rung. At the time it had felt hauntingly familiar to her and now she knew why.

She went back to the report on Kate Wendell and the crime photos. It had been concluded that she was killed nearby and then tossed into the water at the wharf. The photos were old and some of them yellowed with scrawled notes in biro about distances and timelines. Nothing immediately helpful – certainly no mention of a bell. Strike one.

Rudy was killed in her tattoo shop. The amount of detritus on the shelves where a bell could have been left was enormous. Tattoo machines, needles and boxes of ink, personal stuff belonging to Rudy and the other five artists who worked there; the inventory ran to hundreds of items, most of which had never been individually photographed. If there was a bell, it would have been easy to miss. Strike two.

It was all down to Rebecca. Photos, photos . . . Here we are, Rebecca Bradshaw. The girl with no enemies. Glossy shots of her room, of her sitting dead, propped up against the bed in a pool of blood. No, it wouldn't be in any of these – it would have been put elsewhere in the room. On the shelves? They were overflowing with stuffed toys that belonged in a child's room. Sad puppy faces with glass eyes. Family photographs in silver frames. No bell.

The bedside cabinets next. These had been meticulously catalogued and she thanked PC Siskins for his detailed inventory. Given what he'd found when he arrived at the scene, she didn't blame him for going back to website design. Nothing in the bedside cabinets but scented candles, make-up, jewellery and more furry animals. A music box with a ballerina that popped up when you opened the lid. Holly had never had one of those but always wanted one. Maybe she should get one now. Why wait, Holly? Concentrate on the here and now. Tomorrow may never come . . .

And there it was. As if she knew it would be. In the last photo in the stack. Inside the music box, beside three sparkling bangles, a small, rather random brass bell.

Two's company, three's a crime.

Very clever, hiding it in the box, but not clever enough.

Oh, I really am starting to see you now.

She took a sip of cold coffee and the phone rang. It made her jump and coffee spilt over her legs. She cursed, put her cup down and picked up the phone.

'Holly?' A female voice.

'Yes.'

'It's Alex. Alexandra Lymington.'

'Alex, how are you?'

'I hope you don't mind me calling. I know it's late . . .'

Holly checked her watch. Nearly midnight. She could almost hear Alex gathering her thoughts, trying to form the words.

'I got your number from DI Bishop. The other day, when you came to see me—'

'Yes, I'm sorry if I overstepped the mark.'

'No. I wanted to thank you for being honest. Everybody seems to be walking on eggshells around me. Which I understand, but at the same time it's nice to find someone . . . someone real. Someone who understands what's going on.'

'I do.'

'Well, thank you. It meant a lot to me.' There was a long pause. 'I can't sleep. I don't sleep at night or during the day. I keep seeing things when I close my eyes. Things that I shouldn't have seen. I can't take them away, can I?'

'No.'

'I've started taking pills to help. The doctor gave them to me, but I feel like a zombie during the day. I can't do much and I feel as though I should be doing things. Maybe that's a good thing though . . .' Another pause. 'Holly?'

'Yes?'

'I don't think I want to feel any more. I'm all cried out, I'm exhausted. The funeral is next week.'

'Would you like me to come?'

'Please. Connie and Stephen are arranging most of it. They've been so good to me. That's where I am at the moment. I'm with Connie. I don't want to be by myself.'

'It's best to have people around you.'

'I . . . I can't stop thinking about it. How do I stop thinking about it?'

'It's really hard, Alex. Everything takes time.'

'All I do is think about it.'

Holly found herself massaging her forehead without even realising it.

'Do you read?' she asked.

'I'm sorry?'

'Do you read books?'

'Some.'

'Then start reading whenever you can. Take your mind off everything. Read one line of one book. If you haven't thought about what happened in that room for that one line then you can read two lines and not think about it. Two lines becomes three. Three becomes a paragraph, a paragraph becomes two paragraphs and then all of a sudden you've read a page and then a chapter. That's one chapter out of a book that you haven't thought about it. That's the way to do it. An incredible start, and it all begins with one line. One line in one book.'

'Okay.'

'And don't make it fiction. Make it non-fiction. What are you interested in?'

'I like history.'

'Then read about the kings and queens of England. The knights and noblemen. The princesses and their dowries. Try it during the day and each night before you got to bed.'

'I will. I'll start now.'

'Be persistent.'

'Thank you.'

Holly gathered her next words.

'Alex, before you go, can I ask you a question about your uncle's desk in the living room?'

'The one next to the skeleton?'

'That's right. Can you remember seeing a bell on that desk? A small brass one?'

'A bell?'

'Yes.'

The line went quiet then . . .

'No, I don't think so. I think I would have remembered. How big?'

'No bigger than a Christmas ornament.'

'I would have remembered that, I'm sure. I looked at the phrenology head all the time. I don't recall ever seeing a bell there.'

'Thank you, Alex.'

'Why?'

'I'm not sure yet,' Holly said. 'I'll let you know if it comes to anything.'

She hung up. The killer had brought the bell with him. What was it about the bell? She went through all the notes on Sickert again but nothing was mentioned. Definitely the same killer though, the same calling card. But why? Richard Sickert. She needed to talk to Bayview Hospital, but first . . . She dialled Bishop's number. When he picked up, she almost shouted, 'One question. Richard Sickert – he was put away in 2007. Is he still inside?'

'Where's he at?'

'Bayview Psychiatric.'

She could hear him moving about the office, shuffling papers and leafing through them. She wanted him to hurry up.

'Yes.'

'You're sure?'

'Denied parole this year.'

Holly stared at the dead faces of Natasha Sickert and the others.

'Bishop, we've got a copycat.'

Twenty-four

Bishop scanned the photos of Richard Sickert and his victims that had been fanned out across his desk, as Holly and Crane looked over his shoulder.

'Richard Sickert. Triple murderer. A sociopath. Bayview Hospital is a small, privately run clinic in King's Wood near Hastings. Thirty-five patients, all of them considered extreme. It's known as the "Monster Mansion".'

'Jesus.'

'Sickert was convicted of killing three women in 2007. Kate Wendell, Rudy Esters, and his wife, Natasha. All three women were strangled twice. Once to kill them, once post-mortem. Two ligature marks were found on each body, just like Jonathan, Evelyn and Rebecca. Do you have any coffee? I didn't have a chance this morning . . .'

Bishop thumped the side of the coffee machine and it spat out a plastic cup, which filled with steaming black. He handed it over and she took a sip.

'Thank you.'

He gave her a nod to carry on.

'None of them were sexually assaulted but they were all

penetrated. And most importantly they all have burn marks on their inner thighs. The mutilation is almost identical to our victims. Christ, Bishop, this is a copycat, no question . . .'

'Keep going.'

'Sickert was charged and tried for the murder of his wife. He confessed to the other two murders when he entered his guilty plea. That was the only link; the police had never found anything to connect them. All three had different economic and socioeconomic backgrounds, like our victims, and why he chose them is something that is unexplained to this day.'

Bishop said, 'I'll need Angela to compare the autopsy reports to corroborate what you're saying, but so far . . . And you mentioned a bell?'

Holly pulled out a series of blown-up photos from the old case files, and one of Jonathan Wright's living room.

'What am I looking at?'

She pointed to the brass bell in each photograph. 'Sickert left one with his wife and now we've found bells at the Wrights' and in Rebecca's flat. One at each crime scene.'

'Nothing with Kate Wendell or Rudy Esters?'

'No. But it could easily have been missed.'

Bishop looked at her with a tinge of sympathy and shook his head slowly. 'The burn marks and the interference, yes. The bell is way too thin, Holly. I can't . . . I mean, people pick up random souvenirs over the years. There must be a million of those things.'

'I asked Alex about it. She said she'd never seen it before. Sometimes serial killers will leave something behind – a signature – so they get credit for the kill. It could also be a shift in the MO. An escalation.'

Bishop clawed at his hair, trying to comb it with his fingers as he took it all in.

'Okay. I'll buy it. We've got a potential copycat. What's next?'

'We need to look at all of the patients or prisoners who have been in contact with Richard Sickert. I know you're not sold on the bell, but it was never mentioned in the press. Nobody knew about it except the killer, so whoever is doing this, has to be someone he knew. Someone he shared a cell with, someone he spent time with after his incarceration. Sickert has been at Bayview ever since his trial and he's never getting out, so we need to look at all the people who were incarcerated at the same time as him and who have since been released.'

'Crane, have Bayview got back to us yet?'

'Just come through, sir.' He picked up the printout. 'There are three patients regularly on day release: Mark Grey, Daniel Summers and Anton Samnovitch.' His eyes widened – 'Sir, you're not going to believe this ... Daniel Summers has been red-flagged.'

'Why?'

'He's been missing for ten days.'

It was the afternoon now and in the incident room, the wall boards had glossy photos of Richard Sickert and his victims plastered over them. Bishop let the members of the task force settle.

'Right, obviously, there have been some developments. I appreciate you all getting here as fast as you did. I'm going to pass you straight over to Holly.'

She took a deep breath and pointed to the photo of Richard Sickert.

'This is Richard Sickert.' A moment to let the name settle

with them. 'He was convicted of killing three women back in 2007 and was sent to Bayview Psychiatric Hospital. He was denied parole in 2016 and remains there under lock and key. However, we are now working on the theory that Richard Sickert has a copycat. This person knows all about the murders that Sickert committed and is mimicking his crimes. Because of this we are looking at ex-patients from Bayview, or patients who are currently under their care but are on day-release schemes. One of those patients is a man named Daniel Summers. We have been informed that Daniel was held in the same ward as Richard Sickert for two years. They'd have got to know each other, talked to each other, perhaps became good friends.' She pinned a photo of Daniel up on the board. He had long, very pale almost white hair; his face was unshaven and frighteningly gaunt.

'Daniel Summers. Forty-one years old, six foot one, one hundred and seventy pounds according to his last medical. This photo was taken in 2008 when he was charged with murdering his sister. He strangled her, had sex with her corpse and then set her on fire. He was sectioned and sent to Bayview in spring of the same year. After five years there he attacked one of the nurses, a certain Rose Gifford, while she was administering his medication.' She added a photo of a woman, whose face had been horribly mutilated.

'He spent one year in intensive therapy because of this, but in 2014 he was allowed to return to the general population wards of Bayview. A year later, it was deemed that his condition had become stabilised to such a degree that the doctors considered his release. This isn't an easy process – every step must be approved by the Ministry of Justice, but after an intensive review, Daniel was allowed supervised visits to the nearby town of Hastings under Section 17 of the Mental Health Act. He was always accompanied by either the ward sister or the primary care physician, in this case, Doctor Seymour Andell.'

'Who's he?'

'Doctor Andell is head of the Bayview Board of Psychiatry. He is also one of the forerunners of the modern psychology movement.' She took a moment and collected herself. 'When I was at university I read and practically memorised most of his case studies. He's written a dozen or so books on cognitive behavioural psychology, environmental psychology, criminal sociopathy. If there's something worth knowing, he's written a book about it.' She checked the notes. 'Now. Earlier this year, under the Mental Health Discrimination Act of 2013, Daniel was allowed out on unaccompanied visits to Hastings on a bus that stopped at Bayview specifically for him. According to the hospital, there were never any problems. He was always punctual and polite wherever he went and he always returned to Bayview within the allotted time. Last year, he was released from Bayview on his own recognisance, which basically means he was on out his own. Daniel's post-care conditions stipulate he has to report in every week to Bayview for a mental health assessment and his medication. However, he did not make an appearance at the clinic the Saturday before last – which means he has been off the radar for ten days. So, Daniel becomes a man we would very much like to talk to.'

She looked around the room, knowing a word of caution was in order.

'Now. This may not be our man, but at the moment he's the best lead we've got. He has been diagnosed as both a schizophrenic and a sociopath by Doctor Andell, who has also classified him as DOM – dependent on meds – which at the moment we can assume he is without. This means that he may be very, very dangerous.'

Bishop pulled out copies of the photo of Daniel and gave them to Crane to hand around.

'This is nine years old. No photographs have been taken during his time at Bayview, so this is all we have. Sussex CID are cooperating with us on this as it's in their jurisdiction; the local DI is Gary Bright. I don't know if any of you have come across him before but I have and he's one of the good ones. He's sending out preliminary teams to canvass the area and he'll be reporting back to us on their progress. He is also in direct contact with Bayview Hospital. But this is still our investigation. We're pulling everybody back in. Holidays are cancelled, as is sleep. You know your units. Let's go.'

The place was suddenly a madhouse of activity. Phones rang, names and orders were yelled out. Holly watched them for a moment, then began to collect her notes. Bishop came up beside her.

'What time do you think you'll get there?'

'It's a three-hour drive,' she said. 'Nightfall if I'm lucky.'

Twenty-five

Holly thrashed her car engine, pushing it to the max.

On leaving the station she had immediately got snarled up in the Hammersmith one-way system and had sat and cursed as droplets of rain began to splash on the windscreen. The storm never broke but the endless sea of tail lights had made her late and now she was trying to navigate single-lane country roads in unfamiliar territory. Eventually she saw the sign for Bayview Hospital and headed towards the flat squat building that rested within a perimeter of concrete and barbed wire. The gates were solid metal and a camera scanned the entrance. Holly pulled to a halt at the barrier by the security hut and her headlights shone on the guard sitting inside trying to ignore the pelting rain on his roof. He motioned to her that he was coming and appeared out of the hut, raw-faced from the wind. She wound down her window and handed over her ID.

'We expected you hours ago.' He handed her ID back to her. 'Follow the driveway. All the way up to the main doors. I'll let them know you're coming.'

Holly did as she was told, parked and walked through

the rain towards the entrance. She pressed the intercom. A buzzer sounded and the doors opened with a thud of electronic bolts. She stepped into a long corridor, so brightly lit it was hard to see where it ended. Old yellow bricks underfoot. 'Follow the yellow brick road,' she murmured and then she was at another door that buzzed and let her through to the reception area. Comfortable sofas and leather chairs, potted ferns, a vending machine and the ward sister perched behind the main desk.

She was in her fifties with bright red fingernails and her hair was scraped back so hard it seemed to be strangling her ponytail. She scrutinised Holly's ID before handing it back.

'We weren't sure if you were going to turn up.'

'I tried to call but there was—'

'No signal. There never is around here,' she smiled. 'My name is Sister Arlington. I am the ward sister and on duty most evenings. The formalities first.' She started logging Holly in as she reeled off the customary warning: 'Bayview is a secure psychiatric hospital but the prisoners here are all dangerous. On no account must you interact with them in any way without a member of staff being present. You are our guest and you will follow our rules accordingly. Clear?'

'Clear.'

She took a polaroid of Holly and fanned it, clipping it to a security tag when it was dry. 'Wear this at all times and hand it back to me when you're done.'

'Thank you. Are we going straight to see Richard?'

'I'm sorry, Miss Wakefield, but Mr Sickert was put on his medication forty-five minutes ago.'

'But I was told I could interview him tonight.'

'And we were told you would be here two hours ago.' A

pause. 'I'll take you to Doctor Andell. Maybe he can make an exception.'

The security door buzzed as it swung open and the ward sister walked ahead, her heels echoing in the polished corridor.

'You haven't been here before have you, Miss Wakefield?'

'Holly, please. No. I'm aware of Bayview's reputation, though.'

'The Monster Mansion?'

'Something like that.'

'I hate that,' the sister admitted. 'We do house psychologically disturbed patients here, but no more than Belmarsh or Limington. And here we believe in giving our patients as normal a life as possible, allowing them to roam as much of the buildings and wards as they like.'

'When was the last time you saw Daniel Summers, Sister?'

'Ten days ago. He arrived at eleven thirty-five in the morning. I gave him his medication for the week and then he left.'

'Who supervised the session?'

'Doctor Andell. All sessions with Summers are supervised.'

'And how did Daniel seem that day?'

'Seem?'

'Yes. Was there anything in his behaviour that stood out?'

'No. Nothing at all.'

A darker area. The corridor was lonely-looking and cold. There were muffled noises, shouts and cries of troubled sleep.

Sister Arlington smoothed the front of her over-starched uniform as they stopped at a door. She knocked twice. 'We're here.'

Doctor Seymour Andell was attractive, in his mid-forties, with side-parted dark hair and the palest eyes Holly had ever seen, like beaten metal, washed out in the lights of his office. A little stooped as he shook her hand, making them almost the same height. The ward sister exited and Andell ushered Holly into a seat whilst he took his place in a high-backed swivel chair behind his desk. The room was painted a pale yellow with a multitude of certificates lining the walls, alongside a collection of eighteenth-century prints. The rest of the furniture was Danish, mid-twentieth century – upright teak filing cabinets and dressers and a side table with all manner of teas.

'Holly,' he said. Nodding but not blinking.

'Yes.'

'Holly Wakefield.' Another pause. The pale eyes drilled into her. 'I had generously put aside time for you one hour and forty-five minutes ago, but it would now seem your journey has now been in vain.'

'I know, I'm so sorry. The traffic coming out of London was . . .' It sounded lame and she knew it.

'When you've worked in psychiatry as long as I have, in one sense time is irrelevant. But in the other . . . it governs us, dictates our moods, dictates how we see the world. What we think. It also dictates when we take our medications. Richard Sickert is a very dangerous man and his medication protocol cannot be altered or messed with or stopped. Especially if he is about to interact with someone he hasn't met before for an interview that he doesn't know anything about.'

She felt like an idiot schoolgirl. The sort of dressing down you get from the headmaster and you sit there and you . . . She took a breath.

'I can only apologise, Doctor Andell. We only just got the news that Daniel Summers has gone missing today and—'

'Not missing. He didn't show up for his visit on Saturday but he has enough medication to last him.'

Holly took a second, surprised. 'You don't seem too concerned.'

'I'm not. Daniel has a cottage. A place his parents gifted to him. It's out by the coast. He goes there a lot, to think. He meditates, which is something we try to encourage all our patients to try. Our meditation sessions.'

'Do you have the address?'

He nodded. 'As do the local police. I have already forwarded it to Detective Inspector Bright. I will forward it to DI Bishop and I will give you a copy for your records. I'm sure Daniel will be there now and he will come back here in his own time. We have a very different view on treating patients here. It's not exactly conventional.'

'No.'

'You disapprove?'

'I don't know enough about your research to form an opinion.'

'Spoken like a true psychiatrist.' Andell smiled for the first time. It was short-lived but it was there and Holly felt her hands unclench. 'No,' Andell continued. 'The NHS alert was triggered because if one of our patients does not turn up for a scheduled appointment we are required to notify them immediately. We comply because it is required of us, but we are not concerned. You can check the records. He always turns up. More important, perhaps, is that his pathology does not match that of your killer.' He gestured to the folder on her lap. 'May I?'

She opened it up and passed across the contents. Doctor Andell grimaced at the lurid details. 'Rage. Pure and simple. My God, that's ... it's been some time since I've looked at crime scene photos. How on earth have you connected Daniel to this, Miss Wakefield?'

'The crime scene had similar properties to the Richard Sickert murders,' she said. 'Daniel and Richard were housed in the same hospital wing for two years, weren't they?'

'Yes. I'm not sure where you're going with this . . . '

'They must have interacted. Talked. Shared secrets. You don't think it's possible that Daniel was influenced by Richard to kill?'

'To become his copycat?' Andell stifled a laugh. Any ground she had recovered had just been lost. 'The idea of someone coercing Daniel to murder again is bordering on ridiculous.' He got up and pulled a file from the filing cabinet with '*Daniel Summers – Confidential*' on the cover and passed it over. 'Daniel's rigid personality at a pathological level enabled him to kill his sister – but that same pathology won't extend to any other victims.'

'What about the attack on Rose?'

'Nurse Gifford? He saw her as an extension of his sister. They were quite similar in appearance. Daniel's sister was an older, matriarchal woman who belittled and criticised him. They lived with each other and had slept with each other since they were in their early teens. He didn't like the arrangement, but being the structured man he was, he said nothing until one day he was pushed too far. Years of seething resentment turned into anger and indignation. Within months that anger had turned into rage-fuelled violence. In his own mind, he quite easily justified the killing.'

'How?'

'He felt his sister was demanding too much of him. She was controlling him. Which she was. He saw no way out other than to kill her . . . '

He spoke in the same deliberate tone as in the YouTube

videos Holly had studied: straightforward, eloquent and know-ledgeable. And someone Holly desperately wanted on her side. Aside from the videos, she had seen Doctor Andell at several of his lectures and read all his books, and if she had ever thought about meeting him this wasn't how she had envisaged it.

' ... After he burned her body, he began to suffer from remorse. He knew he had done wrong and wandered around until the police picked him up. I was lucky enough to have been on hand and I have helped rehabilitate him to his present condition.'

'So do you believe Daniel has been fully rehabilitated?'

'I do, yes. When he initially arrived here, he needed twenty-four-hour monitoring and was placed on suicide watch. It took several years for me to get through to him, but when I finally did, I found what I nearly always find.'

'Which is?'

'Someone who is lost.' He stared at her and she wasn't sure if he wanted her to say something in response. She could feel her cheeks reddening. 'Would you like a drink?'

'I'm sorry?'

'Coffee? Tea?'

'Tea, please.'

'I have a variety of herbals, Earl Grey if that's—'

'Earl Grey would be perfect, thank you. Milk. No sugar.'

Doctor Andell headed to the rear of the room where he put the kettle on. She wanted to bring up one of his case studies, at least try to converse with him on some common ground, but instead she found herself staring at the photos of his wife and daughter on his desk and then at the prints on the wall.

'The story of Tom Rakewell. Are you familiar with it?' He had turned back.

'No.'

'*A Rake's Progress.* It's a series of eight prints, engraved by Hogarth in 1734. They show the plight of a rich merchant's spendthrift son who has come to London to seek his fortune, or rather spend his fortune. It's perhaps more a morality tale than anything else.'

'And what happens to him?'

'He spends all his money on prostitutes and gambling, ends up in debtor's prison and eventually succumbs to Bethlehem Hospital, or Bedlam, a human zoo that encouraged shameless voyeurism. Where the mad and the sane came face to face.'

'But who is really crazy . . . ?' Holly said softly, entranced by the engravings. A spoon chinked loudly against the side of a china cup, breaking her reverie. She turned and saw Andell stirring in the milk. He placed the cup of tea on the desk, then sat down in his chair. He took one more look at the crime scene photos and handed them back.

'There are very few sociopaths who will kill just for the sake of it. Daniel isn't one of them.'

'But if Daniel didn't kill the doctor and his wife, then who did?'

'You. Me. Anybody.' He said it matter-of-factly but there was a sorrow behind his eyes. 'A psychopath doesn't conform to the normal life structure that we can adhere to. You work at Wetherington Hospital, don't you?'

'Yes.'

'What's it like?'

'Not like this. Larger. More patients. Most of whom are voluntary admissions. We do have a few murderers, but I wouldn't consider them as dangerous as the patients here.'

'Put them in a field of flowers and they'll make a daisy chain. Put them in a crowd of people and they will kill as soon as the handcuffs come off.' A pause. 'I can try to help, offer some names. I don't want to overstep my boundaries here, but—'

'No, Doctor Andell, that would be incredibly helpful. Any insight at all would be ...' She decided to jump feet first. 'I attended your lecture at Nottingham University when you talked about John George Haigh, the "Acid Bath Murderer".'

'Corpus delicti.'

'"If the bodies cannot be found, a murder conviction is not possible."'

'Nottingham.' He smiled wistfully. 'That must have been at least ten years ago.'

'Eight, actually.' She had corrected him but ... 'I found it fascinating. I think we all did. It was a very busy lecture hall.'

He took a moment. Seemed to see her for the first time.

'You think this killer has killed before, don't you?'

'Yes.'

'Why?'

She swallowed hard. It was like talking about space flight to Neil Armstrong. 'I think the murders are too refined for first kills. Too perfect. As if he's already had practice.'

'In his mind, perhaps he has. Daydreaming. Fantasising for years until he is ready.' A breath. 'I don't disagree with you, Holly, but I would suggest expanding the criteria. Merely as a process of elimination, you understand. People who haven't killed before, but who you or I believe could very well take that next step. There are a few that I have treated within the past five or so years.'

'Thank you. The victims appear so random, it's—'

'Have you heard of John Abignail?'

206

'He killed thirteen women. Was sentenced to death in 1967.'

'Do you know what his final words were to the chaplain who tried to give him his last rites?'

'Actually, I don't.'

'He said, "Look, if you come in here, I'm going to have to kill you. It's not personal. I don't hate you and I'm not angry. It's just something I'll have to do."'

'So you don't think this killer is personal? He didn't kill them for a reason?'

Andell shrugged. 'I believe he probably did kill them for a reason, but I'm not a profiler, that's your job.' His gaze fell to his watch. 'Maybe they are random. Maybe there is no link. Perhaps the doctor was killed because he was wearing green trousers, the wife was killed because she liked the Rolling Stones. But if it is a copycat, then you need to understand why this person is copying Richard Sickert. And to understand that, you need to understand Richard himself.' He nodded without warmth, as if unsure of where to begin but then he leaned on the desk and started speaking.

'Richard's story is a complicated one. His mother, Mary, was born in Cricklewood, London in 1957. She left school at the age of eleven to go and work at Barton's Vintners in Cloister Road and stayed there until she became pregnant. She and her husband, Roger, were married on 16 January 1973, and she gave birth at home to her first son, Wilfred, two weeks later.'

'She was sixteen?'

'Yes. Then in the summer of 1974 she was dismissed from Barton's for theft and spent three weeks in Broadmoor Women's Prison. Within six months she was back at Broadmoor, this time on charges of prostitution, and from then on she seemed to spend her life between prison and the unlicensed sex bars in

Soho. In 1977 she fell pregnant again. Whether Roger was the father or not will likely never be proved, but in June the next year she gave birth to Richard. Within a week her husband had filed for divorce and disappeared forever. By this time she had turned to drink and drugs and had become a functioning alcoholic, plying her trade as a prostitute in central London. There appeared to have been no maternal bones in her body.'

'So who brought Richard up?'

'It was his elder brother, Wilfred, who really cared for him. Helped raise him. He must have had a hand in – or at least an understanding of – who Richard turned into and why. A few years later, their mother attempted suicide and Wilfred saved her life by calling an ambulance.'

'What method did she use?'

'The same one as Seneca: a hot bath and a quick blade. It was a shocking time for both children but their mother's actions had far-reaching consequences. For obvious reasons, Mary was considered unfit as a mother and the two children were taken into care and put up for adoption.' Andell took a breath. Frowned. 'They were both placed with foster parents in Battersea' – he checked the file – 'a Margaret and Simon Westall. Are you familiar with the stringent checks for fostering?'

'A little.'

'Well, they had both been cleared by the Social Services, and the two boys were their first adoptees, but sadly within three weeks they began to sexually abuse both of them. They were subjected to all manner of depravity. Not only by the Westalls but by friends of the Westalls. They were handed out at "*parties*" that the Westalls would throw. Wilfred escaped and went to the police but his story fell on deaf ears and social services placed him back with the Westalls. On his second escape, he succeeded in taking Richard with him and the two of them roamed the streets of Soho in a desperate attempt to get help from their mother. She took her sons back to her flat and sent Wilfred out to get food, but while he was gone she tried to commit suicide again. Richard was not as quick as his brother and this time their mother died in the bathtub.'

'Slashing her wrists?'

'Yes.'

The same way Richard killed Natasha Sickert. He re-enacted his mother's suicide attempt every time he murdered . . .

'The police were alerted when a client turned up for sex and found her. By the time they arrived at the scene, Wilfred and Richard were huddled in one corner of the bedroom. Initially, the police thought they had murdered her, and took them into custody, but then the coroner stepped in and determined it was indeed suicide. After her volatile history and previous suicide attempt became known, the CPS dropped all charges against the brothers and they were free to go home.'

'Home?'

'If we take this as a snapshot of their young lives we can see that neither of them really stood a chance. Back with the Westalls, the abuse continued unchecked until Wilfred turned sixteen and left home to join the army. Sadly, Richard was left to fend for himself. Although growing up he was still a child in every sense. A child who could not control any aspect of his life and he became incredibly dependent on his foster parents. Wilfred petitioned the army to let him stay in England to take custody of his brother; but he was ordered to go to Germany to finish his contract. Unfortunately, he was killed two months later in a car accident.

'Richard was ten years old at that point and it could be argued that the psychological damage had already been done. After his brother's death Richard was moved from foster home to foster home. Six in total, but none of them could cope with him and eventually he was placed back with the Westalls. He stayed with them for the next five years. And in those five years the real Richard eventually broke free. He was a paranoid schizophrenic with severe sociopathic tendencies, the likes of which I have never seen before. He had experienced visions and heard voices ever since he was three years old. Untreated, it was a miracle he kept his murderous thoughts in check for nearly fifteen years.'

'And after fifteen years?'

'He snapped. The Westalls disappeared. They were never found. The authorities believed he killed them, but he has never admitted to it, even to me, and so the police could never charge him. After that, he was moved from one foster home to another and then to different adoption agencies, but nobody seemed to want him. Too badly damaged. The flotsam and jetsam of our social system. Forgive me, Holly, but I am not a fan.'

'No. I can understand that.'

'At eighteen years of age the care system spat him out and he was left to fend for himself, living on social security. Drinking. Taking drugs. And then he seemed to have experienced his first years of what I term "reflective sanity".'

'What do you mean by that?'

'A sociopath confined to his abuse will accept it. Live it. Learn to enjoy it even. Not because of what it is, but because of the range of feelings it creates inside of him. When the Westalls were no longer there, neither was the abuse. It was the first time in his life he wasn't being abused and he had the intellect

210

to reflect on that. To think about his current situation. Did he prefer it? Did he miss the abuse? Was it something he needed? Or was it simply nostalgia? His old life. And then there was the tightrope precipice. Would he now become an abuser? Which path would he take?'

Holly leaned forward, listening intently.

'Deep down, he had already decided. He liked being in control. He wanted to kill and he structured his life around that desire. How can I do this and get away with it? I will get a normal job. I will get a girlfriend. I will have friends. I will get married. And yet all the while I will be planning murder and mayhem and nobody will ever know.'

'He was a planner.'

'Oh yes. An extensive planner. He watched his victims for weeks. Months, in some cases. For him, it was like foreplay. Until his body could no longer take it and then he had to strike. To satiate his desire. To fill that emptiness.'

'You believe he killed more women than the three whose murders he was charged with?'

'At the trial, the prosecution tried to link at least three unsolved murders to Richard, but I argued on his behalf that they be dismissed. The pathology simply did not match. But are there others he has killed? Yes. He has told me of some women, but has so far refused to name them or reveal where the bodies are buried.'

She had wondered whether to mention the wallpaper and after a lengthy pause she said, 'Did he ever take a trophy?'

'He did, yes. Clippings. Hair clippings.'

'Pubic?'

'No. From the victims' heads. Does this ... does your killer take trophies?'

'A section of wallpaper has been cut from each victim's bedroom. We're not sure yet if . . .'

'Wallpaper?'

'Unusual, I know. Any insight into that?'

'A flashback to his childhood, perhaps? A killer will normally take something much more personal to the victims though.'

Holly said, 'Can I ask you about the bell?'

'The bell?'

'There was a bell on the stairs at Richard's house. The police officer, DI Combs, kicked it on his way down the stairs. An identical bell was found at the Wrights' residence and also at Rebecca Bradshaw's.'

'Who is Rebecca Bradshaw?'

'A previous victim who has now been linked by the pathologist to the same killer.'

'Three murders so far.' The shadows seemed to deepen around Andell's eyes. 'The bell was Richard's calling card. He also left one at the other two killings but they were never noticed or found. He told me where he put them, but not until long after the trial.'

'So he did leave a bell when he murdered Kate and Rudy?'

'Oh yes. The bell is a fascinating insight into what makes Richard tick.' He glanced at Holly and gave a wan smile. 'His foster mother gave him the bell when he was five years old. He would sit halfway up the stairs in their house and was told to ring the bell when their friends arrived for sex. Sometimes he and Wilfred were made to watch in a mirror, hidden behind a screen. Sometimes they would be told to participate. When Richard was older the mirror and his reflection became the basis of his psychosis. He took a bell when he went to see Kate and Rudy, convinced that, if he rang it, the women would have sex with him, like his foster mother. When they didn't, he smashed the mirrors and killed them.'

'No rape.'

'No. Penetration, but by a foreign body. Yes, it would appear that whoever is killing these poor women now is definitely following in Richard's footsteps. How that person found out about the bell, though ... Was it ever mentioned in the press?'

'Never.'

'Then it must be somebody to whom Richard has spoken, or at least communicated with. Have you thought about the police who worked the case?'

'It's a possibility, yes.'

'There's a tradition within the police of turning from white to black, as it were. Christie, Dorner, Popkov, Middleton, the list goes on and on. Something you can't discount.'

'I know.'

'I understand now why you came here to talk about Daniel. He was close to Richard for two years. But it's not him. I simply cannot see him doing this. His pathology wouldn't let him. I need to collect my thoughts, go through old files – Richard has been here for over ten years, he has come into contact with hundreds of patients during that time.'

He gave a sad little smile. She thought he looked suddenly tired. Then he picked up her teacup as if he had been a bad host. 'Would you like another?'

'No, thank you, Doctor.'

As he was returning the cup to its tray he asked.

'Would you like to see him?'

The corridor was lit like an aquarium.

Weak neon bounced off green linoleum and green-washed

walls. Doctor Andell stopped at a security door, key card in hand.

'I'd ask you to keep your voice down when we enter the corridor. The patients here are all medicated but it's always a delicate balance. They will recognise my resonance but yours will identify you as a stranger.'

She nodded.

Doctor Andell swiped the key card and opened the door. A white-tiled corridor stretched ahead for fifty metres with cells on either side. Walking quietly, he eventually stopped at a door with a white metal viewing panel that he slid to the side.

'Richard Sickert.'

Through the glass she saw a bed with the patient sleeping on his back. Sickert was thin, but tall, his long black hair tied in a ponytail that hung down over his shoulder and fell across the bed. He was breathing deeply and Holly wondered if he was dreaming. She was almost disappointed he looked so normal. There was a bandage on one of Sickert's wrists.

'Is he suicidal?'

'At the moment, yes. I believe he is self-harming in order to stay alive. A coping mechanism for survival and his way of escaping the emotional pain. We've had to place Richard on a new medication regime. It's easier if I explain ...' He sighed. 'Richard has a fear of his own reflection, it's part of his pathology. You may have noticed, there are no mirrors in my office, but glimpsing a reflection of oneself is unavoidable in a hospital and last week he managed to obtain a knife from the kitchens and began self-harming – so we've had to immobilise him. It's a step backwards, which is unfortunate, because it means as an institution we have failed him, and as a doctor, I feel as though I have failed him too.'

'You obviously take Richard's case very personally.'

'I vowed when I testified in his defence at the trial that I would spend my life trying to help him. A case like his is ongoing. He will need constant treatment, assessment and care. I believe he can be rehabilitated, however, and it is my intention to make that so.'

'Would I be able to come back and talk to him at some point in the future?'

'For obvious reasons we're handling him very carefully at the moment. At the weekend he has intensive CBT, but the week after perhaps?'

'Thank you.' She had put the thought to one side but now wanted to bring it up. 'I don't understand why he killed his wife.'

'I'm sorry?'

'Natasha. Why did he kill her?'

'Have you read the court transcripts?'

'Yes. He strangled her, slashed her wrists and then went and sat in the middle of the road. Gave himself up. If he hadn't killed his wife, he probably could have carried on killing. He'd got away with it until then. Why, on that night back in 2007, was he suddenly ready to face trial and go to prison? Sutcliffe didn't kill his own wife. He kept her alive. Kept the anonymity, kept the alibi.'

'How many paranoid psychopaths like Richard have you worked with, Holly?'

'Well, each case is—'

'How many?'

'None, first hand. But Robert Hare's checklist is a reference point. You can—'

'Everybody has read the PCL-R. But some people cannot be put in a box.' She was about to protest when he waved a

215

hand at her. 'I don't mean that to be offensive, Holly. I have been in the business of psychiatry for over twenty years. If I had never met Richard, I would be in the same position you are in now. He is the most unique individual I have come across and, without question, the least understood. Charting him is like trying to sketch the Mariana Trench, the pressure from the depths is agonising and it's so dark that sometimes you can't help feeling lost yourself.' He looked away, shutting his eyes as if fighting the vision. 'Sorry. I honestly don't know the answer to your question. Richard's motivation for killing his wife is like everything here: a work in progress.'

She hoped she hadn't upset him, but he moved on to the next cell and beckoned her over. 'Here is one of my success stories.' Holly looked through the glass panel. A man was sleeping on his side, curled foetus-like. He had his back to them and his head was shaven.

'Herbert George,' said Andell. 'A serial rapist. I don't think he ever sleeps.'

'He's awake now?'

'He will be. He'll be listening. He's been with us for twenty years now and his transformation has been quite remarkable. He asked to be castrated when he first arrived; indeed, the prosecution wanted chemical castration, but that was never an option as far as I was concerned. This isn't America in the seventies. He's been let out every weekend – supervised of course – for the last five years. The ward sister and one of the orderlies have always escorted him. And next week he will be let out on his own for the first time.'

'Aren't you worried?'

'No. He's made remarkable gains in self-control.'

'And he never murdered?'

'That's the fascinating part of his pathology. He considers murder abhorrent.'

There was a sudden thump on the wall of the cell next door. Andell looked annoyed and quickly took Holly by the arm and led her back towards the main door and past a cell where a man's shadowed face was now pressed against the glass panel. The thumping continued and Holly could almost feel the vibrations in the floor. A patient shouted:

'Get in here, bitch!'

As the security door shut behind them, she peered back into the confinement area. The lights had already turned themselves off. It was pitch-black again and quiet as a tomb.

'Who was that?'

'That's Martha Star. Real name Alan Hunter. Our first gender-neutral. That's a textbook all by itself.' He smiled an apology and led her away. 'I'd like to show you something else.'

They walked to a waist-high window at the far end of the corridor that looked out into the blackness of the night. It had been so quiet where they were that Holly was surprised to see it was still raining.

'What are we looking at?'

'Our history,' Andell said. He flicked a light switch and nightlights outside came to life revealing a lawn below them filled with yew trees and a scattering of graves and old headstones.

'In the Victorian era, Bayview was a mining town, but in 1867 a pit explosion claimed fifteen lives. The single biggest mining tragedy in this area. After the disaster, most of the surviving miners suffered from what we would now call post-traumatic stress disorder. They were trapped down there for days. In narrow tunnels, in complete darkness, barely able to move or breathe, trying to keep calm to save oxygen, all the while knowing that they probably would never be found. Resigning themselves to death.'

'I can't imagine how horrific that must have been.'

'After five days a miracle occurred and five men were pulled from the rubble. A small hospital was set up in the remains of the colliery to cope with their needs. Three of them died within a day, one committed suicide, but Stanley Wickes survived. He was the pit boss. A tough old goat but he'd lost his sight in the cave-in and didn't recognise the voice of anyone who spoke to him, even his wife and his closest friends. He would sit in his room all day and gaze blankly out of the window at the remains of the colliery he could no longer see. He said he could hear the ocean and for some reason thought they had moved him back to his childhood home so he could have a view of the bay before he died. They thought he had gone mad, and perhaps he had, but the parish priest didn't give up on him. He used to sit next to him and pretend he could hear the waves as well. He decided to call the hospital "Bayview", and the name stuck.'

'That's a wonderful story.'

Andell smiled. 'Over time, the hospital expanded as other towns heard of the rehabilitation work that was being done with Stanley, and people would arrive with their mentally challenged relatives. By 1896 Bayview was granted its Royal Charter as an asylum for the disassociated. The rest, as they say, is history. We've come a long way since the days of Bedlam.'

'Pay a penny to see the freaks.'

'And be entertained by the inmates at the asylum, yes. Sad days for our profession, indeed. But out of tragedy is born hope, I believe.'

'It's nice to meet someone who thinks he can make a difference.'

'Thank you.' He glanced out of the window again. 'All the patients here take great pains to keep the cemetery neat and tidy. They find it relaxing, peaceful. Lord knows, the majority of them have never known much peace in their lives. There's a fascinating account of the accident by the parish priest at the time, Reverend Leo O'Brian. Only a few copies have survived; I'll lend you mine, if you're interested. It's incomplete, but makes for a fascinating read.'

'I'd like that.'

Andell flicked the switch and the graves were plunged into darkness. He turned from the window and they walked back along the corridor.

'Doctor Andell, may I ask your professional opinion?'

'Please do.'

'One of my patients suffers from acute schizophrenia. He was responding well to risperidone, but recently it seems as though he's taken a giant step backwards.'

Andell creased his brow. 'It's hard to make a judgement call when I haven't seen the paperwork or talked to the patient. Is he hallucinating?'

'Yes. And he's developing delusional ideas to explain what he sees. He's hearing voices as well.'

'I've found citalopram works well. If he can't cope with that, then sulpiride. We're trying it on Richard now, combining it with regressive therapy.'

'How is it working?'

'He's begun experiencing a powerlessness with regard to his emotions. Like most men who were abused as children, he has a lot of pent-up anger. It won't cure him, but . . . '

'In your opinion, is it ever possible to cure?'

'You cannot cure schizophrenics, sociopaths or psychopaths. You can, however, control them.'

They were back at the end of the corridor. Holly could see the ward sister at reception through the glass door. She looked up and waved at them.

'Sister Arlington,' Andell said. 'She's like a modern-day Florence Nightingale. I'd be lost without her.' He smiled. 'It's been lovely to meet you, Holly.'

'Likewise.'

They shook hands and he seemed to choose his next words carefully.

'I must reiterate what I said earlier: it's not Daniel doing this. I would stake my reputation on it. No, Holly. You're dealing with something entirely different.'

'Thank you, Doctor Andell. That's what I was afraid of.'

She walked fast after parking her car in her street. The rain still fell but it was more like mist than anything else and she found it surprisingly refreshing. She turned on to her road, enjoying that feeling of coming home. There was barely any traffic apart from the odd taxi at this time of night but somewhere, echoing in the distance a baby cried. She reached her steps, took one final breath of the cold air and within a few minutes was back in her flat.

Too tired to think, she removed her make-up, got into bed and switched off the light. She lay there for several minutes, her eyes searching the darkness, oblivious to the cold rain that still thrashed outside in the night.

Twenty-six

Holly woke to the sound of the doorbell, followed by a sharp double tap on the front door.

She pushed herself up in her bed, mind groggy, and then appeared a few seconds later in the hallway, fastening her dressing gown as she stumbled like a drunk. She squinted through the spy-hole.

'Jesus . . . ' under her breath. Didn't this guy ever sleep? She opened the door. Bishop was there, dishevelled, exhausted.

'We've got another body.'

'Let me get dressed.'

'There's time for a coffee if you want to put the kettle on.'

'There is?'

'I'll explain on the way.'

She nodded absently. 'Come on in then,' she said, and led him into the living room. She ground some coffee and put two mugs on the counter.

'How do you like it?'

'Milk and two please.'

She watched him sidle over to one of the bookshelves and

stare at the small collection of framed photographs on top. 'Your mum and dad?'

'Yes.'

When she handed him a mug of coffee he was looking at a holiday snap from the beach. Her with her mother and father, all three of them with sandy-faced smiles and wind-blown hair. She wondered if he could see the similarities between herself and her mother. The same brown hair and high cheekbones, full lips and deep brown eyes.

'How old were you here?'

'I was six and a half. Already wanting to take over the world.'

He nodded and when he turned back he noticed the home-made incident board that covered the wall above the mantelpiece. He gave her a wry smile. 'Love what you've done with the place.'

'Thank you. Magnolia is so nineties.' She moved over to the airing cupboard and armed herself with a towel. 'I'll be back in a minute.'

When she emerged from the bathroom, towel-drying her hair, she couldn't see Bishop at first, then noticed the open door to the spare room. Ah, she thought, this could be interesting. She took a deep breath and went inside.

Bishop was standing in the middle of her special room. Her *very special* room. His mouth was open in the proverbial 'O' and she couldn't blame him. The room was an odd museum. Or rather a museum of oddities. Racks of knives and machetes, a Georgian blunderbuss, a pickaxe, a hangman's noose, a ghoul-ish china doll that seemed to follow you with its glass eyes, two Victorian dresses on hangers labelled 'Ripper Victims', glass specimen jars containing bits of preserved flesh ...

Holly flicked a switch and the place lit up like a gallery. Spotlights highlighted some of the more macabre pieces. It was supposed to impress but she thought Bishop looked a little sickly in the light.

'Holly,' he said flatly.

She stared at him, unsure how to play this, but then suddenly dived straight in. 'Well, I might as well let you in on my secret. This is called—'

'Creepy.'

She couldn't say much to that.

'The correct term is "murderabilia". It's all about the history of murder and psychotic murderers. Sociopathic killers. The weapons they used, mementoes from their victims. I collect their things.'

He stared at the hairless china doll and coughed. 'Please don't tell me you slept with that thing when you were a kid?'

'No.'

'You really do bring your work home with you, don't you?' he wheezed. 'Where do you get all this stuff?'

'Internet. Some auctions. Private collectors. There's quite a network actually.'

'Really?'

'Yes. There's a club.'

'I bet there is.' He carried on perusing, as if shopping for a new pair of shoes that he didn't really want. 'What's that?' He pointed to the hangman's noose.

'That was Albert Pierrepoint's. He was Britain's most famous executioner – hanged over four hundred criminals. That's one of his last ropes.'

Bishop nodded, dazed. He saw an old china teacup. It was white with red and yellow roses and had a gold rim. The sort of thing anyone's grandmother might have owned along with a teapot, creamer and a sugar bowl. He picked it up.

'Is this yours?'

'Be careful. It's from Graham Young. He poisoned three people between 1962 and 1971. That's the cup he served them the poisoned tea in.'

Bishop put the teacup down gently. 'You should open this up to the public. Geeks and freaks or whatever.' He gestured toward a two-foot-long serrated machete hanging like a regimental sword on the wall. 'That's not from a film, is it?'

Holly shook her head quickly. 'No. You don't need to know about that one.'

Bishop shrugged and turned back to her. She was sure his smile was meant to be reassuring but it looked a little wonky. 'I tend to leave the murder weapons in the evidence room,' he said. 'But we all collect things, don't we?'

'We do, yes. Maybe we can do swapsies?'

Bishop looked horrified. 'I collect stamps. I don't think anybody ever got killed over a stamp.'

She pointed to a glass display stand in which sat a small black stamp affixed to an old envelope. Bishop shuffled over and gazed at it. Holly came and stood next to him.

'It's from Roland Williams. He was called the Penny Black Murderer. He killed people then sent them apology letters after they were dead. Total psycho.'

'Total.' A beat. 'Do you let other people see this room? It's a bit . . .'

'What?'

'I don't know. It's not normal, is it?'

'Probably not. At least, not in the normal sense of the word "normal".'

'No. It's, er . . . what's the opposite of normal?'

'Paranormal?'

'I don't think so,' he said quickly. 'So, what do you do when you get a date? You don't let guys come in here, right?'

'I don't bring guys home.'

'No, of course not.' He looked embarrassed. 'I mean, I'd be surprised if you did bring guys back— Not bring them back to your house, because that wouldn't surprise me.' Holly could see him beginning to sweat. 'Shit. What I'm saying is, I'd be surprised if you brought guys here and then showed them this room. That's what I meant. That would be . . . weird.'

She'd never seen him so flustered. She was half-expecting him to backtrack some more or perhaps dig an even deeper hole for himself but instead he went quiet and shifted uncomfortably on the spot.

'I don't bring guys back here. I like my privacy.'

'Oh, right. Good.'

There was an awkward silence.

'Do you want more coffee?' she said.

'Do I have to drink it in the creepy-death-room?'

'Your choice.'

She turned and left. Flipping the museum lights off and leaving Bishop in semi-darkness.

He watched her go, stood still for a second and managed one last look at the room. He convinced himself that the china doll had somehow moved closer and felt himself shudder.

'She is so fucked up,' he whispered under his breath, but he couldn't help smiling as he followed her out.

They were in the lift and descending to the mortuary.

Holly had filled Bishop in on her trip last night, Doctor Andell's diagnosis of Daniel and Richard and the fascinating history of Bayview itself.

225

Bishop said, 'He emailed us Daniel's address. It's a crofter's cottage by the sea. A bit isolated. No phone line, so a couple of the local coppers are going to go check the place out. See if he's there. See if he's got an alibi for the night the Wrights were murdered.' He opened a door for her. They went through.

'I saw Richard Sickert in his room,' said Holly. 'Andell let me look at him.'

'You make him sound like an exhibit.'

She smiled at the irony. 'I guess.'

'Well, what was he like?'

'He was asleep, lying on his back. Very still.'

'Yeah, sleep can do that to you.'

'You're in a joyous mood today, DI Bishop.'

'We've got ourselves another victim. Hopefully a break.'

The lift door opened and they walked the short corridor, following signs for the mortuary. They descended a flight of stone steps. The lights were subdued here, softened.

'Ever had to kill a rat?'

'No.'

'Mean fuckers. Hertfordshire Council has a rat problem. Restaurants and houses are getting overrun, apparently. Some hot-shot terminators decided to venture down into the sewers to try to eliminate them and on day three, one of their men discovered what he thought was an old sack of food. Turned out it was a body.' A pause. 'A man's body.'

She took a second. 'Then how do you know his murder is related to this case?'

'He had a tiny brass bell tied around his neck.'

On an aluminium autopsy table lay the remains of a bloated,

blue-green corpse. Swan pressed the flesh on one of its shoulders as if testing the freshness of a fruit.

'A few weeks in a sewer and I'd be happy if I looked this good. Rats have got to a lot of him, although even they left him alone after putrefaction set in. It's going to be difficult to ascertain time of death. His fingerprints are all but eaten, both upper and lower jaw are missing and I've only found one tooth.'

Bishop and Holly stood on the other side of the room. The smell was hideous. Bishop found a vial of peppermint oil in one of the drawers in the bench and rubbed some under his nose. He offered it to Holly who took it gratefully.

Swan switched her microphone on.

'Thursday 16 November 2017. 9.05 a.m. We have a white male, approximately six feet and one inch tall. There is no evidence of any hair on the scalp, which would indicate the victim was either bald or had a shaved head. His eyes are gone, presumably eaten by rodents as both orbital cavities show evidence of small incisor marks. Judging from the condition of his skeletal structure and the traces of osteoporosis, I would put his age at forty at least, more likely fifty plus.'

'Cause of death?'

'Massive cranial haemorrhage due to a severe blow or blows to the head. Can't be more specific on the number of blows, as forty per cent of his skull is missing. Presumably washed away on a tide of feculence.'

'What about a DNA match with the hammer we found?'

'Already sent samples off.' She moved her fingers into the crevice of the neck. 'The hyoid bone is fractured, suggesting strangulation, consistent with the three previous victims. However, the skin has decayed to such a degree that there are no signs of a ligature mark, therefore no signs of petechial haemorrhaging. Impossible, therefore, to tell whether it was pre- or post-mortem. There is, however, subcutaneous evidence of evisceration, consistent with the manipulation of Jonathan Wright's corpse. Due to its poor condition, the body has no identifying scars apparent; however, most of the remaining torso, arms and legs would appear to be covered by a multitude of tattoos. I must say I can't ever recall having seen a body with this many tattoos before.'

She followed the tattoos along first one arm and then the other with the overhead magnifier. 'I got my first tattoo when I was forty-two. On my arse. A scalpel with the word "*mortis*" underneath. Makes me smile every time I look at it in the mirror. Should have had it done years ago. My husband hates it. What about you, Holly?'

'Yes. I have one.' She smiled at the memory. 'It was a group thing at our school. A sort of leaving present for the girls so we'd never forget.' She turned to Swan and lifted her hair, revealing a strip of tattooed blue and red butterflies that fluttered from under her collar and halfway up her neck. She shot a look at Bishop and grinned. 'The boys were too chicken.'

'I like that. Girl power,' Swan said. 'What about you, Bishop? Come on. Show and tell.'

'Got a few from the army but nothing worth talking about.' Holly couldn't tell if he found the subject distasteful or not.

Swan pulled back slightly and raised the magnifier.

'Well, I hate to say it, but as per usual I know everything but always a week too late. Aside from the bell that was found, I would conclude at this early stage that the modus operandi is consistent with the previous victims. It's the same killer.'

'Timeline?'

'Too much degradation for me to give any decent kind of

estimate. But there were fly eggs and pupae in the corpse. I sent specimens over to the forensic entomologist, William Buckley at the Natural History Museum. Do you know him, Bishop?'

'No.'

'Nice chap. He's taken over from Harrison. Never did like Harrison, he could wax lyrical over bluebottles for hours. Should have married one. Buckley will have answers for you by now.'

'What about identifying him?'

'From my end, the chances of that are slim to none.' Swan took a deep breath. 'The face is unrecognisable. Reconstruction would be virtually impossible because of the lack of cranium and soft tissue liquefaction. We can run DNA samples and check the database to see if he had a record, but if that doesn't work my only other suggestion would be to see where the tattoos might lead us. If any of these designs can be identified as the work of a particular artist, and we can track that artist down, they might be able to tell us who our illustrated man is.'

'Thank you, Angela.'

She swung around to look at him. 'I don't normally ask, but how's this one going?'

'Slowly,' said Bishop.

'Holly?'

'We're getting there.' She couldn't think of anything else to say.

Bishop started for the door.

'Come on. Let's go look at some dead flies.'

They walked side by side below the vaulted ceiling of the Natural History Museum's entrance hall. He motioned to the marble steps and they climbed to the third floor, where they were greeted at the lift by William Buckley. He was medium height with greying hair and a pair of thick-rimmed glasses.

'DI Bishop?'

'Yes.' They shook hands. 'And this is Holly Wakefield, she's assisting in the case.'

Buckley smiled and led them along the corridor, away from the throng of visitors and through a security door. At the top of a staircase was an archway into another corridor with windows of frosted glass on one side and doors on the other. It was very warm and Holly could hear a faint buzzing.

'These are the main insectaries where we breed the flies. I apologise for the temperature but we need to keep the heat elevated, I'm afraid.' He opened a door and ushered them inside. It reminded Holly of a school science lab, a dozen or so desks, a whiteboard on the wall and overhead projector at the far end.

'This is one of our classrooms – I thought it best to talk to you here.'

He led them over to a microscope on one of the desks, where numerous flies were stuck with pins on to little blocks of styrofoam.

'So if you don't mind, let me give you a quick entomology lesson. As soon as someone dies, their body starts to decompose, creating chemicals which give off a mixture of very specific odours. These smells are obviously attractive to insects, specifically blowflies, which will lay eggs immediately, sometimes within minutes. These hatch into maggots or larvae, then the pupae stage occurs, which generally lasts from six to fourteen days. It's this cycle or speed of growth from an egg through to the adult that helps us determine the time that a person died.' He gestured to the flies on the pins. 'These flies emerged from the pupae we discovered on the corpse. Initially, we thought the victim had been killed and deposited in the sewer almost immediately because the common green bottle fly eggs were very prevalent. However ...'

He took the smallest of the fly specimens and placed it under the microscope. 'This is where it got interesting. Meet *conicera tibialis*, or the coffin fly, from the Phoridae family, which was also found on the corpse. As you can see, they're less than a quarter of an inch in length, and we nearly missed it. He gestured to Holly. 'Please.'

She leaned forward and peered through the lens, adjusting the ring until it was perfectly in focus. The fly had a hump to its thorax and the magnified bristles on its antennae looked huge against the brown of its abdomen. Holly moved away, allowing Bishop a chance to look, but he declined.

'The female lays one to one hundred eggs at a time and the lifecycle from eggs to adulthood can be as little as fourteen days or as long as thirty-seven. Therefore, we have a two- to five-week time window with gestation. Now, since most of the pupae were empty, we can surmise that the adults had already emerged and left the scene. I believe the deceased was left somewhere secluded and not in direct sunlight for two or three days, which would have generated the initial infestation of bluebottle flies, but then moved and placed into the sewer pipe.'

'So how long has our victim been dead then?' Bishop asked.

'At least six weeks. Possibly more.'

Back in Bishop's car he put the keys in the ignition but instead of starting the engine, he handed Holly the tiny brass bell in a plastic evidence bag. She took it and held it close to her eyes. Plain and simple with no decoration or engravings of any kind. Tinged green where it had oxidised.

'I wonder where he gets them from,' Holly said. He didn't answer. She shot him a look. 'I thought you were in a good mood?'

'I didn't think the body was going to be as bad as that. I thought we'd get a clear-cut victim. Thought we might be nearer the truth.'

'We are.'

'How?'

'All the other kills were out in the open. On show. This guy is different. He doesn't fit the MO.'

'You're right. So?'

'The only reason a killer will break his MO is if the victim didn't match the profile of the other targets. In other words, he wanted him dead but not for the same reasons. Our killer didn't want us to find this one. He was out of sight. Hidden away. There was no show here, no exhibition. But he took a big gamble that didn't pay off. He couldn't resist leaving his calling card, could he. The bell around his neck.'

'This is the second man he's killed that we know of. And he was killed before Rebecca. You still convinced men are not his target?'

'Absolutely.' She lowered the bell on to her lap but continued to hold it tightly through the plastic. 'This one is way more personal,' she added. 'Just for him.'

There was a silence, not uncomfortable, and then Bishop turned the engine on.

'So what makes this dead guy so different?' he asked.

'That's what we need to find out.'

Twenty-seven

Bishop had sent out half a dozen officers to visit tattoo shops in an attempt to identify their victim but so far they hadn't come up with anything. Now he and Holly were back in his office, lunch barely touched, staring at copies of the photographs under magnifiers.

'This guy travelled,' Bishop stated flatly.

'What makes you say that?' Holly asked.

'They're from all over the world, by the looks of things. Fading on the colours. Too much sun.' He fanned the photos out on his desk, went through them one by one. 'This one's Far East. Looks like the tail of a dragon there.'

'China, Japan?'

'Japan. Three claws. Chinese dragons have got five.' The next picture. 'The skulls could be from anywhere. Memento mori, the universal symbol of death or mortality. Nice one of Betty Page there.' He looked at it under a magnifier. 'It's covering up something a lot older, can't see what it is.' He flicked through a few more. 'Fleur-de-lys, typically French but sometimes they're misdrawn as the clubs from a pack of cards. There's another early one underneath. Crudely done. Maybe home-styled. Real early though. It's been covered up pretty good. Hold on ...' He pulled down the overhead magnifier again. 'Looks like a ... maybe it is a series of cards. Poker? I wonder if our guy liked gambling? Where was this one on his body?'

Holly read out the notes from her file. 'On his left arm. Upper tricep.'

'There's something on it. Hard to see what it is. Looks like the outline of an animal of some sort, a crown maybe. And some numbers. Fuck, I've seen something like that before.'

'You have?' Holly leaned forward.

Bishop put the photo down, deep in thought. Turned to her. 'What do you think?'

She leaned into the magnifier, adjusted the focus.

'It's a ... it's a leopard or a lion maybe. Letters or numbers? Three and eight, I think.'

'Hold on.' Bishop moved back in. 'Yeah, there's trace marks there. Ah shit, it's not three and eight, it's three and three. And that's a lion.'

'What are the letters then? B and E?'

'Nope.' Bishop smiled. 'R and E ...' A beat: ' ... 33 RE. Where Duty and Glory Lead.'

'Duty and glory?'

'I'll be damned,' said Bishop. 'RE is the Royal Engineers. Our dead guy was in the army.'

There was a knock at the door. Crane entered. 'Sir.'

'What?'

'No news on Eagen. We're chasing up a lead from a second garage where he used to work, but nothing so far.'

'All right. Thank you.'

Crane left then came back in again almost immediately.

234

'Oh, nearly forgot. Ambrose called. He and Claire had a baby girl.'

'Nice.' Bishop's face broke into a smile. He shared it with Holly and then turned back to Crane: 'How much did she weigh?'

'What? Oh, I don't know, I didn't ask.'

'That's good though,' Bishop said. 'Any names?'

'They're thinking of Lulu, but they don't know for sure yet.'

'Cute. Lulu's a good name.' Crane exited. Bishop sat for a moment then picked up the photo from under the magnifier.

'Royal Engineers,' he mused.

'Do you know people from there?'

He smiled but avoided her eyes.

'I'll make some calls tonight.'

Holly could tell he didn't want to go there. Old memories. Shut away for good and then the lock slips undone and we're back where we used to be. His face changed for the briefest of moments but then became a mask again.

'What are you thinking?' Holly asked.

'At this precise moment, I'm thinking about my favourite sergeant, and how happy he is that he has brought a new life into this world. That's what I'm thinking about. He's wanted kids for years now. They weren't sure if Claire could – there were complications – but now it all seems to have worked out perfectly.' He looked up at her and she saw that a weary anger had replaced the wistfulness. 'And I'm trying to stay thinking about that for as long as I can because when I stop thinking those lovely thoughts I will have to face the bloody reality of what we're all trying to deal with at this station.' He picked up his pen and started to doodle.

'Bishop?'

235

Nothing. Lost in his thoughts.

'Bishop?'

He looked up at her at last and put the pen aside.

'Sorry.'

'What are you writing?'

He didn't answer, raised his eyebrows and gave her a half smile so she went closer. He had written the name 'Lulu Ambrose' in big red letters with a little heart by its side.

But underneath, written in black, was the word 'Darkness'.

They had stayed in the office together for another hour or so until eventually Bishop had told Holly to go home.

'Get some sleep,' he'd told her. 'I'll be out of here myself in a few minutes anyway.' She had left and after half an hour he had started to tidy up his desk. He was almost done when he heard cheers and claps from the hallway. A few minutes later, Ambrose burst into his office, beaming like a kid in a candy shop.

'Evening, sir.'

'Hello, dad!' Bishop stood up, genuinely happy, and came around the desk to shake the sergeant's hand. 'Congratulations, my son. You will now have a lifetime of worry, sleep deprivation and overdrafts. But . . . ' he added. 'It's worth it.'

'Thank you, sir. Wanted to let you know I'm ready to come back to work.'

Bishop half-laughed until he realised Ambrose was serious. 'Jesus Christ, go home. Take care of Claire, go look at your beautiful daughter some more.'

'Sorry, sir, but Claire's the one who sent me out. Her whole family is there taking care of them both. There's seven of them. All women. It's a bit . . . unnerving. Thought I might be more use here.' A hint of desperation in his face. 'How's the case going?'

'No, no, no ...' Bishop said. 'Firstly, how much does she weigh? And where are the photos?'

'Seven pounds and three ounces.' Ambrose pulled out his phone and fanned through a carousel of pink limbs, screaming faces, and an exhausted Claire.

'Did you watch?'

'Yeah. Bloody amazing.' He held up his left hand. Bishop hadn't noticed the scratches on his fingers and the small splint. 'Claire dislocated my third knuckle on the final push. The dangers of offering to hold her hand! Had no idea her grip was so strong. Didn't make a fuss. Popped it straight back in after.'

'The knuckle, not the baby, I presume.'

'Bloody right. Flailing like a banshee when she finally decided to come out.' He stopped talking and was suddenly emotional. 'I'll never forget this,' he said slowly.

'No, you won't.' Bishop patted him gently on the shoulder.

'Right.' Reverie over. 'Let me tell you what's happening.' So he filled him in on everything: Holly finding the link with the bell, the copycat, the body in the sewer. It was when he was talking about bluebottles that his phone rang.

'Sir, it's Doctor Andell for you,' Crane's voice came through.

'Hm?'

'From Bayview.'

'Oh, right. Thank you, Sergeant. Put him through.' A slight delay. 'Ambrose, let me take this. And you – get the hell out of here. That's an order.'

'Thank you, sir.' Ambrose left with a smile and then the phone clicked and Bishop heard Doctor Andell breathing and talking to someone in the background on the line.

'Doctor Andell?'

Muffled voices and then suddenly clarity; 'Sorry, yes. Evening, DI Bishop. I wanted to let you know that Daniel Summers was visited by the police today. I've just got off the phone with DI Bright.'

'Jesus Christ. Where was he?'

'At his cabin, near the woods. And on the night the Wrights were murdered he was at a restaurant in Hastings with the ward sister and an orderly. I believe DI Bright is checking his alibi now.'

Bishop felt like throwing the phone across the room.

'DI Bishop?'

'Yes, sorry.'

'DI Bright seemed convinced of Daniel's innocence. I hope you are too.'

'Yes.' Bishop took a second. Then he said, 'I've known DI Bright a long time. I trust his judgment.'

'Well, are you narrowing down the list of possible suspects?'

'What suspects? We don't have any. We had one, but we had to let him walk.'

'Who?'

'A rapist called David Eagen. He confessed to the murder last week and then changed his mind in the interview room.'

'You had him?'

'We had him, but couldn't hold him.'

'Oh, I see. The frailty of our laws is quite astonishing. What did you make of him?'

'A conceited piece of shit.'

'Yes. He is an interesting character.'

'You know him?'

'He was admitted to Bayview last month when he

238

attacked a prostitute. I was the one who gave his evaluation.'

'I didn't know that.'

'I'll send you a copy. He's quite ... I would have mentioned it to Holly, but I had no idea he was part of your investigation.'

'Well, we've got men out looking for him twenty-four-seven, but ...' Bishop sagged in his chair. 'I'll be honest with you, Doctor, we're wading through a sea of uncertainty. Fetishists, hedonists, rapists who haven't killed—'

'Perhaps not rapists either.'

'Really?'

'Well, he doesn't rape, does he?'

Bishop stopped doodling. Thought for a second.

'No.'

'Which means he's either incapable of doing so himself or doesn't want to engage in that type of intimacy.'

'But he does penetrate them.'

'He does. Yes.' A pause. 'He or she does.'

Bishop put his pen down.

'*She?*'

'A sociopath is a sociopath, regardless of gender. I think it more likely that the killer will be a male, but ... you can never discount the possibility.'

'Never even crossed my mind.'

'Hell hath no fury.' A pause. A hand over the mouthpiece. 'Thank you, darling. The white shirt will be perfect.' His attention came back to the phone. 'Sorry, Inspector, my wife and I are going away this weekend. Another lecture. Wales this time.' A pause that stretched. 'May I ask you a question, please, DI Bishop?'

'Fire away.'

'How long have you known Holly?'

'Known her? Only since the beginning of the case when I asked her to help us out. Why?'

'I see.'

A silence.

'Sorry, Doctor, was there anything else?'

'No, not really.' A pause. 'Actually, yes. How much do you know about her?'

'I'm sorry?'

'What do you know about her?'

'Not much. She's written a book that we've used as a reference. She teaches at King's College, works at a place called Wetherington—'

'—Hospital. Yes, I know,' Andell interrupted. 'I meant personal information.'

'Can I ask why, Doctor?'

'You should really check up on her.'

'What do you mean, check up on her? Like, make sure she's okay?'

'No, I'm sure she's fine. But she's . . . her background . . . '

'Are you saying she's not qualified to help in an ongoing investigation?'

Silence. Bishop was losing patience. He didn't have time for this.

'Doctor, if you have something to tell me, please do.'

More silence. Bishop was on the verge of hanging up when Doctor Andell blurted: 'I recognised her when she came to visit. Not at first. But, after talking to her for some time I knew there was something about her that was familiar. I conducted some research of my own and then it clicked. It's a small world, psychotherapy. I wasn't sure if you were aware, that's all.'

'Aware of what?'

'She's not who she says she is.'

Bishop was hunched over his desk now. He took a moment to register this. He was about to ask another question when Doctor Andell spoke again: 'Look, I feel as though I've said too much. I thought you must be aware, what with her being involved in such a similar case.'

'Similar to what?'

'No. Enough. I feel as though I have betrayed her trust already. I shouldn't have said anything.' He went muffled again and Bishop thought he may have been opening drawers or moving furniture as there was a metallic drag in the background. 'I really should go, Inspector. I'm here if you need me though. Please let me know.'

The phone went dead. Bishop put it back in its cradle and stared at it, frowning. What the hell was that about? It was too much to think about tonight. He just wanted to go home and watch mindless TV for a couple of hours. Read a book. Anything but this. He got up then sank back down. Closed his eyes, his face grim. Holly's background? He dialled her number then hung up quickly.

What was he really annoyed about? They couldn't catch this killer, for a start. That was it. But he knew these things couldn't be rushed. He knew that the tortoise always beat the hare.

Patience, he reminded himself. Patience. One of the many things he had learned in his time in the army and as a police officer. He was very grateful for that. Sitting in quarters at Camp Bastion, forty-degree temperatures outside, watching the sand, waiting for the call. Radio silence on night manoeuvres in Kabul, holed up in some godforsaken dugout. Not talking. Not moving for hours at a time. And then finally home. Back to England and the regiments of Bobby Peel. He had walked the beat for five years and learned patience in the face of public angst. He had learned to remain even-tempered when faced with drunken idiots, resisting the urge to lunge at them with fists swinging. He had learned never to underestimate what someone would do for power, money, sex or drugs. And then he had joined CID and the rules had changed and politics had become the new Everest. Power games inside the small brick building that he now called home. Friends had come and gone. Some had been fired, some had quit and some had stayed on. New people had come in. New blood. New ideas. He felt older all of a sudden. Ambrose's new daughter? The circle of life. Christ. Don't go there, Bishop. Not tonight. Maybe that's why he was so tired. So angry. So frustrated. Life moving on like an irresistible tidal wave that grew and grew in his mind until it would block out the sun and then it would topple in on itself and break into a million pieces when it smashed upon the shore. The room was getting darker. Or maybe that was his eyes. Did he need glasses now? Jesus, Bishop. Enough! Give it a rest. A deep breath. He dialled a number. It was picked up after four rings.

'DI Bright.' The voice sounded alert despite the time.

'Gary. It's Bill. Bill Bishop.'

'What can I do you for?'

No need for pleasentries.

'I hear you visited Daniel Summers. What did you think?'

'I've known him ever since he started coming out on day release. For the first year I had him followed to make sure he didn't get up to anything. Off the record. Still working on the CCTV for his alibi, but . . .'

'But what?'

'I don't think it's your man.'

242

'Shit.'

'Anything else?'

'Yeah,' Bishop sighed. 'Got a body in the morgue with some Royal Engineer ink. Wonder if you could make a few calls for me. Check their database. See if one of your old boys has gone AWOL in the last two months.'

'This tied in with the same case?'

'Could be.'

'Consider it done.'

The phone went dead. Bishop suddenly felt like a drink but shrugged it off. He logged on to the National Police Database and pulled up a photo of DI Bright. Then he went on Facebook, checked out the DI's profile. Scrolled through his photos. Family. Sports. Old army shots in the barracks. R&R in the Middle East. He was a big man. Bigger than Bishop. One photo showed him holding a massive knife and a gutted fish. He was starting to—

A laugh outside the office made him stand up and he walked to his door. Through the glass he could see Ambrose and a few of the night crew laughing as the new dad showed off the photos on his phone, everyone going ga-ga.

'Ambrose?'

The sergeant couldn't hear him. He opened the door. 'Ambrose!' Ambrose turned at the noise, the party broken up. Bishop gestured for him to come into his office then went and sat behind his desk, waiting for him to enter.

'Sir?'

'Close the door and take a seat.'

Ambrose did. Bishop could tell he was still high on new life. He didn't want to dampen his spirits so didn't keep him in suspense. 'Holly. Find out about her for me, do a bit of background.'

'Background?'

'Yeah, you know. Where she was born, education – that sort of thing. I mean, I know a bit about her but . . .'

'Sure.'

'And don't delegate this to anyone else. Your eyes only. Okay? Good. And one more thing. Get out of here. Now. I'm serious! Or I'll take you off as SIO,' but he was smiling. 'Go see the little princess.' Ambrose nodded, his eyes sparkling. Bishop turned back to his computer signalling the meeting was over. 'And shut the door behind you.'

As the door closed behind his sergeant, Bishop turned off his computer and looked around. He hated this office. It was so small, so cramped. He needed to clear his head. He looked at the orchid and tested it to see if it needed watering. The earth was dry around the base but there was a slight acidity there, a slight dampness. 'Tomorrow,' he said. 'I'll water you tomorrow.'

He got outside in time to watch Ambrose drive out of the car park. He lit a cigarette and dragged on it like a greedy schoolboy while staring up at the heavens. At least it wasn't snowing. He took one last draw, then stubbed the damn thing out under his heel.

Twenty-eight

Bishop had arrived at Holly's flat twenty minutes ago, soaking wet, the rain seeming to follow him into the living room as he took his jacket off.

'Sorry,' he said as he collapsed on to her sofa. He had closed his eyes and Holly thought he could have been asleep when she returned minutes later to hand him a mug of coffee.

She sat next to him, took a sip from her own mug. There was something intimate about it. Sharing the first drink in the morning with someone in your home. It felt nice and she tried to remember the last time she had had a man in her flat at this early hour. Through the long windows she could see the rain falling outside but the room was warm and quiet. She sensed something in Bishop and as if on cue he said:

'Good news or bad news?'

'Bad.'

'Got a call from DI Bright early this morning. Daniel Summers went back to Bayview for his meds and his alibi checked out. Bright sent me the CCTV of Daniel at a restaurant near Bayview the evening the Wrights were murdered.'

'Was he by himself?'

'No. he was being chaperoned by one of the nurses. And according to her he was on Lorazepam.'

'Christ. There's no way he could have done it then.' A pause. 'And the nurse never thought to tell us this?'

'She went on holiday the day after the murder and only came back to Bayview last night.' He paused, took a sip of his drink. 'She had no idea what was going on and got an earful from Doctor Andell. He's more than precious about his patients, has the whole of the hospital under a tight leash.'

'Does DI Bright know who Daniel is?'

'Oh, he knows him. Been watching him for years.'

'And you trust him?'

'Who?'

'Bright?'

A slight hesitation. 'Yep. Known him a long time. Ex-army. Old school, like me.'

Old school, like you, thought Holly. A rum baba and black forest gateaux kind of guy.

'Jesus, I was sure it was him.' She took a breath. 'Are you going to get into trouble for this? I mean, I led the charge against Daniel, didn't I?'

'You also spotted the bell connection. We wouldn't have done that without you.' A pause. 'But . . . there's something else.'

'What?'

'Doctor Andell knows Eagen. Eagen was sent to Bayview when he attacked the prostitute last month. Andell's going to send us over his evaluation.' He looked at her solemnly. 'Not Eagen though, right?'

'No.' Adamant. There's no way it's Eagen. No way on earth.

She was still staring at Bishop when she realised that a very small space deep inside was shouting out to her. Gut instinct, warning her against something. The first call of her survival mechanism. Trust me, but be careful, it was saying. Be careful, Holly, or everything will come crashing down.

'Holly?'

'What?' She was lost in thought.

'You want the good news?'

'Sure.'

'Bright got an ID on our tattooed man.'

Twenty-nine

Bishop drove, Holly rode shotgun, reading a report.

Trees flashed by in the background as they cut through the country roads.

'Corporal Brian Reise. Born in Farnborough in 1963. Never married. No kids. He was in the Thirty-Third Engineer Regiment and worked EOD – what's that?'

'Explosive Ordinance Disposal. Bomb disposal.'

'How do we know this is him?'

'A quick show and tell of the photos in the officer's mess. He was famous for his tats apparently. A little background check showed he hasn't been to the veterans' association to collect his pension for the past nine weeks so . . . '

Holly nodded. Back to the report.

'Arrested once at fifteen for a brawl outside a pub in Fleet. Joined the army in 1985, stationed in Aldershot, Northern Ireland and then Germany. Came back to the UK in 1990. Retired in 2013 when he was fifty years old. Got out on a disability.'

'Thirty years in the army and he only made corporal?'

'Is that strange?'

'Very,' said Bishop.

'In 1989 he was listed for a promotion but it never happened.'

'Why?'

'It doesn't say.'

'Then that's what we need to find out.'

It was the last house along a small leafy street.

A sad two-storey building with seventies pebble-dash on the walls that had been painted white at some point but now looked grey. The garden had been neglected; dead leaves and branches were scattered everywhere and the remains of a broken fence sagged on either side of the front gate. To the left, about fifty yards away, was a small bungalow with an empty driveway, and to the right an overhanging forest.

Blue flowers poked their way through the rough grass at their feet as Bishop and Holly walked up the path. A bit of a surprise, the front door was unlocked. They both entered and stood in the hall. A wooden floor, a staircase to the left, two doors to the right, a gloomy passage straight ahead which led to another closed door.

'No post,' Bishop remarked. He slipped on latex gloves and handed Holly a pair. 'Forensics should be here any minute but whilst we're waiting ...' He tried the first door. A bathroom, dusty and cold. The next door revealed a living room with red drapes pulled tight across the windows. He flicked the light on. A heavy rug, a few cabinets with cheap ornaments, and some even cheaper pictures on the walls. Above the mantelpiece were half a dozen framed faded photographs: Reise in a crowd at a wedding, one of him fishing in a stream, a few cityscapes that looked European.

'Some of these pictures are at least twenty years old.' Holly picked one up and drew a finger through the dust. 'Do you have photos of yourself in uniform at home?'

'One in the bedroom. A couple of me with the lads from the station in the living room.'

'Reise hasn't got any. A career soldier with no photos of his army days. That doesn't make sense.' She turned her attention to a bowling trophy that said *2015 runner-up*. A local competition in Guildford. 'This is recent.'

Bishop shrugged, then asked: 'The other victims were killed in their own homes. Why not Reise? This place is isolated. He could easily have been killed here.'

'If Reise had been killed here he would have eventually been found. Then forensics would have combed every inch of this place, and the killer knew that. He changed his MO. I don't think he wanted us to know anything about Corporal Reise.'

'So what exactly do you think we're looking for?'

'I have no idea.'

They searched in silence for another ten minutes, moving furniture, pulling up the corners on the rug, looking through a cabinet full of cutlery and place settings. Then the two of them headed upstairs.

The first bedroom was dingy and cold. The carpet stained and threadbare. A steel-framed bed and an empty chest of drawers. The last bedroom had an en-suite bathroom, a desk and swivel chair, chest of drawers and a standing mirror. Holly went straight for the en-suite. She lifted the cistern and felt around and under the rusty water. She dried her hands on the stiff towel by the radiator. Checked the bath, behind the base panel, and a small cupboard where she found a single razor blade and a hand mirror. She went back into the bedroom. Bishop was at the desk pulling open drawers. A stapler, a hole punch, a writing pad with pages ripped out. He showed it to her.

'We'll take it with us,' he said.

She tried the wardrobe: dusty suits, a military uniform with boots and shoes neatly arranged on a rack. 'Still kept his uniform.'

Another ten minutes of silent searching and then they both shared a weary look. Holly reached her hands under the bed and came out with a handful of old tissues. She wandered over to the standing mirror and stared at its reflection.

'Why would he have a full-length mirror in here?'

'Maybe so he could see himself in his uniform.'

She tried to angle it downwards to see herself but it wouldn't move.

'It's been bolted.'

'What?'

'The mirror. It's been bolted in this position.'

'So?'

She stared at the reflection again, tried to see what Reise would have seen. 'How tall was he?'

'Six foot one.'

'He wouldn't have been able to see himself properly. Come and try it.'

Bishop went over and looked at his reflection but could only see above his waist. He tried to adjust it but Holly was right. It had been bolted into place. 'Well,' he muttered, 'it's not exactly as if this place is full of all the latest mod cons, is it?'

She sat on the bed while Bishop went back to examining the wardrobe. She heard muffled thumps as he moved the heavy shoes about. 'I haven't asked you yet, but how did you get into your job?' he asked.

Holly shrugged. 'I kind of fell into it.'

'Really?'

'Probably read too many Sherlock Holmes and True Detective stories when I was a kid. I wasn't exactly a Barbie type of girl.'

The shoe-moving stopped but he stayed where he was. 'Yes, somehow I can't see you living in the "dream home" with a plastic Ken.'

'No. Just a bunch of old nooses, meat cleavers and bottles of sulphuric acid.' She smiled but then went quiet. 'I don't know. I do question what I do sometimes. Sometimes I wonder if I should pack it all in, start all over again. A second chance, you know.'

He reappeared from the wardrobe and sat at the desk.

'Don't,' he said flatly. 'Don't pack it in. From what I've seen, you're good at what you do. You are making a difference.'

'Thank you.' She looked at nothing in particular and then lay down on the bed and didn't say anything for a while. She adjusted the pillow. It felt damp but she didn't want to move. She noticed Bishop staring at the carpet and wondered what was going through his head. He seemed vulnerable today, sitting by himself, so much smaller somehow, honest and pain-fully real. She found herself staring at him and he happened to glance up at her when he asked:

'What was he like?'

'Who?'

'Your dad.'

She took a second. 'I remember images. Feelings more than how he actually was. Smiling – he always seemed to be happy. Helpful. Always there. I felt safe around him. Secure. I used to think he was the strongest man in the world. That he could lift a house. But a lot of kids think that, don't they? We're all under the illusion that our parents are the best in the world. We all exist in that little fantasy land where everything is magical. There is nothing we cannot do. No mountain we cannot climb. We don't know what the real world is like. We have no idea what we're letting ourselves in for. How about you?'

'My parents?'

'What do you remember?'

'Nothing really. Not too many memories at all.'

She guessed that was it. He obviously wasn't very forthcoming on the subject. Then he said: 'I thought I knew my mother better.'

'What do you remember of her?'

'I think she was sad.'

There was a dull silence that stretched. Holly couldn't look at him. She wanted to go over to him and hold him and tell him everything was going to be all right. She knew she couldn't though, so she stayed where she was and then her tone changed. 'Up there,' she said.

'What?'

She shifted her head on the pillow slightly.

'The fire alarm.'

'What about it?'

'That's what he could see in the mirror when he lay on the bed.'

'So?'

'I don't know. Seems a bit weird, that's all.'

Bishop glanced at it, carried the chair over from the desk and climbed up. He reached to the fire alarm, twisted it and was rewarded by a gentle click as it came away revealing a neatly cut circular hole in the ceiling. He put his hand into the space, fingers fumbling, eyes screwed shut with concentration. Nothing. Something . . . ? His fingertips brushed against a smooth hard object and he pulled out a First World War brass cigarette case.

Holly pushed herself off the bed as he climbed from the chair and opened up the case. Inside was a notebook bound in red leather – a Royal Engineers Diary for 1989. Bishop flicked through the pages. Reise had put his name and rank at the front, but apart from a few words here and there it was sparse, almost unused until 7 August, where there was an asterisk and a continuous line through two weeks until 21 August.

'Not much of a writer.'

'No,' Holly found herself whispering, 'but every night when he put his head on his pillow, he stared up at this book.'

Bishop turned it over and picked out a folded piece of paper that had been tucked inside the back. It was creased and covered with brown spots but it opened to a faded photo of a pretty young woman sitting on a bench by a waterfall. In her twenties, she was staring shyly past the camera. He turned the photo over; written on the back in faded ink was a name and date:

'Mina – 1988.' He passed the photo over to Holly. 'File said he never got married.'

'His girlfriend then.'

'You think she's connected to this somehow?'

Her lips curved into a smile. 'Yes, I do.'

Thirty

They were all back in the incident room.

It had been a long day and most had finished their shifts but some were still there. Die-hards, thought Holly as she moved among them. Die-hards or simply people with nowhere else to go. Bishop, Crane, Jacobs and Williams were poring over old trial transcripts, Kathy was preparing a new press release. Holly had the photo of Mina in her hand; an enlarged copy had been pinned on the incident board.

She fired up the nearest computer and was about to settle down for the night when Ambrose returned. He held a sheaf of papers in one hand.

'From Mr Munroe, the estate agent. The list of people who wanted to view the Pettiman property in Abinger Hammer. Seventeen in all.'

Bishop sighed. 'Christ, it never ends, does it? Have we cleared anybody yet?'

'We've cleared the first fourteen,' Ambrose said. 'Alibis all backed up by numerous witnesses. That leaves three couples who are still of interest. The first are Alan Voysey and Paula Baulch, newly engaged. Live in Sunbury-on-Thames.

Apparently, they're on holiday; we spoke to their neighbours. They had mentioned moving in the past six months so it's a matter of confirming that with them in person and deleting them from our enquiries. The other couple we're still waiting for are a Mr and Mrs Braggs in Kensington. Not picking up the phone. We sent a car. Neighbours said they might be away on holiday.'

'Why is everybody on holiday? Am I missing something here?'

'A policeman's lot is not a happy one, sir.'

'Thank you, Ambrose, I'm glad you're back because your comic routine is much better than Sergeant Crane's.' He forced a smile. 'I don't even know what day it is any more.'

'Thursday.'

'Friday,' Holly corrected.

'Friday it is.' Bishop nodded. 'Happy Friday everybody.'

'And then there's the last couple. Again, not picking up the phone. We sent a car around to their property – no answer.'

'Where do they live?'

'Number 79 Pontefract Court. It's a housing estate off the Linton Road in Barking.'

'Barking?'

'Yes, sir.'

'Bit of a step-up, isn't it? Barking to a little village in Surrey.'

'Who went?'

'Rankin, I think.' Ambrose consulted the notes. 'A bunch of high-rise flats. Bloody dump. Car got keyed as well.'

'The last couple. What were their names?'

'Beverley Allitt and her boyfriend, Leslie Bailey.'

Holly looked up in disbelief and suddenly peeled herself off the chair.

'Sorry, what did you say their names were?'

256

'Beverley Allitt and Leslie Bailey.'

All eyes turned to her. She was shaking her head, playing it through her mind.

'That can't be right.'

'Why?'

'They're both serial killers,' she whispered.

'What?' Ambrose looked at her in disbelief.

'You're joking,' Bishop said.

She felt as though all the blood had drained from her body. When she spoke it was very quiet. 'No, I'm not. Beverley Allitt was "the Angel of Death". She murdered four children in 1991. And Leslie Bailey. Um . . .' racking her brain . . . 'was a paedophile who murdered a young boy in . . . I can't remember the year.'

Bishop stood up. 'Hold on, hold on . . . so . . . Are you sure about the names, Sergeant?'

Ambrose checked again. 'Absolutely positive.'

'Jesus Christ. When was their appointment?'

'Six o'clock on 5 October.'

'Wasn't that the day the estate agent said they redecorated?' Holly asked.

Bishop rifled through the notes on his desk. 'Yes. The fifth.'

'You wouldn't schedule someone the day it was being painted, would you?'

Bishop picked up the phone. It rang three times and Holly heard the dulcet tones of Mr Munroe on the other end.

'DI Bishop here, Mr Munroe. Thanks for picking up so fast. No . . . nothing's wrong, sir. A quick query on one of the couples on your list of potential buyers. They were scheduled for the fifth. Beverley and Leslie, I think their names were.' A long pause. Holly watched him intently, trying to read his face but she couldn't. 'I see. Thank you, Mr Munroe.' He hung up and stared at them with an expression of calm satisfaction. 'Mr Munroe tried to cancel because of the decorating but they were insistent. He couldn't make the viewing himself so he never actually met Beverley and Leslie. He gave them the lockbox combination.'

It was 10.30 p.m. when they arrived at 79 Pontefract Court in Barking.

Rankin had been right in his assessment: the block of flats was indeed a dive. Rusty supermarket trolleys toppled and abandoned, stained mattresses sagging with wet. The normal teenage detritus hanging in the shadows with acid-coloured eyes who slunk away when Holly and the others arrived in a flash of blues.

There were twelve of them in all: Holly, Bishop, Crane, Kathy, Jacobs and seven Met officers. Four were armed with G36 assault rifles, one with a Taser, two with riot shields and the last with the hydraulic battering ram. The flat was three storeys up so they took the stairs. All moving in sync like a well-oiled machine. Quiet as mice, they huddled by the door. Bishop gave a nod to everyone and knocked.

'Police. Open up, please.'

Nothing.

A few seconds passed and he knocked louder. Shouted: 'Police. Open up!'

Silence.

He knelt to the letter box and tried to push it open. 'Holly?' She came straight to his side. 'Letter box has been sealed,' he said.

She crouched next to him, had a look herself. 'It's been glued shut.'

Bishop turned to Crane: 'Where are we on the warrant?'

'Still waiting, sir.'

A man appeared at the end of the walkway, watching them curiously, neither frightened nor friendly.

Bishop spotted him. Pointed to number 79.

'Beverley and Leslie, mate. Do you know them? The couple in here. Beverley and Leslie?'

'I don't know. No.' He disappeared. Closed his door.

Bishop knocked on the neighbour's flat. It was opened by a woman in her fifties, hard-worn and sucking a Marlboro. She had obviously been waiting by the door, had heard them outside.

'Hi there, not a problem,' Bishop said, flashing his warrant card. 'Your next-door neighbours – Beverley and Leslie I think it is . . .'

'Who?'

'Beverley and Leslie.'

'No. Which side next door?'

'This side, love. To your right.'

'There ain't no Beverley and Leslie living there.'

'Who lives there then?'

'Tracy.'

'Tracy who?'

'Tracy Jackson. Why, what's wrong?'

'Nothing, love, do you want to go back inside?'

She shut the door and Bishop spoke into his shoulder radio.

'Control, this is DI Bishop. Confirm there is no Beverley Allitt or Leslie Bailey at this address. Someone called Tracy Jackson is purported to live here. Can we verify, please? Seventy-nine Pontefract Court, Barking.'

They waited in silence. Bishop banged on the door again. 'Police!'

His shoulder radio crackled into life:

'Confirmed. Occupant is Miss Tracy Jackson.'

'Control, this is DI Bishop. We have an NRRK. No Reply Repeated Knocking at seventy-nine Pontefract Court. Request permission to enter without warrant. Initiating a Section 17, under PACE codes of practice. We believe someone's life may be in danger.'

A burst of static. 'Request approved, DI Bishop. You may proceed.'

'Open the bloody door!'

Bishop backed off as the man with the battering ram took up position.

'I want to have first eyes-on, Bishop,' Holly said.

'We go in together, but you stay behind me.'

He gave the man a nod. The ram shot forward like a piston. There was sharp bang and the door came loose with a swift twist and a crash and hung off its hinges like a broken jaw. The man fell back as Bishop moved point, Holly at his heels.

Inside – complete darkness.

He flicked the light switch but it clicked uselessly.

'He's taken the bulb out,' she said. They shared a look. Snapped on latex gloves.

'Okay, everybody, listen up. I want SOCO over here and the area cordoned off, this block and the immediate others.' He handed Holly a torch. 'One room at a time.'

They both flicked on their torches and fanned out the narrow beams. Splashes of orange carpet, red walls and an empty light fixture in the ceiling.

Stepping inside. The bathroom to the left. Bishop pushed open the door. The torches flashed. Holly squinted at the beams as they dazzled the edges of a cracked mirror.

'Bishop?'

'I see it.'

The bathroom was small, cramped. Powder blue toilet, white ceramic basin. A scented candle on the shelf. Toilet paper on the floor.

Moving forward again. No stairs in this place, single storey, but bigger than Holly had anticipated. To the right, the kitchen. Old white-painted cabinets, could be plastic-coated as they shimmered in her torchbeam. Utensils scattered across the work surfaces. A saucepan on the stove, dirty and filled with old soup.

'I can smell something,' Holly said.

Bishop opened up the metal bin with his hand, shone the torch inside. A few flies buzzed free. Plastic take-out containers, eggshells and an empty baked bean tin. Bishop moved on. Opened the fridge. No light came on.

'He's even taken out this bulb. I don't like this, Bishop. I don't like this at all.'

She moved away, found herself edging back to the corridor.

'Stay with me,' Bishop said. She nodded, and saw that Jacobs and Kathy had fallen in behind her. Jacobs was swallowing hard, his eyes like saucers. Kathy was looking all around, both hands out in front of her as if she was waiting to catch something.

Bishop joined them. 'Kitchen clear.' All four of them could see the end of the corridor now. Two doors remained. One on the left. One straight ahead.

Bishop went for the left-hand door. Pushed it open six inches. She heard him flip the switch. Again nothing. He flashed the torch inside. Little pockets of yellow danced across the room. Pink paisley wallpaper. An unmade bed. Exposed mattress and the duvet on the floor. A pyjama case in the shape of a clown lying upside down on the pillow. A bedside table. A clock that didn't seem to tick and three framed photos of a young black woman in her early twenties. Tracy Jackson, Holly surmised. Wearing bright clothes that made her smile seem even brighter. In one photo she was sitting at a bar holding a cocktail in one hand and laughing hysterically, in another she was dressed as a cowboy and trying to look serious. The last photo she stood between an older couple – one white female and one black male – both in their fifties probably; it looked as though they were on a camping trip.

Bishop went around to the other side of the bed to check the wardrobe. Holly stayed put as Kathy moved next to her, her own torch arrowing across the floor and the walls. She pointed to the chest of drawers. Kathy held up her torch while Holly opened each one, her hands moving slowly over the contents. Underwear: panties and bras. T-shirts and sweats in the drawer underneath, half-burned candles, trinkets and old birthday cards in the last. *'Happy Birthday Tracy! Have a great day! Lots of love, Mum & Dad xxx'*. Holly replaced it with an almost religious reverence. She hoped Tracy would get another.

'Jacobs?' she called. 'Give me a hand with the chest of drawers. I want to move it away from the wall.' They shunted it from side to side until she could fit a hand around the back and then she asked Kathy for her torch. Shone the light. The wallpaper looked psychedelic up close and it wasn't blue now, it was a fiery red. No gaps there. No tell-tale cuts in the design.

'Holly?' Bishop was standing by the wardrobe. He pulled aside a dressing gown that was hanging from a hook in the wall. She already knew what he had discovered by the sound of his voice. His torch illuminated a neatly cut square of missing

262

wallpaper against the far wall. She tried to put the horrible thought to one side. Tried to concentrate on the task at hand but she couldn't. The darkness was suddenly stifling and she wanted out but the scenario kept playing over and over in her head.

He's done it again . . . Lights off. The girl comes home. Flick-flack with the switch. Fuse has gone. Where's the fuse box, Tracy?

The others were waiting for her. Half-hidden ghouls by the door. She joined them and they all stood for a second, collecting themselves.

The last door in the flat.

Bishop gave them a look as if to say: This is it.

She knew it had to be. Took a breath as he nudged the handle. It scuffed slowly. A thick carpet, thought Holly. Again, he tried the switch and again there was a useless click and a clack. He pushed the door all the way open and they shone their torches through. Four shafts of light criss-crossed each other like search-lights at sea. Dust motes danced. An opening act.

A sofa, two chairs, a table, a stand with a television on top, a cabinet with hard-bargained keepsakes from car-boot sales. Cheap paintings on the walls. There was an odour though. Holly got it first.

'There's that smell again,' she said.

'I know.'

'Is it the flat or—'

'I got it too,' said Kathy.

'Under the sofa first,' Bishop suggested.

Kathy and Jacobs came forward. Gingerly they each took an end of the sofa and hefted it up. Bishop lit up the carpet with his torch.

'Nothing,' Holly said. They lowered it back down. Under the chair? No, a quick search – nothing there either. They spread

263

out. Kathy tugged on the curtains but they wouldn't open.

'Sir,' she said. 'I think …' She examined the fabric at the side. 'The curtains have been glued shut. Like the letter box.'

'Doesn't want any light coming in here,' Holly whispered. 'Wants to keep us in the dark for as long as he can …'

Jacobs went to the TV and peered behind it. 'Flex has been cut. There's no plug,' he said. He was sweating.

Holly grabbed a corner of the rug under the coffee table and tried to pull it up. It was stuck fast. 'Bishop?'

He came over, hunkered down. Pulled with her. There was a crunching sound as the rug ripped free and dust and fibres zig-zagged around them like fireflies. Bishop coughed, moved away. Holly examined the carpet underneath. No tell-tale blood. She got up as the others met back in the middle of the room.

'That's it, Bishop said. 'There's nothing here.'

'There's got to be something,' Holly said.

Their nerves were frayed. 'Kathy, have SOCO bring some lights in here, extra spots and a K9.'

'You're bleeding,' Holly told him, registering a spot of misty red on his cheek.

'What?' he wiped at it irritably. Checked his ear to see if somehow he had been cut when they had ripped up the rug. There was nothing there. As if in slow motion – a tiny drop of liquid splashed on to his hand out of the darkness.

Holly froze. Looked him in the eye.

The one place they hadn't looked.

Very, very slowly she tilted her head upwards. Towards the ceiling. Bishop's torch followed her gaze. And there she was.

Tracy Jackson.

Like a massive moth, wrapped in white bedsheets stained red.

Jacobs started gagging.

'If you can't hold it in, go outside!' Bishop shouted. 'If you're going to be sick do it into your goddamn hands, but don't let any of it touch the floor! We cannot contaminate this scene. Holly?'

'I'm okay.'

But she didn't feel it and neither did Bishop. He looked white.

Thirty-one

'Tracy Jackson. Nineteen years old.'

Her photo had been tacked up with the others along the top of the incident board; a grisly parade of death on film. Bishop addressed the assembled task force but there was a pall over the men and women there this morning.

'She had recently finished her City & Guilds diploma in hospitality and catering. She wanted to be a chef with dreams of opening up her own business. So . . . same again, people. I know we are exhausted but we have to keep pushing on this, okay? This is a brand-new victim and she's the youngest so far that we know of. Nineteen bloody years old.

'Her parents are coming in this afternoon at two thirty. I don't want any photos of Tracy visible, understood? I do not want them seeing their daughter as we do. I want to make sure we have screens over the windows in here, make sure this incident room is shut off entirely. I will be speaking to them privately in my office. We will funnel them through there. Nobody talks. Keep your heads down and stay out of the bloody way. Right, you've seen the photos. Some of you were there. It wasn't pretty.' He took a breath. 'Now, we don't know for sure if this is the same killer. We have to wait for the official confirmation from Angela. She's there now, conducting a preliminary autopsy, and Holly and I will be going there straight after this. But judging from the circumstances in which the body was discovered, the link with the Pettimans' property, I think it's safe to assume it's our guy.' He seemed to flounder for a second before he found Kathy amongst the sea of faces.

'Kathy, news has already spread about this one. Young black woman. Mutilated on a run-down council estate. There is no way we can deny a link to the other murders, so the word from above is that we go public with this. We have to. The local MP is being drafted in, as is the Mayor of London, and you can expect to see the Chief Constable around these offices a lot more, starting from today. I know what you're thinking: they're only around when there's a photo op. Personally, I'm at odds with this because part of me doesn't want to give our killer the publicity, but the other part of me is trying to be realistic. There are five dead now that we know of, and if we're to stop him claiming more victims we need people to come forward with information. Since you're the one who'll be drafting the release and thrashing out the details with the legal department, do you have any thoughts on the approach we should take, Kathy?'

'I don't see we have any choice but to confirm there is a link; most of the press already know it anyway.'

'Okay fine. Keep the wallpaper connection out though. That detail will weed out the false confessions and idiots wanting their fifteen minutes. Holly, talk us through what we found there.'

'The staging of this killing was the same as the previous murders. Again, the lights were turned off and the bulbs had

267

been removed so we couldn't flick on a switch. How it was prepared and knowing the way we would search systematically from room to room with torches, it makes me believe he set this one up for us to find. The police. The people he knows are after him. As if we were the intended witnesses to his crime. We'll have to wait for Angela's full report to confirm the MO, but I expect it to be similar to the others. As with Rebecca and the Wrights, there was no CCTV in the immediate vicinity of the victim's home. So it seems more and more likely that our killer knows about police procedure. Not only that, he obviously researches the area and conducts some sort of reconnaissance beforehand. How far back this goes, I have no idea. He is meticulous in his planning and perhaps smarter than I first thought.' She glanced at Bishop to say she was done. He was leaning against the wall as if for support and looked at everybody with an expression of melancholy.

'Thank you all for coming in. I know it's stressful, we're limited on overtime as well, but I really appreciate it, as will the relatives of Rebecca, Jonathan and Evelyn.' A second as he looked them all in the eye. 'We are at the end of our tether on this one. I know we are. And I know we are all feeling it, but you are the best lot of bloody detectives and police officers I have ever worked with, so don't let this get to you – that's what he wants. Instead we keep pushing. Pushing. Until we nail the bastard.'

Meeting over.

Everybody started to move. Slowly at first but then it was as if the gears were engaging and momentum started to build. Faster, faster. Voices grew louder. The general hum of the office resumed. Bishop came away from the wall and watched them as they went about their business. As he walked past Holly he gave her a gentle nod so she followed him. She didn't know if he was right or wrong about the press release but she had to bring it up.

'He'll love it – the media attention. He'll feed off it. Want more. You can't saturate him with this. He will soak everything up like a dry sponge. He will never get full.'

'It wasn't my call.'

'I know, but—'

'Who knows, maybe he'll get cocky and make another mistake.'

'He doesn't make mistakes, Bishop.'

'You don't think giving the name of known serial killers to the estate agent was a mistake?'

'No. It was deliberate. He's playing with us now.'

Bishop turned on her. 'Playing with *you*, Holly. Not us. We would never have guessed that link. That was for you. You know that, right?'

She stared into his eyes and saw bad things so looked away. He walked ahead of her and she watched him light up a cigarette before he left the building. He smoked it in silence outside, his face a sullen mask. She could almost see his spirit faltering. She turned away and stared up at the early morning sky. It was sunny for a change but the forecast promised heavy rain and lightning for the weekend.

'You ready?' He stubbed out his cigarette.

'Yes.'

She followed him to his car.

'I am beginning to dislike this person immensely,' Angela said.

They were in the autopsy room and Tracy's body was laid out on the table, covered by a green sheet. Swan pulled it down slightly so that her head was revealed. Holly took one look and turned away. She remembered the photos in the girl's bedroom. So full of life. Now she was a sad hollow of twisted bone and red meat with one eye removed and the other white-rimmed with its lid missing.

'Three successive blows to the head. The first did the most damage and probably killed her outright, the others were purely for the hell of it, but not before he'd spent some time with her. Double strangulation and penetration – again consistent with the others. Burn marks on inner thighs, wrists slashed. The difference here is that the bleeding was pre-mortem. All the cutting would have been done while she was still alive and probably conscious.'

'Fuck,' Bishop said.

Holly felt her hands begin to tremble. She clasped them together to stop them and when that didn't work she folded them under her arms across her chest.

'She would have been fading in and out, but she was trying to defend herself as he was cutting her. There are a few defensive wounds on her hands and fingers, and blood under her nails. She may have scratched him. She put up one hell of a fight. It may not have been enough to do him any damage, but she prolonged her life for another thirty seconds or so. She was a fighter.'

A fighter, Holly thought and it broke her heart.

'How the hell could he be doing that and no one heard her screaming?' Bishop said. 'I mean, Jesus Christ . . . '

'Residual traces of duct tape on her lips, teeth and nose.' Angela took a breath and a step back as if surveying a painting. 'My best guess is: she comes in, he's already there, same as Rebecca, he surprises her, takes her through to the bedroom where he grabs the sheets. Moves into the living room. He ties her up and tapes her. Starts to cut her, she breaks loose from whatever is holding her hands—'

'Trace fibres?'

'None. But her wrists are raw from something, probably a plastic twine of some kind. He carries on cutting until he's done and then mercifully brings in the hammer. All the other activities are post-mortem. The wrist-slashing and penetration. When he's finished, he wraps her up in the sheet and glues her to the ceiling – note the scouring and chemical burns on her skin.'

'How much did she weigh?' Holly asked.

'One hundred and twenty-four pounds. Featherweight.'

'That's heavy for a single man to lift above his head and hold her up there waiting for the glue to dry.' Holly pointed out. 'Could you do that, Bishop?'

'Christ no.' A beat. 'What are you thinking? Someone else there with him?'

'Has to be.'

'Two killers?' asked Angela.

'One to help. One to kill. Or they both kill, acting in synch. They'd have to know each other well. Have spent time with each other. More time than Eagen and Richard Sickert did. Daniel and Richard would be a fit.'

'But Daniel's been cleared and Richard is currently in Bayview,' added Bishop.

Holly nodded tiredly then asked: 'How long would this have taken, Angela?'

'The way he works normally, a few minutes. But it's got to be closer to ten, maybe even fifteen to get this all done and put her up there.'

'What about the glue?' Bishop said.

'A cyanoacrylate adhesive. Industrial. Solvent-free, so it had a quick set time. And the bell . . . ' She removed the sheet in its entirety. 'Around her ankle. Tied up with a piece of blue thread by her Achilles' heel.'

'Any trace fibres?'

'Negative again. However, I think I have an answer to one of your questions. The burn marks on the inner thighs. We found traces of carbon on the bell.'

'That's what he's been using to make the marks?'

'It would appear so.' She took the bell from an adjacent bench and held it against one of the black burns. It matched perfectly.

All three of them stood for a moment, not speaking, gazing down at the body.

'Time of death?' Bishop asked

'Decomposition had already set in so at least forty-eight hours. I can be more specific later.'

'Thank you, Angela.'

'Don't thank me, Bishop. Just find him.'

They walked in subdued silence back to the incident room. Once there they sat at the same desk, both staring at the floor.

'Why do that? Why put her up there?' Bishop said.

'The last place we'd look,' Holly said. 'It's a change in the MO. An escalation. He's trying to shock us more each time.'

'He?'

'They,' she corrected herself.

Holly saw Tracy's parents first when they walked past the open door. Reginald and Alice Jackson. The two from the photo in Tracy's room. The two from the camping holiday. Holly hung her head and muttered.

'They can't ever know what happened to her.'

272

'They'll find out.' Bishop stood up and straightened his tie.

'How?'

'Because they'll ask. And I can't lie to them.'

He went to greet them and Holly watched as he ushered them into his office. She wondered what it was like. She had lost both of her parents but she wondered what it was like to lose a child. A daughter. A son. She couldn't comprehend and found herself looking away. Trying to force herself to make herself busy when there was really nothing she could do.

She got back home and called Doctor Andell.

His answer machine clicked on and she left a message; telling him she understood that Daniel was no longer a suspect but would very much like to talk to him. She could make next week. Whenever was convenient. She hung up, hoping her voice hadn't sounded too subdued, but she felt terrible as she stared at the wall above the fireplace.

She'd been an utter fool. What had she been thinking? Sign up to help with the police? Play at being a profiler. Help catch the killers that scare the normal people in the night. Cause you don't scare, Holly, do you? You don't scare at all. Because you've seen everything. You're an analyst. A sociopath detector! A collector of old nooses and stained teacups. Wow. You're really something special, aren't you? Sitting in your warm flat with your Harland Miller on the floor, preaching death and real dead faces staring at you every night from the living room wall. Judging you.

The phone rang. A text from Doctor Andell.

I'm in Wales but next Tuesday to meet Daniel would be good. Say six o'clock? I'll let him know. Text you his address. And I will arrange Richard for the following day if that suits?

She texted back.

'That's great. Thank you.'

What if this doesn't end? she suddenly thought to herself. What if he is never going to stop killing? She felt worse than she had on her first day almost two weeks ago. She had been nervous but keen, full of ideas and suggestions. Now she … What, Holly? Say it. Now she didn't have the first clue as to what was going on. One killer? Two killers? Three killers? More? This guy was not only killing his victims, he was killing everybody at the station too. And me, she admitted. Killing all of us, destroying our morale with each new victim. A rapid-fire destruction of our confidence. She closed her eyes and gave herself up to the frustration.

People are dead. More victims are waiting their turn with no knowledge of what is coming. If he kept to what he was doing, stuck to his plan – and he did have a bloody plan! – he could already have chosen his next half-dozen victims. Maybe double that. Maybe more.

The case had opened her eyes. She hadn't seen everything and she knew that now.

And she also saw that this was only the beginning.

Thirty-two

Holly and Bishop were in a beautifully kept Grade II listed Georgian building at Brompton Barracks in Chatham, Kent. A British Army base which had originally been built to defend Chatham Dockyard but now formed part of the headquarters of the Royal School of Military Engineering.

They walked beside Brigadier Collins, a fifty-year-old army lifer, who wore his scars with pride. He had met them at the main reception and now led them through a warren of pale corridors. Bishop's limp grew more pronounced as he struggled to keep up.

'I'm sorry I can't be of more help, Detective Inspector, but some personnel files are classified for a reason.'

'I was hoping you would have been more cooperative than this,' said Bishop.

'Calling in a favour? I get it. And normally I would jump at the chance to help you, but this particular individual isn't exactly a beacon for army life.'

'What did he do?'

Collins turned a corner and stopped. The moment Bishop had caught up he started to walk again. Two men in uniform saluted him as he passed, then the brigadier entered his office. He was saluted by a private who stood to the left of the door and exited when waved away. Holly and Bishop entered and Collins poured himself a coffee and sat down behind his desk. He motioned them to sit with a certain civility, despite the scowl on his face.

'Even if I could look at the files, it would take months before we could de-classify them. And once they're de-classified they become part of what's called the public domain and that opens up a whole can of pain.'

'It doesn't have to become public,' Holly said.

'Miss Wakefield—'

'Holly. Please.'

Barely a nod. 'Holly. No disrespect to you, but you're working directly with the police on this – correct?'

'Yes.'

'Excluding our mutual friend here, I'm not too impressed with the relationship between the police and the press, if you don't mind me saying.' A stony look. 'I don't know you. Therefore I don't trust you.'

She smiled wryly. Took an 8 x 10 photo from the folder she was carrying and handed it over. It was an autopsy photo of Reise.

'Our pathologist says he was hit on the head with a hammer, then strangled, mutilated and eviscerated. That's disembowelled—'

'I know what it means.'

'He'd been shoved in a sewer for over a month before we got lucky and found him.'

Collins shrugged and laid the photo on his desk. 'You think this photo shocks me? I've been in Afghanistan and Iraq for the best part of twenty years and I've seen corpses that look a whole lot worse than this. And some of them were men that I knew. Friends even.'

Holly leaned forward, almost pleading.

'It's not just men who have been killed; there are women too, and this killer doesn't do things quickly with a bullet. These are long drawn-out affairs that include sexual assault and torture. He is a sadistic sociopath who doesn't give a damn. He's killed a retired doctor and his wife, an air hostess named Rebecca and now a nineteen-year-old woman called Tracy Jackson. We know he killed Corporal Reise and I'm hoping we can stop him before he kills someone else. And you're right, this isn't the Middle East. Maybe you look at that photo and don't see what I see. Well, forgive my naivety, but I still see a madman on the loose – and it's our job to stop him.'

There was a knock at the door.

'Enter.'

The private was back.

'Sir, Major Welton would like to see you.'

'Tell him I'm on my way.' Collins watched him go, watched the door shut, then turned back to Holly, who was struggling to keep her composure.

'Look, I'm not asking you to give out information that would compromise national security,' she said.

'You don't know that.'

'No, you're right. Maybe Corporal Reise tried to assassinate the prime minister or was selling secrets to the Russians. If that's the case, I don't want to know about it. But I believe he may have been targeted because of something that happened to him while he was in the army.'

'And you base this on ...?'

'A hunch. His body wasn't like the others,' she said simply. 'The rest of the victims had been displayed where people would find them. Where they would shock. Corporal Reise was hidden away in a sewer pipe. I don't think the killer wanted him found.'

'You're a profiler, yes?'

'Yes. I look at the victims and see how or why—'

'I know what you do, Holly. It's pretty simple. There are good guys and there are bad guys.'

'And which are you, Brigadier?'

'That depends which end of my gun you're facing.'

She smiled at that and then came clean. 'And we've got nothing else.'

'Playing a hunch,' Collins mused. He sat upright. Turned to Bishop.

'Read your file. Three tours. Two commendations. A DSO. Had a good career ahead of you.'

'Still do.'

'Yes. Sorry about what happened.' He took a breath. 'What's the hunch then?'

'Why wasn't Reise ever promoted?'

Collins stared at him for a long time before reaching over to his right and opening a drawer. He pulled out a thick folder and placed it on his desk.

'I have to go for a meeting now, Detective Inspector Bishop. I will be gone for precisely five minutes. Judging from the fact that you are hampered by an injury to your leg, it may take you four and a half minutes to vacate my office. I suggest it's four and a half minutes well spent.' He almost smiled as he got up and left the room. 'The copy machine's low on ink, so choose wisely.'

*

278

Bishop was driving back to the station.

Crisp morning light reflected the drizzle across the windscreen as they approached the A289 and began to cross the River Medway. The traffic was sparse but it was denser up ahead. Holly read from the file on her lap.

'Reise's unit was based in East Germany, concentrated in the North Rhine-Westphalia. The HQ for the EOD was at Bielefeld. He was in a specialist unit responsible for counter-terrorist bomb disposal, and recovery and safe disposal of conventional munitions.'

'How long was he there for?'

'Five years, until 1990 when he came back to the UK.'

'When was he listed for promotion?'

'In 1989.'

'Okay, so . . .'

'There are black lines through all of this. A lot of it has been redacted, but hold on . . . ' She turned a page. 'The brigadier has given us copies of some of the originals as well.' She kept reading, more to herself but then she came across a footnote at the bottom of one page.

'Here we go: "Memorandum 7419. Page 103."' She turned to the appropriate page. '"For the attention of Major Anthony Willings. Section 17. Date: 25 June 1989. Subject: Brian Reise."' She flipped the page. '"Loss of seniority (for an officer), or reduction in rank (for a warrant officer or non-commissioned officer) is thereby imposed upon Corporal Reise. He will also be detained in a unit guardhouse, or at the Military Corrective Training Centre, for ninety days from the day of the findings of the jury."'

'The jury?'

'He was obviously on trial for something. "Corporal Reise will be required to carry out extra drill work and is issued with a loss of entitlement to leave. Corporal Reise shall also be fined up to and including twenty-eight days' pay."'

'That's quite severe,' Bishop said.

She flicked past a few more blacked-out pages then stopped and shot a look at Bishop. 'Not when you hear what he'd done,' she said. 'The army had good reason to make Reise's file classified. In 1989 he was accused of setting off a car bomb that killed four people.'

'What?'

'May 15, 1989. The bomb was a homemade IED that Reise had constructed himself in the workshop at his barracks. Comprised of Semtex-H that had been smuggled back from Libya. The bomb exploded and the car was blown off the Johannistal Bridge in Germany and into the river below. They never recovered the bodies.' She paused a moment, took a breath. 'A military lawyer and two military policemen were killed alongside a young private.' She turned another page. 'Reise was arrested and charged with four counts of murder. But his trial only lasted two weeks – August 7–21 . . . '

'The same dates marked out in his diary—'

' . . . Because the jury found him not guilty through lack of evidence. He was, however, demoted and had to face the fines and penalties listed previously. Reise appealed the decision in 1990 and petitioned the Summary Appeal Court where the charge was re-heard by a Judge Advocate and a warrant officer. Nearly all charges were upheld and he was re-posted back to England. He only ever achieved the rank of corporal, even though he served until his retirement in 2013.'

'But who did he kill?'

'Hold on . . . '

She flipped through another ten pages, all of it blacked out.

Another page turned. 'Here we go. The victims were all British officers serving in the army. The first was a lawyer called Nathan Scopes. From Brighton, specialised in military law and was hired by the army legal service to defend army personnel when they were being prosecuted.'

'Okay.'

'Next up are the two military policemen. They were actually brothers. Marcus and Alan Potter. Marcus was twenty-nine, Alan twenty-seven. From Guernsey originally. Joined the military police after a stint in the Met. Both had wives and a child each.'

'They were policemen?'

'Yes.'

'Who was the last guy?'

Holly turned the page and her breath stuck in her throat.

'Jesus . . .'

'What?'

'The last victim. The young private was Wilfred Sickert.'

'Sickert?'

'Yes.' She glanced over at Bishop, eyes wide. 'Wilfred Sickert. Richard's older brother.'

'I didn't even know he had a brother.'

'Wilfred helped to raise him when he was a child. Doctor Andell told me he had been killed in Germany, he thought it was a car accident but . . .'

'This was no accident.'

'No.

'According to his bio, Wilfred joined the army in 1989. He was in the London Regiment of the Infantry. Stationed in Bielefeld with Reise's unit. They obviously knew each other.'

'So out of the four in the car, which one did Reise want to kill and why?'

She carried on reading. Skimming through the court transcripts until ... 'The car that Reise blew up was on its way to the military court in Bielefeld. Wilfred Sickert had just failed a psych evaluation and was being taken there to be charged with the murder of a young woman on 23 April that year.'

'Who?'

'Reise's fiancé. A young woman called Mina Osterly.'

'Mina. The woman in the photo ...'

There was a silence in the car as the information sank in. Holly was joining the dots in her head but it was Bishop who summed it up.

'Brian Reise is engaged to Mina. Wilfred murders her. He's about to go to trial but Brian Reise gets to him first and kills him.' A pause. 'Then twenty years later Reise ends up dead in a sewer pipe.'

'Yes.'

'Jesus.' He banged the steering wheel with his hand. 'How the hell does that help us?'

'Reise knew Wilfred. Wilfred is dead. Now Reise is dead. That just leaves Richard in the equation and he's locked up and we've got logs and CCTV to prove he was there when the murders took place.'

'One step forward. Two steps back.'

'It clarifies a couple of things,' Holly said.

'What? That both Wilfred and his brother Richard were psychos?'

'Yes. Two brothers – both killers – highly improbable but not impossible. Richard was diagnosed as a sociopath at his trial and Wilfred failed his psych evaluation after raping and killing Mina. We have the Menendez brothers who killed their parents in 1989. Anthony and Nathaniel Cook, brothers from

Ohio, who killed at least nine people between 1973 and 1981. We can go way back to the Harpe brothers from—

'Holly?'

'Yes?'

'Again. How the hell does it help us?'

'I don't know.'

A sullen silence between them. They stopped at a roundabout and Bishop unwound the window and lit up. He suddenly turned to her.

'Where was Brian Reise first stationed before he was sent overseas?'

Holly went back through the file again. 'Aldershot.'

'Aldershot,' Bishop said quietly.

'Why?'

'It's a long shot – but Richard Sickert's second victim, Rudy Esters. That's where she was based, right?'

'Of course. The tattoo artist.'

Thirty-three

They had contacted Rudy's old boyfriend, Aaron Esters, and he had been happy to send them all the old boxes and files containing Rudy's drawings and tattoos.

'You can borrow 'em, but I want them back, mind.' There had been a bite to his tone when Holly had spoken to him. 'They were hers. Still are hers, if you know what I mean.'

She promised to take care of them and when three large boxes arrived that afternoon by courier, she and Bishop commandeered a separate office and pulled off the yellowed tape that sealed them. All were filled with coloured tattoo drawings and prints, black-and-white sketches and designs. The boxes were divided into three separate piles and now sheets of tattoos were spread across a table and two chairs, with the rest on the floor and in binders by Holly's feet.

'Appointment books, designs – we've got everything here,' she said.

Rudy had worked as an artist for over twenty years and there had been another five artists at the studio. Thousands of designs, some original, some transfers, it really was needle-in-a-haystack time. They both started going through the boxes and it was hard not to get distracted. The artwork was incredible and because Aaron had put them away they were still in remarkable condition and the colours were pristine.

Holly could tell that a lot of Rudy's clients had been from the army. Many of her designs had military themes; a line of soldiers in shadow with the phrase '*lest we forget*' written underneath, skeletons holding helmets and automatic rifles, fields of poppies, '*death before dishonour*', etc. She thought of her own tattoo and the group of girls who had all had it done together on the same day and allowed herself a small smile. She missed them. The Sisterhood, they used to call each other. Seven girls who had been close. Close in life, close in death, they used to say to each other and she marvelled at how morbid they had been at the time.

The Blessed Home reunion was tonight. She so wanted to go. But part of her knew she couldn't. Not now. Not with this looming ahead of her. After this is over, she thought. After this is done and dusted. After they are either caught or dead. Then and only then will I start to reconnect. To take more care of myself. Try to—

'Got one here,' Bishop announced.

She looked up. He was elbow-deep in a wire-bound book. 'An appointment to see Rudy on 12 May 1986. His name is Brian but no last name.' Holly started searching through the files at her feet.

'What time was the appointment?'

'Three thirty,' he said.

'What day was that?'

'Christ knows.'

'They're listed as days rather than dates in this folder.' She switched to another and fanned through the pages. 'Here we go: 1986. May. Tenth … eleventh … twelfth. Brian … No. Brian Tennyson his name was.' She picked up the sketch – a tattoo of a naked woman sitting astride a tank – flashed it to Bishop and put it back in the stack.

'Semper Fi, my friend.'

She put the pictures down and turned her attention to the appointment books. Each year had four or five books so there were dozens of different volumes to look through. She lugged half of them over to Bishop. 'Do you want another coffee?'

'No.' A dry smile. 'My mouth is so numb I could drink a lava lamp.' He checked his watch. 'After six. You're on the strong stuff now, right?'

'My mistress the cocoa bean.'

'What's that about? Sugar fix? What?'

'It's my go-to drink. When I was at Blessed Home, Maureen would always make me a hot chocolate at six o'clock. I liked routine when I was that age. Mine had been ripped away so I needed something else. Six o'clock every night I'd get my hot chocolate. Something I looked forward to. Something that I've kept going to this day.'

'Every night.'

'Most nights. Yes.'

He smiled again then held up a sheet of paper with the Royal Engineers logo. 'No name on this one but the same design.'

'Date?'

'12 October 1987, 3.20 p.m.'

'12 October 1987.' She found one of the folders for 1987 and flicked through the sketches. She stopped at October and pulled out a file of drawings and went through them slowly. 'Some of them aren't numbered, this is a nightmare. Twelfth, right?'

'Yes.'

She carried on looking through the names. All the appointments were handwritten and a lot of the ink had run and blurred on the pages; coffee-cup rings, tears – they weren't the easiest things to read. Then she found it. 'Here we go. RE Design – 3.20 p.m. Client name Julian Walters.' She lowered the book, disappointed. Took a second. 'Rudy and Brian Reise were killed ten years apart. So if there is a connection between them, what does it even prove?'

'I don't know,' admitted Bishop. 'Is it normal – there's me using that word again – is it normal for victims of serial killers to have known each other?'

'No. Family members, obviously, but we can discount that in this case.' She screwed her face up in thought. Sipped her drink, stared at Bishop, shook her head then stared back at him.

'What?' He took a second. 'Come on. Tell me what you're thinking.'

'Okay.' She gathered herself. 'The man who killed Jonathan and Evelyn, maybe he's not a copycat after all. Maybe he's the original killer.'

'Go on.'

'This guy could have been active back in the eighties, nineties, stopped for whatever reason, possibly because he was in prison, and then Richard Sickert started copying him in 2007. Was put away and now this original guy is back and killing again.'

'It's possible, I guess.'

'So we need to look at unsolved cases before 2007.'

'Going back what? Twenty? Thirty years?' he asked.

'Yes.'

'I mean, that's before my time even. I was stationed in

287

Reading until '95. A whole different set of staff as well who worked this area. Different DIs, chiefs, sergeants. Different coroners.'

'That would explain why we've found no record of similar crimes, Bishop. We've only gone back ten years. Who was the coroner for the Met then? Maybe that's the best place to start.'

'There must have been a dozen or so coroners over those years. Andrea Muster was here when I first started. Sanjay Kapoor, he's still around I think. Demitri Christos, I think he died last year. I don't know Holly. Ronald Anderson was around for a long time.'

'He did the Sickert cases back in 2007. Could you put me in touch with him?'

'I'll get on it.'

She took a breath. 'I mean, I know it's far-fetched but . . . '

'Far-fetched? Jesus . . . Can I get a unicorn with that rainbow?'

She suddenly laughed out loud. So loud and harsh it sounded like a gunshot. And it made Bishop jump. And that made him laugh. And then they couldn't stop. It was as if a pressure valve had been released and everything was coming out through their mouths. She realised they were both so tired they were heading towards hysteria but there was something beautiful about it. Staring at each other. Reliving that moment. Replaying the stupid phrase he had thrown at her again and again in her head. Intimate. Childish. They both stopped after a while and Holly wiped away the tears from her eyes. 'Oh God, I needed that. Seriously. Thank you.'

'Better than sex.'

She laughed again. 'I wouldn't know.'

'That's just sad,' he said, and they laughed some more.

There was a knock at the door. Crane poked his head around. He looked bewildered at the pair of them.

'Everything all right, sir?'

'Yes, Sergeant. Letting off a bit of steam.'

'Right. Kathy needs to see you about the press release.'

'Oh Christ. I didn't realise the time.'

He rubbed his eyes like an old bear and placed the appointment books back on the table. 'Holly, I have to go to a meeting. Why don't we call it a night?'

'Sure. I'll take these home with me, if that's all right?'

'Call me if you find anything.'

'Oh,' an after-thought just before the door closed. 'I got a text from Doctor Andell. He wants me to meet Daniel next Tuesday at 6.00 p.m.'

'Tuesday?' Bishop took a moment. 'Um ... Okay. Sergeant Crane. Do you fancy a jaunt down to a holiday cottage Tuesday evening near the sea?'

'Sounds perfect. Do they do a good breakfast?'

'Easy tiger,' Bishop smiled.

'Six o'clock,' said Holly. 'I'll meet you down there.'

When Bishop and Crane left it suddenly it felt very quiet. She stayed for another few minutes and then began to lag herself. She yawned and went back into the incident room. It was empty and felt cold. More photos had been added to the board. A kaleidoscope of battered bodies and damaged souls. A phone rang unanswered from somewhere. She tried to find it but couldn't and realised it was in another room. She wanted to leave but she couldn't yet. The answers were there right in front of her, right in front of them but they couldn't see it. Can't see the forest because of the trees.

The empty piece of paper.

Still with no name and no photo.

When Kathy left Bishop's office after the meeting he was ready to curl up and go to sleep on the sofa. He'd done it before and it wasn't that bad. You smelled a bit funky in the morning but they had showers and he had a fresh uniform in his locker if he needed it.

The press release looked fine. Kathy had worked her balls off and he had told her so. Damage limitation, because he knew he was going to come under fire for this one. Five murders. How many more? He wasn't in the best of moods when Ambrose knocked and came into his office.

'I'm about to go home, Sergeant. What is it?' Bishop waved him in and then looked up expectantly when nothing was forthcoming.

'What?'

'Not sure quite how to say this.'

'Just say it.'

'It's about Holly.' He took a second. 'I did as you asked. A bit of background. Well, actually I went a little deeper than that because it was hard to find anything, but—'

'Jesus Christ, Sergeant, it's like pulling teeth with you sometimes.'

'Well, for starters Holly's not her real name.'

Bishop put down the press release. 'What do you mean?'

'Her real name is Jessica.'

'Jessica?'

'Yes, sir. Holly's her middle name.'

'Okay, so she goes by her middle name. My father did that.'

'No, but her last name is different too. It's not Wakefield, it's Ridley.'

'Jessica Ridley?'

'Yes, sir. Jessica Holly Ridley. And Jessica Holly Ridley has a criminal record.'

'What charges?' Bishop raised his voice. 'Sergeant?'

Ambrose squirmed.

'Attempted murder, sir.'

Thirty-four

Holly knocked on Bishop's door.

'Come in.'

She entered and shot him a quick smile.

'Morning.'

He smiled back but it was weak. She wondered if he'd missed his coffee. She was in a good mood. She had been up early and determined to find the link between Reise and Rudy. At six o'clock she had.

'There you go.' She placed a copy of the appointment page on his desk, along with the RE logo. 'Reise had an appointment with Rudy on 9 April 1987. Ten a.m. sharp and he paid in cash. They knew each other. I don't know how it helps yet, but—'

'Good. Well done.' He picked up the piece of paper, glanced at it and then put it down. 'Take a seat, Holly.'

She did. He was preoccupied, tidying things on his desk, which made her feel a little apprehensive. She tried to break the ice.

'I feel like I'm back at school in the headmaster's office. Have I done something wrong?'

Bishop took his time and fixed his eyes on her. Clear and intense this morning; maybe he had had his coffee. She suddenly felt herself wilting.

And then he took her breath away.

'Morning, Jessica.'

After the bomb had exploded there was the inevitable silence.

The aftermath. The awkwardness. Thirty seconds passed and Holly suddenly needed a hot drink, or was it simply something that she could wrap her hands around to stop her wringing them together? No drink, so she sat on her hands instead.

'I couldn't tell you. I'm . . . ' she started.

'You have a file with the National Crime Agency. About ninety-nine per cent of it has been redacted and I don't have clearance to get in there. I don't think the Chief does either. All I know is that Holly is not your real name and you have been charged at some point in time with attempted murder.'

'Yes.'

'Okay.'

She nodded. She was trying to read him but it was hard. There was shock there, but something else, a weariness. An inevitability. She couldn't tell.

'Who else knows?' she asked.

'Sergeant Ambrose at the moment. He found out, but I can't keep this a secret, Jessica.'

'Please don't call me that. It's Holly.'

'Right.' Bishop nodded. He was playing it so safe. Kid gloves, and she was grateful for that.

'Do you want . . . ' she stuttered. 'I mean, can I . . . Can we not talk here?'

'I can't leave. Um ... I have a meeting in an hour. There's so much going on ... '

'Of course. Stupid.' Pause. 'Am I off the case?'

'I don't know. I need to know what exactly happened and why. It's not ... if the press got hold of this ... Were you ever prosecuted?'

'No.'

'Did it ever get to a trial?'

'No.' So far so good. Keep the gloves on, Bishop.

'Okay.' He weighed his words carefully. 'I think you had better start at the beginning.'

'Right.' She nodded. She looked at him. Looked away. Giving herself more time to deal with what she was about to say. This is a first, Holly. Here we go. Just say it.

'I lied to you.'

'You did?'

'Yes.'

'What about?'

'My parents.'

'They didn't die in a sailing accident?'

'No, they didn't.' And then suddenly she realised she wasn't scared any more. If she was going to tell her darkest secret, she couldn't think of anyone better to share it with than DI Bishop. What was that old saying? Look before you leap. She turned it on its head. Leap before you look. Jump out of the plane, Holly. Jump without the parachute and enjoy the freefall.

'His name was Sebastian Carstairs.'

'Who?'

'The man I tried to kill.'

'Carstairs?' he sat back slightly. It was jogging something. 'I know that name.'

'You'll know him from the name the press gave him. "The Animal".'

'Jesus.' Bishop shook his head, his eyes wide.

'He had killed seventeen people so far. My parents were numbers eighteen and nineteen.' She sat very still, watching his reactions. His eyes had narrowed, he was hardly breathing.

'It was a school day. I was supposed to walk home with my best friend Jenny. She was meant to be coming for a sleepover, but for some reason her mother said no – I never found out why – so she wasn't with me. I opened the front door, said "Hi", dropped my bag on the hall floor and walked into the living room. My brother should have been home by then and normally when I came back the first thing he did was run out and pull faces at me or pinch me . . . but he didn't this time. I walked into the kitchen. It was always the best room in our house. My mum was a great cook. My dad would help her and they made a great team. It was always warm in there and it smelled of herbs and sugar.

'I opened the door – it was a sliding door – and I saw them. Both of them, hacked to death with a knife and a meat cleaver. And then I saw a man. Standing above their bodies. Him. He turned and looked at me. There was nothing . . . there was nothing about him. I didn't understand what was going on. I could see what had happened in front of me, but I could not comprehend, could not understand what I was looking at. And my parents . . . it was my mother and father in this most brilliant painting in red. And the white linoleum floor. In the kitchen. My father's eyes were open but his head was . . . he had been decapitated. And my mother, she was bent over the kitchen table, she had the knife sticking up out of her back between her shoulders. I found out later he had penetrated

295

her heart all the way through, through the rear ribs, past her lungs and into her heart. She'd died almost instantly, thank God. My father had had a slower death. That was the way he worked. It was what Animal wanted and whatever Animal wanted he got.

'I was rooted to the spot. Time stopped. I felt as though I was there for twenty minutes. I thought he was going to kill me. I wanted him to kill me. I had all these images in my head and I didn't know what to do, so I froze. I literally froze. And then I wet myself. I was conscious of it running down my leg, warm and yellow into my white socks. It was all I could think of. I could feel the heat on my leg, on my inner thigh, as I watched him slowly turn to me. And he pulled a clean knife from the rack and walked towards me. And I thought, this is it – he's going to kill me. What shall I do? But I didn't do anything. I just stood there. My hands clenched together. Fingers twitching. And he put the knife up to my throat and looked at me. He kissed me on the forehead very slowly and said:

'"I've seen things you haven't."

'Then he walked out of the room. And that was it. I think I must have stood there for another twenty minutes. Unable to move, unable to react. I wasn't even sure if he was behind me. I didn't hear him leave the house. I didn't hear the door close. Looking at the remains of my mother and father. On the floor in their brand-new kitchen. Then all of a sudden I thought – my brother! I had to find him. I couldn't see him and he should have been home. I looked around the kitchen but there was so much blood. And then I heard a noise behind me. I thought Animal had come back, but . . . one of the kitchen cabinet doors slowly opened and my brother was in there. White-faced. He'd been sick over himself. Trembling. He'd seen everything.'

'What happened then?'

'Animal was caught two days later. Part of me felt afterwards that he wanted to be caught. He wanted it to stop. I liked to think somehow that whatever he saw in my eyes – the horror that he saw in my young eyes – made him stop. But I was kidding myself. He wasn't caught because of me, though he deliberately allowed himself to be caught. He was getting tired of the incompetence of the police. He wanted the recognition he felt he deserved. He wanted the public to know who he was. For them to know that he lived up to the nickname the press had given him. He was the Animal. The killer who turned up on people's doorsteps and killed everyone inside. So he was caught two days later and he was charged with the murder of nineteen people. It went to trial within six months and on the day I had to give my testimony I went with my family liaison officer – Patty Youngborn from Forest Hill. They wanted me to sit behind a screen so that I wouldn't see him, the trauma would be too much. But I didn't want that. I wanted to see him. Wanted to try to figure him out. Wanted him to make eye contact with me. To look at me. To say something. React in some way. But I don't think he even knew who I was. I don't think he even noticed me.

'So I sat in that box as I testified and I watched him and I watched the lawyers. The defence lawyers said he was insane and while the prosecution presented their case he sat in the dock and did nothing. He didn't smile. He didn't laugh. He sat cross-legged with his hands over his knees, his head back, his eyes closed most of the time, as if he was meditating. As if he was listening – but he wasn't. He was listening in that room but mentally he was somewhere else. Maybe he had transported himself somewhere, I don't know. After two days of deliberation, the jury said they had reached a decision and were all called back in. My foster parents told me that he had been found guilty and that sentencing would take place the following afternoon. On that day I ran away from home and went to the courtroom. I managed to smuggle a fruit knife into the courtroom in my sock. It was the smallest knife I could find at the foster home. And I had been practising for months.'

'Practising?'

'Cutting, Bishop. Stabbing. On fruit and then on bits of wood I found in the garden. I broke three knives in my training, but I felt that by the time that day had come I was strong enough and skilled enough to do it. I researched anatomy. I took out books from the library. I always thought the heart was to the left of someone's chest. It's not, you know. It's way more central than you think and then you have to take the ribcage into account. The sternum. It's a flat bone, like a tie, and then there's the ribs. I counted all the ribs. Had to take them into consideration too. Because if you hit the sternum or a rib, the knife's not going through. It will bounce off and do nothing. So you have to go between the ribs to hit the heart. Between numbers two and three from the top of the left-hand side below the clavicle. In what's called the second intercostal space. It's very precise. So when I was watching him in that courtroom, when I gave my testimony, I was drawing his ribs on to his chest. I was sketching where his heart would be in my mind. Counting it beat. There. Between the intercostals. The aortic valve. The living, pumping valve that kept him breathing, kept him walking, kept him alive.'

She managed to take a breath. Her mouth was dry and she needed water. She felt as though she could sense a coldness growing inside of Bishop. Spreading into his eyes.

'I wasn't sure when I was going to be able to do it but, as luck would have it, his defence lawyers organised a press conference before the verdict and the Animal was deliberately led past the reporters so they could get that prize-winning shot. As he was being jostled and hurried past the clicking cameras I walked straight up to him and took out the knife. I raised it above my head and then, for some reason, I hesitated – I can't remember why – and maybe that changed everything. But then I ran forward and stabbed him in the heart. It was so quick. Beautifully timed. There was no alarm in his face, that was the strangest thing. It was almost as if he had been expecting it. I let go of the handle of the knife and it stayed lodged in his chest, between ribs number three and four, according to the surgeon who took it out of him afterwards. He lowered himself gently to the ground as if he were going to bed and I felt hands grab me and try to pull me away, but he wouldn't let them. He had somehow got a grip of my sleeve and pulled me closer to him. Pulled me nice and close and whispered in my ear:

'"I've been waiting for you, Jessica. I've been waiting."'

'Then he let go of me, and as I fell back bodies swarmed over me and carried me away. But it wasn't as if I wanted to run. I was quite content to be tried for murder. Quite content to meet my fate there and then. I didn't care. All I wanted was for him to pay for what he had done.

'He was six hours in surgery. Six centimetres lower and I would have severed his aortic valve and killed him outright. But I didn't. He lived and survived. He's now serving nine life sentences in Broadmoor. The Crown Court wanted to charge me with attempted murder. My lawyer pleaded down to attempted manslaughter, but because of the extenuating circumstances and the judge's compassion the case was thrown out of court.'

'What were the extenuating circumstances?'

'I was ten years old at the time.'

'Ten? Jesus . . .' She could see him struggling.

'And the fact that both my parents had been victims, and then . . . Sebastian himself.'

'What about him?'

'He refused to press charges. He said he understood my desire. The Crown Prosecution Service had no alternative but to drop the charges due to the mitigating circumstances and me being a minor. Because of my age, the court transcripts were sealed. It was deemed better for me to be given a new identity. Witness protection, of sorts. That's how I became Holly Wakefield.'

Bishop sat in stunned silence for a full minute. Holly watched him, wanting something from him. A flicker of understanding. Anything. But nothing came.

'What . . . I mean, what do I call you?' was all he managed.

'Holly. That's my name. I haven't been Jessica for twenty-seven years. She doesn't exist any more.'

He said nothing but carried on looking at her. Unblinking.

'So what happens now?' she asked.

'What do you mean?'

'Well, you know who I am. So does Sergeant Ambrose. What will you do?'

'I don't know. I honestly don't know yet. Legally, I'm not sure . . . I need to think.'

'I don't want other people to know. I don't want to lose who I am.'

'You have the right to anonymity. That's not an issue. I'll need to tell the Chief though.'

'I understand.'

A moment of stillness.

'I'm sorry. I lied to you about the sailing accident. I lied. I'm so sorry.'

And then he reached over and took her hand.

Thirty-five

It was early afternoon and the station was almost empty.

They hadn't said much more after their conversation. Bishop had asked for privacy as he made some phone calls and Holly had spent the rest of the day in the incident room with the rest of the task force. She had found it hard to concentrate and she became paranoid that everybody in the office knew what was going on. That they knew about her. They didn't, of course. She knew Bishop would keep his word, but it was hard to stay upbeat. She had stared at the incident board for most of the day but instead of Evelyn and Jonathan up there she now saw images of her parents. Butchered. Bloody. Horribly dead. A bitter tide swelled inside her. Anger. Keep it in check, Holly. Bury it. Murderers to the left of me, killers to the right. Here I am. Stuck in the middle of me.

She had been asked by Crane to go and see the Chief and now she sat outside his office. Bishop had been in there for forty-five minutes and Sam Gordon had gone inside ten minutes ago. She played out the various scenarios in her head. Scenario One: she was off the case. The Chief couldn't have anybody with an attempted murder charge working alongside the task force, regardless of the circumstances. If the press got hold of the story there would be a public outcry and an independent investigation. What would happen to her? She would be fired from the college. That much was obvious. Wetherington might be different. Judy Olsen knew the truth, but Max Carrington didn't and she could picture him salivating at her demise. Scenario Two; nothing had changed. She would still be working on the case. Chief Franks would be none the wiser. They would continue to track down the killer and her past would be shielded from everyone at the station. Scenario Three—

The door opened. Bishop stuck his head out.

'Come in, Holly.' He wasn't smiling.

She entered the office. It was big. Twice the size of Bishop's. Franks was behind his desk and gave her a half smile but didn't move from his seat. Gordon was by the window, leaning against the blinds. He was reading a report and didn't look up.

'Take a seat, please,' Franks instructed. So she did and Bishop sat next to her. That felt comforting. She felt as though they were on the same side.

'Quite a few events have happened in the last twelve hours ... ' Franks leaned forward. 'Wanted to bring you up to speed.'

'Okay. Good,' said Holly.

'Let's get to the meat of it first, I think. Sam? The report, please.'

Gordon pulled himself from the window and handed Franks the sheet of paper. He skimmed it, as if for reassurance, handed it back to Gordon and turned to Holly.

'Angela Swan has been busy and has come up with what we like to call the coup de grâce. A piece of DNA evidence that was extracted from under one of Tracy Jackson's fingernails. A strand of hair.' And he smiled. 'A strand of hair that matches David Eagen's DNA.'

Shell-shocked didn't even come near.

'David Eagen. Rapist. Now a killer.' Franks cleared his throat. 'The Commissioner has no doubts about this and the CPS are looking at the evidence as we speak and will be coming to a decision any minute now. I am convinced they will back us up. We also have the address of a second garage where Eagen worked through another PAYE number he was claiming from. He was there last week according to sources, so we will be paying them a visit as soon as we get the warrant. We hope to have him in custody by tonight.'

Holly shot a look at Bishop then at Gordon.

'David Eagen . . . '

'You okay?' Bishop asked.

'Yes.' It wasn't really a lie. She felt okay inside, she just couldn't understand what was going on. 'David Eagen isn't the killer though.'

'Yes, he is, Holly.' This from Gordon. He had his arms folded, head angled to one side. He handed a file to Holly. It had *Bayview Confidential* typed on the front.

'Eagen spent a week at Bayview last month after he tried to strangle a prostitute. His Psychopathy Check List score was off the charts. "A man predisposed to violence and sexual humiliation. It is only a matter of time before he takes the next step and murder is added to his agenda." End quote.' Gordon took a second. 'Everything points to him, Holly. Everything.'

Chief Franks' phone rang. He snapped it up. Listened. Shot Bishop a look.

'That was the CPS. We're on. We appreciate all you've done, Miss Wakefield, but Sam will be taking over from here.'

There was a long and painful silence before Holly finally got up and walked unsteadily to the door. Bishop stood up. It looked as if he wanted to say something but didn't. Holly stopped and turned.

'You're wrong,' she said.

'Thank you, Miss Wakefield. That will be all.' Franks went back to his half smile. She glanced briefly at Gordon who stood watching her, the report still clenched tightly in his hand.

'Come on! You saw him puke up when he saw the photos! He didn't do it.'

'I can't ignore the evidence.'

She was in Bishop's office, pacing in front of his desk.

'Domination. Manipulation. Control.'

'What?'

'It's what he's doing. The killer. Or killers. Not just the victims, he's doing it to us as well. Domination. Manipulation. Control. This is all him. This is everything.'

'Holly, you have to take a step back. You have to look at—'

'No, you don't! It's not him. I'm telling you now: Eagen did not kill Tracy, Rebecca, Evelyn or Jonathan.'

'Then who did?'

'I don't know. That's the bloody problem – I have no clue.'

'We have to arrest Eagen. We have to bring him in.'

'Jesus Christ.'

'Sam thinks it's him. He wants him—'

'Yes, but Sam wants him for the wrong reasons. You know that. Yes, I think it was probably Eagen who was responsible

for the acid attack on Janine. I think that was him. But there's
no way he's the killer.'

'I trust you, Holly, I do.'

'Then why didn't you back me up in there?'

'Because I can't. Not in the face of that evidence. You get
me some different evidence, fine. We've got his DNA under the
dead girl's fingernail. It doesn't get any better than that!' He
rounded on her and their faces were inches apart. She could
see the lines by his mouth, the tiredness in his eyes. He shook
his head softly and backed away.

'All the evidence, everything points to him. It's—'

'Too convenient for me.'

'Oh really? You're talking about planting evidence now?'

'No, I'm not—'

'Come on. Enough. The CPS have said we have an airtight case.'

'It's not over.'

'Holly, drop it.'

'No, I'm not done—'

'You're a volunteer. I called you, remember?'

She sighed. Knew she was beat.

'Am I officially off the case?'

He took his time but nodded.

'That's not fair. You know it.'

'There's nothing I can do.'

'There's more than one killer, Bishop.'

There was a long silence but she could hear him breathing.

'I told the Chief,' he said slowly. 'About you.'

'What did he say?'

'Less than you might expect. Said the past should stay
sealed. Always. And he would do everything in his power to

protect your anonymity if it ever came up. He knows how valuable you've been to this case.'

A sudden thought. 'Then let me still go and see Daniel Tuesday night. Interview him. Sergeant Crane is—"

'Yes, I know. Meeting you there.'

'I still think he could help with the investigation. This isn't over.'

Bishop paced, arms folded. Trying to keep whatever he wanted to say inside. Eventually:

'Fine. Meet with Daniel then. It has to be unofficial though and don't—"

Sam Gordon entered without knocking. He watched them both for a while, then:

'I want to be there when you arrest him, Bishop. I want to see his face.'

Bishop nodded solemnly. 'Fine.'

'Good,' Gordon said and there was malice in his voice. 'Do it. Get the bastard, right?' He swallowed hard, tried to soften his tone. 'Holly, well done for helping out here. Your first case, and you've helped bring a vicious serial killer to justice.'

'It's not him, Sam.'

'Yes, it is. They found a hair under her nail. How can it not be him?'

'I don't like it.'

'Oh, you don't like it – well, I don't care! How many other actual cases have you worked on? I've looked at your record, even glanced at your book. You know what? Sometimes I think you don't know what you're talking about when it comes to serial killers.'

Bishop glowered at him. 'That's enough, Sam.'

'He doesn't fit the profile for chrissakes!' Holly shouted.

'So? Sometimes things just don't fit, do they?' Gordon said, his face red. 'Sometimes there's a piece missing out of the jigsaw, and I know this guy is it! There are always abnormalities. There will always be the one that doesn't fit.'

He stormed out of the room and the door banged shut behind him.

'Shit,' Bishop swore.

Holly sighed and put her head down. She knew Bishop was looking at her. Eventually he spoke.

'Are there? Are there always odd ones out?'

She took a deep breath and locked eyes with him.

'No.'

Thirty-six

'I've done bad things.'

'I know. I know you have.'

'Do you want me to go through them then? Is that what we're doing today?'

'You said you wanted to talk to me. You said you were ready.'

'Yes.'

'Have you changed your mind?' A pause. 'Lee?'

He shrugged. Half smiled.

'Maybe.'

Holly shut the folder in front of her and got up from the desk.

'I don't have time for this. There are only two days left before the board make their decision. You don't want to talk to me? You want to play games? We're done.' She was at the door when he suddenly called out.

'Wait! Wait, hold on. I'm sorry. I didn't . . . ' She turned back. Listening. 'I'm not myself okay? This isn't me. Don't go. Not like this. Look, at the moment the only thing I look forward to is seeing you when you visit. The rest of my time is spent in nothingness. Darkness. Do you know what that feels like?'

'No.'

'But here, where I have to spend my precious seconds . . . no, you don't know what it's like. You've never faced the darkness like I have. It's so tantalisingly beautiful in its emptiness. This place. It's worse than nothing. At least nothing was something at one point. They're killing me.'

'Then talk to me. Tell me what they need to know. Let me help you.' She could tell he was on the precipice. Teetering. One way or the other. Which way would he fall? 'Christ, you're so stubborn,' she said.

He shifted in his seat and came to life. 'Come sit back down. Come on. I'm sorry a million times, okay? Come on.' She paused a second longer then sat down again. 'What do the review board want to know?'

She opened the folder. She had read it a dozen times but when she scanned through it now it felt as if it was the first.

'You were lovers. You and Ryan?'

When he spoke it was between gritted teeth.

'You already knew that, yes, it's not—'

'No, I know. It's not important, but I need to establish some facts.'

'Okay.'

'You believed he was having an affair.'

'He was.'

'With a friend of his called . . . ' flicking over the page. 'Anton Adalbert. A chef at La Rue Est à Nous.'

'Yes.'

'Because of that, you hit Ryan on the head once with a hammer and then you hit him across the chest, arms, abdominals and genitals.'

310

'Yes.'

'Good. Okay. That's good, Lee.'

'No judgements?'

'No judgements.' She looked straight at him when she said that. He nodded slightly, as if relieved, but folded his arms across his chest. Defensive again. 'Let's talk about the room where it happened. A part of your psychosis that they don't understand. This is what they're curious about.'

'*They?*'

'The judicial board. They want full disclosure. The room where you were found when Sergeant Claver came into the house. He said you were sitting on a chair, staring at the wall. And Ryan was . . . well, he was on the floor, dead. And eventually when you looked at Sergeant Claver he said to you: "What are you doing here?" And you said, "Oh, this is my room. *The Red Room.*" Do you remember?'

'Sorry, who asked me that?'

'The arresting officer, Sergeant Claver. He said that. He testified at the trial that that's what you said.'

'Oh. I guess it's true. Yeah, I guess so. I don't remember some of it. The drugs.'

'Why was it the Red Room though, Lee?'

'I used to call it the Red Room. It was *my* room. Maybe because it was red?'

'Was it red?

'Well, it was. After I killed Ryan.'

A pause.

'Right. And Sergeant Claver said you were sitting. Sitting on a chair facing the wall. And the windows were to your right, the door was to your left, but you were facing the wall and it was a blank wall. There was nothing on it. You were staring at

311

the wall. Almost— I mean, he knew you were in shock, but he wasn't sure if it might have been some sort of catatonic state. Catatonic. It means . . . it means – it's like you're asleep.'

'I know what it means. I don't understand what you want to know.'

'What were you staring at? What was it about the wall? Why were you staring at the wall?'

'Why do you think?'

'You have to tell *me*.'

'I *have* to tell you?'

'Yes. It's—'

'Because I would be looking at the pictures.'

A long silence.

'What pictures?'

'The pictures on the wall.'

'There weren't any pictures on the wall. It was a blank wall. An empty wall.'

'You know how good my imagination is. It was easy. I would sit in the chair and . . . '

'What . . . you . . . you'd sit?'

'Yes, when we took drugs I'd always sit in the chair. Ryan would sit or lie on the floor in front of me. That was how we were. So I'd sit there and I'd . . . well, I would sit in the chair and imagine.'

'Imagine what?'

'Imagine I wasn't there. Imagine that I was somewhere else.'

'Where?'

'In the pictures.'

'You imagined you were in the pictures?'

'Yes.'

'What were the pictures of?'

'They were images. But ... images. I'd make them move. They'd be moving.'

'I don't understand.'

'Like cartoons.'

'Cartoons?' She felt herself hunching closer. He was staring at her. It was as if she were seeing him for the first time.

'Yes. I can't, I can't explain it. It's uh ... I can't, you had to see it to believe it. You understand? You have to sit in the chair, stare at the wall and then your imagination would come to life. And it would be fantastic and surreal and the cartoons that I would watch would be so funny. Animals playing music, you know, like an octopus playing the piano or a mouse playing a violin, and they'd all be so happy. And an octopus can't play the piano, but he would. And cows can't dance, can they? But I'd make them. They would all be dancing with each other, smiling, laughing. Applauding. It was ... And then there would be pictures of me as well. I'd never, I never remembered any photos of me as a child, I never remembered things like that but I imagined. I imagined what I would look like. Playing, smiling, dancing with the animals.'

'It sounds incredible.'

'It was. It really was. I was so happy. I'd be so happy I'd be crying. I don't know why, but I always did. There was always this, you know ... when you keep trying, when you don't give up.'

'The human spirit?'

'I don't know. But it was the most beautiful thing.'

'And how long would you watch the cartoons for?'

'Until the drugs wore off.'

She took a second.

'Well done, Lee. Thank you.'

He didn't smile but he blew her a kiss.

'Do you still think he's dangerous?'

This from Judy Olsen as they sat in the cafeteria after the interview. They were both nursing cups of tea and Holly picked at the remains of a sandwich.

'To anybody else? Do I think he would re-offend, is that what you mean?' Judy nodded. 'I don't know,' Holly continued. 'The anger. It feels as though it's too intrinsic in his psychology, but I don't know if he's a danger. I don't know if he will re-offend. It saddens me to say this, it really does, but I don't know.'

Holly left after filing her report. The day had stretched and emotionally she was exhausted. She wanted to go home and sleep, but when she got back to her flat she couldn't. She stayed awake thinking of Lee and then she started thinking about Bishop and how somehow everything seemed to be falling apart.

Thirty-seven

David Eagen stuck to the shadows, his breath smoking in the cold night air.

He was getting tired now. He had been walking since he had left his girlfriend's flat early this morning. Had ended up by the off-licence in King's Cross and managed to bed down with the locals for a few hours' kip. He wasn't a regular there but he'd traded a packet of smokes for the loan of a sleeping bag and recognised enough of the people to know he would be safe. Even so, he'd had trouble sleeping. He kept waking up, thinking the police had found him. He was being stupid. There was no way they could know where he was, but by the mid-afternoon he'd known that it was time to move on. You can never stay in one place too long in this city.

He was grateful when he finally reached a fire pit surrounded by drunks and homeless near Charing Cross later that afternoon. He mingled among them and took a swig of whatever was offered, careful to keep quiet. He handed around a few smokes, his eyes glancing furtively across the crowd until he'd had enough and then he dodged into the blackness below one of the arches, still carrying the bottle. The police had been everywhere looking for him. Asking questions, showing his photo, and he was grateful that no one had grassed him up. Yet. He checked his pockets. Only a few of the blue pills and two packets of cigarettes left. He had needed currency to barter with on the streets and they had done just fine.

He was glad he had stayed with Sasha last night. She was annoying and dumb but she had been his rock these past few months. He couldn't believe he had finally met someone who cared about him enough to lie for him whenever he asked. A woman who would stand by him, no matter what.

He needed a bit of time to get clean again, start afresh, then maybe they could get away together somewhere. Go up north where neither of them were known. She used to make him tea in the mornings when she woke up. He liked that. He regretted going to the police now – Detective Inspector Bishop – but it was a decision he had made when he had been under duress. Not that he'd had much choice? Do as they say or spend the rest of your life in a cell. He couldn't face that.

A noise behind him. He turned quickly. No one. A beer can rolling in the wind. He jammed himself against a wall and zipped up his jacket, angry at himself for being frightened. He pulled a small slip of paper from his pocket and read the address once more. It was only a five-minute walk and he was on time. The last leg of the journey, he reminded himself. He had done everything he was supposed to do and they should be happy with him. Tonight they'd deliver on their promise and let him go. An infrequent smile splashed across his face when he saw that Sasha had drawn a little heart underneath the address for him. Everything was going to be all right, he told himself.

Another noise, this time from within the archway, closer than before. A siren screamed in the other direction. Eagen waited to see if it was for him but it eventually faded away and he knew he was safe for now. He'd planned on coming back here afterwards, but now decided against it. This place was too open, too big; he'd be better off where there was security in numbers or tucked away in a safe hiding place. He made up his mind to head back over the bridge to Sasha's when he was done. Decision made, he leaned against the wall and took a long pull on the bottle. He couldn't stay here too long anyway. Time was ticking.

He started walking and found the block of flats sooner than expected. He approached warily and punched in the number code on the door. It buzzed open and he walked through. Two flights of stairs later and he was at the front door. Number Seven. Lucky seven. He took the key they had given him, put it in the lock and turned. It clicked open and he stepped inside. It was very dark. The curtains were drawn. He couldn't see very well and wanted to call out, but thought better of it. He wondered if they were already there. He flicked on the light.

Click-clack.

Nothing. The bulb must have blown. He took another drink, but as he lowered the bottle, he thought he saw something. Someone?

A shadow in the blackness moving silently towards him.

Thirty-eight

A radio blared.

Men in blue overalls with heads buried under car bonnets. Suddenly a half-dozen squad cars converged. Bishop alighted from the lead car, ID in hand.

'We have a warrant for David Eagen!'

A shake of heads. A few mechanics went back to work, unwilling to get involved. The garage boss came out of his office. Dark-haired and flustered, he was carrying a spanner.

'Are you Nicholas Giorgio?' Bishop asked.

'Yeah. What the hell's this?'

'David Eagen, is he here?'

'He hasn't been in for months.'

'You're lying. He was here last week. Don't play games with me. He's wanted for murder.'

'Shit . . . '

'Yeah. You want to cooperate now? Where he's living?'

'Don't know.'

'He got a girlfriend?'

*

Bishop and Ambrose knocked on the front door of the flat.

A full thirty seconds passed so Bishop knocked again. They heard a chain being pulled back and then the door opened. The woman was in her fifties, not exactly pretty but once cute. She stared at them through bleary eyes.

Bishop held up his warrant card; 'Sasha Bullen?'

Her face dropped at the sight of his identification. She turned to run but tripped over her dressing gown and fell in a heap on the floor. Bishop watched her for a few seconds then took a step inside and helped her up. 'Come on, love. Let's put the kettle on, shall we?'

The living room was stifling. Soot stains on the low ceiling, filthy furniture, old newspapers and hundreds of cigarette burns scattered across the carpet like leopard's spots. A dark passage that led off to the bedroom and toilet. Weak light filtered in through dirty net curtains and the walls shook as a train passed close by.

Sasha squatted on the edge of the sofa, nursing a cup of tea. Moving with the haze of a habitual drug user, she fumbled a cigarette into her mouth. Ambrose was hovering in the doorway. He had a hand halfway over his mouth as if he were stroking his chin but Bishop knew he was simply trying to hide from the overpowering smell of urine and cigarettes. Bishop was being polite and had sat in a chair opposite but was regretting it. What was left of the cushion underneath him was damp and it smelled bad.

'When was the last time you saw David, Sasha?' Bishop asked.

'Last night. When I woke up this morning he was already gone.'

'Do you know where he went?'

'We had sex.' She stared at them both, daring them to contradict her.

'Did David stay the whole night?'

'Maybe. Yeah.'

'Let me tell you why we're here, Sasha. You know about DNA, right?'

'Yeah.'

'Okay. Well some of David's DNA has turned up under the fingernail of a dead girl. The black girl from Barking. Have you read about it in the papers?'

Sasha nodded and started to get teary-eyed.

'We're going to need to talk to David to clear this up. Do you know where he is?' She put the cigarette in her mouth and drew on it like a pro. 'Sasha?'

'It weren't him that did it. God's my witness. He was 'ere.'

'I'm sure he was.'

'Yeah.'

'What did you get up to?'

'Watched TV.'

'What was on. Do you remember?'

She shook her head. Bishop glanced at Ambrose and gave him the heads-up.

'Sasha, can I use the toilet?' Ambrose asked.

She looked at him as if he'd asked for a blow job, then nodded and pointed a finger towards the dark passage. Ambrose crept away.

'How's David been these past few weeks?'

She laughed but it turned into a rattling cough. 'Same as always. He's a good person. He's . . . you know, misunderstood.'

'Right. Did he tell you he came to us and confessed to killing a doctor and his wife. Do you know anything about that?'

'Yeah. He didn't kill 'em.'

'No?'

'No. He was with me again.'

320

'That's right. David changed his mind when he saw the photos. Whoever did that to those two poor people, well ...' He paused. 'I've seen a lot of bad things in my years on the force, but nothing like that. Evil.' He shifted closer to her. 'And you're right, I don't think David could have done that. There was so much blood.'

Sasha looked away, uncomfortable.

'Why would he come to us and say he did it though? I don't get that.'

She shrugged, almost ashamed, took a swig of tea. Then her eyes darted towards the dark passage. Ambrose was coming back, holding two evidence bags in one hand. He looked jittery when he handed them over to Bishop and whispered.

'Under the bed.'

A mix of blue prescription drugs in one and Bishop didn't need to open the other. He could see what they were already. Three small brass bells.

'Have you seen these before, Sasha?' He gave her a few seconds but her face was like stone. 'Come on, Sasha. Where did he get them?'

'He didn't steal nothing.'

'Did he buy them?'

'He didn't. They was given him.'

'Given to him. By whom?'

She sniffed and lit up another cigarette.

'Sasha?'

'I don't know. I never met 'em.'

'Them? Why would "they" give him three bells?'

'Asked him to hold them for a while.'

'Hold them? You mean hide them?'

'No. Hold 'em. He's gonna give 'em back.'

'What about the drugs?'

'They was a present.'

'A present.'

'Yeah. For going to see you.'

'To give a false confession?'

'No. He had to say that to get into the station. He was told to find out something.'

'What?'

'I don't know.'

Bishop watched her, she was shaking now, almost feral. Suddenly she started to cry. 'He's scared though,' she stuttered. 'Scared. Wished he hadn't done it.'

'Done what?'

'The acid.'

'The acid.' Bishop nodded to Ambrose, who moved back into the hallway and made a phone call. 'Who's he scared of, Sasha?' She wiped a sleeve across her red-rimmed eyes. 'Who's he scared of?'

'I don't know.'

'Then we need to find him, don't we?'

She nodded numbly.

'Where else does he sleep? There must be another place. Maybe not another woman, but another place. Right?'

'He's got a key.'

'A key?'

'Yeah. They gave it him.'

Again with the 'they'.

'For another flat? Do you know the address?'

Barely a nod.

Bishop sat and thought for a while. Then he stood up slowly. 'Come on, Sasha. Let's get you down the station.'

Thirty-nine

'We picked up a lead on Eagen.'

Bishop was sitting in an unmarked car, empty coffee cups and plastic sandwich wrappers on the seat next to him. He was watching a block of flats by the old arches close to Waterloo train station. One hand held his phone, the other shielded his eyes from the afternoon sun that was making a splash through the windows.

'Who from?' Holly asked.

'His girlfriend Sasha Bullen. She gave us an address where he's been holing up.'

'You believe her?'

'Yep. That's why I'm spending my afternoon sitting in a car on some crappy street in South London. His girlfriend made a statement. Verified that Eagen carried out the acid attack on Janine. Showed us the bottle.'

'That's good. He'll go down for that.'

'She also said he was given drugs in payment for coming in to talk to us.'

'Do you know why?'

'No.' A pause. 'Something else. He had three brass bells hidden under his bed.'

A long silence. He knew she was still there though.

'Shit,' she said eventually.

'Yep.' A figure on the pavement was approaching his car. Bishop craned his neck for a better view. Kept talking but maintained eye contact. 'One other thing Sasha said: whoever gave Eagen the drugs, he always referred to them as "they".'

'They?'

'As in more than one. That was what you said.'

No answer.

The figure passed by. Some skinny kid with a hoodie and no place to go. Bishop watched him appear in the rear view and keep walking. 'You could be right, Holly. Eagen's got himself involved with a couple of killers maybe. We bring him in, he'll talk. Maybe a plea bargain.' A beat. 'Got the DNA results back from the hammer at the Pettimans' place as well.'

'Go on.'

'Match for Brian Reise.' He took a second. 'Holly?'

'Yes, I'm still here.'

She was being so monosyllabic it was maddening, but he couldn't blame her. She had come up with theories that could yet bear fruit but he had not backed her up. He remembered Gordon sneering at her, belittling her and he hadn't done a thing about it. He felt empty. Empty and dull.

'You still seeing Daniel tonight?'

'Yes.'

'I put in a call to Ronald Anderson as well. The coroner from the original Sickert cases. Thought you might want to talk with him.'

'Why?'

He drew a long breath. 'Christ,' he said, 'I don't know.' *More than one killer, Bishop.* 'I don't like loose ends. Look, if we ever get another case and you get asked to assist—'

'I don't know if I could look at another dead body, Bishop. It's been a bit of a crazy ride. I might stick to the textbooks and the nutcases already behind bars from now on. Bit safer maybe.'

'Yeah,' he laughed, but it was hollow. 'What are you up to?'

Another silence. He could hear music playing in the background. She coughed then spoke:

'Thinking about taking down the rogues' gallery above my fireplace.'

'Back to the safety of the magnolia.' A pause. 'How you feeling?'

'Feeling?'

'Yeah. You know.'

'I'm sure it's not ... so I feel ... yes, I feel as though I have failed.'

'You haven't failed. You've been amazing. You're an amazing young woman.'

'Ha,' she laughed. 'Young woman. Haven't been called that for ... well. Anyway. I'd better go. I've got a busy night. Let me know when you have him in custody.'

'I will do.'

The line clicked off and his radio crackled. He rubbed his eyes, grabbed it.

'Anything?'

'Negative, sir. No movement. No lights. Nothing.'

'Have everybody check in.'

Bishop hung up. He slumped in his seat and checked his watch once more before staring out across the street with very tired eyes.

*

Holly stared at the incident wall.

'Ronald Anderson,' she whispered. Why did Bishop want her to see him? Was he just being nice because he felt guilty or did he really think she might actually come up with something? What could the old coroner tell her? She checked her watch. She would have to be fast. She was tempted to wipe the black marker off the wall and start pulling off all the photos when her eyes strayed onto the one photo of the victim they knew the least about.

Mina Osterley.

The young German woman for whom they had no autopsy photographs. She poured herself a glass of wine but it tasted bitter.

Mina stared back at her. Long dark hair. A wisp of a smile. They both stayed like that for several minutes. Holly taking her in, trying to feel her. A connection. How was she linked to all of this? What was it about Mina?

She fired up her computer. A quick search and she had the number she wanted. She checked the time and hoped they were still at the office. They were one hour ahead of England this time of the year. When the line clicked on and the operator spoke, she thanked God that he spoke perfect English. She asked to be put through to the relevant department, told them what she needed and was put on hold for several minutes. Then a voice came through loud and clear.

'This is Anton Fischer from the Bielefeld coroner's office in North Rhine-Westphalia. You wanted to know details about Mina Osterley's autopsy?'

'Yes please. One specific question about her injuries.'

'Go ahead.'

'Was she raped?'

Forty

A fire glowed in the hearth, casting little light and longer shadows.

Ronald Anderson was in his seventies now. He sat in an armchair in his dressing gown, a blanket over his knees. The living room was as it had been in the fifties. Heavy rich curtains and carpets, brown furniture and old stained oil paintings on the walls. Holly placed a cup of tea by his side and sat opposite. He held a cigarette in his right hand that had a long drooping ash at the end.

'Richard Sickert?' he asked.

'Yes. The crime scenes and autopsies, I understand you covered all three?'

'If you want to read about the Sickert cases they're on file at the National Archives in Kew.'

'Actually, I wanted to ask you about some of the other murders you worked on, if you don't mind. Before the Sickert ones.'

'Go on.'

'Were there any that had a similar MO? Particularly ones that went unsolved?'

'How far back are you asking?'

'Ten, twenty years before Sickert.'

He looked away from her. Stared into the fire and pulled his dressing gown tighter.

'I still have my original notes, although it's not exactly light reading.' He shifted in his seat. 'Over there on the shelf. The books that have a red binding. They're all date-stamped. Bring me 2005. I think it's March, but I'll need to have a look.'

Holly did as she was asked, opened the book for him and placed it on his lap. She leaned over his shoulder as he turned the pages slowly, only stopping when he found the information he was looking for. 'There you go. I performed the autopsy on 21 March, I'm not as senile as I think I am.'

He had turned to a black-and-white autopsy photo of a woman's body. She had long blonde hair and her skin looked pale blue in the cold light.

'Her name was Marjory Dawson. She was a librarian in Islington. She wasn't the first one they found like that. Strangled, wrists slashed. But she was the first we managed to ID.'

'There were others?'

'Several.'

'Was there penetration with Marjory?'

'Sex, you mean?' She nodded. 'Yes. He had sex with all of them. Didn't leave any DNA though, no traces, nothing. We found particles of lubricant, so he used a condom.'

'Could you tell if the intercourse was pre- or post-mortem?'

'While they were alive. It was rape.' He took a moment to take a drag on his cigarette.

'How many others were there?' Holly asked.

'That I identified? Four that I remember.'

'All in 2005?'

'Perhaps 2006 for the last. There may have been more.

I wasn't the only coroner then.' He took a moment and lit another cigarette from the tip of the last. 'Fiona Lewes and Amanda Bines were the other two I autopsied that had similar injuries. A horrible affair. I believe the other one was taken care of by the Sussex county coroner Martyn Bloom. Haven't heard from him in years now. Used to keep in touch. Christmas cards. The victim's name was Rachel. Rachel Marcher I think.'

'Rachel?'

'Yes.' There was the slightest hesitation. 'Your killer. I've read about him in the newspaper. Is it the same man?'

'Our man doesn't have sex with them.'

'Not him then. But the injuries are consistent?'

'Yes.'

Anderson shrugged. 'Two different people perhaps. Two different psychoses. Can't help themselves, can they.' It was a statement, not a question.

'Richard Sickert was never charged with killing Rachel or any of the other previous victims. Why not?'

'When it went to trial, the prosecution tried to link Rachel and others to Richard Sickert but they couldn't because of the sexual assault. Richard was not a sexual predator. He liked to kill. Rachel was raped, so were the other three women, but Natasha, Rudy and Kate Wendell were not. Sickert's defence argued that the previous crimes did not fit Sickert's pathology. They were backed up by their defence psychologist.'

'Doctor Andell.'

'A brilliant orator. Ran rings around the prosecution's psychologist – Lawrence Branyan, I think his name was. Dead now. So the previous victims all went into the cold case files. I mean everybody thought it was Richard Sickert, but he never confessed to it.'

'Do you think he killed Rachel and the other women?'

'No, I don't. And if whoever did was never caught, and hasn't died, then he's still out there.'

An idea was forming. A small seed had been planted in the soil and she was waiting for the first green shoot to show. Highly improbable but not impossible.

The wood fire suddenly spat and Holly jumped at the noise. She hadn't realised she was so on edge, hadn't realised it was getting so late either.

'Doctor Anderson, thank you, I have to go now.' She put the book back on the shelf. 'There's one other thing I don't understand. Richard was getting away with murder, so why didn't he cover his tracks this time? Why kill his wife and then sit in the road waiting for the police?'

Anderson pulled his gaze away from the fire to face her, his eyes ancient and rheumy.

'I've often asked myself that question but could never come up with a suitable explanation. But I have no doubt he did it for a very good reason.'

A modern building made of glass and stone loomed in the middle of Kew, '*The National Archives*' stamped across the pediment. The rain had started to fall and Holly stood in the doorway, shielding her phone.

'Bishop?'

'Yes.' His voice was crackly with static, going in and out.

'I think Wilfred Sickert is still alive.'

'What?'

'I think he's still alive. I don't know how but . . . The MO on Mina is almost identical to three women that were killed in 2005 and possibly one in 2006 but I haven't been able to verify that.'

'How can you be sure?'

'I can't. I'm clutching at straws here but I think I'm right.' A pause. 'Bishop?'

'Yes. Sorry. Go on.'

'I need to do some more digging. I'm over at the archives. I'll call you later.'

'Okay.'

The line went dead.

She knocked on the front door. An elderly guard unlocked it and beckoned her inside. The place was huge. A labyrinth of corridors, stairs and dusty shelves, all emanating a stale air of importance. Someone coughed and it echoed as she was led through the archive of books. It was near to closing time and a few people lingered, replacing books on shelves, packing up their notes and snapping shut briefcases.

She had already called ahead and the four case files had been located and piled in a neat stack on a table in a private room. The guard left her in peace and closed the door. The overhead light was off and the lamp cast a yellow glow but it was good enough to read by.

Marjory Dawson. Fiona Lewes. Amanda Bines. Rachel Marcher.

She started with Marjory Dawson. Photos of the crime scene, the body, police notes and evidence. Twenty-two years old and a librarian at Conner House in Islington, where she had worked for four years. She had been strangled, raped and her wrists had been slashed. She was found by a neighbour from the same block of flats, shoved behind the washing machine in the utility room. No parents or next of kin, so she had been identified by a friend from college, an Angus Grant. Behind a washing machine.

Fiona Lewes was the same. Rape, strangulation and wrist slashing. Twenty-nine years old. A lawyer from Kent who worked in London but was found in a field near her home in Sevenoaks. A dog walker stumbled upon her remains at five thirty in the morning. Police thought she had only been dead for thirty minutes or so before the discovery.

Amanda Bines. A school teacher from north London. Thirty-three years old and married. She was three months pregnant at the time of her murder. Her husband, Ian Sumida, was questioned extensively as it was discovered he was having an affair with his secretary at the time, but he was soon released as he had an alibi for the two other previous crimes. A clairvoyant, Edith Clancy, was brought in by police as she claimed to have information regarding Amanda's death, but she was deemed a time-waster. Clancy later admitted she was writing a book and wanted the inside scoop. She was never charged with wasting police time.

Rachel Marcher was a Bosnian immigrant who had come to England in 1995 after her parents had both been shot dead during the Siege of Sarajevo. She had been put into the foster care system and adopted and raised by Mike and Susan Marcher from Bath. She was eleven when she had come to England which put her at thirty-two years old when she had been killed. After leaving college she became a successful linguist and worked as a translator for the NHS and assisted in court cases involving Bosnian immigrants and refugees. She lived alone in a flat in Winchester; her parents found her dead in her bedroom with her wrists slashed and a belt around her neck.

Holly flicked to the back of Rachel Marcher's file and glanced at the last page. It was yellowed and tatty and the old staple was coming loose. It was a copy of Rachel's adoption papers with her CR number. She felt an immense sadness. The poor child. Surviving Sarajevo, working hard and then dedicating her life to others who faced a similar plight. And ending up what? Being brutally murdered in a foreign country for no reason. What a waste. What a tragedy. But there was a reason, wasn't there. There was always a reason, Holly.

She sat and stared at Rachel's photo again. She had a sudden thought and went through the three other folders once more. Slowly. Methodically. One by one. And when she had finished reading, she closed her eyes and dipped her head as if incredibly tired.

How could she have been so stupid?

It was raining, the wind was blowing.

Her red MG followed the A37, hugging the outside lane. Overtaking whenever she could, but it felt like she was driving through a car wash. She had her phone on Bluetooth and Bishop's number on speed dial.

'Pick up . . . pick up.'

He did.

'Holly?'

'Bishop!' She shouted. 'Evelyn Wright, Rebecca and Tracy. Were they adopted?'

'What?'

'Were they adopted?'

'Christ, I don't know! How the hell do I find that out?'

'They'll all have a CR number by their names. Every adoptee has a CR number. A Contact Register number. Marjory Dawson, Fiona Lewes, Amanda Bines, Rachel Marcher.'

'Who the hell are they?'

'The 2005 and 2006 unsolved cases with similar MO's. They were all adopted.'

'What?'

'All the victims are adopted. That's the link.'

'How is that even—'

'It is the link. That's why he's after them. I know it is.' The phone cut out. A burst of static.

'Bishop?'

'Yes?'

'That's why he hates them so much! That's why he's so damn angry. He didn't get their life. He didn't have the chances they had!'

'What do you mean?'

'Because he was adopted himself, Bishop! The killer was adopted too! But something went wrong. Horribly wrong.'

'I can barely hear you!'

She hoped he understood her. She let out a deep breath as the last veil was finally lifted. 'I have to go.'

'Holly, you're breaking up.'

'I have to go . . . ' she whispered.

She finished the call.

The road ahead was black but she drove even faster.

Forty-one

Bishop stared at the phone incredulously.

He had no idea what Holly had been trying to tell him. A series of garbled shouts as the phone went in and out of reception. He dialled her number but it went straight to voicemail. He tried twice more. God, that was infuriating.

He called Sergeant Crane. He was already on his way to Hastings but he hadn't checked in yet. Again – straight to the answer machine. Long live modern technology. Then he called dispatch and asked the relevant question about Evelyn Wright and the others. He hung up and stared out at the miserable night. Streetlights gleamed on the black pavement. Bits of rubbish skittered and swirled and a mangy dog came by and barked. Bishop felt like barking back. A train rumbled over the arches above him and suddenly, in the distance, a hooded figure appeared walking down the street. A black shadow in the shifting rain. His radio squawked. He quickly took it from its holster and turned it down as a voice told him:

'There's someone approaching.'

'Do we have a visual confirmation?'

'Negative. He's wearing a hood.'

He watched closely as the figure passed within twenty feet of his car, turned up some steps and entered the flats.

'Get ready.'

They were already positioned inside. In the corridors, in the staircases. On Bishop's command, they would be going through their final checks. Prepped with shotguns, bulletproof vests and helmets.

'Have you got eyes-on?' Bishop asked.

'He's going up the second flight of steps. Coming into view now. Walking along the concourse towards the target house. Checking over his shoulder. Stopping. Looking at the numbers as he goes. He's stopped. Confirm he is standing at door number seven.'

'What's he doing.'

'He's knocking.'

'He hasn't got a key?'

'Doesn't look like it. He's knocking on the door. Hold. He's trying the letter box but he can't open it. Turning to us now. Checking his watch. Seems agitated. He's pulling down his hood.' A pause. 'Jesus. He's wearing a white mask, Bishop!'

'I'm coming in!'

The rain hit Bishop like a punch in the gut but he needed it after being marshmallowed in the car for the past six hours. He sprinted up the steps as fast as his knee would let him. Passed the first SWAT in the corridor and up ahead he could see the figure had been de-hooded and was surrounded by armed police and being held up against the wall. Bishop pushed through. The kid was spotty. Twenty maybe. Skinny as a rake and wet through.

'Who the hell are you?'

'Jesus Christ – what is this?' He was wide-eyed and shaking.

336

'Answer the fucking question.'

'John. My name's John Foster.'

'Address, John Foster.'

'Um . . . 137 Nightingale Terrace. It's in Lambeth. I live with my mum.'

Bishop turned to Mosely, who was relaying all the information into his shoulder radio. Ten seconds of silence then a crackle and it was confirmed that John Foster lived at 137 Nightingale Terrace in Lambeth with his mother.

'What are you doing here?'

'I work up the road at the carpet shop. I have done for six months. Some guy paid me to come here and knock on the door at six o'clock.'

'Paid you?'

'Yeah. Fifty quid. "Six o'clock sharp," he said.'

'Who?'

'I don't know. I've never seen him before. He came into the shop this afternoon.'

'What did he look like?'

'He was wearing this mask. Like a Phantom of the Opera kinda thing. Gave me one and told me to wear it. Said they were all playing a prank on a mate who lived here. Like a stag do or something.'

'Who's that then? Who lives here?'

'Am I in trouble?'

'No. Tell me who lives here.'

'It's a policeman.'

Jesus, Bishop thought, Holly was right.

'What's his name, John Foster?'

'DI Bishop.'

*

SWAT rammed the door open.

A flashbang was thrown inside and the first three men rushed forward into the noise and the smoke. Assault rifles up, elbows tight, flashlights barely making it through the haze. Bishop came in behind them, deaf from the noise, holding his breath so he wouldn't choke on the smoke.

'Armed police! Armed police!'

'Room one – clear!'

They moved forward, heel to toe, covering every angle. For the first time in a long time Bishop felt as though he wanted his old SA80 rifle in his hands. His adrenalin was through the roof and he could feel his heart beating in his chest. The men moved like shadows, a choreographed dance from room to room.

'Kitchen – clear!'

'Bathroom – clear!'

They converged on the door at the far end of the property. The bedroom, thought Bishop. Holed up like an animal in its den. He saw one of the men reach out and try the handle. Locked. An order was given and the same man leaned back and kicked the door. His foot bounced off, left a meaty imprint. Another kick. Something splintered and on the third attempt the door cracked in half and was flung open.

After that everything happened very fast.

Bishop saw a shadow in the darkness swing towards them in a rush of air. The flash of a knife. And then there was light and noise like a million fireworks. Bullets chewed up the air. A nightmarish squeal from close by, punctuated by the rapid sound of bullets thudding into heavy flesh. The shadow was pushed back as if hit by a water cannon. Then it pivoted and swung at them again.

Another burst of gunfire. Bishop was almost blinded. Could

only see in black and white and his ears were ringing. He could taste metal in his mouth. Realised his hands were shaking but at the same moment realised he had never felt so alive.

'Cease fire!'

The silence was deafening.

Smoke. Cordite. A dirty haze of death.

'Sir?'

One of the SWAT team was calling to him. They were already standing down. Threat neutralised. Bishop stepped up as they swung their flashlights and helmet cams on the mess in front of them.

The figure was twisted horribly, blood running into its dead eyes, hanging like a grotesque puppet. Twitching without a sound.

'Can we get a visual confirmation, please sir?'

Bishop put a hand out and lifted the remains of the face. He nodded once.

'Yeah. That's him.'

He left the flat and swallowed the fresh air outside. It felt clean and cold and he suddenly started shivering. Somehow his jacket had come off in there. A large crowd had gathered in the car park and news crews were jostling amid the spectators. Ambrose came up to him and said something but he couldn't hear. The ringing in his ears wasn't going to get better anytime soon.

'I can't . . .' he pointed to his ears.

'Sam Gordon wants to talk to you, sir! Wants to see—'

'Tell him it's Eagen.' He shook his head. 'But Gordon's not seeing a damn thing.' He was about to call Holly again when he saw the SWAT leader waving him over.

The flat had been lit up like daylight and forensics were

already taking photographs and fingerprinting. He was led back into the bedroom. 'Careful sir, there's a wire on the ground there. Tread over it.' Bishop did and looked up at Eagen. The dead man looked like a pathetic scarecrow. His mouth had been gagged and he was tied up to some sort of wooden mount. A Y-frame with a heavy spring at the back. His arm was stretched out, the knife still gripped in his hand.

'What the hell is this?' Bishop asked.

'I've never seen anything like it. There was some sort of trigger wire attached to the door. When we broke it down, it got released and he was swung forwards. It's a pretty simple mechanism.'

'I'm guessing he didn't hook himself up to this?'

'No.' The SWAT Leader pulled the bloody clothing to one side.

'Jesus,' exclaimed Bishop.

'Yeah. Guy was nailed to the wooden frame whilst he was still alive. Then gaffer-taped for good measure.'

'What about the knife?'

'Glued to his hand.'

Bishop tried to take it in. He frowned. He wanted them to open the windows, let in some fresh air. He turned away. Needed to get out now. Needed to get back to the cold night air. He was wasting time. Sasha's words kept coming back to him: 'they'. Two people. And Eagen wasn't one of them. Two people killing. Eagen was only the runner.

'Sir? One last thing.'

He turned back. Leaden feet.

'We found this in his other hand. Stapled to his palm.'

He handed over a plastic card covered in blood. Bishop wiped it clean. It was a Polaroid security pass for Bayview Hospital and when he turned it over he saw a photo of Holly.

Forty-two

Sky and water merged into a sheet of grey, broken only by the dark lines of cliffs in the distance.

Holly's car drew to a halt. She turned off the engine and sat in silence while her eyes became accustomed to the gloom. To the right she saw Daniel's two-storey crofter's cottage standing blackly against the night sky. Nothing stirred and no lights showed. To the left, the jagged coastline and the boiling sea below. Muffled explosions. Deep and dark.

She got out, pulled her jacket tight around her and cupped the torch beam with her hand to shield the light. There were two cars in the driveway. She played the light over their interiors. One had a police radio that flashed sporadically. Sergeant Crane. He must already be inside. She headed to the pale strip of mud that led to the cottage and then disappeared into a thick forest behind. The front door was closed but unlocked and she stepped inside.

The torch's narrow beam cut weakly through the darkness illuminating old furniture. Peeling paint. Soot stains by the chimney. Decades of dust and dirt. It looked lived in but unloved. She tried the light switch. A dull flick-flack as it clicked uselessly and she got a quick jolt of fear.

'Sergeant Crane?'

A slight hesitation. She pulled out her phone. No signal.

'It's Holly Wakefield.' A breathless pause. 'Sergeant?'

This felt all wrong. Her instincts were telling her to get the hell out but her feet were carrying her across the room until she felt her foot kick something. It rolled across the wooden floor. She shone the light towards the noise and caught sight of a bowling ball as it finally stopped and bounced gently into an armchair. Shiny and polished, it conjured up an image of Brian Reise's bald head. Dead Brian Reise from the drain pipe.

A gust of wind suddenly slashed the rain against the door and it sagged and swung shut behind her.

'Sergeant Crane?'

Where the hell was he? She looked around, half-expecting him to suddenly appear with a carefree grin in her torch light, but all she saw were deeper shadows. Photos of Daniel on the wall above the fireplace. Wooden frames. He looked similar in each one, as if the photos had all been taken on the same day. Slightly different from the mugshot they had – a heavier jaw, perhaps, and the eyes ... there was something wrong about them. Something sullen. Daniel standing in the garden. Daniel in town outside of a hobby shop. Daniel resting up against a tree. He looked the same in each photo. No smile. No real emotion at all. Hollow memories for one man by himself.

A single staircase ahead. Old and rickety, the wood exposed like the remains of a skeleton. And on either side a door. Both of which were closed.

She listened at the left one first. Then the right. No sounds. She went back to the left door, wondering if she should have gone to the right. Her hand was already on the handle. Too late now. She turned it gently and the door opened inwards.

342

A kitchen beyond. Farmhouse style, with two levels of wooden cabinets and dusty glass doors. A few cups across the countertop and in one corner an electric oven and a silent fridge. A chopping board on the countertop with a large cleaver sticking out of it like an axe. Freshly cleaned, glinting dully in her torch beam.

Movement to her right. The scurrying of tiny feet. A rat caught in the torchlight as it slunk behind the oven. She could almost smell the loneliness. The despair.

Dust motes danced in the yellow beam as she returned to the main room. She passed the staircase and opened the other door. A dining room. Chairs stacked at one end and a glass chandelier that glittered like diamonds. A drop cloth draped across a table below with a place setting for two. A dinner and side plate, knife, fork, spoon and a wine glass, freshly cleaned. Someone's coming to dinner. She had a sudden niggling feeling that she was supposed to be the guest tonight. Domination Manipulation. Control. What had come before was merely an interval in a macabre show. A spectacle that she had somehow become part of.

'Sergeant Crane!'

Her voice was loud and echoed forever.

Where was he? Perhaps he was hurt? He could be lying somewhere. She should search the living room again then—

A noise.

From upstairs? So faint it could have been her imagination.

'Sergeant?'

What was she doing? Get out now, Holly. Get back in your car and drive away. But she couldn't. She lifted a foot on to the first step. Swore softly as the wood splintered under her shoe. She raised the torch; rotten wood and silver cobwebs.

She made her way up as silently as possible. Constant shifting shadows. Her imagination playing cruel tricks. On the landing, she could make out three doors. A faint strip of yellow light under the closest one. She gathered herself.

'Sergeant Crane? Daniel? It's Holly Wakefield.'

She knew there would be no reply but she had to know for sure. She had to—

'Come in.'

The voice surprised her. She pushed open the door and saw him immediately. A figure hunched in the far corner, writing in a large wire-bound book. She turned off her torch. The light she had seen was from a small white candle that burned on the desk. His shoulders tightened visibly as she entered, aware of her presence.

'I'll be with you in a minute.'

His voice was strange, muffled. And then he turned.

Doctor Andell was wearing the same clothes as the last time they had met, but seemed slightly taller somehow.

'Hello, Holly.'

For a moment she doubted her eyes but then she nodded. It was all or nothing now. Leap before you look. A slight hesitation. Then:

'Hello, Wilfred,' she said.

His response was halfway between a smile and a sigh.

'Wilfred?'

'Yes.' She tried to swallow but her throat was very dry. For the first time real fear gripped her. 'You're Wilfred Sickert.'

'Am I?'

A nod. 'You joined the AAC in 1989 The Army Air Corps.' Bishop had told her that. He had known what AAC had meant. Where was Bishop now? Where the hell was Crane? 'You were stationed in Bielefeld with Reise's unit in Germany. How well did you know each other?'

Doctor Andell pursed his lips.

'Well enough, I imagine. You were in different units but on the same base camp. Maybe you knew him from before that. Rudy Esters gave him his tattoo. Did you know Rudy too?'

Nothing.

'Brian Reise blew up the car you were in. The car that was taking you to a military court to be tried for the murder and rape of his fiancée, Mina Osterly. It was 23 April 1989. You were sixteen years old.' Holly brought the photocopied sheets from her pocket. 'DI Bishop and I got copies of everything from Brigadier Collins.'

'Brigadier who, sorry?'

Holly smiled but she thought she was going to be sick. 'I don't know how you survived the car bomb. Luck. Providence. It doesn't matter. But you came back here. Changed your appearance. Took on someone else's identity or simply made up a new name for yourself. Then you set yourself up as a doctor. Took your exams. My God, you're a planner, aren't you?' Holly was thinking a mile a minute. Her brain on overdrive. 'What better cover? What better role to hide in plain sight. A doctor. A psychologist whose life ambition is to help the mentally sick and fucked-up.'

'And why on earth would I want to do that?'

'So you could help the one that meant the most to you. Your brother: Richard Sickert.'

His eyes were cold. As cold as the sea.

'You argued for his defence when he was charged with the murder of three women. You even managed to get the charges for the murders of Rachel Marcher and the others dropped, didn't you? Because the rape didn't match his pathology. But it matched yours.' A pause. 'And it didn't stop there. You've been helping him by letting him out. Helping him by allowing him to satiate his hunger. Letting him out to kill again – and you've been doing it with him.'

'You're either very tired or mentally unstable. Which is it?'

She turned to the door. 'A quick DNA test will prove you're related. There's no court in the world that will let you go free.'

'Please stop, for God's sake, Holly! You're making a fool of yourself.'

'Is that all you have to say?'

She could feel her legs trembling. Her hands were clenching and unclenching and her palms were sweaty. He moved closer to her. Only a few steps but it was enough to make her bolt. She grabbed the door handle and pulled but it wouldn't budge. She shook it and she could hear the lock jangling from outside. She turned back to face him.

'He's locked it, Holly.'

He?

Wilfred didn't come any closer. He seemed content to let her stand by the door. An animal cornered in a trap. And she saw the madness flash in his eyes. But then the immediate calm afterwards. So controlled, she thought to herself. *So* controlled. Anybody else would have thought it was a trick of the light, but she saw it. She caught a glimpse of the horror.

'Are you wondering if the police officer whom Bishop sent will come to your rescue? He won't. He was put to sleep long before you arrived.'

She felt herself faltering. She'd been a fool to come here alone. They should have driven together. At least then—

'How did you find out?'

The question surprised her. She almost choked on the name: 'Mina.'

He nodded. 'Jolly little Mina. I saw her at a dance with Brian. "Tiptoe through the Tulips", that sort of thing. She was with friends and I happened to ask about her. Who would have thought?'

'There were always two killers. One was a rapist. The other wasn't. Your brother can't or won't rape—'

'Can't.'

'But you always did. All the way back to Mina. The injuries to Mina were almost identical to the autopsy reports on Rachel Marcher and the others. It had to be the same killer. It had to be you. No two MOs can ever be the same. Therefore, by definition – you had to be alive. It makes sense, right?' She couldn't believe she was asking him, but she was. She had to hear it.

'Are you disappointed in me?'

A slight nod. 'Yes.'

'Every man has his passion. Some like fly-fishing. I prefer killing.'

'Brian Reise? That was a huge risk.'

'He spotted me. On a bus, of all things. I wasn't sure if he recognised me, but I couldn't take the chance.'

'Which bus?'

'The number 38 to Guildford. It passes through a serene village called Abinger Hammer. You should go if you ever get a chance.'

'Checking the route from the Pettimans' house to the Wrights'.'

'Have you worked out the connection?' he said suddenly. 'Evelyn, Rebecca, Tracy, Marjorie Dawson . . . ' A beat. 'You.'

Finally, after a long moment, she gave a slight shrug.

'Yes.'

'And still you came,' he said calmly. 'You understand I'm going to have to kill you now.'

Suddenly he was holding a small brass bell. He shook it. It rang – loud and tinny. Then he blew out the candle. She turned her torch back on. Shone it into his eyes, but he shrugged it off. 'Keep the light on and you're going to make this way too easy.'

She clicked it off.

Darkness.

She tried to remember what she had seen of the room. It was rectangular and dilapidated. There had been an old dining-room table with chairs and crockery on top. Drawn curtains on the windows but a skylight above. The rain was pounding on the window so hard it seemed it would break the glass. What had been background noise sounded deafening now.

'I'm so glad I got to know you a little, Holly. So glad.'

His voice was loud. Close.

Holly stayed still. Then she started to move. Kicked off her shoes. Backwards towards the door and to the left. Keep your eyes open and they'll adjust to the light, she told herself. She felt something brush against her arm. She jumped back and felt the air whoosh where her head had been. She fell against the wall. Reached out a hand but the door wasn't there. She must have misjudged. Something brushed past her again. She leaped to one side. Moved away. Scurrying little steps, side to side. Then she stopped. Crouching. Breath in ragged gasps. Trying to slow down her heart. Almost impossible. Where was he? She realised the rain had covered the sound of her own footsteps but it was also covering the fall of his. She was still holding the torch. Wondered if she could use it as a weapon.

Somewhere in the middle of the room a floorboard creaked. He was moving in the darkness. Moving towards her. She turned and began to feel her way around the walls away from him.

'I can hear you.'

She stopped moving, not sure if he was lying. And then thunder boomed from outside. Three seconds later and the room was lit up like daylight with a flash of lightning. He was facing away from her but turned quickly. Saw her crouched in the corner. She struggled up as the lightning faded into blackness.

She moved to her right. Stopped. Moved some more. Felt something touch her leg. One of the chairs? There was a creak on the floorboards directly in front of her. She froze. Then another creak to her right. Further away. *How was that possible?* She shuddered. There was someone else in the room. Richard Sickert had joined his brother. Summoned by the bell. She hadn't seen him come in. Hadn't heard him. They weren't talking but she knew they were working together. They liked the darkness. Made it work for them.

'There is only one door. All we have to do is wait for the lightning.'

A scuffing to her right. A footstep to her left. Thunder boomed. Three-second warning. Three seconds, Holly. What do you do? She grabbed the chair. Two seconds. She lifted it above her head. One second. Lightning flashed. A split second to orientate herself. Wilfred was to the left, the shadow of Richard to the right. She jumped forward and swung the chair on to Wilfred's head. There was loud crack and he went down like a rag doll. Richard turned and lunged at her as the light disappeared again.

She skittered away like a frightened deer. Into the table, on to the table, the crockery, everything scattering like a

349

flock of pigeons disturbed by a gunshot. Over the table on to the ground. Gasping. Panting. She could hear Richard behind her. Furniture bumping into him. She found the door. Wrenched it open and went through. Tried to close it behind her. Fingers numb. Tried to work the lock. Such a simple lock but it wouldn't close! But now it will! Now it's done. There was a fierce bang against it. She lowered her shoulder into it. Dug deep with her heels. Another bang on the door. Her body shook with the impact and she could hear the lock breaking. He was hitting it so damn hard. She pulled away and felt along in the blackness. The walls. The landing.

Behind her – Crash!

She didn't need to look. She knew what that sound meant. Completely blind. Hands splayed and groping. There. The railing on the landing. She started down the stairs and tripped almost immediately and tumbled forward. She rolled and rolled, cartwheeling down, knocking into the bannisters until she finally lay motionless at the bottom. Her body checking itself automatically as she bit her lip and choked on dust. No broken bones. No fractures. Lungs were good. Hold on … Argghh. She almost passed out. Her left leg. The shin. Something wasn't right. She pushed down with her hand. Felt something ragged and wet and the searing pain struck again.

'H-Holly!' It was Richard. He was halfway down the stairs already.

She pulled herself to her knees. Too far to get to the front door. There was no way her leg could support her, so she dragged her body across the floor towards the kitchen. Thunder boomed. Move faster, Holly. Move! She fell through the doorway and lay on the ground as lightning lit up the whole house. In that brief moment of fluorescence she saw Sergeant

Crane slumped against the far wall. Sergeant Crane! Richard must have put him there whilst she was upstairs with Wilfred. He looked somehow alive but was sitting in a heap. Eyes open. The whites reflecting like cat's eyes. A second later the darkness enveloped everything again. She wanted to call out but scrambled over instead. He had to be alive. Had to be. But his skin was cold. Clammy. Water was dripping from somewhere and had soaked his uniform. And then she saw the knife sticking out of his stomach and knew he was dead. Christ, she didn't even know his first name. She stifled a scream. Moved away. She didn't want to die like that.

She felt along the walls. The oven. The silent fridge. Don't open the door just in case the light is still working. Countertops. A saucepan. The bread board. The meat cleaver. Heavy and solid. She grabbed it like a life raft, pulled it to her chest. Kept quiet when she heard a footstep from the living room and then hunkered down and held her breath. Lightning flashed again and she saw Richard illuminated in the doorway with his back to her. His head roving from left to right. The lightning faded and ever so slowly she edged towards him in the blackness, the pain in her left leg coming in blinding flashes. She thought of Bishop and his dodgy thigh and wondered where he was. Wondered if he'd laugh when he saw her limping pathetically across the room.

Thunder boomed and lightning followed but now Richard was gone. The front door was open. She sensed movement to her right and then something hard hit her on the cheek. There was a crack and she reeled backwards, dropping the cleaver. Eyes streaming and semi-conscious, she managed to crawl over to the stairs. Had to get away. Started to climb on her elbows and knees. One at a time.

She didn't hear him but by the time she was halfway up the stairs she knew he was behind her. Standing over her. And then she felt a thin snake twist itself around her neck. Coiling into her pale skin. Its teeth sinking into her flesh. Her whole body was yanked upwards and she thought her back would snap. She tried to forget about the pressure around her neck. Tried to forget that she couldn't breathe. That her throat was being crushed shut. Cinched like a wet towel. She flailed her arms, knowing that she was about to die. Knowing that she had to get some DNA out of the bastard who was behind her. Anything. Trace fibres from his clothing. Skin. Blood. Hair. She thought of Tracy Jackson. A fighter. That was how she wanted to be remembered at least. She knew she would never get out of here alive. Would never be able to escape. She waited for the final crunch of her larynx and she wondered if Angela Swan would do her autopsy. She liked Angela. She prayed it would be Angela taking care of her battered corpse. Her whole body felt dead already and red fireflies burst inside her head. She took her last breath. Pulled up her legs to her chest and twisted herself to face the man trying to kill her. It was pitch-black and he was a shadow but she suddenly kicked out. There was a massive crash. Was it the lightning or . . . no, it was the bannister. She had kicked it loose and now the shadow stood on the edge of the stairs, one arm arcing backwards like a rodeo rider trying to keep his balance, the other clutching the belt around her neck. Tied together like the Gordian knot. He saw what she was thinking. Their eyes met. Shades of intimacy. And she saw a pleading in his face. She lifted a hand to the belt around her neck and gripped it tight in her white-knuckled fingers as if her life depended upon it. And she knew that it did. With a rush of energy, she ripped the belt from his hands. Severed the knot. He hung on the edge of the landing for a few seconds as if suspended from invisible wires. Arms cartwheeling, mouth in a silent scream – then his foot slipped. Wood splintered. And with a terrible yell he fell backwards and disappeared. There was a sickening crunch from below.

She took a breath. She was alive. One more breath and somehow she blinked. There was still pressure on her neck. The belt was there but it wasn't as tight. Nowhere near. She put a finger under the thin coil and pulled it away. Threw it as far as she could. Pulled herself over to the edge of the landing and stared down as thunder cracked above. The lightning came after two seconds this time. The storm was getting closer and with it came the flash of light. She saw Richard's body. He was lying on his back, arms by his sides, his legs obscenely sprawled. He had fallen twenty feet and landed on his head.

He was twitching when she made her way down the stairs and dragged herself over to him. A hand was working. His arm was trying to move but the bones wouldn't let it. She edged closer on her belly. Adrenalin firing. The pain in her body reduced to a whimper. By the time she got to his face she was exhausted. His eyes were fully open, but somehow not registering. Lightning flashed and she saw him properly for the first time. It was Richard but it wasn't. He had blond hair. Dyed. She could see the black at the roots and she suddenly realised how they did it. How Richard managed to get out of Bayview without being noticed.

'Holly . . .'

She leaned down closer to his lips. She didn't want to miss what he said. It was obscene but she didn't want him to die alone. She wanted him to know that someone was there.

'Yes.'

'You w-were one of the l-lucky ones.' His broken hand reached out to touch her cheek, almost gently.

'I used to w-watch … the aeroplanes in my room. There were hundreds of them on the wall. In my bedroom. Then I'd close my eyes. I used to … f-fly away with them. I used to f-fly and never come back. But I did, Holly. I always came b-back.'

His face was so pale now.

'Did you manage to fly away?' A beat. 'Watch the … bluebells again, Holly,' he whispered.

'What …?'

'Watch the … b-bluebells.'

Stunned, she felt his body quiver as if suddenly cold and realised he was dead. For several seconds, she lay there next to him, wondering what to do.

'He remembered you …'

She spun around with a gasp, almost passed out with shock. Wilfred was emerging from the shadows at the bottom of the stairs. His head was at an awkward angle and he had a hand pressed hard against his neck. 'That's why you were so special. *So special.* Your first day at "Blessed Home". My brother was there. Only for three weeks. He was ten years old. He told me you looked so sad and alone. You looked how he felt. He was asked to carry in the plate of biscuits for the newborns. That's what he called you all, the ones who had just arrived. The newborns. He saved you a biscuit. Do you remember?'

She shook her head.

'He saved it all for you and when you took it you said something. You said, "I miss my mother and father." And he said, "I know. But one day you'll be free."'

'He was insane.'

Wilfred gestured to the body. 'Not any more.'

He edged closer. She pushed herself away from Richard's corpse and pulled herself to her feet. Pain ratcheted through her leg as if someone were trying to prise off her kneecap with a knife.

'Don't waste your energy.' His voice was soft. Almost pleasant. The caring doctor on his rounds. 'The door is locked. You won't make it.' She knew he was right. She thought she probably had one burst of energy left in her, one last leap. He was expecting her to run into one of the other rooms, expecting her to stay trapped inside. She deliberately relaxed her body, shoulders drooping in submission as if accepting her fate.

'Good girl.' He half smiled. He took another step towards her. It was a fumbling one and she realised he was still hurting. He was blinking rapidly as well, clearing the fog from his eyes, but his voice was chilling. 'Although it will be violent, there is a peace about death which is quite soothing. I promise.'

She nodded. Counting the seconds. Unable to take her eyes off him and praying that she had remembered the room layout as well as she hoped. A flash of lightning would be helpful right now, she thought. Come on thunder. Play with me. Please . . . Nothing. Just the unbroken splashing of the rain outside. Another few seconds and he would be able to lunge at her, she could almost feel his arms dragging her to the floor and his strong hands around her throat. Time's up, Holly. She couldn't wait any longer. She turned away from him and ran towards the wall in total darkness.

One. Two Three. Staggering steps but she needed to get her speed up. Four. Five. Six. Faster. Faster. Come on, Holly! Seven. Eight. Pitch-black ahead. One more step? Two more? Two more, her instincts cried out and then she leaped forward with a cry of pain and anguish. Hands covering her head.

Eyes screwed shut. This is the end, she thought. This really is the end now. She had misjudged. She was too long in the air. She wasn't going fast enough and then she felt herself smack into concrete. Concrete that suddenly shattered and exploded like fireworks and before she knew it she had broken through the window. Smashing into the open air, getting sliced and diced and landing in a heap of blood and sweat in the mud. She rolled over and over, the momentum carrying her further away from the cottage until she finally stopped and lay gasping, her mouth stretched open in a cry of pain. Everything was numb. Her forearms were in ribbons and she could feel the exhaustion sweeping over her. But she couldn't stop now. She mustn't. She pushed out of the pain. Started pulling at the wet ground with her hands and for whatever reason Holly thought of herself as a child again – digging in sand on the beach with her brother, but in those days they had been smiling and now she couldn't make herself smile. Slimy wet mud between her fingers, scraping the earth to one side as she tottered to her feet. She looked back. The rain still fell. The moonlight was dull but bright and she could see him watching her from the broken window. A silhouette against the shards of glass that stuck up like impossible teeth.

Get away, Holly. Move your wrecked body. One foot in front of the other. Don't stop now. She staggered along the path, leaving a heavy trail of mud. The rain felt like a monsoon and she could smell the wet earth and rotting leaves. Get to the treeline. Once you're there you can hide. Hide and catch your breath. A startled deer appeared from nowhere and bowled her over. She scrabbled to get back up, kept on moving. Her clothes were caked with mud, her breath was a shallow gasp and her leg felt raw every time she put weight on it. Past the first trees, her fingers white from the cold. Moving into the forest, into the shadows. As lightning flashed she looked back over the rain-drenched landscape of dead trees behind her.

Nothing.

She had no idea where he was. No sound but the rain.

She started running. Her leg screamed with every step as twigs and branches snapped on her head and hands. And then her leg gave way and she collapsed behind a massive oak tree.

Silence for a few seconds but the unmistakable rustling noises of his determined pursuit. Her hands fell on to a small rock as a twig broke close by. He could sense her somehow. She slowly stood and threw the rock at the noise. It clunked into a tree and she saw Wilfred look up and see her. She cursed, turned away and then felt herself fall backwards. The ground disappeared and she kept falling until she landed on her back with a splash and a yelp like an injured dog.

She was in a pit of some kind. A wet pit of mud and rain. Six feet deep, cut crudely into the earth. Water sloshed up over her body, she staggered to her feet and tried to get a handhold on the sides. Roots, stones, moss, but her fingers could find no purchase on the rain-slick surface. She slipped and went under the water. Hands scrabbling through the black mess until she pulled up something shiny in the moonlight. A fractured skull. The top half of it missing, the jaw still managing to smile despite the rain. And then she uncovered the body that it belonged to. Dead and decayed many years ago now. All that was left were a few sodden rags of cloth and a grey skeleton.

She sensed him before she saw him. Watching her from the edge of the pit like a predator watches an animal caught in a trap. He was on his stomach, leaning forward over the edge, and they held each other's gaze as if they were lovers in a tryst.

Then he lowered himself down until he was in the pit and slowly turned towards her.

She was struck so fast and violently she suddenly found herself cowering against the other side, crumpled and tear-streaked. The air was a blur of red mist as he gently pulled her away from the wall. He was smiling. It was obscene. Water flushed across her face and she spluttered and moaned as he placed one hand lovingly around her throat. Her fists tried to push him off but he was too strong. She tried to punch him but the blows were weak and eventually her hands fell to her sides. Her fingers brushed against the bones of the skeleton underneath her. Wet and slippery like sticks in the mud. The ribs. The pelvis. Another victim. Another woman. And somehow she felt an affinity to whomever they belonged to. You were like me once – young, hopeful – and now you're here. Lost and forgotten in some pit in the middle of nowhere. But she wasn't lost any more. Holly had found her, and as her hands stretched out she came across the shattered remains of a thigh bone. Still hard and fibrous, with a wicked point. And she suddenly thought of Sebastian Carstairs – the Animal – and how she had tried to kill him. Stabbed him in the heart with a tiny fruit knife. Ten years old. A child. She knew where Wilfred's heart was. Of course she did. Just as she had known where Sebastian Carstairs' heart had been.

But now she wasn't a ten-year-old girl.

Wilfred tightened the grip on her throat and Holly gripped the piece of bone with her right hand. She wondered if trying to kill Sebastian Carstairs all those years ago had simply been a test, a rehearsal to get her ready for what she was about to do now. She felt more animal than human. Primal. Bloody. Frothing with anger. No hesitation, Holly.

Not this time. She looked Wilfred in the eye and from somewhere found the strength to lever one hand on to his chest and push him up. Then she stabbed the thigh bone between his ribs. Numbers two and three. Past the intercostals where she knew the aortic valve was pumping. She saw the surprise in his eyes and felt his body tense, his lips parted in pain, or it could have been rapture. His hands clenched her throat and shoulder as if in the throes of a climax and then his whole body shuddered as she twisted the bone and felt it break and splinter inside him.

They stayed like that for some time. Eyes locked. Bodies stiff. She had never seen someone so still before. It was as if he had set eyes on the Gorgon and had been turned to stone. He stopped blinking, and the rain washed over his pupils as they slowly turned grey. She realised she was the only thing holding him up so she let him go and he slipped gently past her and disappeared into the mud.

Her eyes fluttered for a few seconds. A deep breath came next and she exhaled through her mouth as if it were a relief. She took another gulp of fresh air. The rain felt suddenly wonderful but then, within a single breath, it turned cold. Swallowing mud and blood. Eyes glazing over, knowing she might never be found. She had to get out of this pit but she couldn't move. Paralysed with pain and exhaustion. She felt herself slipping underneath the water. The clouds parted overhead and the full moon shone down on her. It looked so beautiful. Like a pale face. It had never looked so alive.

She felt her eyes closing as the water continued to rise. And at that moment she was content to die. She regretted a few things but it didn't matter any more. We're all looking for something special, she mused. Why do we spend our lives doing that? The pain in her body was becoming less, fading like an old memory. It's like when we're walking on the road. Eyes down on the pavement. See if someone's dropped a coin. Her body was growing colder by the second. Walking along by the river, trying to see some fish. Walking on the beach, trying to find the shell. We always look down. We're always looking for something, Bishop. Something sparkly. Something that we want to take home.

Forty-three

A cluster of fuzzy, flashing blue lights appeared through the drifting rain.

One car was ahead of the rest as it skidded to a halt by the front of Daniel's cottage. Bishop pulled himself out and started moving, the wet earth spitting up against his feet with every step. A stumbling run that ended with him falling against Holly's car. It was locked, so he battered on the windows, cleared the rain to see inside. Empty. He ran to the house. Checked the two cars in the driveway then noticed the jagged window frame and the shards of glass on the ground.

Two more vehicles pulled in behind him. Ambrose, Lipski and Jacobs in one. Kathy, Harrowman and Mosely in the other.

'Mosely, Lipski, the house with me. The rest of you search the area!'

They all scattered, boots slipping, flashlights fanning out like fireflies blown away on the wind.

Bishop shouldered the cottage door open. Pulled himself inside and floated his torch to the left and right. He felt

Mosely next to him like a block of oak. Strong and reliable. Unflinching. He couldn't see Lipski but he could see the light from her torch. It was shaking.

'Holly! Sergeant Crane!'

He wiped the rain from his eyes, nodded to them both. They went left and right. He walked straight, lifted up a drop-cloth that was lying in the centre of the room—

'Over here!' he shouted as his light illuminated a body of a man dressed in black. Face bruised and gory. White hair, almost silver in the light.

'Is that Daniel?' Mosely was by his side.

The cheekbones. The eyes. The hair. Bishop reached down ever so slowly to the hand and checked for a pulse. Half expected the eyes to suddenly flicker open. The twisted hand to straighten and grab his wrist. He could hear his own breath, see it misting in front of him. He pressed his shoulder radio, eyes refusing to move from the body. Still expecting it . . .

'This is Ambrose,' the voice crackled.

'Call the county coroner, Sergeant,' he said it casually but his heart was in his mouth. He turned the radio off. Let go of the dead man's wrist. Thought he heard Lipski say something from another part of the house. Couldn't work it out.

'Lipski?'

Mosely was coming out of the darkness, walking towards him. Face ashen.

'It's Sergeant Crane, sir,' he whispered. 'Lipski found him. In the kitchen.'

Bishop followed the big man. Saw the young sergeant with the knife sticking out of his stomach. Said a prayer to himself and wondered how he was going to tell Crane's mother and father. Lipski was hovering by his side. It looked as if she wanted to hold the dead man, take the knife out, say comforting things to him.

'Don't touch him,' Bishop said.

'I won't.' Her voice a flat, robotic monotone. 'I'll secure the room, sir. Make sure no one disturbs the evidence. Await the coroner.' Straight out of the textbook.

He nodded.

Mosely emerged from the dining room. Nothing in there. Bishop squeezed past and headed up the stairs. Treacherous planks of old wood. Half the bannister missing. He got to the top, Mosely close behind. He motioned the big man to go to the end of the landing. Bishop went to the first room.

The door had been smashed. The lock was on the floor. He stepped inside and heard the rain scattering like pebbles on the skylight. He flicked his torch around the room. A table, overturned. Smashed plates and cups, chairs upside down on the floor. A desk at the far end. His torchlight caught a reflection of something shiny on one of the chairs. Blood. Still drying. Deep red. He felt sick. Holly. Please don't say she's here. Please tell me that she managed to get away and everything's all right. But his gut was telling him everything was wrong. Everything. She was dead. And he was responsible. He had made that phone call asking for her help. Without him, she would never have got involved. He wouldn't be searching for her. Worrying about her. Looking for her in this abandoned house by this forsaken shoreline. She would be at home in her flat watching crap TV or checking in on the creepy fucks in her murderabilia collection. He didn't think he could face being the one that found her.

His light flickered away from the blood and on to the desk in the corner. A cold candle, an old large wire-bound book the size of a photo album. The cover was a simple blue. Plain.

The words 'Exercise Book' written on its front. Like an old school book. He opened it up. A list, handwritten, of locations: Hammersmith, Fulham, Kew, Streatham, Old Kent Road . . . Monopoly for beginners. The contents went on for a few pages. Different towns, some outside of London. And the writing got smaller, as if the author was concerned that they were running out of space. He carried on turning pages and then the contents changed.

There was a single page for the first entry: Erica Preston. Thirty-nine. Born 1958. Address: 357 Oldham Road Hammersmith W6 0AS. Telephone number: 020 887 9989. She was an aerobics teacher at Dance Attic. Frank Syson, Annette Messenger and Sylvia Plantain were her neighbours. And underneath this information was a square piece of paper. Grey, perhaps, but it was hard to see in the torch light. Bishop touched it. It was paper, but it was harder than normal. Had been glued into place. In that moment he realised what it was. And he knew what the list was. What it meant. He turned the page: Juliette Stokes. Born: 1976. A civil engineer from Windsor. Another square of wallpaper beneath her name. Another page: Abigail Brewer, a school teacher from Manchester . . . Nicky Thomas . . . Alison Zorensky . . . He flicked through the pages, feeling sicker and sicker. This was the killer's keepsake. His trophies. The book must have had over twenty names. He found Rebecca then Evelyn and Tracy. Then he flipped to the last entry and almost dropped the torch. A block of white wallpaper with tiny blue flowers. Today's date was written at the side and underneath:

Holly Wakefield. Flat 3, 22C Northwest Lane. SW12 1PQ.

Standing by the deserted desk, in the empty, silent room, Bishop was too choked up to speak.

*

The wind howled. The rain was blinding.

Bishop was crouched at the cliff's edge, his face drenched with uncertainty and rain. He had spotted what he thought could have been a body in the rocks below but in the crashing waves it had all but disappeared. Sergeant Ambrose approached, shaking his head, both hands holding on to his hat. He had to shout to be heard.

'We're waiting for NPIA to get back to us with an official ID on the body. There's a chopper coming and DI Bright is en route with thirty men.'

Bishop nodded, but he knew it wasn't enough. He turned away from the cliff, and walked back to the cottage, clutching at Ambrose to steady himself as the wind buffeted them. By his car, the others were talking. A pantomime out of earshot. Kathy broke away from the group.

'Sir, we've checked east and west. No sign. Only the forest left, but it's so hard to see. Should we wait for the others?'

Bishop cursed. 'We go in now! Every second counts. Grid formation. Thirty feet apart. On my lead!'

The rain had turned to snow. Gentle flakes melting on sweating bodies. Water dripped from his hair and the tip of his nose as he led the group into the forest, their torches scouring the trunks and hanging branches. Intermittent shouts of 'Holly' then silence as they waited for an answer. He slipped and went down on one knee. Struggled to his feet, dropped the torch, scooped it up and carried on hobbling.

'Holly!'

Deeper into the woods. The forest seemed to get denser the more they carried on. Like something out of an old Disney movie. Sleeping Beauty – the hedge of thorns. This place was too big. There weren't enough of them . . .

His radio crackled and he heard a familiar voice.

'DI Bishop – Inspector Bright here. We've fallen in behind you, flanking north and south.'

He turned and heard boots trampling through the mud and men shouting Holly's name. A dog barked. Movement either side, and he saw the forest was alight with flashlights. Thank God.

'Holly!' he screamed. The snow was settling. A fine mist of white on the mud. 'Holly . . . !'

He started to run but felt his leg go. Managed to stay on his feet. The sensation in his knee made him wince and lean up against the nearest tree. The pain was gone in seconds as the adrenalin kicked in, and in a way the pain was cathartic now. He didn't mind damaging his leg while he ran, he didn't mind being on crutches for the rest of his life, but he was not going to let her—

A call rang out: 'Dog's got something!'

Bishop surged towards the sound until he finally pushed through a circle of bushes and saw:

Holly.

A swampy mixture of flesh and mud and rain. Barely walking. Eyes closed. He caught her as she sagged into him. She felt cold and slippery, like wet rubber. But somehow she was managing to keep standing by herself. God knows what was keeping her up. Bishop stared at her, her eyes swollen into slits, her mouth and nose bloody. He wiped her face and she suddenly coughed and spat up black mud. Slumped down on one knee and gasped for air.

'They're dead, Bishop . . .'

Another great gulp of air and he had one arm around her and held her hand with the other, wishing that she would turn

366

and see him, so she would know that everything was all right. As if hearing his thoughts her eyes opened in her damaged face. Their eyes met but then she stared past him and he saw the beginnings of her childlike smile.

'It's snowing . . . ' she whispered.

'Yes,' Bishop said, cradling her head. 'And it's beautiful.'

Forty-four

The phone call didn't wake him.

Bishop was lying on his sofa in the semi-darkness with his eyes open, listening to the rain. He was in his house. It was a small mid-Victorian terrace and the room was sparsely furnished with a desk and computer, a chair and a TV. The sofa was a sofa-bed that he pulled out some evenings when he fell asleep watching old movies. There was only a single photo in the whole place. A blonde woman wearing a black dress and smiling from ear to ear. It hung on the wall above the fireplace so he could see it whenever he was in the room.

A coffee filter brewed from the kitchen and it reminded him of Holly. Strong and sweet. Beautiful but damaged. With a kick like a mule. He was looking forward to it. The phone rang. He took the receiver gently.

'Yes?'

He arrived at the station and Chief Constable Franks was waiting for him. A warm handshake and the offer of another coffee.

'Cream and sugar, William?'

'No thank you. Black, sir. Trying to lose a bit of weight.'

'How's that knee?'

'Still bending at the right moments, sir.'

'Good, good.'

Franks coughed and it seemed to echo in the large office. He lifted a file off his desk and stared at the photos of Wilfred and Richard Sickert. He raised his eyebrows as he put them back in their folder and closed the file. Sealed it with an elastic band and placed it neatly in a drawer.

'You have conducted yourself with distinction and integrity throughout this very complicated murder investigation. Even the Commissioner has been singing your praises. Congratulations are in order. There is talk of a commendation for you, Detective Inspector.'

'Thank you, sir. I couldn't have done it without the team.'

'The team.'

'Yes, sir. And Holly.'

'How is Miss Wakefield?'

'Recovering. She seems to be remarkably resilient.'

Bishop was about to say something but then saw that Franks was flicking through his calendar, checking dates. 'There's a charity ball next weekend. Rotary Club sort of thing. I won't be able to attend. Miriam is insisting we see the grandchildren again. Some Mozart recital in B Major performed by nine-year-olds. Forty-five minutes of auditory agony. Therefore, I have two tickets to the charity ball available. I thought of you and Holly. I'm sure she'd like it. Mixing with the top brass. Get her out of the house sort of thing. The two of you could let your hair down a bit.'

He passed over the two tickets and Bishop took them.

'That would be lovely, sir. Thank you.'

'Hmm.'

Bishop felt as though he had been patted on the head and he wanted to rub it raw but instead stayed seated and stared at the tickets as if they were an invitation to Willy Wonka's Chocolate Factory.

'That's all, DI Bishop.' Franks' phone rang. He was waiting for Bishop to leave.

'Sir.' He got up and retreated to his office. Ignoring Kathy and Mosely, he slammed the door shut with his foot. He poured himself a drink from a hidden stash of brown bottles behind one of the cabinets and sat back and sipped it. He didn't even know what it was but it tasted wonderful. Strong and rasping on his throat. Like petrol but it smelt of amber.

Holly Wakefield.

Jessica Ridley.

For the first time in a long time he didn't know what to do. He sat upright in his seat, face impassive as the minutes slipped by. Ambrose knocked and entered so Bishop downed the drink and pushed the empty glass away from him. He fumbled for his cigarettes but his hands were shaking and he dropped the packet. Ambrose leaned forward and picked it up for him.

'All right, sir?'

Bishop stared at him as if he was a stranger then suddenly blinked and came back into the room.

'Sorry, Sergeant. Yes,' he lied. 'I'm fine.'

'SOCO have finished at the pit. Recovered two skeletons, not one. A man and a woman, both mid-thirties. We're running a fast-track DNA through missing persons. You never know. We might get lucky.'

'That's my line, Sergeant.'

Ambrose smiled and left, closing the door behind him.

Bishop logged on to his computer, started to read his emails then slouched wearily in his chair.

He stared at his pink orchid and felt the soil. A little dry. He filled up a cup from his cooler, dribbled some water into the pot then sat on the desk when he was done.

A wave of dizziness hit him. The room seemed hot – or was it him?

He really needed a bigger office.

Forty-five

Holly was in bed.

She had no idea how long she had been asleep but the bed felt comfortable, warm and clean. Her eyes were closed. She had the worst headache, and she was beginning to be aware of the pain in her left leg as the anaesthetic wore off. The doctors had told her she had fractured her tibia, the front part of her shin, when she had fallen down the stairs, and they had pushed it back together and she now had a lovely chainmail of black stitches running from halfway up her calf to the base of her knee underneath a thick plaster cast. She had lost a tooth somewhere along the way, had severe swelling in both orbital cavities, another possible fracture, and her jaw and cheeks had taken a vicious bruising. All in all, she didn't feel like going out for drinks tonight wearing her best party frock.

The night at the cottage was a blur. After she had killed Wilfred, she'd been certain she would die. How she made it out of the pit, she had no idea. But she remembered walking for what seemed like an age, until she heard dogs barking and wandered in that direction. She knew it was Bishop the moment he held her. Recognised his grip although she had never so much as held his hand before. He had carried her out of the forest and an ambulance had spirited her away. She thought he was still with her in the ambulance because she was holding someone's hand but when she opened her eyes there was no one there.

He had visited her the next day, or so the nurse had informed her. She had been so drugged up, she hadn't known what was going on around her. She had a vague recollection of answering questions but couldn't remember if her answers had made any sense.

They'd be doing more tests today. Someone with a white coat would prod her and tell her she was really lucky – and maybe she was. She didn't feel lucky at the moment. In fact, she felt broken. Not in half. But the edges. Neatly fractured corners that hurt in places that no one else could see.

She heard footsteps near her. Movement by the bed. She opened one bleary eye and had to blink the redness away. And there he was.

Bishop.

Standing at her side, looking half asleep.

'Hey,' he said. All gravelly and rough.

'Hey back,' she managed.

He had a bunch of flowers that he put into a vase. Purple gladioli and black calla lilies. They sat nicely by her bed and she could smell the freshness. He managed a flicker of a grin. The cheeky schoolboy had returned.

'How you doing?'

'Leg feels like jelly. And I keep thinking my head is going to explode.'

He nodded and smiled. Patted one hand gently on to the covers. With the other he revealed a gift bag neatly tied with a red ribbon.

'Brought you a selection of coffees yesterday but the nurses said no.'

'I'm not allowed caffeine for a week. This place is full of sadists.' She pulled herself up a bit, wincing as she did. 'What did you get me instead?'

'Hot chocolate.'

'Hot chocolate?'

He nodded.

'What am I – ten?'

He shrugged, passed the bag over. She opened the ribbon and put her hand inside. Her eyes were so gritty she couldn't focus properly on the writing.

'Read it to me.'

'Seriously?'

'I nearly died.' She smiled. 'Read it to me.'

He cleared his throat. Then, 'This hot chocolate is really expensive and comes all the way from Belgium.'

'Does it say that?'

'I'm ad-libbing. Here we go. "Ever want to relax and sink into the sofa when it's time for bed?"' He paused. 'Jesus . . . '

'Keep going.'

'"Well now you can. Four varieties from the four corners of the earth. Cinnamon, gingerbread, mint and Nutella."'

'Nutella?'

'Apparently. "Made with seventy per cent Columbian chocolate – these drinks are smooth and rich. You can even add marshmallows for that extra-special treat or for those extra-special occasions."'

'Extra-special occasions.'

He gave her a look. 'We could have hot chocolate nights. You know? Try them out – see what works.'

'Sounds perfect.' She took a breath. 'Thank you.'

He sat on the edge of the bed. A moment passed before he said:

'I came to see you yesterday, but you were pretty messed up. Wanted to know if you could bring us up to date. I've got a lot of assumptions but no real answers. It appears that Wilfred wasn't killed in Germany. Made his way back to England and became qualified as a psychologist. The insane running the asylum. How am I doing?'

'Good. Can you—'

He passed her a glass of water and she took a sip. It hurt to swallow and it made her cough, but when she cleared her throat she was ready to continue.

'How long they killed for or how many people, perhaps we'll never know. But Wilfred saw his role as protector and guardian of his younger brother. So when Richard was charged with killing his wife, Wilfred brought him safely into the confines of Bayview. Perhaps that's where they hatched their plan.'

'The plan being?'

'The scorpion and the frog. They both wanted to kill. It was in their nature. Wilfred was able to do as he wished. A new name, a new identity. Perfect anonymity within the world of psychiatry. But his brother Richard was a triple murderer. A prisoner for life. Wilfred couldn't bring women back to Bayview, so he had to come up with a way to get Richard out. When Daniel was incarcerated at Bayview he saw the perfect opportunity. Physically, they were the same height, the same build. With a little help from a surgeon's knife, a change of hair colour, contact lenses, a shave ... Richard became Daniel. It was as if he'd been given a free pass to kill. Every time Daniel was due a visit into the outside world, he'd be drugged and left in his room while Richard took his place. For the first few years they must have played it safe. Didn't kill anyone. Had to be sure they could get away with the deception. Maybe they suspected DI Bright was watching.'

'Makes sense.'

'So the local police came to the conclusion Daniel wasn't a problem, having no idea that it was actually Richard who was on the loose.'

'And the night the Wrights were killed, the real Daniel was at the restaurant?'

'The perfect alibi. Daniel was drugged and sent out with his chaperone while Richard and Wilfred carried out the murders.'

'I still don't see why Wilfred and Richard preyed on adopted kids?'

'Because they were the ones who got away, Bishop. Marjory Dawson, Amanda Bines, Rebecca . . . Me. All the victims were adopted children who got good parents. They weren't abused. So Wilfred and Richard wanted to punish them. Why should they have suffered when others didn't?

'When you're put into foster care you can be lucky or unlucky. But one thing is always the same. You never know what's going to happen to you. You wait and wait. Put your best dress on, comb your hair. Come downstairs and serve coffee or tea and sit and smile with the other children. Bright-eyed and young. All of us hopeful. Then we would go back upstairs and wait again. It never got any easier. I was so lucky. Maureen was amazing. I just wanted to stay with her and she let me. The most brilliant woman I have ever met. So brave. In the cottage, Wilfred told me Richard was at the same home as me. Only briefly, but he was there. By then he had already been classified as unfit for adoption. No one wanted a boy with psychological problems. No one was ever going to give him a chance.'

'What about the wallpaper? His trophy?'

'When he was a child it helped him escape from what was happening to him. The abuse. He told me he used to fly away in the aeroplanes. Closed his eyes and took himself away. He created a fantasy to deal with the situation, to take away the pain. I used to stare at my wallpaper and imagine it was a field of flowers that I could walk through with my parents. I was somewhere else. Lost. For those precious moments I forgot what had happened. I was in my imaginary world. Richard . . .' she faltered. A half-smile. 'He never stood a chance, Bishop.'

She closed her eyes, her face pained for a second. Then the moment passed and she blinked rapidly.

'You okay?'

'Flash-bangs. Mini migraines. They only last a second or two. I'll be all right.'

'Will you?'

Something passed between them. It was hard to say what it was, but at the end of it they both smiled slightly. Then Holly said:

'And the ultimate thrill for Wilfred was to have me working on the case. The icing on the cake. He planned the acid attack on Janine so that Sam Gordon would take compassionate leave and I would be brought in. How did he get Eagen to do it?'

'Eagen was a patient there, remember? During that week Eagen confessed on video to raping three other women. Wilfred said he would tell the authorities unless he did exactly as he was told. Eagen would have been facing life in prison.

377

Didn't see a way out. We found more hair samples from Eagen in "Doctor Andell's" office. We can safely assume he planted the strand under Tracy's nail.' He sighed. 'Wilfred was the one who told me to look into your past, by the way.'

'Makes sense. Maybe he thought I was getting too close.'

'Maybe.'

He stared at her. Dipped his eyes, then told her.

'Suits you, by the way.'

'What?'

'The plaster-cast. The missing teeth.'

'Tooth.' She smiled and showed him.

'You look like a weird creepy doll.'

'A *weird creepy* doll? Not just a doll, but a weird creepy one? Like I belong in some strange person's murderabilia collection?'

'Ah, Jesus . . . '

'Could you check in on them, make sure they're okay? Some of the dolls get really lonely at night.'

'You're such a freak.'

'I know I am,' she said. *But so are you, Detective Inspector Bishop.*

He smiled and put his jacket on. 'Get some rest, I've got to get back to the office.'

'Another case?'

'Finishing up this one. We managed to get a DNA match on the two bodies in the pit. Margaret and Simon Westall.'

'Wilfred and Richard's foster parents.'

'Yep. Probably their first kills. As for the rest of the victims . . . ' He held up the wire-bound book he had found back at the crofter's cottage. 'Not sure where to start with these. Fifteen names. Fifteen bodies. I'll see you tomorrow.'

'Wait.'

Bishop came back. Hovered at the end of her bed.

'The bodies in the book. I think I know where they are.'

'Where?'

'In plain sight.'

He didn't question her. Simply drove.

They got to Bayview an hour later. Neither spoke much during the journey but Holly had already told him what she was thinking. The building was on lockdown when they arrived and there were a dozen police cars in the car park. The authorities were moving fast.

DI Bright and the local SOCO team met them at the main doors and ushered them past reception, the ward sister, and into the building's corridors. Holly moved as fast as she could on her crutches but felt herself flinch as she passed Wilfred's office. She gritted her teeth until they were in the corridor with the window in the far wall. She and Bishop looked down upon the miners' graves in the lawn.

'You sure about this?'

'His beautiful little secret,' she said. 'Has to be.'

They took the lift down to the lower levels and she pushed open the maintenance door. The sunlight felt warm on her face as she stepped into the cemetery. Bright green grass speckled with the old headstones. There was something peaceful and beautiful about it. Holly limped to the nearest grave. She reached out and touched its rough surface. Moss, flaked cement and a name impressed in the middle.

'Erica Preston.' She read aloud. She turned back to Bishop. He opened the wire-bound book. Flicked a page. Squinted, then looked up at her and nodded. He turned to the forensic team.

'Start digging,' he ordered. 'Dig them all up.'

SOCOs moved like moths across the lawn as Bishop came and stood next to her. She didn't see him but she felt him. She could feel the warmth coming from within. She stared at the headstones and let the enormity of what she was seeing sink in. At least these women would have some sort of peace now.

She had changed so much in the past few weeks. She had been to places she never thought she could. Overcome obstacles, thoughts and feelings. She wondered if Bishop felt the same. They stood like that for a moment. Neither of them needing to do anything. Then she said:

'We're not who we used to be, Bishop.'

He nodded solemnly. She felt his fingers brush against hers. 'I know.'

Forty-six

The house was old and dilapidated.

Someone had tried to repaint it a while ago but never finished. The garden was neat, however, and the roses had been pruned back and were already showing fresh buds in the winter air. Holly walked the path to the front door and automatically looked up above the lintel where the words *'Blessed Home'* were impressed in the stone. The mat at her feet said *'Welcome'*. *Always*, she thought to herself. She knocked on the door and it was opened by a long-limbed woman in her seventies, a hippy if there ever was one. She squinted at Holly. It had been such a long time, but then Holly felt the warmth of her smile.

'Holly . . . ?'

'Hello, Maureen.'

Holly sat on the sofa, Maureen next to her. They had enjoyed an hour-long catch-up and were on their second cup of tea when the girl entered again with a plate of biscuits. She exuded confidence but there was a wariness in her eyes.

'Thought you might like a biscuit, Miss Wakefield.'

'Thank you.'

She offered the plate to Maureen as well and then left.

'How old is she?' Holly asked.

'Lizzie? She's eleven. She's only been here six weeks. She's had a rough time of it but she'll be all right. She's a fighter. Like you.'

Holly didn't feel like one at the moment.

'I'm sorry I missed the reunion.'

'It was nice. Only six boys showed, but seventeen girls turned up. Women now. It's funny, I recognised all of them. As if it were yesterday.'

'I should have come.'

'Next time. There's always next time.'

They sat in silence for a while. Holly knew she should get going but there was one more thing she wanted to do but wasn't quite sure how to ask. 'Maureen, would it be possible for me to—'

'Yes.' Maureen interrupted.

'You don't know yet what I'm going to—'

'You want to see your old bedroom.'

Holly entered the room and the nostalgia swept over her like the summer sun.

She found herself rooted to the spot, staring at where she had slept when she was a child, where she had been moved when she was ten. The room had hardly changed. The carpet and the curtains had been replaced but they had the same pattern and were exactly as she remembered them. She touched the desk by the far wall, then slowly made her way over to the bed. It was new but remarkably the bedside drawers were the same, made of old oak. She remembered how the top drawer would always judder whenever she pulled it open to reach for a pair of socks. She wasn't sure whether to smile or cry, so she did neither, content to soak up the energy and relive the memories. But the room didn't feel quite right, there was something different.

'What's changed?' she asked.

Maureen nodded. 'My goodness, you have a good memory. Yes. We had to move the desk over to the other wall. Unfortunately, someone vandalised the wallpaper.'

Holly turned swiftly. 'What?'

'Someone cut a square out of it. It was the strangest thing.' Maureen walked to the desk and shifted it to one side. 'One of the younger boys no doubt. See?'

Holly forced herself over, her feet like lead. Maureen was right. A neat four-by-four patch of wallpaper had been removed.

'Holly? Are you all right?' Holly had started to wring her hands together. Maureen took them in her own and gave them a squeeze. 'It's always a bit of a shock coming back.'

She nodded numbly. 'Sorry, Maureen. Can I have a moment please?' The last word died to a whisper.

Maureen retreated, watched her from the doorway then stepped away to leave her in peace. Holly stared at the wallpaper, her jaw hung open and she shuddered. She suddenly looked around, scared, until her vision finally blurred behind tears. She wanted someone to hold her, to make her safe, and she immediately thought of Bishop. Detective Inspector Bishop, the man who had saved her life. But it wasn't his voice that she heard playing softly in her head. It was Richard Sickert's.

'*Watch the bluebells again, Holly . . .*'

She squeezed her eyes tight so she wouldn't cry and walked slowly over to the bed. Lay herself down and fixed her gaze on the opposite wall. The wallpaper had never been changed.

It was the same as when she had been a child. It's was white with tiny little bluebells printed on to it. She thought of the aeroplanes that Richard had had in his own bedroom when he had been with the Westalls. Thought of him flying away.

And when she lay back and lost herself in the past, she saw her parents again and it was as if the bluebells were swaying in an imaginary wind.

Lee Miller was playing cards when Holly entered and sat down.

He stopped, immediately sensing something. Narrowed his eyes as he took in the limp, the crutch and the bruises on her face. There was a hardness when he asked, 'What happened to you?'

She shook her head dismissively.

'We've only got five minutes. This isn't an official interview but Max Carrington has let me come in.'

'Carrington? His balls have finally dropped? How wonderful . . .'

'How are you today, Lee?'

'No.' Anger flashed in his eyes. 'You are my guest here and you do not get to control the conversation!' He slammed down the cards. Then regretted it and looked up at the camera. 'I'm fine. I'm merely expressing an emotion, which I'm allowed to do. In fact, it is actively encouraged.' Back to Holly. 'Tell me who did that to you.'

'Don't, Lee. You know I can't. It's a conflict—'

'Of interest.' A pause. 'Love it when we finish each other's sentences.' He sniffed and gathered the cards, squared them off at the edges and put them in the middle of the table. 'I think I have a right to know.'

She stared at him.

'It doesn't matter. He's dead.'

Lee nodded. Exhaled.

'The case you were working on?'

'Yes.'

'Did you kill him?'

She didn't do anything but somehow he knew.

'Welcome to my world.' He nodded slowly. 'Mum and Dad would be so proud.'

'Don't!'

She shot out of her seat and instantly regretted it as the pain ripped through her leg. God, he could wind her up so easily. Lee stood up too, raised his hands in an apology. 'I'm sorry, I'm sorry, I'm sorry. It's not ... They would be proud. You know that.' He licked his dry lips. 'Of you anyway.'

A guard opened the door and stuck his head around.

'Everything all right?'

Lee sat down immediately. Hands face up on the table. Holly shot a look at the guard and nodded. 'It's fine. Everything's fine.' The guard exited and closed the door. Holly sat back down. There was a lull between them. Seconds passed before Lee spoke.

'You said you only had five minutes. Why did you come?'

'The judicial review.'

Lee shrugged. 'Our conversation was going so well and you had to ruin it, didn't you? "Mad, bad and dangerous to know."'

She stared him down.

'Come on, Holly, play the game. Who said it?'

'No games today, Lee.'

'Then what do you want to tell me?'

'They made their decision. I'm sorry. No parole.'

She felt his eyes staring through her. 'That doesn't surprise me somehow. Dangle the carrot. Hit me across the shins with the heavy stick. I never had my hopes up. Never. Look at what's become of me.' A pause. 'Look at what's become of you.'

'Don't start, Lee.'

'Lucky, lucky you.'

'Is that what you truly believe?'

His expression was half fearful as he studied her face and Holly could feel the anger rising inside her. 'If I had come home five minutes earlier, I would have been dead,' she said. 'Like them.'

'But you didn't, did you? You're alive. More than me. And you didn't see what I saw. Didn't see Mum and Dad walk into the kitchen. I was hiding in the cupboard – wanted to make them jump like Dad used to do to us. Remember? And then the devil came from nowhere and killed them.' He drew a hissing breath. 'You didn't see them fall to the floor. Dad was unconscious. But Mum ... You didn't hear her gasping. Gasping.'

'No.' She looked away. Blinked. Then back with him again. 'Do you hate me for that? Do you wish I'd been there?'

'Yes.'

'But I wasn't.'

'No. It was just me.'

'Just you.'

There was a moment of complete stillness. Then Lee wiped a hand over his face. He was sweating. 'There's something about you today. What is it?' he said. 'Come on, Sis. Why so glum?'

'I've met someone.'

A shadow crossed his face almost immediately. 'And that makes you sad?'

'Yes.'

'The thought that, if you love them, history will somehow

repeat itself and this person will be ripped from your life and you will once again be left with nothing.'

'I'll always have you.'

'That's not enough and you know it.' He half smiled. 'I want you to be happy, Holly. Above all else. You know that, right? Above all else. Above me.'

'Don't say that.'

'What? You think I don't have moments of happiness in here? *Au contraire. Je suis* very happy in my little perfect house. My home of contemplation. But I will be overjoyed if you are happy. Who knows? You may even get married. I'll have to come to the wedding. Give you away. I'm sure they'd let me out for the day. Suited and booted. I'm quite a catch still, I think.'

His face looked so young when he said that. So innocent. It was as if they were planning their lives all over again and they were children. Sitting in her bedroom waiting for Mum and Dad to call them down to dinner. Her eyes filled with tears.

'Don't fucking cry!' he turned on her. 'I hate it when you do that.' He gave her a handkerchief. She took it and wiped her eyes. Offered it back but no.

'Keep it. Keep it close to you. Always.'

He looked away from her for the first time and contemplated.

'This man. Does he like you too?'

'I think so.'

Stillness. He never seemed to blink these days.

'Then be careful, my dear sister. "We are what we pretend to be, so we must be careful about what we pretend to be."'

She tried to sleep when she got home.

First night back in her old bed. First time away from the watchful eye of the nurses and doctors. First time alone. After

387

three hours of tossing and turning she took a pill. An hour later she was so tired she couldn't work out whether she was asleep or awake. Fully clothed, she had forgotten to get undressed and was sprawled on top of her duvet. Suddenly, she sat bolt upright. *What was that?* A noise. *From where?*

She heard a whisper that sounded like her name. And again, this time from a different corner of the room, then from behind her, then from the foot of the bed. She fell back on to the mattress, her body shaking and sweating. She pulled the covers over her head and curled into a tight ball.

And then, as gentle as a snowflake falling, she thought she heard the soft, tinny ring of a small brass bell. The duvet was thrown to the floor. Hands instinctively bunched into fists. The bell was still ringing. But it was the phone. Just the stupid damn phone. She answered it, her voice quavering. It was Bishop.

He came to see her that night.

He didn't stay long and didn't say much. Wanted to check in on her. Make sure the flat was secure. Make sure she felt safe.

'I'm fine,' she insisted, but she liked him being there. She made him hot chocolate and they sat and sipped it together in silence like conspirators.

'The charity ball on Saturday. I'll come pick you up.' As he got up and left her flat. 'Seven o'clock?'

'Sounds good,' she replied.

The door closed. The shadows deepened and the darkness was complete, but she allowed herself a small smile.

'Night, Bishop,' she said under her breath.

Acknowledgements

I would love to thank Luigi Bonomi – my superhero of an agent at LBA – who read the first five thousand words of this novel and suggested it might be a good idea to finish it. His ideas, help and humour have kept me married to my Mac – in sickness and in health – and without him this story would not exist. And Alison, Amanda, & Danielle at LBA and my foreign rights agents ILA who always have a brilliant answer for every question I ask. Two more supportive agencies I could not ask for.

A massive heart-felt thank you to Emma Beswetherick, my publisher over at Little, Brown – who did an amazing job of editing and encouraged me throughout the process and was always only a phone call away. She also helped me get rid of the dog. Dominic Wakeford, Irene Rolleston and the wider team over at Little, Brown, the sales team, marketing, cover design, foreign rights, and everyone who has made this book a reality.

Sources

Fredric Wertham, *A Sign for Cain: An Exploration of Human Violence* (New York: MacMillan Publishing Company, 1966)

Robert D. Keppell and William J. Birnes, *Signature Killers* (New York: Simon & Schuster, 1997)

Reading Group Questions

1. Why do you think Holly Wakefield makes an interesting series heroine?
2. Can you comment on the burgeoning rapport between Holly and Bishop?
3. Does setting play an important role in the book?
4. Did you feel scared at all during your reading of the story? Do any particular scenes spring to mind?
5. Did you find the research into serial killers interesting?
6. Can you talk about the role of family and childhood in the book?
7. Can you comment on the relationship between the role of a forensic psychologist and the police?
8. Did you work out who the killer was?

Author Q&A

How does it feel to see you first book in print?

It's wonderful. Whatever I write, I never actually think anybody will ever read it, let alone turn it into a book, so it feels surreal to be honest.

What did you do before you became an author?

I was and still am an actor and have been writing on and off for the past twenty years. When I lived in Los Angeles I worked for CAA as a *reader*, where I would read up to ten scripts a week with a view for development at the major studios. It was the best training I could ever have had.

Have you always been a fan of crime fiction and is that why you chose to write in this genre?

I love crime fiction! The first detective books I ever read were the Hardy Boys, which I began reading when I was about nine. I took out the *Mystery of the Whale Tattoo* from the school library, and after that I devoured the series. By twelve I had moved on to *Sparkling Cyanide* by Agatha Christie and then I went with *The Adventures of Sherlock Holmes* and stories by Edgar Allan Poe. I'm a massive Scandi-thriller lover as well – *The Girl with the Dragon Tattoo*, *The Bridge*, *The Killing* – and when I need to relax I delve into Ian Rankin, Ann Cleeves and Val McDermid, as well as Edward Rutherfurd, Ken Follett and Bernard Cornwell. As for writing crime fiction, I think it's the best genre for red-herrings, sudden twists and unexpected heroes.

Did you set out to write a crime series?

Originally *When Darkness Calls* began as a street-theatre event in Edinburgh when I was living up there. Back then it was called *The Man In The Mask*, then it progressed to a screenplay called *The Neverfind* which eventually morphed into the novel. And then there was interest in it, so it just kind of progressed and found its own path.

Who is your favourite character in the book and why?

That's a tough question. I love all of them. I look at Holly as a bit of a superhero, but by that definition it also means that she'll only ever be as good as her antagonists. You always need bad people to bring out the best in us, and I know Holly is up to the test. I love Bishop as well and their relationship is one that I really enjoy writing. There has to be something in each character that appeals to me though. Even the bad seeds have to have a splash of vulnerability otherwise they are one dimensional.

Did you have to do a lot of research when writing this book? In particular, the research into serial killers and their cases?

Yes. God knows what Google analytics thinks of me. I have some very bizarre searches in my web history no doubt. I also have quite an extensive collection of true crime books.

What has been the hardest part of the process?

Having faith and trusting myself to step away from whatever I'm writing for a day or two and then re-reading it again with fresh eyes.

What has been the most enjoyable part of the process?

Meeting new people who are in the business. This is all so new to me I'm still finding my feet, but, in the same way that it's great to hang with actors backstage and on set, I'm finding the same camaraderie with other authors, my agent and publishers.

What do you do when you're not writing?

I write every day. I'm working on a YA fantasy book at the moment and I have a play to finish, as well as half a dozen screenplays that have been staring at me rather rudely for years. I'm also a working actor so it's been a busy year. I've just finished a run in the West End with a play called *Soldier On* at The Other Palace theatre in Victoria about veterans returning from Afghanistan, and next year I have a few projects lined up already. What I do need to do though is to learn to relax more. Any suggestions would be welcome!

Are you working on a new story at the moment?

Yes, I am. The third adventure for Holly. I know how it begins and how it ends and I know who the killer is. Now I just have to find the other 98,000 words that go in the middle ...

Turn the page for the opening of the next
chilling **Holly Wakefield** thriller

When
Angels Sleep

Coming in November 2019

One

The man sang to himself on the drive home from work.

He had a lovely voice. Mellifluous, his singing teacher had once told him – a nightingale set free in the dark. When he had sung at school he had always closed his eyes and fantasised.

My life is not beautiful. He used to think. *It is not magical. But I can feel the love. Coming closer. Closer every day.*

He had been asked to join the choir when he was thirteen – high praise indeed for a school of four hundred pupils. And when he sang a solo in St. Mary's church that Christmas Eve, and his mother had watched from the wooden pews amongst the other mums and dads, he had thought for the briefest of moments that he actually was in heaven. There had been no applause or welcome hug after, but the fleeting smile had been enough. That was twenty-two years ago. How he had grown since then.

He turned into his driveway, parked the car and got out. It was February and cold. Blobs of cloudy snow littered the grass and the ground was slippery with wet. A quick wave at the light-sensor so he could see the lock, then he turned the keys and pushed open the front door. The house was dark. It always was. Black wood paneling, dark brown floors. A Gothic hall stand with an elephant's foot base. He switched on the hall light. Tiffany-stained glass that splashed gummi-bear colours all over the walls. He placed his suitcase on the hall stand and called up the steep stairs.

'Hi Mum!'

'Is that you?'

'Yes!'

'You're early.'

'I'm going out tonight.'

'What?'

'I'm going out. Remember?'

He went into the kitchen, put the kettle on the stove and made himself a cup of tea. Five minutes later he put two sausages in the frying pan and watched them sizzle like fat fingers until they were brown all over. He boiled some peas, cut the sausages into edible-sized chunks, buttered two slices of wholemeal bread and put everything on a tray with some cutlery.

The stairs were surprisingly noiseless for a house this old: a Victorian throwaway that was neither loved nor lost. He hoovered twice a week, but the dust always seemed to settle as if dropped by a sieve, and he couldn't help running his finger over the bannister when he got to the top. He took a left on the landing, passed two bedrooms, the bathroom, and entered his mother's room. The curtains had already been drawn, and the only light was from a lamp on the bedside table. The seventy-year-old woman was perched like a giant crow in the bed. Propped up by pillows, her emaciated arms draped across the duvet and her nightdress was buttoned to the neck. Her head hung forward and was tilted slightly to one side. Her eyes seemed to follow him, but her head never moved.

'Where are you going then?'

'I've told you, Mum. It's a works do.'

'Works do?'

He placed the tray of food gently on her lap.

'Come on, eat up before it gets cold.'

His mother stared at the food, then picked up the knife and fork and started to eat. She chewed a piece of sausage loudly.

'What time will you be back? Last time you left me I thought you were dead.'

'I'll probably be late. We're all going to the Cosy Club, it's—'

'You needn't go into detail. I hope I didn't raise one of those boys who always tells you exactly what they're doing when you ask them?'

'No, Mum. Of course not.'

She had spilled peas onto the duvet and they rolled around like baby marbles. The man started to scoop them up but was interrupted by a quick rap on his knuckles with a fork.

'I haven't finished with them. Stop hovering! And where's my tea?'

'I forgot,' he said, and quickly left the room.

Downstairs he re-brewed the kettle and made his mum a cup of tea. He put two Jammy Dodgers on a small plate and headed back up the stairs. She was fiddling with the bedside lamp when he entered. The light was flickering like an SOS.

'What are you doing, Mum?'

'Trying to fix the . . . It's always doing this.'

'It's fine. Just . . . hold on.' He put the tea and biscuits on her lap. Went to the other side of the room and pushed her wheel-chair to one side. Knelt down by the wash basin and opened a small door that was hidden behind. He went through to the next room and when he came back about a minute later the

401

light had stopped flickering. He closed the door and pushed the wheelchair back into place. 'There you go. Nice and quiet. I need to get ready now.'

He had already showered and shaved that morning and opened the suitcase he had left on his bed. Looked at the meticulously folded clothes and added a pair of flat shoes and an iPhone. He shot himself a smile in the mirror but it ended abruptly when he felt suddenly sad. *Stop it*, he said, and grabbed the St. Jude medal around his neck. *Stop it. Stop it.* His eyes went to the ceiling where the painted angel murals were watching and he gave himself a minute.

By the time he went back into his mother's room she was asleep, as quiet as the dead. The man wasn't sure whether he should wake her, but—

'I'm off now, Mum.'

'Hmm . . .' his mother stirred.

He leant in closer and gave her a kiss on the cheek. Smelt her breath, her old hair. She stared at him with rheumy eyes and wiped a bit of sausage fat off her chin.

'Where's Stephen?' she whispered.

'Don't wait up for me,' he said, his breath catching in his throat.

He took his mother's tray and went downstairs. Washed everything up, put it all away, and placed a box of Weetabix on the kitchen table ready for breakfast.

'Bye, Mum!' he shouted up the stairs as he made his way into the hall, but he didn't leave just yet. He opened the front door then slammed it shut and stood in absolute silence, listening for a soft footstep or a scrape of furniture, barely daring to breath. Five minutes. Ten. Nothing. Then he caught a glimpse of himself in the hall mirror and the sadness came back like a black wave. His head fell forward onto his chest and he cried for a full minute. The sort of crying where he had no idea if he would ever stop and his head hurt and his heart pounded and his face was a mess but he just didn't care. And he couldn't see because everything was blurry and nothing looked real and he couldn't feel pain because pain didn't exist anymore – there was only the never-ending slog of sadness.

'What am I like . . .' he sniffed. And after several minutes he rallied bravely, because deep down he knew exactly what he was like.

He was a lonely man with so much love to give, but nowhere to put it.

Two

'Are you drunk?'

It was a good question.

Someone had banged a nail into Holly Wakefield's head about two hours ago and no matter how much she tried to find it she just kept grabbing tufts of hair. Dirty hair. Smelly hair. Cigarettes and rhubarb gin.

'I think I might be,' she managed.

She pulled herself upright and her eyes flipped open, timid and confused, like a newborn shrew. And then there was something she hadn't felt in a long time: the stomach lurch, and she shut her eyes as the room spun and wondered if she was going to be sick.

'Are you going to be sick?'

Another really good question. Detective Inspector Bishop was on fire today.

'Possibly.'

Hold it in. Hold it in. For God's sake, hold it in.

Who had suggested shots at four-thirty in the morning? It had started with gin and tonics at 8.00 p.m. last night. A reunion with the girls from Blessed Home, her foster home from when she had been a young girl. Valerie, Sophie Savage, Michelle, Joanne, Zoe. Sixty-two flavours of gin? Who even knew that was possible.

Then they had all decided on something to eat.

Soho – where else?

Balans on Old Compton Street – it had to be.

And after they had been kicked out at 2.00 a.m. they had gone to a members-only club on Shaftesbury Avenue. The Connaught, or something. No – The Century Club, that was it, and they had stayed there until they went on lockdown. Valerie was a member and got them in and then the party had really begun. Sophie had fancied one of the waiters and he had told them one of the funniest jokes about a deer, a skunk and a cuckoo. How did it go? A cuckoo, a skunk and a deer went out for dinner at a restaurant one night and, when it came to pay, the deer didn't have a *buck*, the skunk didn't have a *scent* – and the cuckoo? No, that's not right.

'The cuckoo . . .'

'What?' said Bishop.

'Shush. It was a joke from last night. Trying to remember. It was funny.'

Was it a cuckoo? Maybe it was a blackbird or a partridge? It would come back to her. If it didn't she could always ask one of the girls. Ah – the girls. Her girls. All grown up now. All beautiful and smart and strong and lovely. And hard as nails when they needed to be. Good company. Nostalgic until the last round. By four o'clock it had been free drinks, cigars on the terrace and then the singing had—

She was being guided. Gentle hands. One on her shoulder. One on her lower back.

'Where are we going?'

'Toilet.'

'I think I'm okay.'

Stomach lurch number two and then that metallic taste at the back of her throat and she could feel her jaw beginning to lock open as her body was about to—

'Don't watch me, please don't watch me,' she whispered.

The hands lowered her to the floor and she could feel the fluffy bathroom mat under her knees. Her fingers automatically gripped the rim of the bowl and then it all came up.

He held her hair as she vomited.

And kept vomiting.

'Good shot,' he said. And she had no idea if he was being sarcastic.

I wonder if he still fancies me?

And when she finished she found her laugh, because she had just remembered the punchline to the joke. It wasn't a cuckoo! It was a duck! The deer didn't have a *buck*, the skunk didn't have a *scent* and the *duck* didn't have the *bill*.

'That's brilliant,' she said as she wiped her mouth with the back of her hand, and all of a sudden everything made sense.

'Better?'

They were sitting in Brickwood Coffee & Bread, an artisan breakfast café with exposed bricks and wooden planks on the walls and a never-ending supply of healthy food and slow roast coffee. Holly had passed on the food but had taken a kale smoothie. It had tasted like lawn mower leftovers but she had held it down. *Good stomach. Love you.* Now she was nursing a black coffee.

'Do I smell of sick?' she said.

'Coffee and lack of sleep. That's what I'm getting from over here.'

'I'm a classy chick. What can I say?' she smiled and was suddenly conscious that she hadn't even brushed her teeth yet. Their waitress brought out Bishop's full English breakfast. Holly flinched as if it were part of a horror movie.

'Is that black pudding?'

'Yeah, you want some?'

'I'd rather eat my own feet.'

'What happened to the "hot chocolate and possibly a quiet movie if our mood takes us" evening with the girls?'

'We started with good intentions but then it quickly descended into chaos. It was good food. Good drink. I like my girls.'

'I know you do,' he smiled. 'Did you forget about our breakfast?'

'No.'

Yes.

She had vaguely remembered at six-thirty this morning when she had collapsed through the front door and belly-dragged herself into the bedroom.

'I've got something for you,' he said.

'Another coffee?'

'If you want.' He ordered one then handed over a thin paper folder with no labels or words on the front cover. She started to open it but he closed it gently in her hands.

'Not over breakfast,' he said. 'It's the final report from the Sickert case.'

There was a mood breaker if ever there was one. Wilfred and Richard Sickert.

Doctor. Bastard. Patient. Bastard.

It had been nearly four months since she had first got the call from DI Bishop of the Met Serious Crime squad and been asked to walk into a living room containing the freshly murdered and mutilated bodies of Jonathan and Evelyn Wright. He had been a doctor, she his loving wife. Forty years with each other wiped out by a flathead hammer and a wicked blade.

Angela Swan, the coroner, had concluded at the autopsy that the injuries to Evelyn were consistent with a previous murder; that of a British Airways flight attendant named Rebecca Bradshaw. Rebecca had been killed three weeks previously, left sitting propped up against her bed like a life-sized plastic doll. Wrists slashed, head resting against her chest as if she were asleep. Three murders, similar MO, and all of a sudden Holly had had a serial killer on her hands.

Before that her life and been quite simple really. Well . . . both her parents had been murdered by a serial killer and she had been brought up in a foster home . . . but she still considered herself one of the lucky ones. She had stayed in school, worked hard and went on to major in criminology. Having had first-hand experience of death, she always wanted to know why. Why do you kill, Mr Sociopath? What makes your brain go tick-tick instead of tick-tock? Now she taught behavioural science to students at Kings College in London and the rest of her week was spent at the Wetherington Hospital taking care of mentally challenged patients who had the propensity to kill.

The phone call last November had changed everything, and alongside DI Bishop, she had helped track down two of the most brutal and clever killers England had ever seen. Two brothers: Wilfred and Richard Sickert. Born of the same womb, living by the same code. It had taken her to a small crofter's cottage by the sea near Hastings – how romantic – and ended with Richard breaking his neck and her stabbing Wilfred in the heart with the broken thigh bone of one of his previous victims. All in all – an eventful two weeks.

The CPS had briefly considered prosecuting her over the deaths of Wilfred and Richard, but the Commissioner and Chief Constable Franks had stepped in and all charges had been dropped. It was the first time in a long time that Holly had felt as though she had had help from other people. That she wasn't alone. That she had a family.

She was toying with file. Wanted so much to read it.

'I don't want to know where they're buried,' she said.

'I didn't think you would.'

Her next coffee arrived and she downed it in one.

'I'm living life, William,' she said. 'Not staying in the confines of my flat anymore. It's quite nice out there. With people.'

'People are nice. Most of them. When's your next doctor's appointment?' he asked.

'Forty-five minutes.'

'You want me to drive you?'

'Yes please. I might get lost,' she smiled, and then his phone went. Holly watched him as he talked. He looked younger than his forty-three years. Maybe he'd had a haircut or maybe he was just sitting in good light. He listened for a while longer then frowned and hung up. Shot a look at Holly and then went back to his breakfast. Indecision – fleeting – but it was there.

'I have to go.' He waved a hand to get the bill. 'I'm sorry, Holly.'

'What is it?'

'It's a body. Another case.'

'Can I come? I should come. Hold on, let me get ready—'

'No, Holly, stay. Go to your doctor's appointment. Make sure everything is fine.'

'Everything is fine, Bishop. I want to help.'

'I'm sure you do, but not yet.'

'At least tell me what it is—'

'I'll call you later.'

He left enough money on the table and walked away. The waitress returned before the front door had even closed.

'More coffee?'

Holly managed a smile but thought it might have looked a bit wonky.

'Keep it coming.'

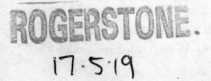